THE WEDDING
OFFICER

ALSO BY ANTHONY CAPELLA

The Food of Love

THE WEDDING
OFFICER

Anthony Capella

TIME WARNER
BOOKS

TIME WARNER BOOKS

First published in Great Britain in April 2006 by Time Warner Books

Copyright © Anthony Capella 2006

The moral right of the author has been asserted.

A CIP catalogue for this book
is available from the British Library.

C Format ISBN-13: 978-0-316-73095-2
C Format ISBN-10: 0-316-73095-5

Typeset in Galliard by M Rules
Printed and bound in Australia
by Griffin Press

Time Warner Books
An imprint of
Time Warner Book Group UK
Brettenham House
Lancaster Place
London WC2E 7EN

www.twbg.co.uk

'I am concerned at the increasing number of applications by officers or other ranks to marry Italians. COs must realize that everything possible will be done to discourage such marriages.'

Bulletin issued by the General Officer Commanding,
No.3 District, Naples, 5 September 1944

PART ONE

One

The day Livia Pertini fell in love for the first time was the day the beauty contest was won by her favourite cow, Pupetta.

For as long as anyone in Fiscino could remember, the annual Feast of the Apricots had incorporated not only a competition to find the most perfect specimen of fruit from among the hundreds of tiny orchards that lined the sides of Monte Vesuvio, but also a contest to determine the loveliest young woman of the region. The former was always presided over by Livia's father, Nino, since it was generally accepted that as the owner of the village *osteria* he had a more subtle palate than most, while the latter was judged by Don Bernardo, the priest, since it was thought that as a celibate he would bring a certain objectivity to the proceedings.

Of the two competitions, the beauty contest was usually the more good-natured. This was partly because it was unencumbered by the accusations of fixing, bribing and even stealing of fruit from another man's orchard that dogged the judging of apricots, but also because the girls of the village were remarkably similar in appearance – dark haired, olive skinned, and built along the voluptuous lines that a diet of fresh air and pasta invariably produces – and it was thus a relatively simple matter to decide which one combined these features in the most pleasing way. The apricots were another matter altogether. Each time Vesuvius erupted, it covered its slopes with a deep layer of a remarkable natural fertilizer called potash, and as a result the mountain supported dozens of species of fruit and vegetables which grew nowhere else in all Italy, a culinary advantage which more than compensated for the area's occasional dangers. In the case of apricots, the varieties included the firm-fleshed *Cafona*, the juicy *Palummella*, the bittersweet *Boccuccia liscia*, the

3

peach-like *Pellecchiella* and the spiky-skinned but incomparably succulent *Spinosa*. Each had their ardent champions, and the thought of the honour going to the wrong sort of apricot provoked almost as much debate as the decision over which farmer had produced the finest specimen of fruit.

Livia was too busy to pay much attention to either contest. A feast day meant that the little *osteria* would be even busier at lunchtime than usual, and she and her sister Marisa had been up since before dawn preparing the dishes that would be spread out on the tables lining the length of the terrace, where vines provided shade from the fierce midday sun. In any case, she had a rather low opinion of both kinds of competition, her view being that in the case of apricots it very much depended on what kind of mood you were in, while in the case of female beauty all the girls in the village got stared at quite enough already. Besides, everyone knew that one of the Farelli sisters would win in the end, and she didn't see why she should give them the satisfaction of beating her. So, while everyone else was out in the piazza, arguing, cheering, booing and clapping the contenders, she concentrated on preparing the antipasto, deftly wrapping *burrata* in fresh asphodel leaves.

'Hello?' a male voice called from the little room which doubled as a bar and a dining room. 'Is anyone here?'

Her hands were full of wet *burrata* and shreds of leaf. 'No,' she shouted back.

There was a short pause. 'Then I must be talking to an angel, or perhaps a ghost,' the voice suggested. 'If there's no one around, I don't usually get an answer.'

Livia rolled her eyes. A smart-arse. 'I meant, there's no one to serve you. I'm busy.'

'Too busy to pour a glass of *limoncello* for a thirsty soldier?'

'Too busy even for that,' she said. 'You can help yourself, and put your money on the counter. It's what everyone else does.'

Another pause. 'What if I'm not honest, and don't leave the full amount?'

'Then I will curse you, and something very unpleasant will happen. I wouldn't risk it if I were you.'

She heard the sound of a bottle being uncorked, and the sound of her father's lemon spirit being generously poured into a glass. Then a young man in a soldier's uniform appeared in the kitchen. He was holding a full glass in one hand and some coins in the other. 'It occurred to me,' he said, 'that if I left my money on the counter and some other rogue came along later and stole it, you would think that it was me who was the dishonest one, and something unpleasant would happen to me after all, and that would be a terrible thing. So I thought I'd bring you the money myself.'

She pointed with her elbow at the dresser. 'You can put it over there.'

He was, she noticed, quite extraordinarily handsome. The black, tailored uniform recently redesigned by Mussolini showed off his lean hips and broad shoulders, and his dark eyes grinned at her from beneath a soldier's cap that was set at a jaunty angle on the back of a mass of curls. Caramel skin, very white teeth and an expression of confident mischief completed the picture. A *pappagallo*, she thought dismissively, a parrot – the local expression for young men who spent their time trying to look handsome and flirting with girls.

'What are you doing in here?' he asked, leaning back against the dresser and watching her. 'I thought everyone was outside.'

'I shall pray to Santa Cecilia for you,' she said.

'Why's that?' he said, surprised.

'Because you are clearly afflicted by blindness. Either that, or you're a cretin. What does it look like I'm doing?'

This sort of remark was usually enough to deter unwelcome visitors to her kitchen, but the young soldier didn't seem at all put out. 'You look like you're cooking,' he remarked.

'Brilliant,' she said sarcastically. 'The saint has performed another miracle. You can go now, you're completely cured.'

'You know,' he said, crossing his legs at the ankle and taking a swig from his glass, 'you're much prettier than any of those girls in the beauty contest.'

She ignored the compliment. 'So that's why you're here. I should have guessed. You came to stare at the girls.'

'Actually, I came because my friend Aldo wanted to come, and there's not much else to do around here. I'm stationed in the garrison at Torre El Greco.'

'So you're a fascist?' she said disapprovingly.

He shook his head. 'Just a soldier. I want to see the world. All my life I've lived in Naples, and I'm bored with it.'

'Well,' she said, 'you can start by seeing the world outside that door. I don't have time to chat to you.' As she spoke she was putting balls of *burrata* inside the asphodel leaves, weaving the leaves through each other so that they formed a natural basket for the cheese.

The handsome soldier was unperturbed. 'You're very rude,' he said conversationally.

'No, just very busy.'

'But you can be busy and talk to me at the same time,' he objected. 'Look, you've done a dozen of those already. And I can take away the plates you've filled and bring you new ones.' He fitted his actions to his words. 'See? I'm making myself useful.'

'Actually, you're in the way. And those plates need to go on the other table.'

'I'll tell you what,' he said. 'I'll go away if you give me a kiss.'

She glared at him. '*Quanne piscia 'a gallina**, *cazzo*. Not in a million years, dickhead. Now get out of here.'

'But my intentions are completely honourable,' he assured her. 'You see, I've fallen in love with you. And what's wrong with kissing someone you're in love with?'

She couldn't help it. She smiled slightly, then put her stern expression back on. 'Don't be ridiculous. We don't know each other from Adam.'

'Well, that obstacle is easily removed. I'm Enzo. And you are—?'

'Busy,' she snapped.

'I'm very pleased to meet you, Busy. Would you like to kiss me now?'

'No.' She had finished the antipasto, and began to chop lemons to accompany the *friarelli*, a kind of bitter broccoli.

'Then I shall just have to use my imagination instead.' He leant back and closed his eyes. A smile played across his face. 'Mmmm,' he said thoughtfully. 'Do you know, Busy, you're a very good kisser. Mmmmmm . . . Let's do that again.'

'I hope that hurt,' she said pointedly.

'What?'

'I just imagined kneeing you in the *coglioni*.'

Enzo clutched his privates and fell to the floor. 'Ow! Ow! What have you done? Now we'll never have those twenty adorable *bambini* I was planning.'

'Get up,' she said, laughing. 'And get out of the way. I have to drain this pasta.'

He jumped up. 'Tell me one thing, Busy. Do you have a boyfriend? Am I wasting my time here?'

'The answer to one of those questions is no,' she said, 'and to the other one, yes.'

* Literally, 'When the chicken pees.'

For a moment his brow furrowed as he worked it out. 'Impossible,' he said firmly. 'Anyway, one good answer is sufficient to be going on with. Aaargh!' He leapt back. 'What in God's name is that?'

Hearing an unfamiliar voice in the kitchen, Pupetta had put her head through the window to see what was going on. Her head was rather large, and was topped by two massive horns, backswept like bicycle handlebars. The horns were considerably wider than the window, but she had long ago worked out how to ease one in before the other. It was this horn which had just claimed Enzo's hat. The soldier turned and regarded the beast with horror.

'That's Pupetta,' Livia said, reaching across to give the buffalo's massive forehead a friendly scratch, retrieving the hat at the same time. 'Haven't you seen a buffalo before?'

Enzo shook his head. 'Not this close. I'm from Naples, remember? We don't have buffalo in the city.' He took the hat and arranged it on Pupetta's head, where it looked almost comically small, then saluted the animal ironically.

'Then we certainly couldn't get married and have those twenty *bambini* you wanted. I could never leave Pupetta.'

'Hmm.' Enzo scratched his head. 'In that case,' he said to Pupetta, 'you'd better be the first buffalo to come and live in Naples.'

Suddenly serious, Livia said, 'Anyway, we shouldn't be talking like this. You're a soldier, you're going to go off and see the world.'

'Only for a little while. Then I'll come back and have *bambini*. And *bufale*, of course,' he added quickly.

'What if you have to fight?'

'Oh, we never fight,' he said casually. 'We just march around and look fierce.'

There was the sound of a clock striking, and Livia rushed over to the stove. 'Now look what you've done. It's almost lunchtime, and I've stopped cooking. My father will kill me.'

'You still haven't kissed me,' he pointed out.

'And I'm not going to,' she said, pulling saucepans out of the cupboard. 'But if you like, you can come back later, and we'll have a coffee together.'

He snapped his fingers with delight. 'I knew it!'

'And don't get any funny ideas,' she warned him, 'or I really will knee you in the *coglioni*. I've had plenty of practice.'

'Of course. What do you take me for?' He finished his drink and set the glass down by the sink. 'It's excellent *limoncello*, by the way.'

7

'Of course it is. Everything is good here.'

'I can see that,' he said. He kissed his fingertips and blew the kiss at her as he walked backwards out of the door. After a moment she noticed that Pupetta was still wearing his hat.

Soon after midday Don Bernardo and her father broke off from their separate deliberations, and a great crowd of people surged across the dusty piazza towards the *osteria*. Within moments every place was filled, and Livia began to serve the food.

Most of the ingredients she cooked with came from the tiny farm immediately behind the restaurant. It was so small that the Pertinis could shout from one end of it to another, but the richness of the soil meant that it supported a wealth of vegetables, including tomatoes, courgettes, black cabbage, aubergines and several species that were unique to the region, including bitter *friarelli* and fragrant *asfodelo*. There was also a small black boar called Garibaldi, who despite his diminutive size impregnated his harem of four larger wives with extraordinary diligence; an ancient olive tree through which a couple of vines meandered; a chicken or two; and the Pertinis' pride and joy, Priscilla and Pupetta, the two water buffalo, who grazed on a patch of terraced pasture no bigger than a tennis court. The milk they produced was porcelain-white, and after hours of work each day it produced just two or three *mozzarelle*, each one weighing around a kilo – but what *mozzarelle*: soft and faintly grassy, like the sweet steamy breath of the *bufale* themselves.

As well as mozzarella, the buffalo milk was crafted into various other specialities. *Ciliegini* were small cherry-shaped balls for salads, while *bocconcini* were droplet-shaped, for wrapping in slices of soft prosciutto ham. *Treccia*, tresses, were woven into plaits, served with Amalfi lemons and tender sprouting broccoli. *Mozzarella affumicata* was lightly smoked and brown in colour, while *scamorza* was smoked over a smouldering layer of pecan shells until it was as dark and rich as a cup of strong espresso. When there was surplus milk they even made a hard cheese, *ricotta salata di bufala*, which was salted and slightly fruity, perfect for grating over roasted vegetables. But the cheese the Pertinis were best known for was their *burrata*, a tiny sack of the finest, freshest mozzarella, filled with thick buffalo cream and wrapped in asphodel leaves. People came all the way from Naples just to experience its unique taste. Sometimes they would even buy a few to take back to the city but, as Nino always told them, it was a futile exercise: by the time the *asfodelo* started to turn brown, which was after just a few hours, the cheese was already starting to lose its flavour.

Business was always good, not least because of the prodigious appetites of the Pertinis' neighbours. Visitors from the city might come and go, but the mainstay of the *osteria*'s business was the villagers themselves. At noon each day every last one of them, from Don Bernardo the priest to the widow Esmerelda, the village prostitute, stopped work and strolled over to the Pertinis' vine-shaded terrace, where for two hours they ate like royalty and drank wine made from the same grapes which ripened above their heads.

It was sometimes said of the Vesuviani that, labouring as they did under the ever-present threat of annihilation, all their appetites were gargantuan – whether for wine, for food or for love. They were also much more superstitious than other Neapolitans, which was to say, extremely superstitious indeed. Every lunch began with a dual offering: a grace offered up to heaven by the priest, and a small libation of wine poured onto the earth by Ernesto, the oldest labourer in the village, a tacit recognition of the fact that here on Vesuvius the ground beneath their feet was considerably more threatening, and closer to their thoughts, than heaven. Like every other village on the volcano, Fiscino was protected by a little circle of shrines, some containing statues of the Virgin, others little effigies of San Sebastiano, who had been protecting them for as long as there had been people on the mountain. Other Neapolitans might object that in that case he had not been doing a very good job, since there had been a catastrophic eruption as recently as 1923, but to the Vesuviani the very fact that eruptions were not more frequent was proof of his remarkable efficacy. However, they were not above hedging their bets, just in case, and many of these protective shrines also bore a little mark depicting a horn, a symbol already old when Christianity came to these parts.

Similarly, it was accepted that while doctors might be good for certain straightforward medical problems, such as a wound that needed stitching, more complex maladies required the intervention of a *maga,* or healer. The *maga* fulfilled many of the functions of a pharmacist, dispensing herbs and recipes to treat everyday ailments such as toothache or the flu, as well as potions that would make a woman fall in love or a man stay faithful. On Vesuvius, the magical powers of the *maghe* were even more widely distributed than usual, so that one family possessed the secret of medicine for warts, while another had the cure for earache, and another the remedy for the evil eye. Within each family it was a matter of some speculation as to who would inherit the gift. For the Pertinis, the matter resolved itself early on. Both Livia and Marisa helped their mother in the kitchen, but while it soon became clear that Livia had inherited her mother's ability at the stove, Marisa preferred to concoct recipes of a different kind, involving the blood of a cockerel, dew harvested at dawn on the Feast of St John, or obscure herbs gathered from the depths of the pine woods that covered the slopes of the mountain.

Livia could not remember learning to cook. Agata had begun to teach her when she was very small, bringing a wooden step into the kitchen so that Livia could reach the stove. By the time she was twelve she had graduated from helping out when the restaurant was busy to being in charge when her mother was ill – a circumstance which occurred increasingly often. She no longer had to bring any conscious thought to what she was doing, nor was she ever aware of following a recipe. As a mathematician is said to be able to see complex equations in terms of patterns, or a musician can improvise melodies from a dozen different scales, she knew instinctively how to bring out the best in whatever ingredients she was using. When she was asked how she had cooked something, or what it was called, she would simply shrug and say 'It's *sfiziosa*,' – a Neapolitan word which has no exact equivalent in English, or even in Italian, but which means roughly 'for the hell of it,' or 'as the fancy takes me.' The restaurant's customers soon learnt not to ask, and were simply grateful for the presence of such precocious talent in their midst, even if the owner of the talent was something of a *scassapalle*, possessed of a fiery temper and a sharp tongue.

During the meal Livia noticed that Enzo was sitting with a group of other soldiers, and that he was easily the most handsome of any of them. She also noticed that the beauty pageant contestants were sitting nearby, shooting the soldiers limpid glances out of the corners of their eyes; glances that did not go unnoticed by the young men, who responded by indulging in increasingly raucous horseplay, which the girls then pretended to be offended by. The three Farelli sisters, of course, were flirting more than anyone. Livia sighed. It seemed to her unlikely that Enzo would come back for that coffee after all. Colomba, the eldest of the sisters, was clearly setting her cap at him – or rather, her bonnet, a ridiculous concoction covered with glass fruit and feathers. So that was that. It was Colomba who had coined the nickname *stecchetto*, little toothpick, for Livia, because she was so scrawny. She had filled out a little since her sixteenth birthday, but she would never have Colomba's curves.

Then she saw that Enzo was getting up from his place and coming towards her. She turned away. He did not stop, but as he passed her he whispered, 'I was right the first time, when I called you an angel. Because surely only an angel could cook like that.'

'Save your flattery for whoever wins the beauty contest,' she said. But she flushed with pleasure despite herself, and when she saw Colomba Farelli looking at her with daggers in her eyes, it was nice to be able to smile sweetly in return.

As she was serving the huge platter of sliced apricots in wine which was the inevitable *dolce* of the feast-day lunch, something rather remarkable happened. A row had broken out between Colomba and her two sisters, Mimi and Gabriella. And not just a row: within moments it had progressed from name calling and screaming to hair pulling and scratching, much to the amusement of the watching soldiers. It required the intervention of Don Bernardo himself to calm the warring parties, getting to his feet and thumping the table with an empty bottle of wine until there was silence.

'This is a disgrace,' he thundered. 'And as a consequence of your appalling behaviour, I shall not be awarding the prize to any of you.'

'So who will you give it to?' a voice asked from the crowd.

'To no one.'

'But if you don't give it to anyone, it'll be a draw, and they'll all have won,' the voice pointed out. There was a murmur of agreement at the irrefutable logic of this.

'Then I shall give it to . . .' Don Bernardo's gaze raked across the terrace, and came to rest on Livia. 'I shall give it to someone who truly deserves it, because she provided us with all this food.'

Oh no, Livia thought. To enter and not win would have been bad enough, but not to enter and to win because the priest was angry with the Farelli sisters would be completely humiliating. Colomba, for one, would never let her forget it.

The same thought must have belatedly occurred to Don Bernardo, who was quailing slightly before the ferocity of Livia's scowl. 'Um . . . er . . .' he said.

Enzo jumped to his feet. 'He means Pupetta,' he shouted. 'Pupetta the wonder-cow, who provided the milk for our wonderful *burrata*.'

'Exactly,' Don Bernardo said, relieved. 'I mean Pupetta. Where is she?' Pupetta, hearing her name, looked up from the end of the terrace, where she was just wondering if she could pretend to be a goat and eat the soldier's hat.

11

'*Viva* Pupetta,' someone shouted. There was a general shout of agreement, and people started to clap. The Farelli girls rearranged their bonnets, and settled down again to flirt with the soldiers. After all, there was no shame in losing to a buffalo.

Two

After lunch the accordions and the castanets came out, as they always did on a feast day. Someone began teasing out a low, throbbing rhythm on the *tammurro*, the goat-skin drum shaped like a huge tambourine, and everyone, young and old, began to dance. Children partnered their grandparents, the little girls putting their feet on their grandfather's shoes until they had learned the steps for themselves; mothers swayed with their babies on their hips, while the soldiers and the beauty contestants took the opportunity to show off to each other, the girls with the sinuosity of their movements and the boys with their acrobatics.

'Will you dance the tarantella with me, Busy?' Enzo asked Livia, as she passed him with a pile of dirty plates in her arms.

'Certainly not. People will gossip. Anyway, you can stop calling me that. My name is Livia.'

'So you're not really Busy?'

'You know I'm not.'

'Well,' he said reasonably, 'if you're not busy, you've got time to sit down and take that coffee with me.'

She smiled, and came back and sat down. 'Thank you for getting Pupetta that prize.'

'Not at all. She was definitely the best cow in the whole contest.'

Livia's younger sister, Marisa, brought them two cups of espresso with a knowing smile. When she had gone Enzo fixed Livia with his big dark eyes and said seriously, 'What do you want to do with your life, Livia?'

No one had ever asked her a question like that before. Taken by surprise – she had assumed that they were going to go on talking nonsense – she said, 'Is there a choice?'

13

'Every girl has a choice,' he said. 'Particularly one as beautiful as you. You must have dozens of men wanting to be your beau.'

She was pleased by the compliment, but chose to ignore it. She had always hated the way Colomba Farelli simpered and shrieked every time a man paid her any attention. 'There have been some,' she admitted. 'Although none that I liked. But anyway, having a choice of men to marry isn't the same thing as being able to choose what to do in life. Whoever I end up with, I'll have to keep his house and cook for him.'

'Then you must make sure you marry a man who loves you,' he said.

'Yes,' she said doubtfully. That hadn't been what she'd meant, exactly. She tried to explain. 'I've been used to cooking for a lot of people, here at the restaurant. It's going to be very different when I get married.'

'Ah,' he said. 'Now I've realised why you were so rude to me earlier. You don't want to get married, because it means leaving here.'

'Possibly.' She shrugged, amazed that he had understood her so quickly.

'I'm exactly the same,' he said, leaning forward. 'Only for a different reason. I don't want to get married, because I *do* want to leave here, and if I get married I'll have to leave the army and live at home with my wife, just like my older brother Ricardo.'

'This is very romantic,' she said, laughing. 'We hardly know each other, and already we're telling each other that we don't want to get married.'

He shook his head. 'I'm saying that I'm as surprised as you. I wasn't on the lookout for someone, but when you meet the right person, you have to grab the opportunity while you can.' He reached across and took her hand in his. 'You are the most beautiful girl I have ever met, Livia.'

It was the kind of remark that, had it been made by one of the young men she usually served at the *osteria*, she would have dismissed with a mocking comment. But now she felt a wave of heat rising from her neck to her ears.

'I've made you blush!' he said delightedly. 'It's a good sign. You know what they say: if you can make a girl blush, make her laugh or make her cry, you'll be able to make her—'

'I know that saying too,' she interrupted. 'And there's no need to be obscene.' But even as she said it, she had a sudden mental image of the two of them in bed together, and she blushed again.

'Wait here,' he said, jumping up. 'I'm going to buy you a ribbon from Alberto Spenza.' He went over to where a plump young man was hanging around with the soldiers. She saw Enzo offer him a coin. The plump boy glanced across at Livia, then opened his jacket to reveal a dozen yellow and red ribbons. Please let Enzo choose me a red one, she thought, because red will look better in my hair; and she was absurdly pleased when she saw him coming back across the square towards her with a long red ribbon dangling from his fingers. 'For you,' he said, presenting it to her with a bow, a salute and a click of his heels, all at once.

At that moment Pupetta lowed mournfully from her pasture behind the house. 'Thank you,' Livia said, taking the ribbon and tying it in her hair. 'But now I'm afraid I'm busy again.'

He frowned, inspecting her face, then carefully looked behind her. 'How strange, Busy. You still look exactly like Livia.'

'I have to go and milk Pupetta and Priscilla,' she explained.

'Then I'll come and help,' he said.

'Don't get any ideas,' she warned. 'Just because you've bought me a ribbon, it doesn't mean I'm going to kiss you.'

'On my honour as a soldier, I promise I won't try anything.'

'Hmm,' she said. She wasn't surprised when, the moment they were alone in the barn together, he did try to kiss her. But since she had rather been hoping he would, she allowed him to embrace her briefly, and even to touch his tongue against hers, making her gasp with pleasure, before she pushed him away firmly and said, 'The milking has to be done.'

'And I'm the man to do it,' he said, pulling up a milking stool. 'Show me what to do.' They were both rather out of breath.

She pulled up a bucket and another stool and sat down next to Priscilla, who was less patient than Pupetta and liked to be milked first. 'You've never done this before, have you?'

'No,' he said, scooting closer. He rested his head on the buffalo's flanks, taking the opportunity to study Livia's profile from very close quarters. 'But I'm very good with my hands.'

She giggled. 'Go on then, maestro. See if you can milk her.'

He put his hands tentatively on Priscilla's teats and squeezed.

'Not like that,' she said. 'You're meant to be milking her, not fondling her.'

He smiled at her. 'I wouldn't know anything about either one.'

'I'm glad to hear it, even though I don't believe you for one moment. All soldiers have lots of girls; they're famous for it.'

'Not true,' he protested. Then seeing that she wasn't cross with him, he added, 'Well, a little bit true.'

She put her hands on his and showed him. 'Like this,' she explained. 'Squeeze, pull and twist . . . then release.' There was a ping! as a thin squirt of milk hit the bottom of the bucket. The rich, clean odour of it rose into their nostrils.

'So this is different from the way a woman's breast likes to be touched, is it?' he wondered aloud as they milked, an innocent expression on his face.

'I'm not answering that,' she said. 'Pay attention, or you'll knock the bucket over.'

Their heads were very close, and the pressure of her hand on his, alternately squeezing and releasing, was rather pleasant. He turned his head to look at her profile again. With her hair pulled back by the red ribbon, he could see where the hairline around her ears became softer and more downy as it merged into the fuzz of her skin, soft as an apricot. Impulsively, he leant forward and placed a kiss on her cheek. She turned her head to him, her lips parted and her eyes shining.

That day poor Priscilla was not milked very effectively, although it was one of the longest milking sessions the buffalo had ever known.

Three

Something unprecedented had happened: Livia had burnt the onions. And not just any onions, but the ones in her famous *sugo genovese*, that wonderful sauce of reduced onions, flavoured with beef stock, celery and chopped parsley, that together with *pummarola* and *ragù* form the holy trinity of Neapolitan pasta sauces. To make a true *genovese* the onions have to be cooked for around five hours over the gentlest heat, stirring occasionally to prevent them from sticking to the bottom of the pan and splashing them with water whenever they look like drying out. Onions are remarkable things, for cooked like this they lose almost all their familiar oniony taste and become an intensely sweet, aromatic jam, yet if a single piece happens to burn in the cooking, the acrid taste will permeate the whole dish.

Not since she was a child had Livia burnt the onions in her *genovese*, yet today the customers at the restaurant were all too aware of a faint, bitter aftertaste in the sauce as they forked the pasta into their mouths. They exchanged glances, but nobody said anything.

'How was the meat?' Livia said, coming out to collect some dirty plates. She did not wait for an answer, but started stacking the dishes up on her arm.

'Livia,' an old farmer called Giuseppe said gently, 'we haven't had the meat yet.'

'Haven't you?' She looked surprised. 'Oh, nor have you. I'll get it.' She went back into the kitchen.

After ten minutes someone stopped Livia's father as he brought in more wine. 'Nino, what's wrong with Livia? She's acting very strangely. That pasta didn't taste right at all. And she still hasn't brought out the *secondo*.'

Nino sighed. 'I'll go and have a word.'

He went into the kitchen and found Livia staring out of the window as she absent-mindedly stirred a saucepan. 'Livia. Are you all right?'

'Mmm? Yes, of course.'

He glanced into the pan. 'I never knew you had to stir boiling water before.'

'What? Oh, of course. Well, I'm boiling an egg. Only I forgot to put in the egg.'

Nino tapped his forehead. 'If you ask me, it's your head that's boiled. There are people out there waiting for food.' He suddenly noticed that her hair, which was tied back with a red ribbon he had never seen before, smelt of rosemary, and that there was a rhododendron flower tucked behind her ear. 'Are you waiting for that boy to come back?' he demanded.

Livia blushed. 'Of course not.'

'Livia,' he said gently, 'he's a soldier. He'll probably never come. And if he does, what happens when he gets posted somewhere a long way away?'

'Wherever he goes,' she said, 'he'll come back eventually.'

Nino raised an eyebrow. 'So you're thinking seriously about him?'

'Perhaps.'

He watched her thoughtfully for a moment. 'I think,' he said, 'that when this lad does turn up I'd better have a word with him myself.'

When Enzo returned to Fiscino the next day, having toiled in the sun all the way up from Torre El Greco, he was slightly perturbed to discover, first, that he had to have a discussion with Nino before he could see Livia, and second, that the interview was to take place in the field where Nino was supervising the mating of Priscilla with another farmer's bull.

'Come on, boy, you can give me a hand,' Nino said, looping the bull's halter around his own wrist as he led the way. Enzo followed at what he hoped was a safe distance. He had thought Pupetta and Priscilla were huge, but they were positively svelte compared to the buffalo bull, whose vast, muscular shoulders were covered in a shaggy pelt like a lion's mane, and whose forehead resembled nothing so much as a massive rock crowned with two fearsome spears.

Nino thumped the bulging muscle on the bull's neck appreciatively. 'He's called Dynamite,' he told Enzo. 'Best damn buffalo sperm this side of Caserta.'

Enzo nodded thoughtfully, trying to look like a connoisseur of buffalo semen. It was hard enough picking his way through the vast buffalo cow-pats without getting any splatters on his uniform.

Nino led the bull into the field, then shouted to Enzo to shut the gate. Dynamite trotted forward on surprisingly dainty legs, then opened his mouth and bellowed, causing Enzo to look around apprehensively as the huge sound echoed off the woods around them.

'He's scented them,' Nino said with satisfaction. 'That's good.'

'How often do you do this?' Enzo asked, eager to make a good impression.

Nino gave him a surprised glance. 'Every year, of course. The females won't produce milk unless they're in calf.'

That the production of milk was directly related to calving had never really occurred to Enzo before. 'And what happens to the calves?' he asked.

'We eat them,' Nino said bluntly. 'Eat them before they've even tasted grass. I cut their throats and bleed them myself, in the barn. They're sweetest like that. Good, he's interested.'

Enzo watched, slightly overawed, as Dynamite's interest manifested itself all too clearly beneath the beast's shaggy belly. With another almighty bellow, the buffalo levered himself onto Priscilla's back, jabbing at her hindquarters with his enormous pizzle until he managed, more by luck than judgement, to lodge himself inside her. Priscilla grunted, and lowered her head to chew at the grass.

As the bull rutted, Nino turned his attention to Enzo. 'So you're the lad who's got Livia in such a spin,' he commented.

'Yes, sir,' Enzo said, his heart lifting at this confirmation that Livia really did care about him.

'Going to marry her?'

'Er,' Enzo said, 'I've only just met her. But I hope to. Assuming she'll have me, of course, and that you give me your blessing.'

Nino looked at the young man shrewdly. 'You probably think that's what a marriage is all about,' he said, jerking a thumb at Dynamite's energetically swaying hindquarters.

'Oh, no, sir.'

'Of course you do. Every boy does, at your age. But watch what happens.'

Dynamite's forehooves scrabbled at Priscilla's sides. Then, with another almighty bellow that sent birds shooting from the trees, his buttocks shuddered and he slid off her. A few moments later, both animals were contentedly grazing the lush, humid pasture, Dynamite's pizzle drooping onto the grass.

'Doesn't last long, does it?' Nino commented. 'Bit of a stupid reason to get married, really, when you think about it. If that's all you're after, you'd do better to visit the widow, Esmerelda.'

'That's not what I'm after at all, sir,' said Enzo, who together with his friends had visited the widow Esmerelda on several occasions already. 'I love her.'

'And as for a dowry, forget it. I'm just a poor farmer who keeps a little country bar.'

Enzo scratched his head. 'No dowry at all?'

'Well, maybe just a token one. Say a thousand lire.'

'What about two thousand?' Enzo said, desperately trying to negotiate.

'I thought you said you loved her,' Nino said.

'Oh, I do. It's just that—'

'Well, if it's love, where does money come into it?' Nino demanded belligerently.

'It doesn't,' Enzo assured him. 'Er – a thousand is fine.'

Nino regarded the young man anxiously. He was handsome, certainly, but his negotiating skills were non-existent. Here in the countryside, where even settling the price of a chicken could take all day, such things were important. He suspected that Livia might end up wearing the trousers in this relationship. Still, he knew his daughter well enough to know that there was no point in trying to change her mind.

'I'll have to think about it,' he said grudgingly. 'And if it ever occurs to you to dishonour her before her wedding day,' he added, looking the boy hard in the eye, 'just remember what happens to the calves.'

Enzo and Livia spent the afternoon together, and that evening the first customers at the *osteria* were pleased to hear the sound of singing coming from the kitchen.

Livia was so happy that she was barely aware of what she was cooking. But everyone remarked on how her lemon pasta seemed even sweeter than usual, whilst the baked mozzarella with roast peppers was a triumph. Admittedly, Livia absent-mindedly ate all the cheesecake that was meant to be for dessert herself, while she was sitting in the kitchen daydreaming about Enzo, but as the customers later agreed, it was worth it just to see her so happy, not to mention to avoid the risk of any more burnt onions.

Four

Fiscino etiquette was both very liberal and very strict. Once they were formally engaged, it was completely accepted that Livia and Enzo would sneak off to roll around in the hay barn, kissing and working each other up into a frenzy. It was also expected that they would both be virgins on their wedding night. Anything in between, however, was a grey area.

One of the many advantages of this tried-and-tested arrangement was that it forced the young man to be a lot more inventive than he might have been if he had simply been able to make love in the conventional way, and then fall asleep. Enzo soon discovered that beneath Livia's practical exterior she was extremely passionate.

'Now listen,' she said, the first time they went to the hay barn. 'Let's get something clear. I've come here because I don't want my sister rolling her eyes and giggling every time she sees us together, not because I want you to stick your tongue down my throat. And I'll thank you for keeping your hands to yourself.'

'So no tongues, and no hands,' he agreed. 'Are there any other body parts you'd like amputated? My legs, perhaps?'

'Your legs are acceptable,' she said, 'so long as you don't try to grope me with them.'

'That's not very likely,' he pointed out, 'since if I did, I'd fall over.'

'Good. That's settled, then.'

Enzo sighed. Much as he adored Livia, life with the Pertinis seemed to be one long negotiation in which he always seemed to come off worst. 'May I kiss you now?'

'If you like.' She came into his arms, and he pressed his lips against hers. She gasped, and after a moment he felt her tongue pushing between

21

his lips. Experimentally, he put his hands on her back, then slid them around her waist. Livia squirmed, but it seemed to him to be a squirm of pleasure rather than disapproval. He kissed his way down her neck, and when she moaned with delight he thought he might as well continue towards her breasts. To his amazement, those seemed to be up for grabs as well. After a few minutes of him kissing and stroking them through her dress, she was clearly impatient to have the material removed, so he pulled her dress down over her shoulders before continuing.

'I thought you said no hands,' he murmured as he lavished attention on her beautiful little nipples.

'Yes, well, that was before I realised how much fun it was going to be,' she said with a shiver as he did something particularly pleasant with his teeth. 'Pupetta always makes it look rather boring, and really it isn't boring at all.'

Livia had a very good time indeed in the hay barn, and by the time she came to be married she was already fairly sure she was going to enjoy that side of things. Meanwhile, she and Enzo were not allowed to kiss in public, and when they danced the tarantella at a *festa* they had to keep a handkerchief between them, holding one end each so that their hands never actually touched. This Livia found rather amusing, as Enzo's big blue handkerchief also featured, necessarily, in some of their more enthusiastic encounters in the barn.

A fortnight before their wedding, Enzo took her to Naples to meet his family. She had not realised from his descriptions quite how poor they were, or what cramped conditions they lived in, sleeping three and even four to a bed in a tiny three-roomed apartment in the slums of the old quarter. But she was in love, and she was determined to make the best of her new life.

Enzo's mother, Quartilla, was a typical Neapolitan, sharp-eyed and shrewd. The first time they met she asked Livia to help her by making a *sugo*, a tomato sauce, while they talked. Of course, she didn't really need any help, but she had been told that this country girl was good in the kitchen and she wanted to see if it was true. 'Help yourself to whatever you need,' she said, and sat down to peel some *fagiole*. So Livia cooked, and Quartilla watched her like a lizard watching a fly.

Livia could have made a *sugo* blindfold – she had been making it almost every day for years. The only difficulty was, there were as many different kinds of *sugo* as there were days in a month. There was the everyday version, which might be no more than a handful of ripe tomatoes squashed with the tip of a knife to release the juices, then quickly fried in oil. There was the classic version, in which the tomatoes were simmered along with some garlic and onions until they had reduced to a thick, pulpy stew. Then there was a richer version, in which pieces of meat were cooked for several hours to extract all the flavour, and so on all the way up to *ragù di guardiaporte*, the gatekeeper's sauce, so called because it required someone to sit by it all day, adding little splashes of water to stop the rolls of meat stuffed with parsley, garlic and cheese from drying out.

Livia knew that whichever recipe she chose now would be taken by Enzo's mother as a kind of statement about her character. She quickly rejected the rich version – that would look extravagant. The classic version, on the other hand, would look as if she wasn't putting any thought into it, whilst the simplest one, although her own favourite, might look as if she wasn't prepared to make an effort. So she decided to follow her instincts.

'Do you have any anchovies?' she asked.

Enzo's mother looked as if she was about to explode. 'Anchovies?' In Naples, anchovies were only added to tomatoes if you were making *puttanesca*, the sauce traditionally associated with prostitutes.

'Please. If you have some,' Livia said demurely.

Quartilla appeared to be about to say something else, but then she shrugged and fetched a small jar of anchovies from a cupboard.

The sauce Livia made now was not *puttanesca*, but like *puttanesca* it was powerful and fiery. It was also remarkably simple, a celebration of the flavour of its main ingredients. She tipped the anchovies, together with their oil, into a pan, and added three crushed cloves of garlic and a generous spoonful of chilli flakes. When the anchovies and garlic had dissolved into a paste, she put in plenty of sieved tomatoes, to which she added a small amount of vinegar. The mixture simmered sluggishly, spitting little blobs of red sauce high into the air, like a pan full of lava. After three minutes Livia dropped a few torn basil leaves into the sauce. 'There. It's finished.'

Instantly Quartilla was standing next to the pan, dipping a spoon in to taste it. For a brief moment her eyes registered surprise. Then she recovered, and made a show of smacking her lips thoughtfully while she considered her verdict.

'Well,' she said at last, grudgingly, 'It's a bit showy, and it's got too much heat in it – it needs to be reined in a bit. A lot of men would think it was quite tasty, but that's men for you, they can easily mistake chilli and strong flavours for good solid nourishment, particularly when it's made to look all pretty on the plate. But it'll do.'

And you're an old witch, Livia thought. Quartilla must have read her mind, because she added, 'And if you don't make my Enzo happy, girl, I'll put you over my knee and beat you with that wooden spoon myself.'

Naples, Livia realised, was going to be very different from the country. She noticed, too, that whenever they went out together for the *passeggiata*, the evening stroll along the Via Roma that was a ritual for all betrothed couples, Enzo seemed to take great pleasure in the admiring glances he himself received in his uniform, whereas whenever a look or a smile came Livia's way he was unhappy, and hurried her along.

The night before the wedding Livia wore green, and when she walked to the church a veil covered her face, so that evil spirits would not see her happiness. Enzo, meanwhile, carried a piece of iron in his pocket to ward off the evil eye. Their families walked with them, the little children running alongside catching the sugared almonds that were thrown up into the air. Afterwards there was a big party, for which Livia had cooked all the traditional dishes. Each one had a symbolic or superstitious meaning. The sugared almonds meant that there would be bitterness as well as sweetness in their lives. The soup of chicory and meatballs which started the feast symbolised the pairing of complementary ingredients. Even the pastries, fried twists of dough dipped in sugar, were supposed to ensure fertility. The happy couple were toasted by the families with the cry of '*Per cent'anni!*', and Enzo had to make a formal announcement that Livia was now no longer her father's daughter, she was Enzo's wife. Then there was a great chant of '*Baci! Baci! Baci!*' to encourage them to kiss in public for the first time, which they did to great applause.

I'm Signora Pertini now, Livia thought – for in Italy a woman keeps her father's surname after her marriage, her change in status denoted instead by the fact that she is no longer called *signorina*.

It was the custom that when they went to bed, the wedding guests came into the bedroom with them and placed gifts around the room – money, mostly, but also cloth, chinaware and sweets – so that when they were finally left alone, with many a ribald comment from the departing guests, they first had to clear all the coins and sugared almonds off the bed. The ribald comments had made Livia rather shy, in fact, and she was glad to have had all that rolling around in the hay barn to give her confidence. But she was also glad they had not gone any further than they had: in the morning, as Neapolitan custom demanded, she had to take the sheets to her mother-in-law to wash, so that if Quartilla wished she could satisfy herself that Livia had been a virgin. Quartilla only gave her a nudge in the ribs, and commented slyly, 'There'll be a lot more washing from now on, I hope. I want a grandchild.'

Livia blushed. 'There's plenty of time for that.'

'Not this month there won't be. Enzo goes back to the garrison next week.'

'Next week?' Livia had not realised their honeymoon would be so short. But Enzo reassured her that he would be home again after a fortnight, and a fortnight was not so very long to wait.

When he came home from the garrison, however, something seemed to be worrying him. He cross-questioned her about who she had seen, what she had been doing, and which of his male friends she had seen when she was out shopping in the market.

The next day Quartilla announced that from now on, one of her other daughters would be doing the shopping.

'But why?' Livia asked, appalled. Now she wasn't cooking for all the *osteria*'s customers, going to the market was the only real pleasure she had when Enzo was away.

'People have been talking. Apparently you're too friendly.'

Livia searched her memory. She had been polite, certainly, and since she was herself bursting with happiness she had probably smiled at the stallholders. But there had been no flirting, of that she was absolutely certain.

She protested, but Quartilla simply said, 'It's different in the city. Besides, you're Enzo's husband, and this is his wish.'

Livia accepted the inevitable, and waited another week for Enzo's next leave. But it was no different this time – again she was cross-questioned about who she had seen, what she had been doing, whether she had been out, and if so what she had been wearing.

'Enzo,' she cried, 'This is ridiculous. I married you because it was you I wanted, not someone else. What makes you think I'd even look at another man?'

He refused to answer, until eventually she coaxed it out of him. 'If *I* seduced you,' he said glumly, 'it stands to reason someone else could too.'

She laughed, although the assumption that it had been his choice that they were together now, rather than hers equally, actually made her rather cross. 'Don't be crazy. It's you I fell in love with, and there's no one else like you in all Naples.'

He smiled, and looked happier. 'Yes, that's true, isn't it?' Then his features clouded again. 'But I'm not here most of the time.'

'Well,' she said, 'if you're really worried about me being bored while you're away, I think I have the answer. I'm going to get a job in a restaurant, as a cook.'

Enzo looked appalled. 'You, go to work in a restaurant? God forbid!'

'Why not? Most of your sisters work.'

'Yes, but that's in the factory. The lines are separated – the men work on one side, the women on the other, and they all keep an eye out for each other to make sure nothing goes on. If you were in a restaurant, anything might happen.'

She wanted to explode, but she had an idea that she had to be quite careful how she handled this. 'Believe me,' she said, 'I am quite capable of looking after my own honour. I'm not like those other girls, who simper and flirt and make eyes at any man who smiles at them.'

After a moment he nodded. 'That's one reason I liked you, right from the start. I could never have married one of those girls who showed themselves off in the beauty contest.'

Again, Livia felt a pang of irritation – not because she had a very high opinion of beauty contestants, but because it seemed to her that a double standard was being applied here. But she contented herself by saying, 'Tell you what. How about if I do the shopping in the market, but I take your sister with me? Then everyone will be satisfied.'

Enzo agreed that this was a good idea, and Livia decided to leave the question of working in a restaurant for another occasion. It was the first disagreement the two of them had ever had, and she wanted to think it through before she worked out how to proceed.

On reflection, though, she decided that it had not been such a very big matter. This trait of Enzo's was by no means uncommon amongst Neapolitan men, and she felt that her ability to handle the situation probably boded well for their married peace together. Things would be better once he had left the army, as he had promised to do by the end of the year.

So in all in all things had worked out satisfactorily, and even Quartilla turned out not to be such a dragon when you got to know her, apart of course from her incessant demands for a grandchild, which would happen soon enough anyway if Livia and Enzo went on making love at the rate they did. Although Livia sometimes missed the excitement of

26

cooking for dozens of people at once, she was happy, and her life would probably have followed much the same course as Quartilla's or her own mother's, had it not been for a series of events which turned out to be even more cataclysmic than an eruption of the volcano.

PART TWO

FEBRUARY 1944

'. . . The main effort must, however, be directed against hoards in the hands of farmers and black market operators. This problem has been discussed at length, but, with the exception of sporadic efforts in various provinces, no positive general vigorous action has been initiated. The position indicates that the matter is now one of the gravest urgency.'

Memo, AMGOT headquarters, 15 October 1943

Five

'This is as far as we go,' the driver said, pulling the truck over to the side of the road. He pointed. 'The Riviera is down that way, if you can get through the rubble.' He watched as James climbed down from his perch on top of a pile of ammunition boxes, then gave a cheery half-salute before putting the big K-60 into gear. 'Good luck, sir.'

James Gould picked up his kitbag and knapsacks and arranged them around his body in the position of least discomfort, the heavy roll of the kitbag balanced on one shoulder and the knapsacks slung over the other. ''Bye,' he called, attempting to return the driver's salute over the kitbag. 'Many thanks.' As the truck drove away an old woman's face, weather-beaten as a pug's, appeared at a nearby window and peered at him fearfully. He nodded politely. '*Buona sera, signora.*' The face vanished abruptly.

He had been warned about the smell. As they'd retreated from Naples the Germans had blown up the sewers – those that hadn't already been destroyed by weeks of British and American bombing. Burning braziers stood outside some of the buildings to counteract the stink, but they seemed to have little effect. In the gloom of the narrow streets, with half-destroyed ruins towering precariously on either side, the inky flames only added to the apocalyptic atmosphere. As he gingerly picked his way through the debris James saw one building, now reduced to rubble, which appeared to be still smouldering. Only when he got closer did he realise that what he had taken for wisps of smoke were actually streams of flies, busily zooming in and out of the rubble. The smell was particularly bad just there.

He continued to nod at the Italians he passed: an elderly man, who scuttled past with his eyes averted despite James's polite '*Buona sera*'; a couple of *scugnizzi*, street urchins, who stopped to stare at him, their arms draped insolently around each other's shoulders; an ancient woman, indistinguishable from the one who had appeared at the window earlier – the same lined face, the same dumpy body, the same shapeless black dress. He stopped her and tried to ask for directions. '*Scusi, signora. Dov'è il Palazzo Satriano, per cortesia?*' He had been practising his Italian on the troop ship from Africa, but the flowing consonants still felt strange and chewy in his mouth. The woman gave him a glance in which terror mingled with incomprehension. He tried again. 'The Palazzo Satriano? It's on the Riviera di Chiaia.' It was no good: he might as well have been speaking Swahili. '*Grazie mille*,' he said resignedly, and pressed on.

Knowing that his destination was on the seafront, and reasoning that he couldn't go far wrong if he kept downhill, he continued the way he was going. All around him were signs of the city's recent history. On one wall a giant mural depicting Mussolini's *fascio* symbol, an axe surrounded by a bundle of sticks, had been overpainted with a German swastika, and on top of that, a hastily whitewashed panel bore a crude Stars and Stripes and the words *Vivono gli Alleati*, Welcome to the Allies. The mural was decorated with a spray of bullet holes, though it was impossible to tell at which point in the wall's artistic evolution they had been added.

Two young women were coming towards him. They were dark-haired, dark-skinned and dark-eyed, beauties of the type that one saw in pre-war photographs of the country, although he noticed that they were wearing what seemed to be American military jackets, brightened up here and there with twists of coloured fabric. Each of them had a flower tucked behind one ear. They glanced at him, the nearest smiling shyly, and he tried the same sentence on them. '*Scusate, signorine. Dov'è il Palazzo Satriano?*'

The girls' reaction was very different to the old woman's. The one who had smiled was instantly in front of him, standing very close, her fingers playing with the buttons of his uniform and her voice murmuring something so quietly that he had to put his head close to her mouth to hear.

'Tree teen russians. Ver' cleen, ver' cleen.'

He realised too late they were prostitutes. Her soft fingers brushed his hand, and even as he pulled away from her he felt her slender leg still pressing against his. 'You like?' she murmured eagerly, pointing at herself and then her companion. 'Both tree teen russians.' Three tins of rations: it was nothing, it was less than five shillings.

32

'I'm sorry,' he said, taking a step away from her. '*Sono un ufficiale inglese.*' He hesitated. Had he just said that he was an English officer, or an official Englishman? '*Mi sono perso*, that's all.'

The girl smiled, a little ruefully, as if to say it would have been nice to meet him on an evening when he was neither an official Englishman nor *perso*, lost. He had come across whores before, of course – the dour-faced women back home who put cards in their windows that read 'Soldiers' washing dealt with', the heavily made-up caricatures who prowled Piccadilly and Regent Street, the well-padded *lucciole* of his last posting – but never had he come across such beauty sold so cheap, or such a wistful, resigned shrug at his refusal.

He turned the next corner and found that he was in a street crammed with bars and restaurants. It surprised him: the briefing notes had said such premises were still officially closed. 'Naples is the first major city to be liberated by the Allies. The free world will be watching to see how we conduct ourselves,' the notes had gone on to say. On the evidence before him now, James thought, the free world might be a little shocked. The street had narrowed even further, so that it was barely wider than a desk, and the ubiquitous braziers gave off a stifling heat. Even so, the little thoroughfare was thronged with people. Pressing past him were uniforms of every hue and nationality – British khaki and American olive green, but also a melee of Poles, Canadians, New Zealanders, Free French, Highlanders, even a few diminutive Ghurkhas, all picking their way cheerfully through the rubble. And the girls – everywhere he looked there were more dark-haired, dark-eyed young women with flowers tucked behind their ears, strolling in pairs, hanging on the arms of the soldiers, or leaning languidly against the doors of the bars, waiting for customers. Dresses cut from army blankets, or adapted military uniforms, seemed to be the order of the day, which gave the little street the air of a bizarre military camp.

It was hard getting through the crowd with the kitbag over his shoulder: whenever he turned one way or the other it bashed against someone, like Charlie Chaplin and his ladder. He found himself apologising left and right to those he was assaulting. There appeared to be no particular regard for rank here, which was just as well given the difficulty of returning salutes around the kitbag. Once he thought he felt light fingers tugging at his knapsack: when he looked around a *scugnizzo* was already slipping away through the crowd, casting James an affronted look over his shoulder as if it was hardly sporting of him to have fastened his luggage so tightly.

At an intersection a street trolley rattled past, unbelievably full, a trio of nuns hanging off the running boards, its klaxon lowing as it attempted to clear a way through a tangle of traffic. Convoys of trucks were being directed by an American military policeman in a white tin helmet and, opposite him, an Italian *carabiniere* in an elaborate band-leader's uniform. The American had a whistle in his mouth: shrill blasts accompanied his gestures, impatient and stern. The Italian, by contrast, seemed almost apologetic as he shrugged and gesticulated at the traffic. Long-horned oxen, harnessed in pairs to wooden carts like something out of an Egyptian watercolour, defecated lethargically as they waited their turn. Small boys darted amongst the mayhem selling lipsticks and lucky charms.

Eventually a friendly British fusilier pointed him in the right direction. The way led down a side street barely larger than an alley, then followed a dizzying series of zigzagging stone staircases. It was a relief to be out of the din and the crush, and it was a little while before James realised that he was no longer hemmed in on every side by buildings.

He stopped, momentarily taken aback by the view. In front of him, a vast orange sun was setting over the bay of Naples. Under the red sky the sea was as smooth as a saucepan of boiled milk. Along the seafront, palm trees nodded in the evening breeze. And on the other side of the bay, the vast bulk of Mount Vesuvius loomed abruptly out of a distant peninsula, like an egg in its eggcup. A tiny question mark of smoke hung over its summit.

'Gosh,' he said aloud. Then, conscious that one was not here to admire views but to finish a war, he descended the steps towards the large building he could see at the bottom.

Six

The Field Security Service had done itself proud, that much was immediately apparent. His new headquarters was an ancient *palazzo*, somewhat dilapidated in appearance but still bearing signs of its former grandeur. Inside the imposing entrance, a faded fresco showed nymphs and satyrs engaged in some kind of food fight. James wandered into an inner courtyard, which contained a lemon tree and four brand-new jeeps.

'Hello?' he called cautiously.

Through one of the windows that gave onto the courtyard he spotted an orderly in an American uniform scuttling from one room to another, bearing an armful of files. 'Excuse me,' James said, leaning through the window. 'I'm looking for FSS.'

'Try upstairs,' the orderly said uninterestedly over his shoulder.

So much for information sharing between Allies, James thought. 'Any idea where?'

'Third floor, maybe.'

James heaved his kitbag onto his shoulder again and trudged up the huge staircase that filled one corner of the courtyard. His nail-soled boots echoed on the stone – the American's rubber soles had made barely a sound.

On the third floor he opened a door and stepped into a large, barely furnished salon. It contained an elegantly dressed woman, who was sitting by the window in an equally elegant chair, and an emaciated old goat, which was tethered to the chair by a chain. A child was sitting cross-legged on the floor next to the goat, milking its teats into a bucket. All three looked up at him as he entered, although only the goat looked particularly surprised. '*Scusi*,' James muttered, withdrawing quickly. He had forgotten that when an American said the third floor, he actually meant the second.

On the floor below the tapping of a typewriter indicated that he was now in the vicinity of an office, an impression confirmed by a printed sign on the door bearing the words '312 Field Security Service (British Army)'. Beneath it a second, typewritten notice said: 'Wedding Officer. Appointments only. Office hours 3.00–4.00'. The same information was repeated in Italian. At some point the notice had been torn into several pieces, as if it had been ripped from the door in exasperation, and then stuck back together. James put down his kitbag and knocked.

'*Avanti*,' a voice said.

He opened the door. It was a large room, and a long table running down the middle of it was piled high with files and papers. A dark-haired man was perched on the side of the table, shuffling papers from one vast pile to the next. He had a coloured neckerchief pushed into the collar of his shirt, which gave his uniform a faintly raffish air. 'Yes?' he said, looking up.

'Hello. I'm Captain Gould.'

'Oh.' The man seemed surprised. 'We weren't expecting you until tomorrow.'

'I got a lift from Salerno. A supply truck on its way to the front.'

'Ah. Rightio.' The man gestured at the papers. 'I was just sorting things out for you, as a matter of fact. I'm Jackson.' He stood up and offered his hand.

James stepped forward to shake it. 'Looks like quite a job,' he suggested, eyeing the mounds of paper.

'It is that.' Jackson ran his fingers through his hair. 'I'm a bit behind, actually. I was going to write you a note. But since you're here, shall we do it over dinner?'

James had not had anything that could properly be described as 'dinner' for a very long time. 'Do you have a mess?' he asked hopefully.

Jackson laughed. 'Not exactly. That is, there's a man called Malloni who cooks our rations for us, but his culinary skills aren't up to much. We suspect he's skimming off the corned beef and selling it on the black market – the locals have somehow become convinced it's an aphrodisiac, I suppose on the principle that anything that tastes so vile must somehow be good for you.' Jackson had a slight twitch, which punctuated every other sentence with the faintest of pauses. 'No, I was thinking more of a restaurant. There's a place called Zi' Teresa's, down in the harbour. Black market, of course, and priced accordingly, but that needn't worry us. It's one of the better perks of the job – just ask the owner to sign the bill, and he'll knock fifty per cent off straight away.'

'But isn't that just the sort of thing we're here to stop?'

'Believe me,' Jackson said with a lopsided grin, 'kicking out the Jerries is nothing compared to the job we'd have if we tried to separate the Neapolitans from their grub. And we've got bigger headaches to worry about. How about it?'

'Take a look at the pictures, when you get time,' Jackson suggested as they walked back towards the stone staircase. 'Some of them are rather racy. If you like that sort of thing.' Now that James looked more closely, it was not only food that the nymphs and satyrs were fighting over in the frescoes. 'Your transport.' Jackson pointed to where a Matchless motorbike was propped underneath a statue of Proserpine, her naked buttocks pockmarked with bullet holes. 'Whatever you do, don't keep it in the street. The Yanks have had three jeeps stolen already. Not to mention several trucks, a freight locomotive and a couple of class C warships.'

'How come you're both in the same HQ?'

'The theory is that their Counter Intelligence Corps and our Field Security do pretty much the same job. Some bright spark thought we should do it together.'

'And do you?'

Outside the *palazzo* Jackson turned left, marching briskly along the seafront. Automatically, James fell in beside him, their arms and legs swinging in unconscious military unison. 'Well, we try not to step on each other's toes. It's a marvellous set-up they've got – twenty-five staff to our three, and a filing system that takes up a whole room. How's your Italian, by the way?'

James confessed that so far, he had barely understood a word that had been spoken to him.

'That's probably because what you were hearing was Neapolitan – it's almost a separate language, and some of the older folk profess not to understand anything else. Don't worry, you'll soon pick it up. But CIC are hampered by the fact that not a single one of them even speaks standard Italian.'

'That's rather odd, surely?'

Jackson gave a bark of laughter. 'Not so much odd as fortuitous. There are plenty of Italian Americans in the Fifth Army, but they've all wangled positions in the stores. The last thing they want is CIC sticking their noses in.'

'You mean – they're pinching their own supplies?' James said, appalled.

Jackson stopped. 'Do you know, I think we should take a detour. There's something I ought to show you.'

He took James up the hill into the old quarter, a mass of dark medieval buildings piled on top of each other. Zigzagging erratically through the middle of this labyrinth was an alleyway that seemed to have become the main street by virtue of its length rather than any claim to magnificence. It resembled nothing so much as an African souk, James thought: narrow, chaotic and unbelievably crowded, both with buyers and sellers. Market stalls roughly assembled from a couple of suitcases and a plank of wood were piled high with every item of army equipment conceivable – ration packs, blankets reworked into dresses and coats, boots, cigarettes, phials of penicillin, toilet paper, even rolls of telephone wire. Passers-by picked over items of military underwear, or haggled vociferously over candy bars filleted from American K-rations. The stallholders eyed the two officers warily as they pushed through the crush, but apart from one shifty-looking gentleman who slid a couple of British bayonets out of sight as they approached, they made no attempt to conceal their wares.

'We used to round them up occasionally,' Jackson was saying, 'but a different set of faces simply came and took their places the next day. Penicillin's where the real money is, of course. So much has gone missing our medics sometimes have to come here and buy it back from the black marketeers, just to keep the field hospitals supplied.'

James nodded. Penicillin: it was the word on everyone's lips. Before penicillin there had been no effective way to treat the infections caused by bullet wounds or bomb shrapnel, so that even a relatively minor injury could lead to the loss of a limb or death. An American company, Pfizer, had now found a way to manufacture the wonder drug in huge quantities, and was even running advertisements in magazines and newspapers boasting of the difference their product could make to the war.

'Why do the Italians want so much of it?' James asked. 'After all, it's not as if they're fighting now.'

'It's not injuries they want it for, it's venereal disease. It's rampant here.'

'Oh. Of course.' James remembered the girls who had approached him earlier. *Ver' cleen. Ver' cleen.* 'There's a fair amount of . . . fraternisation, I take it?'

They had turned off the street market now and were walking down through the old town. As if to illustrate his words, a raucous group of

GIs rounded the corner. Each had a bottle in one hand and a laughing girl in the other.

Jackson shrugged. 'It's simple economics, I'm afraid. The Jerries conscripted all the able-bodied Italian men and shipped them off to labour camps or to fight in Russia. After that, the economy collapsed – prostitution and black marketeering are pretty much all that's left. According to the latest Bureau bulletin, there are over 40,000 prostitutes in Naples. That's out of a total female population of 90,000. If you exclude the very old or the very young, almost any woman you see here is on the game.'

'And there's nothing we can do about it?'

Jackson shot him a glance. 'Well, winning the war would be a start,' he said mildly.

'I meant nothing we can do here, in Naples?'

'We do what we can.' Jackson pointed at a sign above a shop. The original lettering had been painted out and the words PRO STATION daubed on top. 'Officially, prostitution is illegal and we don't tolerate it. But we give out free prophylactics to any soldier who wants them. And there's a sort of fungicide, too, which the girls can use to clean themselves – blue powder, the men call it. But that's as far as our interest extends. At the end of the day, all that concerns Allied Military Government is keeping the soldiers on their feet. After a couple of weeks here, most are headed back to the front. So long as they can stand up and fire a rifle, that's what matters.'

Back on the seafront he ushered James through the doorway of a restaurant. Behind the blackout blinds it was packed with people. Most were officers, but there was a smattering of GIs entertaining local girls, and several tables of surprisingly prosperous-looking Italians, some of whom were eating with American or British staff officers.

'You'd hardly know there was a war on, would you?' Jackson said, enjoying James's surprise.

'Signore Jackson. How very nice to see you.' The maître d' was shimmying between the tables towards them.

'A quiet table please, Angelo. My colleague and I have business to discuss.' The Italian smiled and led them to a table at the back.

'The women look pretty good, don't they?' Jackson commented, looking around him as they sat down. 'They call it the Kraut diet – they're all on the verge of starvation.' A handwritten menu was placed on the table. 'Be careful what you order, though. There aren't many cats on the streets of Naples any more.'

A waiter was passing through the tables with some fish on a platter, showing them to the diners to attract their admiration. Jackson stopped him. 'And take a look at these,' he said to James. 'Notice anything strange about them?'

'They seem all right to me.'

'The heads don't match the bodies.'

Now that James looked more closely, he saw that each fish did indeed consist of two separate pieces, carefully fitted together at the neck. The join was almost invisible. 'Dogfish, probably,' Jackson said dismissively. 'Edible, but hardly a delicacy.' He spoke sharply to the waiter in very fast Italian. The waiter shrugged and said something back – once again James found himself quite unable to make out most of the words. Jackson nodded. 'It seems they have sea urchins today, though I'd advise you against those as well.'

'Why's that?'

'They have a rather inconvenient effect.' Seeing James's incomprehension, he lowered his voice. 'On the libido. Unless you intend to visit one of the rooms upstairs later, I'd steer clear.'

'So this is a – well, a brothel?'

The other man shrugged. 'Not as such. But every black market restaurant has a few girls hanging around. There's a rather notorious beauty at this establishment, as it happens, with a glass eye and a famously supple throat. If you like that sort of thing.' He sat back and regarded James anxiously for a moment. 'You married, Gould?'

'Um,' James said, taken off guard. 'Not exactly.'

'But you've got a girl? Back home, I mean?'

'Absolutely.' Jackson seemed to be waiting for more details, so he added, 'Her name's Jane. Jane Ellis. She's a land girl.'

'Engaged to her?'

'Pretty much.'

'Good. You'll find that comes in useful. In the wedding interviews.'

'Yes, I was going to ask you—'

'My advice to you, Gould,' Jackson said with sudden urgency, leaning towards him, 'is to steer clear of seafood, stay out of the sun, and *think of your girl*.'

'Well, of course. But what I don't quite understand—'

'At the first sign of trouble, just tell them you're *fidanzato*. Engaged.'

'I'll bear it in mind,' James said, completely mystified.

'Got to set the right example. You're the wedding officer now, you see.' Jackson appeared to give a kind of shudder.

'Actually, I don't see,' James said. 'The first I knew of it was that sign on your door—'

'Not *my* door, old thing. Your door, now.' Suddenly, Jackson's mood seemed to brighten. 'Do you know, I think I might have those sea urchins after all. Since it's my last night.' He gestured to the waiter. 'What about you? They do a perfectly acceptable sausage and egg.'

'That sounds wonderful.' When the waiter had taken their orders, James persisted, 'Tell me, though – what *is* a wedding officer, exactly? There wasn't anything in the briefing notes.'

'Ah.' Jackson seemed unsure where to begin. 'Well, it's rather an odd one. Ever since the Allies arrived, there have been a number of soldiers wanting to marry local girls. Quite a *large* number – in fact, it looked as if it might be starting to get quite out of hand. Of course, any serviceman who wants to marry has to get the CO's permission. So, in an attempt to stem the tide, the CO decided that every potential fiancée has to be vetted to confirm that she's suitable and of good character.'

'But what on earth does "good character" mean?'

'Basically, that she isn't a whore.' Jackson shrugged. 'The fact of the matter is that she's bound to be, given what we were saying earlier. Your job is simply to gather the evidence. If she's got enough food, or if there's any furniture left in her apartment, she's a tart. If she can afford soap rather than cleaning herself with charcoal, she's a tart. If she can afford olive oil, or white bread, or lipstick, she's a tart. Just ask her what she's living on. Nine times out of ten she'll tell you there's an uncle somewhere, but that story never stands up to much scrutiny.'

'Doesn't sound too difficult.'

Jackson stared at him. For a moment his eyes had the vacant, dispossessed look James had seen on the faces of Blitz victims and battlefield casualties. Then he passed his hand over his face, and seemed to recollect where he was. 'No, I suppose it doesn't.' A jug of red wine arrived, and Jackson poured them both large glasses, splashing some over the table-cloth in the process. '*Per cent' anni.*'

'Cheers.'

As he set his glass down James noticed that a man at a nearby table was watching them with an amused expression on his face. From his expensive suit James deduced that he was both a civilian, and someone of importance. He was dining with a group of American staff officers. The man caught James's eye, and raised his hand in ironic greeting.

'Who's that?' he asked.

'Who? Oh, him. His name's Zagarella. He's a pharmacist, though his real occupation is professional cockroach. He's the man behind most of the stolen penicillin.'

'Can't you arrest him?'

Jackson smiled mirthlessly. 'I did, once. It didn't get me anywhere. As you can see, he has some rather well-connected friends.'

Their food came. The sausage and egg was, as Jackson had promised, perfectly acceptable, and seemed to be made with real eggs, not dried, and genuine meat instead of bully. After months of tinned rations James devoured it eagerly.

Jackson picked up his sea urchins, avoiding the violet spikes, and spooned the brightly coloured insides into his mouth. James had never seen anything like it. Presumably it was an austerity measure, like the cafés at home that served whale meat pie. 'May I taste that?' he asked curiously.

'All right,' Jackson said somewhat unenthusiastically, passing one over. James dipped his knife into the soft yolky innards and touched it to his tongue. There was a taste of seaweed, but also a rich, salty creaminess, strange but not unpleasantly so. He struggled to think of anything in his experience it could be compared with.

'It's like – like whelks with custard,' he suggested.

'If you say so.' Jackson ate the rest of his sea urchins quickly, without offering to share any more.

As they ate he explained what James's other duties would involve. Notionally, FSS were responsible for anything that could affect the security of the Allied Military Government. 'In theory, that means intelligence gathering. But there isn't any intelligence in Naples any more, only wild rumour. Just last week the Americans produced half a dozen so-called reliable reports that a suicide panzer division had holed up in Mount Vesuvius and was waiting to come out and pounce on our rear. It took me three days to verify what I knew all along, which is that it was all a piece of nonsense.'

'You don't seem very impressed by our Allies,' James said.

'Well, we do have more experience of this sort of thing. Africa and India and so on.' Jackson poured himself some more wine. 'We're just naturally better suited to running an empire.'

James murmured something about the Germans having had a similar notion, but Jackson was disinclined to pick up on any irony.

'Actually, the Krauts ran this place pretty well. They didn't have any trouble with VD, for example. They simply imprisoned any girl who passed on an infection, and gave the soldier concerned a field punishment

42

for good measure – despoiling the purity of the master race and so on. We're supposed to be more civilised, which gets us into all sorts of trouble.'

There was a curious incident when Jackson asked for the bill. Before it could be drawn up, Angelo, the maître d', sidled over to the table and said that there would be no charge 'for the British secret policemen'. He bowed to James. 'A very warm welcome to you, Captain Gould. I hope we'll see you here often.'

'How does he know my name?' James asked when Angelo had gone.

Jackson shrugged. 'It's his business to know everyone.'

'I'm not really happy about this,' James said.

'Why not?'

'It's my first evening in Naples. I don't see that I can start off by accepting – well, what could be construed as a bribe.'

'That's the way it's done here, I'm afraid. You grease my palm, I'll grease yours. Angelo doesn't mean any harm.'

'But technically, this place shouldn't even be open.'

'They're getting back to normal. It's just not the same as our normal, that's all.'

'I still want to pay my half,' James said doggedly. He called to the waiter, who went to fetch a bill.

'*Il conto*,' he said, putting it on the table with a smile. James looked at it: it came to more than two weeks' army wages.

'Can I give you one last piece of advice, Gould?' Jackson said when James had finished paying.

'Of course.'

Jackson hesitated. Then he said slowly, 'This place isn't like home. There aren't any rules here, only orders. Just follow the orders, and you'll be all right. But if you try and make sense of it – well, you'll go completely mad.'

As they left the restaurant they came upon a scuffle – two British soldiers beating up a local boy, no older than fifteen. One of the soldiers had him by the arms, while the other was setting about him with a chair leg. Blood was streaming from the boy's head. A dark, pretty girl not much older than the boy watched helplessly from a few yards away.

'What's going on?' Jackson called sharply. 'Stop that at once.' The soldiers backed off reluctantly, and the two FSS men hurried forward to question them.

It turned out that earlier the boy had pimped his sister to them. A price had been fixed, but the boy had taken the money – or rather, the three packets of cigarettes that had been agreed as payment – and made a dash for it. The soldiers had come across them again later, and had set about teaching them a lesson. James made a show of taking their names and numbers, but it was clearly going to be impossible to do more. He sent them on their way and they left, still muttering threats.

While he was dealing with the men Jackson had been talking in a low voice to the girl and her brother, who then slipped off into the shadows themselves. 'Not a happy story,' he said as James rejoined him. 'And not as straightforward as it looks. The children are *scugnizzi* – haven't seen their parents in over a year. The girl has syphilis, so she was at least partly motivated by a desire not to spread it any further when she ran off. I gave her the address of a hospital that may be able to get her some penicillin, though I doubt she'll be able to afford it. It's a classic vicious circle. She'll have to sleep with a dozen more soldiers to get the funds to clear up her own infection, by which time those men will have infected a dozen more girls.'

'You must be pleased to be going home,' James said. 'Nice to get back to England, after all this.'

'I suppose so,' Jackson said. He looked up at the crumbling buildings around them – the bombed-out windows, the balconies strewn with washing and geraniums, the walls pockmarked by the ordinance of three armies – and then at the crush of humanity streaming past in both directions. 'It's strange how it grows on one, though.'

Seven

Livia Pertini crashed the pans together and glared at her father. 'How can I cook without food?' she cried.

Her father shrugged. 'Alberto Spenza is here, and he wants to eat.'

'That gangster! He's had his snout in the trough for so long, it's a wonder he can fit any more in his fat stomach.'

'Try not to shout,' Nino suggested, although the truth was that Livia was making so much noise banging pots and pans around that nothing either of them said could be heard outside.

'You'll have to tell him to come back another time.'

'And have him go somewhere else? He's one of our best customers – one of our only customers, now.'

Livia sighed. 'I could make a *sugo*,' she said reluctantly. 'But you'll have to tell him there isn't any meat.'

'And some *melanzane farcite*?' Nino said hopefully. 'You know how Alberto loves your stuffed aubergine.'

'I suppose.'

'Good girl. And perhaps a *budino* for afterwards?'

'No! I don't have time. And there's only one egg.'

'Then maybe—'

'And I don't have time to talk to you now,' Livia added bluntly as she started chopping tomatoes for the *sugo*. Nino smiled and withdrew. He knew full well that when the pasta was sorted, his daughter would make a *budino di ricotta*, a cheesecake, somehow cooked with only one egg. This was partly because Livia was a good girl, who listened to her father even when she claimed not to, but also because there was almost nothing else to cook. It had been three weeks since they had last been able to buy supplies. People bartered what they could with their neighbours,

45

but now that food was meant to be sold through government-approved agencies, it was simply impossible to obtain what you needed legitimately.

The sauce that Livia cooked now was a simple one, but thanks to the quality of the ingredients it was also extremely good. She chopped up a handful of *pomodorini da serbo*, a tiny tomato unique to the slopes of Vesuvius. These she fried quickly with some garlic in a little of the Pertinis' own olive oil. At the last moment she threw in a few torn leaves of basil from the bush that grew just outside the kitchen door. In less time than it had taken to cook the pasta, the sauce was done.

Marisa took the dish out to serve it, and Livia got on with the other courses. First, though, she poured the hot oil from the frying pan into a steel container – an old shell casing, which she had found in the fields and carefully cleaned out. She topped up the oil with a little cold water. It was an economy measure: the impurities from the cooking would sink to the bottom along with the water, allowing the precious oil to be reused time after time.

Later, as she washed the dirty pans, she became aware that someone had come into the kitchen.

'Oh,' she said. 'It's you.'

Alberto Spenza was watching her from the doorway. She was not surprised – the kitchen was in any case always open to customers, who liked to see what was on offer before deciding what to eat. But the former ribbon seller was a more frequent visitor than most.

Since Enzo went off to fight, four years before, Alberto had rarely passed up any opportunity to drop by. As the war progressed and he prospered – it was widely known that he was a gangster, and possibly even a *camorrista*, a member of the Mafia – the visits had become more frequent. Livia saw the way he looked at her, and it made her fearful. All Italian men stared – but there was something unpleasant about the surreptitious glances Alberto gave her when he thought she wouldn't notice, the way a greedy man might eye his neighbour's plate.

Today, at least, he seemed to be on his best behaviour. 'A fine meal,' he said with a smile, easing his vast bulk into the room. 'Is there perhaps some coffee?'

'Only from acorns,' she said sharply. She pushed some pans around on the stove. There was no one else to cook for, but pretending to be busy meant she didn't have to look at him while they talked.

'Then it's fortunate that I brought some myself.'

She did look up then, surprised. Alberto was taking a twist of paper out of his pocket and unwrapping it. An aroma filled the little kitchen that Livia had not smelt since before the war. Despite herself, she inhaled the deep, rich flavour, and her features softened.

'It's called Nescafé,' Alberto said. 'The Americans get it in their rations. It's not really coffee, to tell the truth, but it's better than acorns. You have to sweeten it with sugar before it tastes all right.' He smiled, showing his teeth beneath the pencil moustache he grew to hide his double chins. 'But luckily I have sugar too.' He put another twist of paper on the counter. 'Perhaps you'll join me.'

Livia hadn't had sugar for over a year. For any recipe that needed sweetening, she used a tiny dab of honey. 'I'll get a coffee pot,' she said, reaching into a cupboard for a *napoletana*, the traditional hourglass-shaped jug in which coffee was made.

'No need. You just add boiling water. So simple!'

She shrugged, and put a pan of water on the stove.

'You know,' Alberto continued, 'It's a shame you have no customers here. If this goes on much longer you'll start to get rusty.'

The same thought sometimes occurred to Livia as well. 'I've had no complaints. Anyway, the war will be over soon,' she said doggedly.

He raised one eyebrow. 'Will it? My sources say otherwise. Another year at least, perhaps three. The Americans are in no hurry to get killed, and the Germans are in no hurry to surrender.'

Livia thought of Enzo. Dear God, would she really not see him for another three years? It had already been four years since they were together.

As if reading her mind, Alberto said, 'That's a long time to try to keep this place going. You must be losing money hand over fist.'

'We'll manage,' she said defiantly.

He picked at his teeth with a knife. 'Of course,' he said thoughtfully, 'you could always come and cook for me.'

'For you? At your *casa*?'

'Why not?' He crossed his thick arms. 'The war has been good to me. I can afford a . . .' He hesitated. 'A housekeeper. I'd much rather it was you than someone else.'

She busied herself making the coffee, pouring it into two tiny espresso cups. It smelt delicious, but when she put her nose into the cup the aroma quickly dissipated, leaving only a faint whiff of chemicals. She tried some. It was thin and bitter, delivering far less taste than the smell had promised. 'A housekeeper,' she repeated. 'So I wouldn't only be a cook?'

He shrugged again. 'I have some other needs as well.'

She shot him a glance. 'Such as?'

47

'Some washing, some cleaning . . . the kind of things my wife would do, if I had one,' he said casually.

She felt a hot blush turn her face red. Alberto stirred his coffee. 'The kind of things you did for Enzo,' he said softly. 'He told his friends that you were quite a . . . quite a *catch*.' He smiled knowingly. 'Though come to think of it, that might not have been the exact word he used.'

Her heart sank. What sort of stupid things had Enzo been saying? That part of their life was private. Why couldn't he keep his mouth shut? Her cheeks flushed again, this time with shame.

'I heard he had a special nickname for you,' Alberto was saying. '*Vesuvietta*. His little volcano.'

'Enzo's my husband,' she said loyally.

'Of course. And he'll still be your husband when he comes back. In the meantime, though, you should be looking after his interests. Who knows – he could come back with no legs, or blind, or with his hands shot off.' Livia put her hands over her ears to block out the terrible words, but she could still hear him. 'Shouldn't he return to find you've managed to put something aside, instead of running up huge debts? I'll pay you enough to recoup everything you've lost. No one else will help you. Your father's working himself into his grave. As for your sister – no one's going to marry Marisa, she's too strange, and I don't think she's the sort who wants a husband anyway. Who's going to look after her when the restaurant closes?'

'It's quite impossible—'

He shook his head. 'It happens all the time now. Haven't you been to Naples recently? The girls there are selling themselves for a mouthful of bread. It's the same even in Boscotrecase. After the war, we'll all pretend it never happened.'

'This is ridiculous—'

'And if by some sad misfortune Enzo never does come back – well, you'll need a husband who can look after you.'

'Stop this,' she said. 'I can't possibly do what you're suggesting.'

'Yes, you can. Talk to your father.'

'My father *knows* you were going to ask me this?'

'He's a sensible man. Of course, we don't need to involve him in the precise details.' He ran the point of the knife under his fingernails. In that moment she knew that he revolted her. But for her father's sake she tried to keep her temper.

'Alberto Spenza,' she snapped, 'I wouldn't go to bed with you if you were the last man in Italy – which, given that you're already the fattest man in Italy and everyone else is starving, is a distinct possibility. Now get out.'

He shrugged, apparently unconcerned. 'We'll see if you're so fastidious when you've been hungry for a few weeks.' He opened the door and went outside. 'Nino, your stubborn daughter doesn't want my job,' she heard him saying. 'In fact, she's been so rude to me that I doubt you'll see me for a while. Try to talk some sense into her, will you? And if she wants to come around and apologise – well, that would be best for all concerned, although of course I might have found another cook by then.'

When Alberto had gone Marisa and Nino came into the kitchen. Livia was so angry that for a little while she couldn't talk to them. Instead she crashed some plates into the sink and began to wash up. Only when one of the plates cracked in two did Marisa say evenly, 'So Alberto offered you a job?'

'If you call whoring for him a job.'

'Ah.'

'Livia, I didn't know—' her father began.

Livia laughed bitterly. 'And you couldn't guess?'

Marisa said thoughtfully, 'Livia, we all have to survive.'

'What's that supposed to mean?'

'The Farellis have sent all three of their daughters to Naples, did you know that? They send back a little money every month. Where do you suppose that money's coming from? Alberto was right – everything's different now. No one would blame you if you decided to accept his offer.'

'I don't see you volunteering to sleep with that fat pig.'

'Well, if it came to it—'

'None of us is going to do anything like that,' Nino said with finality. 'Let other people do what they like. So long as we still have food to eat, the Albertos of this world can go hang themselves.'

That afternoon a truck came up the road to Fiscino. It drove slowly right around the village, so slowly that Livia could see the faces of the six soldiers sitting in the back, each one holding a rifle. Then it stopped outside the *osteria*. The soldiers jumped down. An officer wearing the khaki shorts and lopsided beret of an Australian regiment climbed out of the front.

'We've been told you're hoarding food here,' he said to Nino. 'I have to requisition it for my men.'

'Livia, Marisa, go upstairs,' Nino said quietly. 'Go to your room and lock the door.'

Livia felt the stares of the soldiers following her hungrily. 'This is Alberto's doing,' she said bitterly to her sister.

'Almost certainly.'

'As if I'd agree to go with him after he did something like this. He's stupid as well as fat.'

'He's not stupid,' Marisa said quietly. 'He knows he disgusts you, so he's not bothering to try to make you like him. He's trying to make you so desperate that you'll have no choice.'

For three hours the soldiers went through the *osteria* and the farm methodically, picking it clean. They took all the tomatoes, both the ripe and the unripe; all the zucchini and aubergines, even the tiny ones. They pulled potatoes out of the soil, roughly shook them free of dirt, and tossed them into the back of the truck. They threw the chickens in as well, picking them up by the legs and tossing them in with the vegetables as casually as if they had been cabbages. At this Nino tried to protest. The officer drew his pistol without a word and casually pointed it at the old man, raising his eyes as if to enquire whether being shot was something he really wanted. He might have been offering Nino a cigarette rather than a bullet.

The soldiers worked on. They broke down the door of the barn, and took all the fruit that was stored in the hay. They approached the bee hive, but having no protective clothing, and no idea how to get at the honeycomb without getting stung, they simply pushed it over, breaking the combs. In the dairy they found a day's worth of *mozzarelle* sitting in a bucket: they took those, too, and a pail of milk left over from the cheese making. Then Livia, watching from the upstairs window, saw one of the soldiers undoing the gate which led to the buffalo pasture.

'No!' she cried. Marisa put a warning hand on her arm.

The soldiers tried to herd Pupetta and Priscilla towards the truck, but of course the two buffalo were big, stubborn old milkers who had absolutely no desire to be manoeuvred into a vehicle. One of the men picked up his gun. Two others grabbed the nearest animal, Pupetta, and held her by the horns. The one with the gun steadied the muzzle against her forehead. 'Steaks tonight, boys,' he called.

'I can't stand this,' Livia said, breathless with horror.

'Wait,' Marisa said. 'Don't be stupid—'

But Livia had already unlocked the bedroom door and was running downstairs. As she came out into the yard she heard a shot and saw

Pupetta's head jerk back. The animal's eyes rolled wildly, her huge bulk swaying on her legs. But she did not fall.

One of the soldiers picked up a rifle and fired into Pupetta's body. Then, suddenly, all the men were firing wildly, the bullets tearing little pieces of skin from Pupetta's hide. Dark spots appeared across her ribs. The men were cheering and whooping, reloading and shooting again. Pupetta sank to her knees, wearily, and lay on the ground. Her legs twitched, like a dog running in its sleep. Then she was still. There was a sudden silence, broken only by the echo of the shots bouncing back from the woods.

'We'll need a saw,' one of the men said to Nino. He mimed a sawing gesture. 'A saw, capeesh?'

'You bastards,' Livia sobbed, shaking her fist as she ran forward to kneel by Pupetta.

'Livia, go back inside,' her father said. But it was too late. One of the soldiers had already grabbed her, laughing as he lifted her off her feet. She hadn't realised before how strong he would be – when she hit him with her fists, it was like hitting a tree. Then another pair of arms had grabbed her too – two men now, whooping as they casually tossed her into the back of the truck along with all their stolen food. She yelled angrily, and the other men cheered. One of the pair who had tossed her in the truck climbed up after her and pulled her arms behind her back, pinning both her wrists in one of his hands.

'Let me go,' she screamed. But the soldiers only cheered more. For the first time she began to feel afraid.

'OK, boys, that's enough,' the officer said casually. 'Throw her out.'

'I'll only be five minutes,' the one holding her said.

'I doubt you'd be five seconds, but that's not the point. You want a girl, there are plenty in Naples. We've got work to do.'

Reluctantly the soldier released her, though not before he had pushed his hand up her skirt. One of the other men was already sawing off Pupetta's hind legs.

When the legs had been thrown in the back of the truck along with everything else, the officer pulled out a pocketbook and peeled off some notes, which he handed to Nino without a word. It was a hundred lire – not remotely a fair price for everything they had taken.

The officer's hand hesitated over the pocketbook. 'How much for the girl?' he asked in a low voice.

'She's not for sale,' Nino said.

After a moment the man shrugged and put the pocketbook away.

Saluting ironically, he climbed into the front of the truck. As it drove away one of the chickens, unsettled by the movement, jumped out over the tailgate with a flurry of wings. The truck didn't stop. Soon the only sound was Livia's sobbing as she cradled Pupetta's great head, still warm but completely lifeless.

'We were lucky,' Nino said heavily when the truck had disappeared from view.

'You call that lucky?' Livia cried. 'They've taken everything we have.'

'Not everything.' Nino crouched down next to her and stroked her hair gently. 'Don't you understand? It could have been so much worse.'

Eight

In just four years, everything had changed completely.

When Mussolini first declared war, some of the women said that he was just like any other Italian man who was feeling a bit cocky: he was starting a fight to show off. But you couldn't say that to the men, most of whom believed *Il Duce* had rescued the country from collapse. Alliance with Hitler was simply yet more evidence that Mussolini knew which side his country's bread was buttered.

Enzo had left with a kiss and a wave, confident that he would be back within a couple of months. Then came the first reports of setbacks. From Africa, from Greece, and then from Russia, the news came back. *Esteemed Signore and Signora, it is with the deepest regret that the government has the honour of informing you of the heroic sacrifice of your son . . .* Even worse, in some ways, was the not knowing: when the letters from your loved one simply stopped arriving, as they did in Enzo's case. Marisa wrote to Livia that sometimes in Fiscino the villagers begged her to use her gifts to tell them whether their husband or son was still alive. She always refused, saying that her sight would not reach so far, though she sometimes confided in Livia that such-and-such a person would never be coming back.

There were German soldiers in the garrison at Torre El Greco, the first blue-eyed men Livia had ever seen. They seemed friendly at first, despite their uniforms and their guns – after all, they were all on the winning side together. But young men who failed to join up voluntarily were taken anyway in huge *rastrellamenti*, labour round-ups. The Germans searched from house to house in the small hours of the morning, opening cupboards and knocking on walls for secret hiding places, kicking in doors with their jackboots, their dogs barking dementedly and waking the whole neighbourhood.

The white bread produced by local bakers before the war disappeared. Your ration coupons only got you a hard black loaf, the iron crust disguising the fact that the inside was mostly air mixed with a stringy dough that provided no sustenance at all. There were just four of them in Enzo's parents' apartment, once the men had gone, but all their coupons combined only got them one loaf a week, together with some pasta and a few beans.

One night Livia had been woken by a strange light coming through the window, along with a deafening growl. Getting up from the bed she now shared with Concetta, Enzo's younger sister, she went to see what was happening. She gasped. Under a black cloud of aeroplanes the sky was full of beautiful light – a ghostly, silvery, sparkling luminescence that fizzed from hundreds of tumbling flares.

She knew what she was meant to do: get to the safety of the big road tunnel that ran through the hillside below Naples. She quickly pulled on a dress and shook Concetta awake, but the pathfinder flares had done their job and the first bombs were already falling as they ran up the hill to the tunnel. Buildings were spitting out mouthfuls of stone and timber, the sky was full of the whistle of falling objects, and down by the harbour the silvery light of the flares had been replaced by the yolky orange of a dozen fires. Yet the streets were crowded with people, running in all directions, just as if it were daytime. As Livia ran past a gap in some buildings, the hot gust of a nearby explosion almost knocked her off her feet. She heard metal ping against the wall behind her. It was like a storm – a storm of steel and high explosive, through which you had to force yourself, bent double, as if you were running against a high wind.

When they reached the tunnel they found it crammed with people. A few had brought blankets, but most simply stood there in the dark, dripping gloom, waiting for dawn – even after the planes had gone it was too dangerous to venture back out.

In the morning they found a city transformed. It was as if Naples had been pulverised by giant fists. Even streets that had not suffered damage were covered in thick red dust. In some places the road itself had caught fire, and the blackened cobbles now smoked gently in the sunshine. Glass crunched underfoot. They passed a shop where a display of four tins in the window had melted into one solid block. Two women were trying to loot it, wrapping their hands in their dresses because it was still too hot to touch. A little further on, a dog was licking the pavement. Some German soldiers were loading bodies into a truck.

After that, the four women had taken their mattresses to the tunnel every night and slept there. It was pitch-black, dank, and it smelled – a mixture of faeces, bodies and God knew what else – but it was safe. Up to a thousand other people did the same thing, while even more crowded into the old aqueducts and catacombs that were carved out of the tufa rock underneath the city. Livia grew accustomed to the incessant noise – the snores, the fights, the couples making love, the cries of infants, even the occasional baby being born. She grew used to the way the ground moved under her as she slept, and the intermittent trickle of mortar from between the bricks above her head whenever a bomb fell particularly close. Far more irritating were the lice: big, fat white creatures that infested every blanket, every mattress and every stitch of clothing, and were spread – or so people believed – by the rats that ran around in the darkness, biting babies' toes off in their hunger. And night after night still the Allied planes came back, the throb of their engines penetrating deep into the tunnel, followed by thuds and bangs and waves of pressure as their bombs gradually reduced the city to ruins.

As the war continued, relations with the Germans soured. They shot people on a pretext, or for the tiniest infringement of martial law. There were no men around to stop them, apart from a few fascists and officials who had been excused conscription, but the *scugnizzi*, the street urchins, formed a sort of unofficial resistance. They attacked German tanks in swarms, pushing bottles full of burning petrol into the slits below the gun turrets. The Germans, for their part, opened up on them with machine guns, and left their bodies where they fell.

Quartilla's nerves had been stretched to breaking point by the constant bombardments, and after a body was found on her own doorstep she told Livia that she should go home, back to Fiscino, where she would be safer. Livia suggested that she should bring her family and come with her, but Quartilla wouldn't hear of it. 'I was born in Naples,' she said firmly, 'and I'll die in Naples, if that's what God demands of me.'

The railway tracks had been bombed, and travelling was slow. But in the countryside it seemed they had not suffered as much as the Neapolitans had done. Dishes had to be cobbled together from poor ingredients, though, and Livia often found herself serving meals she was frankly ashamed of. Even Garibaldi the pig looked emaciated now that the supply of scraps and leftovers had dwindled to almost nothing. There was nothing for it but to turn him into sausages, but even those only lasted a few weeks.

The worry over Enzo was ever-present. She begged her sister to tell her whether he was alive or not: Marisa always shrugged and said, 'It's like a radio signal from a distant station. Sometimes I just know, sometimes I'm not sure, more often there's a sort of echoing fuzziness. Enzo's one of those. Wherever he is, it's a long way away.'

The German soldiers who were the restaurant's main customers now were usually polite. But one night they heard drunken shouting in German coming from somewhere in the village, and then a fusillade of shots. Next morning the widow Esmerelda was lying in the road outside her house, quite dead. That night Marisa took some engine oil that had dripped into the dust of the piazza and cast a spell on it, mixing it with the blood from a cock's comb and the smashed shell of an egg. Whether it was coincidence or not Livia was never quite sure, but when the Germans' tanks drove through the village one of them suddenly spluttered and broke down in a paroxysm of foul-smelling smoke.

At last the day came that everyone had been waiting for. A mass of warships appeared in the bay, the bangs and flashes from their guns like a thunderstorm, making Priscilla and Pupetta bellow and stamp their feet. The next day there were more explosions – from the direction of Naples this time, as the Germans blew up what they could not keep. At long last, the Allies had invaded.

For a while the atmosphere had been almost like a carnival. People said the Nazis were surrendering in their thousands, that the Allies were landing all along the coast, that Rome itself had fallen. None of these rumours turned out to be remotely true. Instead, the British and Americans had to fight for every inch of ground. Earlier in the year there had at least been some food, but as autumn gave way to winter, people starved. The *osteria* stayed open only because of the patronage of a few well-connected men of business like Alberto, who often sent along beforehand the ingredients they wanted cooked. For the other customers, the menu was limited to whatever the Pertinis could lay their hands on. Sometimes there might be a soup made from the water in which yesterday's pasta had been boiled, flavoured with herbs, or a salad made from crusts of stale bread soaked in milk. It took all Livia's skills to make these meagre dishes palatable, but by Christmas even pasta was hard to get hold of, and a bag of flour cost more than a week's wages.

Even before the Allied soldiers came to take away the Pertinis' remaining stocks of food it was clear that liberation was going to be no better, and in many ways far worse, than occupation by the Germans had been. Now Italy was a battleground in which neither side was Italian, and for both sides, the needs of the civilian population came a poor second to the importance of winning the war.

Nine

A tiny lizard, seeing that James was awake, scuttled into a crack in the wall. It was the first time in months that he'd had the luxury of sleeping in private, let alone in such an enormous bed, and for a moment he couldn't recall where he was. Then he saw painted shutters enclosing tall windows. Getting out of the bed, he went to pull them open. The painting was a kind of *trompe l'oeil*, the scene on the inside exactly matching the view of the Bay of Naples outside, though with naked nymphs frolicking in the sea instead of bombed-out ships. Across the bay, Vesuvius puffed a tiny, perfect smoke ring.

He put on his uniform and shaved in a foxed, silvery mirror under the inquisitive gaze of a cherub. It annoyed him that he still needed to do this only once a week. He squinted at his reflection. With the soap covering his chin, it was possible to see what he'd look like with a beard – older, more authoritative. When he had scraped the soap off, the face that stared back at him was once again that of a boy. It seemed to him, though, that the curly ginger-brown hair on the top of his head was already thinning. Some of the men believed that the army-issue shampoo made your hair fall out. He couldn't be going bald, he thought, not yet: he was only twenty-two.

At school he had been a classicist. He found both the history and the language of ancient Rome reassuring, dealing as they did with an empire not dissimilar to the one his school had been founded to serve, but with the added advantage that nothing about them ever changed. Latin was like cricket, only more so: once you had mastered a set of fixed grammatical rules, everything made perfect sense, even if it wasn't actually possible to find an ancient Roman to make perfect sense with. When he was called up, his linguistic skills were enough to get him assigned to an intelligence corps – or, more exactly, to the Field Security Service – where he had been given a choice of learning Italian, French or Arabic. Italian seemed the most similar to Latin, so he had chosen that. He had spent several pleasant weeks under the tutelage of a lugubrious Tuscan count, who had made him read Dante aloud until he was fluent. Then, with typical FSS bloody-mindedness, he had been posted to Africa. It had taken the intervention of his commanding officer to get this transfer.

He went to see if Jackson was still around, but the other man had mentioned an early start and it looked as if he had already left. James decided to start by inspecting his new quarters. On this floor there seemed to be about a dozen large rooms, grouped around the courtyard below. The first room was a kitchen, which also contained a tin bath. Presumably this was the domain of Malloni, the orderly. He looked in the cupboards, which were empty apart from a few tins of army rations. His heart sank a little – they were all marked 'Meat and Vegetables', a tasteless slop he had become all too familiar with over the past eighteen months. Apart from that, there seemed to be precious little for Malloni to work with.

The next room was one of the larger ones. Two men in plain clothes looked up from their desks as James entered. 'Hullo,' he said, somewhat surprised to see them – Jackson had mentioned a couple of civilian staff, but James hadn't expected them to start so early. 'I'm Captain Gould.'

The Italians did not seem particularly interested in this information. 'Carlo,' one of them said curtly. He nodded at his companion. 'And Enrico.'

According to James's watch it was not yet eight o'clock. 'What are you working on?' he asked politely.

Carlo seemed quite taken aback to be questioned in this way. 'Filing,' he said economically.

'Filing what?'

'Expenses.'

'May I?' James took the piece of paper Carlo was writing on. '"Captain Teodor Benesti, informant, two hundred lire,"' he read. '"Marshal Antonio Mostovo, contact, two hundred lire. Carla Loretti, gift, one cheese and a blanket, value fifty lire." What are these?'

'Payments,' Carlo said, taking the paper back.

'Payments for what?'

'For information.'

James experienced a sinking sensation. 'Bribes, you mean?'

Carlo shrugged. 'If you like.'

'I don't like,' James said firmly. 'I don't know how Jackson ran this show, but paying informants is completely against the rules.'

Carlo looked at him without expression. 'You are mistaken. These figures do not relate to the payment of bribes. They are a record of the bribes we have been *offered*.'

'Oh, I see,' James said, relieved. It was clearly correct to record any attempt at corrupting FSS personnel, even if no money was actually changing hands.

'And the money we are given,' Carlo continued, 'goes into a tin in the cupboard. So we always know exactly how much there is.'

The sinking sensation returned. 'What happens to the money in the tin?'

'We use it for the bribes we give out,' Enrico said. The two men watched James impassively.

He took a deep breath. 'There must be no more payments. Of any kind, given or received. Is that clear?'

'*Si*,' Enrico muttered.

'Of course,' Carlo said. But he carried on writing out his list, just the same.

'While I am here, we will . . .' James struggled to think of an appropriate metaphor. 'We will play with a straight bat,' he suggested. No, damn it, that wasn't right. He had just told them that he would be playing with a straight owl, or possibly a straight pigeon. 'With a straight mallet,' he said, miming helpfully.

'Ah, your English cricket,' Carlo said, with a practised lack of interest. 'Unfortunately we cannot play today. We are much too busy.'

The two Italians said nothing more for several minutes. But when James left the room Enrico murmured under his breath, '*Ogni scupa nova fa scrusciu*.' Every new broom makes a noise.

By noon James had sorted the mess of papers into three large piles, which he had mentally dubbed Fascists, Criminals and Madmen. Most important of all, he had located the Black Book, the log of known criminal elements in the area. Unfortunately, Jackson seemed to have been less than meticulous about this as well. It started reasonably enough, with a neat list of names and addresses, and 'fascist' or 'mobster' written next to each one, together with a brief summary of the evidence against them. As James turned the pages, however, the information became more and more scant. Against one man's name Jackson had written 'believed to have three nipples'; against another, the single word 'effeminate'. A certain

Annuziata di Fraterno was 'aristocratic; known to have nymphomaniac tendencies', while one Giorgio Rossetti was 'pathologically afraid of wasps'.

Fascinated despite himself, James had sat down to read further when the door opened and three men walked in. As one of them was a major, and presumably James's CO, he jumped to his feet and saluted sharply. Carlo and Enrico glanced up disdainfully, before carrying on with whatever it was they were doing.

Major Heathcote was a harassed-looking man of about forty. 'Frankly, I don't give a duck's arse about the Eyeties,' he told James. 'I simply want to get this district under some semblance of control. We all thought we'd be in Rome by now, but unfortunately the Jerries have dug in about sixty miles north at Monte Cassino and it's getting pretty grim. Come to me if there's anything you can't handle, but I'm really hoping you won't have to.'

James agreed that he would probably need to bother the major very little, and the CO started to leave. 'Oh, and weddings,' he said, suddenly swivelling round and fixing James with a steely expression. 'Try not to let the men get married. It causes no end of resentment, and it makes the soldiers soft. No one wants to die when they've got an Italian senorita keeping the bed warm for them sixty miles behind the front lines.'

'Signorina, sir.'

'I'm sorry?'

'Signorita would be Spanish.' Conscious that Major Heathcote had probably not come there to have his Italian corrected, James moved swiftly on. 'Don't worry, sir, Jackson briefed me very thoroughly on the marriage situation.'

'I'm glad to hear it.'

The major left, accompanied by one of the men. The other man, a captain with startlingly blue eyes, stuck out his hand.

'Tom Jeffries, A-force,' he said cheerfully. 'Jumbo to my pals. My office is just upstairs, though of course I'm not there much.' He winked conspiratorially.

A-force were the cloak-and-dagger boys. Presumably Jeffries meant that he was usually away doing top-secret work behind enemy lines. 'Oh, of course,' James said. 'Pleased to meet you.'

'Listen, do you fancy a spot of lunch? There's a place down the road which does a very nice veal chop.'

And so, for the second time in twenty-four hours, James found himself being ushered into Zi' Teresa's. If the maître d' was surprised to see him he didn't show it, through Jeffries looked a little nonplussed when Angelo showed them, with a hint of a wink, to 'Captain Gould's usual table'.

As they ate Jeffries quizzed James about his combat experience, which up to that time had been limited, to say the least.

'Not to worry. We might be able to slip you into something of ours now and again,' Jeffries said. 'We've usually got a few people popping in and out of EOT, killing Jerries, and to tell the truth an Italian speaker's always welcome. It gets our boys into no end of trouble, not being able to speak the language.'

James made some vague noises of enthusiasm intended to imply how much he regretted that he was too busy to pop into Enemy Occupied Territory alongside a bunch of bloodthirsty maniacs who didn't speak Italian. In an effort to change the subject he lowered his voice and said, 'Shame what Major Heathcote was saying about the advance.'

'What about it?'

'Well, that it's got bogged down at this Monte Cassino place.'

Jeffries' eyes twinkled. 'That depends on how you look at it. Think about it. Why are we here?'

'To beat the Germans?'

Jeffries shook his head. 'To tie up as many Germans as possible while the main show gets underway in France, that's why. The last thing Churchill wants is for the Jerry divisions in Italy to nip back over the Alps and reinforce their defences over there. So while they think they're holding us back, they're actually *falling into our trap*. Look, Gould. Can I give you some advice?'

Zi' Teresa's certainly seemed to be the place for being given advice. 'Of course.'

'This whole show,' Jeffries said, 'this whole country, in fact, is just a massive ruddy diversion. If I were you, I'd allow yourself to be diverted. Enjoy it while it lasts.'

A woman approached the table. She was tall and extremely beautiful, with long black hair artfully pinned and curled around her head, and a slim dress of some slinky material that wouldn't have looked out of place in a Mayfair dance hall. She also, James noticed, had a glass eye, which looked at him fixedly as she bent down to kiss Jeffries's cheek. There was a faint waft of expensive perfume.

'Speaking of which – may I introduce Elena, my girl?' Jeffries said. 'Darling, this is Captain Gould.'

'Pleased to meet you,' James said, getting to his feet.

'Actually, she doesn't speak much English,' Jeffries said. 'Completely charming, though. She's a schoolteacher.'

'*Buongiorno, signorina,*' James said. '*Molto piacere di conoscerla.*'

Elena smiled. '*Voi parlate Italiano?*'

'Not as well as I thought, it seems,' he said in Italian. 'Your local dialect takes some getting used to.'

'Well, you speak it a lot better than Jumbo does. Will you tell him I'm going to the ladies' room, please?'

'Of course.'

'What did she say?' Jeffries asked as Elena left them.

'She said she was going to powder her nose. Look, is she really a schoolteacher?'

'Why shouldn't she be?'

James thought of mentioning what Jackson had told him the previous night about Zi' Teresa's celebrated glass-eyed employee, but Jeffries was glaring at him fiercely and he thought better of it. It was possible, after all, that this was how schoolteachers dressed in Naples. 'Perhaps I'm mixing her up with someone else,' he said lamely.

'Actually,' Jeffries said, 'I wanted to talk to you about Elena. There's a bit of a language barrier, you see.'

James tried to look as if this possibility had only just occurred to him. 'Really?'

'I need a few phrases translated. Only some of it's a bit delicate.'

'That's all right,' James said dubiously.

'For example, how would one say, "I'm feeling a bit tired actually"?'

'*Mi sento stanco, veramente.*'

'And what about, ah, "That's very nice and all that, but I'd really rather you didn't"?'

'Well, it's difficult without knowing the exact context, but it's something like, "*È molto bene ma non farlo, grazie.*"'

'And what about "It's actually getting rather painful now"?'

'*Mi fa male quando lo tocca.*'

'And "Please stop"?'

'*Smettila, per favore.*'

Jeffries's lips moved as he silently practised the unfamiliar phrases. 'Well, that should cover it,' he said at last.

Elena rejoined them, her nose sufficiently powdered. She and Jeffries smiled at each other coquettishly, holding each other's hands across the table. 'Tell me, James,' she said in Italian, 'how do I tell him "*Aspetta!*"?'

'Er – "Wait", I suppose.'

'Wet?' she said, trying it for size.

'Wait.'

'Wayt. Wayt! And how do I say "*Non smettere!*"'

'Don't stop.'

'And "*Facciamolo ancora ma più piano*"?'

'That would be – "Let's do that again but more slowly."'

'Slewly,' she repeated. 'Slooowly. Good. And "*Svegliati, caro*"?'

'Wake up please, darling.'

'Wek erp plis dah'leeng. OK, I think I have everything.'

'Jumbo?'

'What?'

'Anything else I can assist with?'

'No, I think I'm fully kitted up now. Thanks.'

'In that case,' James said, 'I'd better be getting back. Can I pay my share?'

Jumbo rolled up his left sleeve. His forearm bore no fewer than six wristwatches, each of them, James saw, of impressive proportions. 'No need, old chap,' he said, unbuckling one and laying it on the table. 'I met some Germans recently, up in Abruzzo. This one's on them.'

As James entered the Palazzo Satriano he became aware of a commotion echoing down the marble staircase. It sounded as if there was some kind of party going on – no, not a party, he decided: the voices he could hear were raised in anger and alarm, some of them shrilly.

He rounded the first floor landing and found his way blocked by a mass of women – young women, all dressed to the nines. They appeared to be pushing and shoving with the intention of getting closer to the door of the FSS office. Near the front, a fight had broken out, which provided an opportunity for those not directly involved to try to slip past the protagonists and take their places, which in turn was leading to yet more altercations. With some difficulty, James battled his way past waves of scent, screeching voices and glossy black hair.

'What on earth is going on?' he asked when he reached the safety of his office.

Carlo shrugged. 'It's three o'clock.'

'I'm aware of the time, Carlo. Why are there so many women outside?'

'They are the *fidanzate*. The women who want to marry Allied servicemen.'

'What, all of them?'

64

'No, these are just the most recent ones, the ones who have not yet been given a time when they will be interviewed.'

'Then – Good Lord – how many have we already arranged to see?'

Carlo rummaged in a cupboard and produced a thick sheaf of papers. 'Forty? Fifty?'

'And how long has this been going on?'

Carlo shrugged again. His shrugs, James was coming to realise, were remarkably expressive, almost a dialect in themselves. Sometimes they communicated that Carlo did not know the answer to whatever you were asking him, but more often they suggested that he either did not wish, or did not deign, to enter into discussion on the subject.

No wonder Jackson had been unable to do anything about the black market, James thought. All his time must have been spent on processing would-be war brides. The uncharitable thought crossed James's mind that Jackson, knowing he was about to be posted home, might even have allowed a backlog to build up, secure in the knowledge that it would be his successor who would have to deal with it. 'Right,' he said. 'The first thing to do is to make a list. Carlo, could you go outside and tell those ladies to form an orderly queue?'

Carlo's face was expressionless. 'I could. But first you will need to explain to them what an orderly queue is.'

It took nearly three hours just to take the girls' names and addresses, and by the end of it James was exhausted.

At seven o'clock precisely, a tiny Italian man entered James's office. He was wearing a very ancient tuxedo and a white bow tie, which was almost exactly the same size and shape as the moustache on his upper lip.

'Dinner she served,' he said darkly, as if announcing the death of a favourite pet.

'Ah,' James said. 'You must be Malloni.'

'I 'ave the honour, yes. Wet there.'

Malloni vanished, only to reappear a moment later with a steaming tureen in his arms. 'Ees dinner.'

'Right. Where do you usually . . .?' James gestured at the table, which was still covered in Jackson's papers, albeit sorted into piles. He watched as Malloni pushed them haphazardly towards the centre of the table to make room for his tureen. From behind the door he produced a small bronze gong, which he struck with great ceremony three times.

One by one a handful of other British officers appeared and introduced themselves as his dining companions. Kernick, Walters, Hughes and French occupied offices in various other parts of the building, carrying out bureaucratic duties even more obscure than his own. They all seemed quite haggard with exhaustion.

Malloni produced some rather green-looking silver cutlery and some ancient chinaware and proceeded to lay the table, putting a plate in front of each person. There was also a candelabra, which he did not light, and a number of smaller dishes with lids. James touched the plate in front of him. It was quite cold.

Eventually Malloni wrapped a white cloth over his left arm like a matador's cape, and with his other hand triumphantly raised the lid of the tureen.

It contained, as James had suspected it might, several portions of 'Meat and Vegetables' removed from their tins, mixed together and warmed through. Surreptitiously, he lifted the lid on one of the side dishes. It, too, contained 'Meat and Vegetables'. He tried another. 'Meat and Vegetables' again. He looked up. Malloni was going round the table, standing next to the left side of each man and holding the tureen for them to spoon some onto their plate.

'Jackson warned me this fellow wasn't up to much,' he muttered to Kernick.

'He's better than the last chap,' Kernick whispered back. '*He* used to put garlic in it. Said it made it taste more Italian, but actually it just made us all stink.'

'Why do you keep him on?'

'He's a very good source of Scotch. And occasionally he can lay his hands on a few cigars.'

With even more ceremony, Malloni placed a bottle of Vat 69 whisky on the table. Producing a stiletto knife, apparently from nowhere, he cut the seal with a casual wave of his hand and poured generous measures for each diner. James sipped his. He was not a great drinker, but even so this seemed to him to be a particularly poisonous brand, with a distinct after-taste of petroleum.

He was grateful to have filled up at Zi' Teresa's, and ate as little as possible. His companions, however, consumed theirs with enthusiasm, a haste later explained by the eagerness with which they pushed their plates aside to get on with the real business of the evening, playing cards. Malloni, too, seemed newly galvanised as he opened a large ledger in which to record the bets.

'*Scopa*,' Kernick explained. 'Local game. Really quite addictive. You'll play, Gould, won't you?'

French turned on the wireless. The clipped tones of a BBC presenter said, 'And now some messages for our friends in Northern Italy. Mario, your mother's cow is unwell. Guiseppe, it may rain by dawn.'

'Giuseppe's going to have a busy night,' Kernick commented. He caught James's blank look. 'Instructions for the partisans,' he explained. 'All in code.'

'I had rather a rum do today,' Hughes said conversationally as he shuffled the cards. 'Had to arrest an entire orchestra for promoting Hun culture. There'd been a complaint that they'd been playing Beethoven.'

'Did you charge them?' Kernick asked, studying his hand intently.

'No. Turns out Malloni here knows a thing or two about classical music, and Beethoven is actually Belgian.'

'Bravo, Malloni.' The cook shrugged modestly.

There was a deafening crash from downstairs, followed by a painful squealing noise. A second crash echoed up the stone staircase, accompanied by more squealing. 'What on earth is that?' James asked.

'According to the Americans,' Walters said, 'it's called jazz.'

Now that James listened more closely, he could just make out a hint of a melody in the strangled squeaks, which were presumably coming from a clarinet, although the drums still sounded as if they were being used in the manner of a punch bag rather than a musical instrument.

'They've not been at it very long,' Walters added unnecessarily. 'Quite keen, though. They practise every night.'

After he had lost half a crown at *scopa* James went to bed. The jazz continued late into the night, making sleep difficult. When he did finally drift off he found himself dreaming of Neapolitan fiancées.

He woke with a start, just as the clarinet downstairs gave a sudden squeal of excitement.

But it wasn't the clarinet that had woken him. He listened. There it was again: a soft tapping at the door. Getting out of bed, he went to open it.

There was a child standing there, her ragged clothes, grubby bare feet and tangled hair immediately marking her out as a *scugnizza*. His first thought was that she was stealing. But then he remembered the knock. Presumably even in Naples thieves didn't announce themselves before they robbed you. '*Buona sera*,' he said gently. '*Come sta?*'

The girl seemed undecided between advance and retreat, like a deer startled at its grazing.

'I've come for my blanket,' she said, in a Neapolitan dialect so thick he could barely understand her.

'What blanket?'

She pointed at the bed. 'The man who lives here gives them to me.'

As blankets were a recognised currency in every occupied country, James understood that she was talking about some kind of transaction. 'What does he give them to you for?' he asked. She looked at James, and he suddenly felt foolish. Her eyes were not those of a child, but of the women who walked arm-in-arm past the bars. 'Oh,' he said.

'Are you going to give me a blanket?' she asked.

He went and fetched all the blankets he could spare. 'Take these,' he said, as kindly as he could. 'I'm afraid there won't be any more.'

She nodded, and carefully shook each blanket out and refolded it before vanishing as quietly as she had come. James remembered what Jackson had said, the night before he left. *There are no rules here, only orders.*

Knowing that sleep was unlikely now, he reached for his shirt and undid the pocket, searching for a cigarette. Like everyone else, he had abandoned the British-made Bengal Lancers for the superior soft-wrapped Camels and Chesterfields the Americans got in their K-packs. He lit one, letting the smoke mingle with the scents of jasmine and bougainvillea that wafted through the open windows.

Next to the pack of cigarettes was a letter. He hesitated, then drew it out. The letter had been travelling with him so long, and had got damp and then dried out again so many times, that it had started to come apart along the seams and now resembled one of those lacy patterns made by tearing folded newspapers. But the words were legible enough.

Wendover Farm,
Wendover,
Bucks
14th November 1943

Dear James,
This is a beastly letter – beastly to write, and even more beastly to get, I suppose. I wish I could have said this to your face, but I've thought and thought about it and it seems to me that it's better to let you know how things stand now than to wait until I see you, which mightn't be for months. Besides, I don't want to do anything behind your back, and it wouldn't be fair on Milo either to keep him waiting for your next home leave, whenever that might be.

Dearest James, please don't be upset. Of course your pride will be hurt at being jilted (hateful word, but I can't think of a better one) but apart from that I have this feeling that you're going to absolutely understand. Now that I'm away from home, and able to talk to other girls about their boyfriends (I didn't gossip about you, I promise, but the work is very boring and some of the girls just like to talk anyway), I realise that what we had together was really a lovely warm friendship rather than a love affair. In fact, I still feel exactly the same way about you that I always did – absolutely fond & affectionate, as if you're my brother, and a very nice brother at that. It's just that now I've got a whole new set of feelings as well – my feelings for Milo, I mean. If it hadn't been for the war I would probably never have met him, and you and I would have got married without even thinking about it very much, and you would have gone on calling me 'old girl' just the way your father does your mother, and we would have managed to have some children and it would never even have occurred to us that anything was missing. I suppose I'm talking about passion. But please don't think I'm trying to reproach you, James, I'm just trying to explain why it's a good thing that we've come to this parting of the ways sooner, rather than waiting until we'd got more deeply involved with each other before we'd found out . . .

There was more, three or four pages of it, but the gist was that she'd met a Polish airman who was able to supply whatever it was James had not been able to. Passion, he supposed. It was true that their kisses, when he took Jane to the back row of the pictures or to a dinner dance, had been a little awkward. But he had put that down to their mutual inexperience. He had assumed in his innocence that a well-brought-up girl would not want to be taken advantage of until their wedding night, an occasion he had looked forward to with warm anticipation. Perhaps he should have discussed it with her? But she had never given any indication that she would be anything other than mortified if he had raised the subject. Indeed, the extraordinary frankness of the letter had itself been a shock – as if this other man had been able to stir up not just a new set of feelings, but a new openness about them as well. Or perhaps it was being a land girl that had done that.

It was obvious that one reason Jane had written to him was to clear her conscience before she made love to her new boyfriend. That was almost the first thing that had occurred to him when he read it: she will have slept with him by now. Perhaps the very night after she posted this letter she had . . . No, he must not think about it. He put the letter away, and lay down on the bed again.

'Passion,' he said out loud, around a mouthful of cigarette smoke. But what was passion, when it came down to it? Surely it just meant making a spectacle of oneself – it wasn't that the feelings were any different, just that one allowed them to go on display, as it were. And what was so wonderful about that? These Italians were passionate, he supposed, but as far as he could see that simply meant they were over-excitable, talked too much, and treated women with a complete lack of respect. What was even more extraordinary was that the women seemed often not to mind.

He sighed. Sex was yet another thing that this war had turned on its head. Many of the men saw anyone who was still inexperienced as simply needing a push in the right direction, such as being dragged to the nearest brothel. Even before his dinner with Jackson, whenever James was asked if he had a girl at home, he said he had. Having a girl at home got you out of all sorts of difficulties.

Ten

After the soldiers had shot Pupetta and sawn off her hind legs, the Pertinis had the problem of what to do with the rest of her. There was no market to sell meat at any more, and even if the official food agency had been prepared to expend petrol on coming to pick up the carcass, the family would have been given only a few lire for it.

It was Livia who decided that they should hold a *festa*.

'But how will anyone pay us?' her father wanted to know. 'No one has any money, these days. Not to buy meat.'

'We'll let them pay whatever they can afford. After all, it's better than letting good food go to waste. After the war, perhaps they'll remember that they owe us a favour.'

'And who will we dance with?' Marisa said. 'There are no men any more.'

'There are a few. And they'll all come if there's going to be meat.'

They levered Pupetta's carcass onto a huge spit made out of X-shaped pieces of wood that straddled a pile of oak kindling. The fire was lit at dawn, and by midday the unfamiliar smell of roasting beef was spreading through the village. Their neighbours helped them bring out tables and chairs, and there was no shortage of volunteers to stoke the fire or keep Pupetta turning on her spit so that she wouldn't dry out.

Meanwhile Livia and Marisa prepared the other dishes – delicacies prepared from Pupetta's heart, diced into cubes and served on skewers made from rosemary twigs; from her tongue, boiled and pressed under heavy stones in a saucepan; from her brain, cooked with tomatoes, *pioppino* mushrooms, and *munnezzaglia*, odds and ends of pasta; and from her liver, ground up and fried with shallots. No part of the buffalo was wasted. Vegetables were still in short supply after the hardships of the previous winter, but there were *cannellini*, served with a little of the beef fat, and whole bulbs of fennel baked in the cooler ashes at the fire's edge. There was plenty of *coccozza*, a pumpkin-like vegetable, and *tenurume*, the tender spring shoots of the courgette plant. And of course, there was fresh mozzarella, made with poor Priscilla's milk – so miserable since Pupetta's death that she was only producing half as much as before, but still alive at least. All in all, it was a feast such as none of them had eaten for many years, and although the circumstances were far from ideal, Livia felt that it marked a turning point. From now on, perhaps, things would start to get better.

All the men in the district came, just as Livia had predicted. There were precious few of them – only the maimed, the sickly, the very old, the very young, those in protected professions, and those with enough influence or cash to avoid the *rastrellamenti*. Alberto and his fellow *camorristi* were there, of course – Livia would have liked to have banned them, but she knew her father needed their money. Of more interest to most of the villagers were Cariso and Delfio, the Lacino brothers, who had escaped from a prisoner-of-war camp in the north and walked the two hundred miles home, right though the German and Allied lines. If they could make it back safely, how many more might eventually return?

The Neapolitans say that hunger is the best sauce, and it was not until all the food was eaten, and a respectful interval had elapsed to pay homage to its excellence, that the music began. Livia took off her apron, eager to dance, but to her surprise she found she had no partner. She looked around, hoping someone would try to catch her eye. But instead, all she caught were glances that shifted away from her, and a sudden furtive movement in the trouser pockets of the older men. Whenever she looked at them they were grabbing their testicles. It would have been funny if she had not known what it meant. It was a gesture even older than Christianity. They were warding off the *malocchio*, the evil eye.

'Who will dance with me?' she demanded, looking them straight in the face, one after another. 'Felice,' she decided. 'You were happy enough to eat my favourite cow. Will you be my partner?'

The man shuffled his feet, and did not reply. 'Franco,' she demanded in exasperation of another of her neighbours. 'What about you? You've danced with me a hundred times.'

'That was before Enzo went away,' Franco said quietly.

'What does that have to do with it?' She glared at him, but he too dropped his gaze. Continuing on around the men, she came to Alberto.

He was smirking. Suddenly she guessed that this was something to do with him.

'Alberto,' she said.

He nodded. '*Si?*'

She let him think she was going to ask him, spinning out the moment. 'Nothing,' she said, contemptuously. 'Marisa, you'll dance with me, won't you?'

There was a low chuckle from the other men as they glanced at Alberto's furious face. It was a sweet moment, and sweeter still when she and her sister danced the *tammorriata*, the sinuous, seductive dance of courtship, without any man at all. She saw the dark glitter of desire in the eyes of the men watching them, but they still grabbed their balls superstitiously through their trousers whenever she came near.

'We have Alberto to thank for this,' she muttered in her sister's ear as they spun back and forth to the throb of the *tammurro*.

Then, as they were walking back to their seats, another explanation suddenly struck her. Enzo.

She ran to where the Lacino brothers were sitting with their family. 'Please,' she begged them. 'If you know anything at all, you must tell me.'

Cariso looked embarrassed, but Delfio spoke up. 'We don't know for sure,' he said. She noticed how his voice had changed since he went away to war – it was cracked and hoarse, as if he had been shouting too much. 'In the camp, we naturally asked anyone we met for news of people from round here. There were a few there who'd been with Enzo in Russia.'

'And?' she cried.

'I'm sorry, Livia,' Delfio said. He held her gaze and she thought: he was a boy when he went from here, but now he has talked about death and seen it, and maybe dealt it out, many times. 'He's dead,' Delfio said simply. 'He was in a position that came under fire from a British fighter pilot. None of them survived.'

She turned to Marisa. 'Can this be true?'

Marisa was staring at her anxiously. 'Livia, I'm so sorry,' she whispered.

'Poor Enzo,' she said numbly. So it had happened. What every woman dreaded, what so many women had been made to endure, had happened to her at last. She was a *vedova*, a widow. It seemed impossible. For the rest of her life she would wear black, and sit at the front of the church during Mass, like an old grandmother. And Enzo – poor Enzo – was dead. That beautiful body, the body she had kissed, made love to, slept alongside, laughed with – that young, virile body was already under the ground, his flesh decomposing, in a grave that was itself in some distant country she could not even picture.

Thoughts tumbled into her brain, one after the other. Why had no one told her earlier? Because of the feast, she supposed. No one had wanted to come and interrupt the preparations with this terrible news, in case they were the cause of the *festa*'s cancellation. And why hadn't Quartilla written? As his mother, she would have been sent the official notification. For a moment she clung to the hope that Cariso and Delfio were wrong, that the reason Quartilla hadn't been in touch was because there had been no letter, but looking at their sombre faces she could tell that they weren't.

She had seen the grief of women many times over the least few years. After the initial shock, the wife or mother usually collapsed, shrieking and howling, tearing at her own hair and clothes in a public display of pain and misery, shouting at God and the saints, cursing and weeping. It was accepted, and looking at the faces around her she could tell that it was even expected.

But she did not howl. Instead, a deep and murderous resentment filled her heart. This was the Allies' doing. Allied bullets had killed Pupetta. Now an Allied pilot had, from the safety of the skies, shot her poor husband, while he fought in a war that was none of his making. And these people had the nerve to call themselves Italy's liberators.

She turned and walked away from the fire, into the darkness, so she could be alone. It was only then that her legs gave way and she fell into Marisa's waiting arms. She allowed her sister to help her into the house. Outside, the square slowly emptied as the villagers slipped away quietly one by one.

She did cry then – she howled and wailed and cursed. But it was not only Enzo she was crying for. Until that day, she had been able to hope that when the war was over, and Enzo returned, things would be better. Now she knew that life was going to get hard, harder than she had previously ever imagined it could be. She grieved for Enzo, but she was also crying for herself.

Eleven

'Do you know why I'm here?'

The girl nodded. '*Si*. You're the wedding officer.'

'The Field Security Officer,' James corrected. He had already decided not to continue using the phrase 'wedding officer', which surely made it sound as if arranging other people's matrimonies was the sole extent of his job. 'I need to write an official report saying whether you are a suitable person to marry Private –' James glanced down at his notebook – 'Private Griffiths.'

The girl, whose name was Algisa Fiore, was very pretty. He had to resist the temptation just to stare at her, drinking in the details of her face – those fragile cheekbones, that dark, glossy hair, those extraordinary eyes, so dark and huge. Now, as she gazed at him, the big eyes were full of happiness. 'Do you know Richard?' she asked eagerly.

James admitted that he had not yet made Private Griffiths's acquaintance. At this, a brief cloud of incomprehension crossed Algisa Fiore's lovely features. 'Then how will you know if we are suitable for each other? Never mind, I will tell you about him. I like talking about Richard. He is *molto gentile*,' she explained. 'He loves animals. As I do.' She folded her long, pretty fingers over her knee, and looked at James as if daring him to suggest that a shared love of animals were not sufficient basis for a life together. 'Really, you must try to meet him. I think you would get on so well. Everybody likes Richard.' One of the fingers had a ring on it, and she regarded it dreamily for a moment. 'And he's so brave. Once he killed three Germans with only his bare hands and a spoon.'

'I'm sure Private Griffiths is a wonderful chap,' James agreed. 'But I'm afraid I need to ask you some questions of a more practical nature.'

'Ask me anything.' She lay back in her chair and began to play with a small silver cross that hung at her neck.

'Do you speak English?'

'A little.'

'What does this mean?' Switching to English, he said, slowly and clearly, '"I'd like two lengths of curtain material please, and half a dozen slices of bacon."'

Algisa Fiore laughed delightfully. 'I've got absolutely no idea.'

'"You appear to have given me the wrong change entirely."'

She shrugged. 'Sorry.'

'Does Private Griffiths speak Italian?'

'Not really.'

'How do you communicate?'

'He can make me understand what he wants,' she said with a faint smile.

James coughed. 'What do you know about England?'

'I know it's where Richard comes from.'

'Did you know, for example, that it's a lot colder than here?'

'I know the women are ugly. At least, that's what Richard says.'

James gave up. He was never going to get anywhere at this rate. What had Jackson said? 'Basically, your job is to discover whether or not she's a tart.' He looked around. Algisa Fiore's apartment was small, bare, and spotlessly clean. 'Do you have a job?'

Her big eyes were suddenly unreadable. 'There aren't any jobs in Naples any more.'

'What do you live on?'

She blew out her lips. 'I manage.'

'I'll need you to be a bit more specific, I'm afraid.'

'I have an uncle in Sicily. He sends me money.'

Jackson, he recalled, had been particularly scathing about uncles. 'May I have your uncle's address?' James asked, his pen poised over his notebook. 'Then, you see, I can check with him, and if his account matches yours, there shouldn't be a problem.'

There was a long pause. Algisa Fiore tugged at the cross on her necklace, and tapped her foot in the air. 'I can't remember.'

'You can't remember where your uncle lives?'

'He moves around a lot,' she said defiantly.

'Well, what was the last address you do remember?'

There was another long pause. He said gently, 'Where does the money really come from, Algisa?'

76

She crossed her legs and smoothed her dress towards her knees before replying. 'Soldiers,' she said at last.

'You take money from soldiers?'

'If they offer it to me.'

He wrote in his notebook, 'A. F. all but admitted living off prostitution.' He stood up. 'I'll need to look round your apartment.'

'Of course,' she said, standing up too. The strap of her dress had fallen off one shoulder. 'I'll show you round.' She reached across him to open a door. Whether it was the honey-coloured skin of her bare shoulder, or simply the unaccustomed proximity of a very beautiful girl, James felt a sudden uncomfortable stirring of desire.

'I'll do it myself,' he said gruffly.

She shrugged. 'As you wish.'

He made a quick tour of the apartment. It was so bare that it didn't take long. But he noticed the bar of soap in the bedroom, and in the kitchen he found half a loaf of white bread and a small jar of olive oil. He wrote these details in his notebook. Returning to the main room, he found her waiting for him, quite naked, the first naked woman he had ever seen. She was holding the dress bunched in front of her so that it preserved a tiny scrap of her modesty.

'Oh,' he said.

She smiled at him, and the room lit up. 'I think you like me.'

'That isn't . . .' he began.

'You can finish interviewing me in there, if you want.' She indicated the bedroom with a tilt of her beautiful eyes.

'Please. You must get dressed. This really won't help.'

She pouted, and let the dress drop to the level of her waist. 'I'm sure you can think of something you want to ask me.'

'If anything, you see, it rather proves my CO's point,' he explained, taking a step back.

'Aren't I pretty enough?' She did a slow pirouette to show him what was on offer.

'You're very attractive, but it's completely out of the question—'

'We're in Naples,' she said, coming closer. 'Nothing's out of the question.'

James took another step backwards and found that his back was now against the wall. And then the dress had been dropped to the floor, her arms were snaking around his neck and her soft, fragrant breasts were pressing against his chest as she kissed him. For a moment he felt almost giddy with the physical presence of her. Then he recalled the advice Jackson had given him.

'Besides, I've got my own girl,' he said. '*Sono fidanzato*. I'm engaged to be married.'

The effect was remarkable. Algisa instantly stepped back, clapping her hands with delight. 'But that's wonderful. Tell me all about her. Is she pretty? What does she look like? Isn't being in love the most wonderful thing?' She sat down again, evidently convinced that her problems were over.

James picked up her dress and handed it to her. 'Here. You'd better put this on.'

Her eyes registered surprise, and then fear. 'You're not going to write me a good report, are you?'

'I'm afraid not.'

'Then you can't be in love,' she said bitterly. 'You were lying.' She threw the dress to the floor. 'I didn't want it to be like this. None of us did. What choice were we given? I'll be a good wife to him, I'll make him happy. Can't you help me?'

'I'm afraid I don't make these rules. If you really want to marry each other, you'll just have to wait until after the war.'

'What makes you think either of us will still be alive after the war?' It was said without self-pity, just the faintest of shrugs.

'I'll see myself out,' he said, closing his notebook and getting to his feet. As he closed the door to the apartment he thought he heard her weeping.

Twelve

The next morning, as James wrote up his report from the day before, a dapper gentleman was shown into his presence.

'An informant,' Enrico said tersely.

The dapper man introduced himself as *Dottore* Lorenzo Scoterra. He was, he said, an *avvocato*, a lawyer, and he wished to give the British some information about known fascists in the area.

James made it clear that he was unable to pay for this information, at which Dr Scoterra became quite impassioned. He did not want money, he said, and even if James had tried to give him some he would certainly have been obliged to refuse it, since the disbursement of funds, however innocently intentioned, might tarnish the validity of his information in the eyes of those James shared it with. He was motivated, he explained, purely by his regard for justice and the rule of law – the calling in which he had spent his professional life – and his admiration for the British, not to mention a strong desire to see the fascist bastards who had profited from the German occupation brought to account. Dr Scottera indicated, however, that he would not say no if James wished to carry on their discussion over a glass of marsala.

Since it was by now quite late, and James had had no breakfast, this seemed a reasonable suggestion, and they repaired to the bar at Zi' Teresa's, where Angelo the maître d' greeted James with the casual wave afforded to an old friend.

James duly ordered two glasses of marsala, a drink he had not tried before. It was sweet, but not unpleasantly so, and rather fortifying. The barman broke a raw egg into each glass just before serving it – a remarkable thing, given the scarcity of fresh eggs at that time. Dr Scoterra seized his even before the barman had finished stirring it, downed the egg in

79

one swallow, and paused reverently to savour the experience before turning to James with a smile of gratitude. He was, James noticed, almost painfully thin.

He proceeded to give James an exhaustive list of people who had benefited from the Germans' presence. James's ear was by now becoming accustomed to the rapid torrents of the Neapolitan dialect, which filled every potential pause for breath with a *senz'altro* or *per forza* or *per questo*, and which replaced every full stop with the briefest of commas, and he found he was able to follow without too much difficulty. The more notes he took, the more details Dr Scottera seemed to be able to remember, and they consumed several more glasses of marsala before the lawyer finally ran out of information.

'Well,' James said, putting down his pen and gesturing to the barman for a bill, 'that's been extremely useful, *Dottore*. But I'm sure you've got clients to attend to.'

'Yes, of course,' the lawyer said, a little reluctantly. Then he brightened. 'But I forgot – there's something I haven't told you.'

'Really? What?'

The lawyer leaned sideways so that he could whisper conspiratorially into James's ear. 'There is a division of German tanks hiding inside Vesuvius.'

It seemed to James that someone had already mentioned German tanks to him during the last few days, but he could not at that moment remember who it had been. 'Do you have any proof?'

'I have been told by a highly reliable source, whom I have entrusted on many occasions with my life.'

James paused in his note-taking. 'Who's that?' he asked, his pen hovering over the paper.

'They are going to attack you from the rear. They know they will all be killed, but it is a point of honour with them – they want to die for their Führer.'

James remembered now: Jackson had specifically told him not to listen to any stories about German panzer divisions holed up in Vesuvius. 'I'm afraid your source is misinformed,' James said. 'That's been looked into, and it isn't true.'

Dr Scoterra looked wistfully at the bottles behind the bar.

'There is just one other thing, though . . .' James said.

Dr Scoterra brightened. 'Yes?'

'This trade in black market penicillin. Do you have any idea who's behind it?'

Dr Scoterra laughed. 'But of course. Everyone does.'

'Who is it?' James asked, nodding to the barman for two more glasses of marsala-and-egg.

'The pharmacist, Zagarella. He runs it on behalf of Vito Genovese himself.'

'Would you say so in court?'

Dr Scoterra looked alarmed. 'If I attempted to do anything of the kind, I would be killed long before I got to the courtroom.'

'Well, where can I find Signore Zagarella?'

'You are not seriously considering arresting him?' Dr Scoterra was now so perturbed that he was getting to his feet, despite the fact that the barman had not yet finished pouring his marsala. 'I had no idea that you were thinking of such a rash course of action. Really, as a lawyer I must advise you against it.'

'But the man is a crook, surely?'

They stared at each other across an unbridgeable gulf of understanding. 'At least promise me that you'll keep my name out of it,' Dr Scottera said, fumbling for his coat buttons.

'Since you're not prepared to give evidence, that shouldn't be too hard.'

'You think I'm a coward?'

'I think the penicillin market should be stopped. This stealing could put soldiers' lives at risk.'

Dr Scoterra sighed. 'When you've been in Naples a bit longer, you'll understand. To survive in this city, it is necessary to be *furbo*, crafty. That's the way things are around here.'

When Dr Scottera had scurried away, James signalled to the barman for the bill.

'*Duecento lire*,' the barman said impassively, placing a ticket on a saucer. James stared at him. Two hundred lire? It wasn't possible. '*È troppo.*'

The barman shrugged. Drinking eggs were expensive.

'*Momento.*' It was the maître d', Angelo, hurrying across the room with an anxious smile on his face. 'Please. Today they are on the house.'

'I have to pay,' James said doggedly. 'Although I shall need a receipt.'

Angelo sighed. From behind his ear he produced a pencil, with which he proceeded to make some calculations on a napkin. The calculations went on for a very long time, and seemed to involve several complex equations, complete with brackets, percentages and conversions in and out of various currencies. Eventually Angelo cried, '*Aha*,' and struck the barman triumphantly around the head. '*Attenzione, cretino!* You added it up all wrong.' The correct sum, he informed James with an apologetic smile, was actually forty-five lire.

James handed over a fifty-lire note. 'Please, keep the change.'

'You're very kind.' Angelo hesitated. 'Incidentally, I could not help overhearing some of your conversation just now.'

'From all the way back there?'

'I have very keen hearing. I should probably not say this, but Doctor Scottera is right about one thing, at least. To take on the black market would be a very large undertaking, and would make you many enemies.'

James noted that 'at least'. 'That's a risk I'm prepared to take.'

After a moment Angelo nodded. 'Then may I give you some advice?'

'In this place, I would expect nothing less,' James said drily.

'When it comes to anything to do with the *camorra*, think carefully about whether to involve your Allies.'

'Why?'

But Angelo's shrug was all the answer he was going to get.

James went back to the Palazzo Satriano, his mind made up. Jackson had let things slide, clearly, but there was no reason for him to do the same.

'We are going to raid the pharmacist Zagarella,' he told Carlo and Enrico. 'I have reason to believe that he may be connected with the black market in penicillin.'

Carlo yawned and scratched himself. 'Of course he is connected with it. He runs it.'

'Then why haven't we put him in prison?'

Carlo shrugged. 'We are just three men, and with respect, if we were to start taking on the *camorra* we'd need an army.'

The more he thought about it, the more Angelo's suggestion that he involve the Americans sounded like good advice. 'This may have escaped your notice, Carlo,' James said stiffly, 'but as it happens, an army is just what we have.'

He went downstairs and knocked on one of the windows in the central courtyard. As Jackson had said, the Yanks' set up was impressive. Doors opened and closed busily, revealing a succession of bustling offices. Orderlies hurried to and fro with piles of papers; pert stenographers busied themselves at typewriters; men in olive green uniforms snapped terse orders at each other. James was suddenly rather ashamed of the comparative lethargy of his own operation upstairs. The surly indifference of Enrico and Carlo – he still had no real idea of what they actually did most of the time – was surely no match for this.

No one came to the window, so he wandered into what seemed to be the main office and waited for someone to talk to him. Eventually he stopped a passing orderly and asked if he could see someone in charge.

'Got an appointment?' the orderly snapped.

'No, I just—'

'I'll get the book.' He bustled off. James made a mental note to get FSS an appointment book as soon as possible.

'Hey, buddy.'

The voice had come from behind him. James turned. The speaker was a young man of about his own age, seated at one of the desks. He wore a pair of steel-rimmed glasses that at some point had been mended with a piece of copper wire. Even seated, James could tell that he was tall and lanky, an impression confirmed when the American got to his feet. James saluted just as the American stuck out his hand. The American laughed, and saluted too.

'Eric Vincenzo. You're the new guy at FSS, right?' He waved at a chair in the corner. 'What's up?'

He sat down and swung his own feet up onto the desk. Behind him, a clarinet was resting on a shelf. This, James deduced, must be the perpetrator of the insomnia-inducing jazz that drifted up the stairs each night.

Following James's gaze, Vincenzo looked alarmed. 'You're not here to complain, are you? Have I been keeping the neighbours awake?'

James assured him that he was not there to complain about the noise, and explained about his planned raid on the pharmacist. The American stroked his chin thoughtfully.

'So you're thinking of a joint operation? Well, the first thing is to check out this informant of yours. Let's take a look.' He had pulled the drawer of a filing cabinet, which slid open effortlessly on its runners, and was leafing through some files. 'Would that be the same Doctor Scoterra who was the secretary of the local fascist party?'

'I don't think that sounds right.'

'Hmm.' He pushed the drawer shut. 'Well, there's an easy way to check. Come with me.'

James followed him through a succession of rooms, all as busy as the first, until they reached an enormous salon, presumably once the palazzo's ballroom. In the centre of the room was an equally vast filing system, nearly eight feet high, around which more secretaries flitted like bees servicing a honeycomb.

'Goodness,' James said enviously.

'Oh, it's not ours. We took this from the German Consulate. I'll say this for the Krauts, they kept immaculate records.' As Vincenzo spoke he was locating the right drawer. 'Here we are.' He handed James a folder.

The first item was a letter in Italian from one *Dottore* Scoterra, addressed to the German Consul. James quickly scanned it. Doctor Scoterra wished, he said, to offer his services as an informant. He made it clear that he did not expect to paid; indeed, even if Herr Hitler wished to give him some reward for his services, he would be obliged to refuse it, since the disbursement of funds, however innocently intentioned, might tarnish the validity of his information in the eyes of those his handlers shared it with. He was motivated purely by his regard for justice and the rule of law, the calling in which he had spent his professional life, and admiration for the Germans, not to mention a strong desire to see the socialist bastards who had profited from the years of softness and corruption brought to account. There followed a long list of names, many of which were familiar to James from his own conversation with Dr Scoterra, except that on that occasion he had described them as fanatical fascists rather than fanatical communists. The letter ended with a suggestion that the Germans might like to interview him further in a quiet place, such as a bar.

'The little prick,' he said, with some feeling. 'He's been trying to use us to settle his own scores. He even got me to buy him a glass of marsala.'

'That's the one where the barman puts an egg . . .?'

James nodded. 'You know, I thought at the time he seemed rather emaciated. It was probably the first food he'd eaten all week.'

Eric Vincenzo laughed. 'You've been *fottuto*, as they say in these parts. That means—'

'I know what it means,' James said tersely. 'Fucked. Screwed over.'

'Yeah – you speak Italian, don't you?' Eric said, eyeing James carefully. 'I noticed that letter didn't give you any trouble.'

'Don't you?'

'I'm learning, but it's a slow business.'

'With a surname like Vincenzo?'

'I'm third generation. My folks wanted me to be a proper little American, so they refused to speak Italian at home. Not that it stopped them from being locked up for six months as enemy aliens when war broke out.' He offered James the file. 'Want to trade?'

'Trade what?'

84

'Well, I reckon that even though your informant's motives may be less than honourable, he could be quite useful. We'd need to clear it with our COs, but it seems to me a joint operation could benefit both of us.'

Both COs endorsed the notion of a joint operation against the black marketeers, so long as it was under one command. Curiously, the American CO seemed to think this was a job for the British, while Major Heathcote had a strong feeling that it was a task better suited to the Americans. After some internal wrangling, it was decided that for the time being James and Eric would report to Major Heathcote.

The operation took place the next morning at dawn, and was divided into two parts. The Italian *carabinieri*, under Carlo and Enrico, had been given the task of rounding up the black marketeers on the Via Forcella. Rather to James's surprise, Carlo and Enrico accepted their mission with enthusiasm, dressing for the occasion like extras from an Al Capone movie, in boaters, blazers, bow ties and spats. From a cupboard somewhere they also broke out a fearsome arsenal of tommy guns, which James hoped they would use with rather more restraint than their matinée idols – although from the way in which the Italians waved the weapons around, he rather doubted it. Meanwhile, James and Eric were to search the pharmacist's premises.

Signore Zagarella was having his breakfast when they knocked on his door. He received the news that they intended to look for contraband penicillin with equanimity.

'Go ahead,' he shrugged. 'You'll find nothing here.'

They searched for an hour. The apartment was not only bare of penicillin, it was bare of contraband goods of any kind. With a sinking feeling James realised that they had been expected. At last, in a wastepaper basket under the sink, he found a single used phial of penicillin. He showed it to Zagarella, whose expression did not change.

'You'll have to come with us,' James told him, unable to keep the satisfaction out of his voice.

'To where?'

'To the Poggio Reale, initially,' he said, naming the city prison. 'You'll be held there while we make our enquiries.'

Zagarella said agreeably, 'My friend, if you are tired of life in Naples, I can arrange to have you sent away.'

'On the contrary,' James said. 'I think that life in Naples is about to get much better.'

The pharmacist shrugged and held out his hands for the handcuffs.

'You can put me in Poggio Reale if you like, but I can assure you I won't be there when you come back.'

It seemed only reasonable to celebrate the success of their collaboration over a drink at Zi' Teresa's.

'What are you going to do when the war's over, James?' Eric asked as they finished off a bottle of wine.

James shrugged. 'I haven't really given it much thought. Go back to university, I suppose. They gave us a promise that we could finish our degrees when the war's over. What about you?'

'I'm going to be a jazz musician. Or possibly a spy. I haven't decided which yet.'

'Really?' They both seemed unlikely career choices for a grown man. 'Presumably you need a degree to be a spy? And being a professional musician can't be easy.'

Eric shrugged the question aside. 'It's what you decide to do that matters, isn't it? After that it's up to you.'

'It is?'

'Of course. This war's going to change everything, James. Everything's going to be blown wide open.'

'I was rather hoping everything would go back to the way it was before.'

'Come to America,' Eric said, shaking his head. 'You don't have to go to university in America. You can be whatever you want to be.'

'Well, thank you for the invitation. But I don't think I'm ready to stop being British just yet.'

Eric laughed and poured some more wine. The bottle was almost empty. He made an imaginary gesture of wringing the bottle out to get the last few drops. 'After this, we'll try the cocktails,' he announced. 'They do a pretty good Tom Collins in this place.'

'What's a Tom Collins?'

Eric laughed again, although James had not in fact been joking. Then, abruptly, his face clouded. 'You got a girl, James?'

'Oh, yes,' James said automatically. 'Back home, that is.'

'Name?'

'Jane. Jane Ellis.'

'Good name,' Eric said approvingly. 'Is she pretty?'

'I suppose she is, rather.'

'Shit, I need a pretty girl,' Eric said. 'I haven't had a pretty girl in weeks.'

'As long as that?' James heard himself saying. 'Goodness.'

'An Italian girl, that would suit me. Though not speaking the language doesn't help.' He raised his glass. 'To Allied cooperation, the beginning of our friendship, and Jane.'

James raised his glass. '*Per cent' anni*, as the Italians say.' He felt bad about perpetuating the myth of his fictitious fiancée with Eric, but if his work had taught him anything, it was that one couldn't pick and choose whom one told a particular lie to.

All the same, it was extraordinary how, sitting here in Zi' Teresa's, basking in the warm glow of Eric's Yankee optimism, and with a successful operation against the black market under his belt, the misery over being jilted which he had been carrying round with him for so long seemed suddenly less crushing, and he could almost contemplate a future in which an imaginary Jane was no longer necessary.

As they went to the bar to order their cocktails James spotted a face he recognised. Jumbo Jeffries was sitting on his own, working his way through a large plate of sea urchins.

'Oh, there you are,' he said without much enthusiasm.

'Enjoying your meal?' James enquired.

'Not much.' Jumbo gestured at the plate in front of him. 'Elena's got me eating these. Apparently they're good for the libido.' Now that James looked more closely, he could see dark rings under Jeffries's eyes. A religious medal hung around his neck. Jumbo touched it self-consciously. 'This too, apparently. It's all your fault,' he added glumly.

'Mine? Why's that?'

'It's those damn English phrases you taught Elena. When I could pretend I didn't understand her, everything was fine. Now everything's got much more difficult.' He pushed the plate away from him. 'It's no good. I'm sick of the bloody things.'

Thirteen

James was still in a buoyant mood next morning as he set off with Eric to interrogate the prisoners rounded up in the raid on the Via Forcella.

On their way they dropped in on Zagarella in the Poggio Reale prison, where they found him as imperturbable as ever, and working his way through an excellent breakfast. He had been given a cell, or rather a suite of cells, which was larger than Algisa Fiore's apartment. One of the warders was busy making up his bed with fresh linen. James noticed that the prisoner also appeared to be wearing a freshly laundered shirt.

'Have you come to release me?' he wanted to know.

'Our enquiries are not yet complete,' James said. 'You'll stay here until they are.'

Zagarella dabbed at his lips with a napkin. 'I doubt that very much,' he assured them. 'I must say, I am surprised that you are still here yourselves. I imagined that you would have been transferred out of Naples by now.'

'You'll find the Allied Military Government rather different from anything you're used to dealing with.'

'You are referring, I take it, to your famous incorruptibility,' Zagarella said, 'which, to be sure, has already cost me a great deal of money.' The warder, having finished making up the bed, produced a bowl of water, a shaving brush and some soap, with which he began energetically lathering the prisoner's cheeks. 'You should remember,' the pharmacist continued, 'that we Neapolitans have been occupied before. The Aragonese, the Austrians, the Bourbons, the Italians – yes, even the Italians – the Germans . . . and now, of course, the Allies. So you see, we have had plenty of practice at it.' The warder applied his blade to the side of Zagarella's cheek. The pharmacist closed his eyes with a grunt of pleasure, and made a little gesture of dismissal at James and Eric.

'It will give me great pleasure,' James said as they left the prison, 'to put that man behind bars.'

'He already is behind bars,' Eric pointed out, 'and to be honest, it doesn't seem to be inconveniencing him that much.'

'They're only treating him so well because he's convinced them he'll be out soon. If we get a conviction, he'll be just another prisoner.'

'James,' Eric said, 'do you know how many mobsters we've actually managed to convict since we came to Naples?'

'How many?'

'Three.' Eric frowned. 'Papers go missing. Witnesses don't turn up, or change their stories at the last minute. One had an epileptic fit in the middle of giving evidence and had to be excused. Then there are the accused who turn out to have such astounding war records working for the resistance that we have to give them a medal instead of a prison sentence. And that's even before you get to the judges who appear to have selectively misheard the evidence, or the prisons which turn out to have faulty locks. And yes, there have been guys from CIC who have been transferred after a word in the right ear. This man Vito Genovese who runs it all, he's in with AMG at the highest level – I mean the very highest level. They say that when General Clark first arrived in Naples, he expressed a wish to eat some seafood. Well, all the fishing boats were grounded, because of the mines. Vito organised a great feast to celebrate the general's arrival, by the simple expedient of stealing all the fish from the Naples aquarium. Shortly afterwards, he was given the post of official advisor to the high command. If someone like Zagarella is really under his protection, there won't be much we can do about it.'

At the Questura, the main police station, James explained that they wished to interview the suspects rounded up in the raid on the Via Forcella. After much paperwork they were taken to the cells, where they were shown a very old man who was sitting in the holding pen, completely alone.

'What's going on?' James demanded. 'Where are the others?'

The policeman who had brought them down to the cells shrugged. 'What others?'

'There must have been dozens of people trading on the Via Forcella yesterday. Where are they all?' Seeing that he would get nothing out of

89

the policeman, he spoke to the old man. 'When you came in here, how many were with you?'

'Oh, twenty or thirty.'

'Where are they now?'

'They all went in the night,' the old man said sadly. 'I would have gone too, but I couldn't afford the fine.'

'What fine?'

'Fifty lire.' The old man spread his arms. 'I'm just a scrap metal dealer. I don't have fifty lire.'

Expressionless, the policeman said, 'He is mistaken. No one has been fined. You can inspect the books if you wish.'

James sighed. 'What's this man charged with?' he asked the policeman.

'Selling copper telephone wire.'

'Nothing to do with penicillin?'

'It would seem not.'

'If you please,' the old man said, 'I'm very anxious to get out of here. My wife, you see, is getting on, and we have no neighbours. I'm afraid that if I don't get home, there'll be no one to cook her a meal.'

The policeman brought them a roll of telephone wire. 'This was found on him.'

'I cut the German wire,' the old man said proudly. 'That's what I'm meant to do, isn't it? We don't like the Germans.'

James translated what the old man had said to Eric, who scratched his head. 'That was before the Allies arrived. We dropped leaflets telling the Italians to do as much damage as they could. But after we arrived, we obviously wanted the wires left alone so we could use them ourselves.'

'Here,' the old man said, producing a dog-eared leaflet from an inside pocket and unfolding it proudly. 'See? It says to cut the wires. Will I get a medal?'

'You can't cut telephone wires any more,' James explained. 'They're ours now.'

'But it's German wire.'

'Yes, but . . .' James sighed. 'Oh, never mind.'

They all looked at the old man, who seemed completely unaware of what was going on.

'Can't we just kick him out?' Eric suggested.

'That won't be possible,' the policeman said sternly. 'He has been charged with destruction of Allied military property. The penalty is up to ten years in jail.'

90

'What do we do?' Eric asked.

'There's not a lot we can do,' James said glumly. 'Officially, it's out of our hands.'

The old man had given an address in a village to the south of Naples. When they got back to their HQ, James took the FSS motorbike off its stand, pushed it down the stone staircase, and set off. The main thoroughfares out of the city had been cleared of rubble now, and there were a number of trams working. The rule seemed to be that the driver of any kind of two-wheeled vehicle considered himself entitled to drive alongside them and hold on, getting himself towed along for as long as he felt like it in order to save on either petrol or leg power. James was relieved when he finally left the city and found himself in the countryside. It was a beautiful spring day, and with the sun on his face it was possible to believe himself a thousand miles from any war.

The landscape he was driving through could not have changed much since medieval times. The fields were tiny, and the doubled-up women working in them were dressed in the same shapeless black dresses and headscarves they would have worn in the time of Boccaccio. Occasionally there was a bullock or a mule to help with the labour, but most of the work seemed to be done by hand.

Eventually he found the village the old man had named, and by asking around located his house. It stood on its own in the midst of a few weed-strewn fields: James guessed that he had simply become too old to work them any more. Small piles of scrap metal – the wreckage of a burnt-out truck, a couple of pieces of twisted metal from a German bomb, an empty American ammunition box – testified to his new profession. The whole place was eerily silent.

The house was barely more than a byre with a couple of rooms attached. James knocked on the door. 'Hello?' he called. There was no reply.

He pushed the door open and went inside. When his eyes had got used to the gloom he made out a bed underneath the window, covered in rags. A faint protuberance in the rags resolved itself into the outline of a wizened old face. Sightless eyes, ghostly with cataracts, peered unblinkingly at the ceiling. '*Buongiorno, signora*,' he said softly. The old lady gave no sign of having heard him. She appeared to James to be very close to death. When he looked in the kitchen, there was absolutely no food in the place.

*

91

'You want to do *what*?' Major Heathcote stared at him, boggle-eyed with disbelief.

'I want to ask the Italians to have him released, sir,' James said. 'Even if he has done something wrong, which is debatable, he could be freed on compassionate grounds.'

'Compassionate grounds?' The major had gone red in the face. 'Captain, sixty miles away at this very moment there are over five thousand soldiers sitting in foxholes full of freezing water, being shelled night and day by the Germans, unable even to stand up for a piss in case some sniper puts a bullet through their heads. Why don't you ask *them* about compassionate grounds?'

'I'm aware the fighting is quite tough at present, sir.' The major grunted incredulously. James pushed on, 'All the same, it's surely the duty of the military government to act fairly. And this man has been locked up for all the wrong reasons.'

'By his fellow Italians.'

'As a result of *our* operation—'

'Which you now tell me was an abject failure,' snapped the major.

James said nothing.

The major sighed. 'And you've absolutely nothing to charge this pharmacist Zagarella with?' He looked from one to the other of them.

'No, sir,' Eric muttered.

'Do I take it, then, that he has finally been released from his incarceration?'

'Yes, sir,' James said between gritted teeth.

'So you have at least ended one illegal imprisonment,' the major said pointedly.

'Yes, sir.'

'Whilst in the process making AMG a complete laughing stock.' The major gestured at the door. 'Get out of here, Gould. You too, Vincenzo. I don't want to see either of you again for at least six months.'

'Yes, sir.' James hesitated. 'About this wire-cutter, sir.'

The major glared. 'I'll make a phone call, though God knows I've got more important things to think about.'

That night, Malloni appeared as usual on the dot of seven. But there was an air of suppressed excitement about him as he ceremoniously struck the gong for dinner. All became clear when he came to put out the crockery: instead of the usual flat plates on which they ate their 'Meat and Vegetables', the British officers were being given soup bowls.

92

'I say, Malloni, what's all this?' Kernick asked.

'Eezer zoop,' Malloni said, with just a touch of pride. 'Meet zoop.'

He left the room, and returned with a cracked soup tureen so big he could barely carry it. It was, James thought, the size and shape of a German shipping mine. But sure enough, when Malloni lifted the lid James could see within it a puddle of dark liquid, not unlike a Brown Windsor.

'Makes a change,' Walters commented approvingly. 'Well done, that man.'

Malloni staggered from person to person with his tureen. As they served themselves, however, a strange silence fell on the table. Kernick, inspecting the contents of his bowl, muttered, 'Ah.'

As James ladled the soup into his own bowl, he became aware that it had an unusual consistency. It seemed to contain parts that were almost jelly-like, and others that were remarkably thin. Examining it more closely, he saw that Malloni had created his soup by the simple expedient of taking rather fewer tins of 'Meat and Vegetables' than usual, and adding to them a large quantity of warm water.

'Meter zoop – wit veg'balls,' Malloni said proudly when they were all served. 'Enjoy.'

Polite to the last, the British officers obediently picked up their soup spoons and dipped them in their bowls.

It soon became apparent that Malloni's meter zoop tasted quite as vile as it looked. Watering down the tinned slop had not diluted the taste at all, yet if anything it had somehow exacerbated the rancid, greasy texture. It was, James reflected miserably, a perfectly bloody end to a perfectly bloody day.

Fourteen

Livia wrote to Enzo's family in Naples telling them what she had learned about his fate, but there was no reply.

Once Pupetta had been eaten, the Pertinis had to face the fact that there was almost no food apart from the mozzarella that they made each day from Priscilla's milk. In normal times, such cheese would have sold for enough to buy them the other basics they needed – flour, salt and so on. But without any way of transporting it, they had to eat it themselves or see it wasted. Sometimes there seemed to be simply no point in enduring hours of backbreaking work just to produce something that would be left to go rancid, but Priscilla still had to be milked or her udders would hurt.

The lack of a tractor preyed on Livia's mind almost daily. With a tractor, they could get their cheese to market. With a tractor they could work the fields, and recoup some of their losses.

Alberto waited a week after the news about Enzo came through, then resumed his campaign with renewed vigour. As if to mock their lack of transport, he arrived one afternoon in a magnificent new Bugatti. When he had eased his vast bulk out from behind the wheel, he presented Livia with a loaf of white bread – the first she had seen for years. She wanted to refuse it, but the thought of her father and Marisa reminded her that she was no longer in a position to be so high and mighty. So she swallowed her pride and reached for the loaf, determined to accept it with good grace. Alberto smirked triumphantly. She said sharply, 'I want to be clear with you, Alberto. I'll take your bread because I have no choice, but I'll never share your bed.'

The smile on his face didn't falter. For a moment he pulled the bread away, out of her reach, the way a boy might tease a younger sister by

94

withholding a toy. Then, seeing her hand follow it involuntarily, he laughed and let her take it.

'One day you will realise you have no choice about that, either,' he said in a low voice. 'It's no different from catching a robin. First you lay a trail of breadcrumbs, to get it used to eating from your hand. Then – pfft.' He mimed closing his fist.

'Alberto,' she said wearily, 'Why me? Surely you must be fed up with this by now, and there must be a dozen girls you could have without nearly so much difficulty.'

He put his face even closer, so close she could feel his breath on her cheek. His hand slipped around her waist. 'Of course there are. But I've decided I want you, and what's more everyone else around here knows it. If I don't succeed now, I'll be a laughing stock. And in my line of work, being laughed at could be fatal. I have to have you, Livia.' His big, fleshy lips and bristly moustache pressed against her ear, his tongue darting in to caress her lobe lasciviously. She shuddered, and she could tell from the way he grunted that her revulsion was almost more exciting to him than her acquiescence would have been. Marisa's right, she thought: he doesn't want me to desire him, he wants to conquer me. She thought of the soldier who had held her wrists in his hand as Pupetta bled to death, the way he had been aroused by her struggles, how even the officer had become excited by watching. What was it about some men and war, that they loved so much this sudden power they had? And now that they had tasted it, would they ever be prepared to let it go?

Fifteen

Rather to his surprise, James had at last met a young Neapolitan woman of unquestionably good character.

The address was an elegant house in the suburb of Vomero. When he arrived for the vetting, James was shown into a drawing room furnished with great taste and an obvious abundance of wealth. Emilia di Catalita-Gosta was engaged to a staff officer; she spoke a little English, and was clearly well educated. Her delicate features, in fact, reminded James a little of Jane. Her father was also on hand, a distinguished gentleman of about sixty who was wearing an immaculate suit. He spoke to James about the family estates in Tuscany – at the present moment, of course, regrettably cut off by the front line – and they soon discovered a common interest in the works of Dante.

It was a pleasure to spend time in the company of civilised people. When the fading light finally indicated that it was time for James to leave, he was almost reluctant to go. As delicately as he could, he hinted to the father that his report would not pose either Signorina di Catalita-Gosta or her fiancé any problems, and gave her his best wishes for a long and happy marriage. With equal delicacy, the father nodded to show that he had understood.

James asked if he might see some more of the house before he went. Emilia's father hesitated. 'Unfortunately some German officers billeted here during the Occupation,' he said quietly. 'I should be ashamed to show the other rooms to you in the state in which those animals left them. However, I would be honoured if you would come to dinner in a week or two, when everything will be back to the way it should be.'

James told him he quite understood, and they made a firm arrangement for two weeks' time.

'There is just one other thing,' Signore di Catalita-Gosta said. 'It is, I suppose, a kind of favour, although I am wary of presuming further on your kindness.'

James assured him that he would do his best to consider the request favourably.

'I don't want to prejudge your report, of course. But if it does happen to be positive, as we dare to hope . . . my daughter, who is very religious, has set her heart on marrying on the first Sunday in Lent. There is a sort of tradition that people from the better families are wed on that day, in the Duomo.' He shrugged. 'As, indeed, I was myself. It is only a tradition, you understand, but I know it would have meant a lot to Emilia's mother, God rest her soul.'

The first Sunday in Lent was less than a week away. 'I'll see what I can do to hurry the approval along,' James promised.

Signore di Catalita-Gosta bowed. 'You're very kind.'

'Not at all. It's a pleasure to be able to achieve something useful in all this mess.'

As James made his way back down the hill to the Palazzo Satriano, he felt a sense of good cheer that even the anticipation of Malloni's warmed-up 'Meat and Vegetables' could not entirely dissipate.

On Sunday morning he was woken at six a.m. by the telephone. It was Major Heathcote, and he got straight to the point. 'What do you know about this mob at the cathedral?'

'I didn't know there was a mob at the cathedral.'

'The MPs are worried it could turn into a full-scale riot. Take a look, would you?' The line went dead.

James got dressed and went downstairs. Deciding that if there was really going to be a riot it would be more safely witnessed from a jeep than a motorbike, he went to wake Eric.

The American came awake groggily, and James had some difficulty persuading him that attending to a potential riot was more important than having a cup of coffee. Even without the coffee, it was a good fifteen minutes before a grumbling Eric was finally driving the two of them towards the Duomo.

Near the cathedral their way was blocked by a solid mass of people. As Eric edged the vehicle forward, James became aware that the mood of the crowd was strangely fraught. Women were tearing at their clothes and sobbing. Elderly men were stabbing their hands at the sky. Young girls, their heads covered with scarves, jabbered and shrieked hysterically at

97

each other. There was a high proportion of nuns and priests amongst the crowd, he noticed, and everywhere the sign of the cross was being made. It was all very mystifying.

Suddenly James saw a familiar face. Telling Eric to pull over, he swung the door of the jeep open. 'Doctor Scottera,' he called. 'Get in.'

The lawyer looked slightly embarrassed, as if he had been caught doing something slightly disreputable. But he climbed into the jeep and pulled the door closed quickly. 'You should go back,' he said.

'Why? Is it dangerous?'

'For you? Yes, perhaps a little. The crowd is very over-excited. But at the moment I am more concerned about myself. I would rather not be seen with you, after your ill-advised attempt to control the penicillin dealers.'

'Ah. You heard about that,' James said.

'My friend,' Dr Scottera said disdainfully, 'the events of that day have already been turned into a fine ballad, which is being sold in the municipal gardens for five lire a sheet. Your own name features heavily, not only in the lyrics of each verse, but also in the chorus, where it is accompanied by certain gestures which are always guaranteed to cause amusement. You will recall that I advised against the operation at the time. Now, shall we go?'

'What's going on here?' Eric asked, putting the jeep into reverse.

'It is the liquefaction of the blood.' They must have looked perplexed, because Dr Scoterra added, 'The blood of the saint. A famous relic, which is kept in a special chapel of the cathedral. Twice a year, absolutely regularly, the dried blood becomes liquid. If, as now, the blood starts to liquefy at the wrong time, it means a great tragedy is coming to Naples.'

'You mean, something worse than being occupied by the Germans, having your young men conscripted to fight in Russia, and having Naples blown up by three different armies?'

'It is, of course,' Dr Scottera said stiffly, 'only a superstition, which an educated man such as myself would never give credence to.'

'You just happened to be up early?'

Dr Scottera sniffed.

Eric pulled the jeep over and turned off the ignition. 'We'd better go take a look, anyway.'

The two of them pushed their way through the crowd towards a side door of the cathedral. Inside, things were no calmer – a wailing sea of people surging from side to side, aimlessly, but with palpable tension. Eventually, they found a priest.

'It is the saint,' he sighed. 'The blood. For certain, a terrible fire is coming, in which many people will perish.' At these words, a great weeping arose from those near enough to hear. The priest brightened. 'However,' he said loudly, gesturing towards another priest who was emerging from the vestry with a tray around his neck, like a cigarette girl at a cinema, 'it may be that a relic from one of the Christian martyrs will offer the faithful some protection.' There was a rush towards the priest with the tray.

Fighting through the throng, Eric and James found that the tray was laden with small white objects. 'If I'm not very much mistaken,' Eric said, picking one up and examining it, 'these are human bones.'

'Relics, *signore*, relics of the early martyrs,' the priest confirmed. 'Free to anyone who makes a donation of fifty lire to the offertory.'

'Are there any catacombs around here?' James asked Eric.

'Miles of 'em. All stuffed to the ceiling with bones.'

They looked at the tray of bones again. 'I suppose even priests have to eat,' James said.

'Screw that,' Eric said. Taking a priest in each hand, he pulled them towards the vestry. 'See if you can locate this blood, will you?' he called over his shoulder.

The saint's blood was encased in the stem of a magnificent silver reliquary, which was in turn being clutched reverently by another priest.

'Tell them if this goes on they're going to have a riot on their hands,' Eric suggested.

James did so, but the priests just shrugged. 'It is the saint,' one repeated. 'He is trying to warn us.'

'I've had enough of this bullshit.' Eric pulled his pistol out of its holster and pointed it at the priest holding the reliquary. The other priests crossed themselves in unison. 'Tell him that if that blood hasn't unliquefied within two minutes, they're going to have another Christian martyr to sell off in little pieces.'

'Are you sure this is a good idea?' James asked.

Eric waved the pistol in a threatening manner. 'Tell him I haven't had any coffee yet and I'm extremely grouchy.'

'What I'm trying to say is, *I* think it's a really *bad* idea,' James said nervously.

'You're not telling me you think this blood liquefied all by itself?'

'Possibly not, but we came here to *prevent* a riot,' James pointed out. 'And I think that by any measure shooting a priest, in a cathedral, during the middle of a miraculous event, with around a thousand witnesses, many of whom are already in a somewhat agitated condition, might well not be the most effective way of achieving that. Particularly as there are just two of us.'

'You think I should put the gun away?'

'That's what I think, yes.'

'I reckon that blood would unliquefy in about two minutes if this priest just set it down. It's because he keeps shaking it around that it's gone like that.'

'Quite possibly,' James agreed, 'but if the Italians choose to believe in this stuff, that's their business.'

'So how do you propose we deal with this situation?'

'Well,' James said, 'it seems to me the priests have taken care of that already. They've allowed the crowd to get worked up into a frenzy, admittedly, but they've also provided a solution, in the form of these relics. So long as they don't run out of relics – and from the sound of it, they've got an inexhaustible stock – it looks as if everyone's going to be happy.'

Somewhat reluctantly, Eric put his gun away.

'Many apologies,' James said to the priests. 'My friend has not had any breakfast.'

The priests looked sympathetic. One of them impulsively stepped forward and pressed a piece of bone into James's top pocket. 'It will protect you from the coming fire,' he whispered, 'just as you have protected us from the American with no breakfast.' They all shook hands formally, and Eric was blessed by the priest with the reliquary.

'Incidentally,' James said as he prepared to go, 'I believe I may know someone who is getting married here today. A Signorina Emilia di Catalita-Gosta.'

The priests looked blank. 'Who?' one said.

'Emilia di Catalita-Gosta. She's marrying an English staff officer today, here, in the Duomo.'

The priest shook his head. 'Not today. It isn't possible. Not in this part of Lent.'

'But it's a tradition, I understood? That the brides from the better families get married here today?'

'On the contrary,' the priest said. 'Today, and for the whole of this week, there are no marriages in the cathedral. Whoever told you otherwise was mistaken.'

As they walked back to the jeep James said slowly, 'I think I may have been *fottuto* again.'

'In what way?'

'I don't know exactly, but I think I need to visit Signorina di Catalita-Gosta and find out.'

'Oh, shit,' Eric said suddenly.

'What's up?'

Eric pointed. 'You won't be going in that.'

The jeep was now a foot lower to the ground than it had been when they'd left it, owing to the removal of all four of its wheels. The head-lamps, windscreen wipers – indeed, the windscreen itself – as well as the doors, bonnet, engine and seats were all gone. It was a mere skeleton, a husk of a car.

'Got a gun in that holster, James?'

'Yes. Why?'

'Please, shoot me right now. Because if you don't, the quartermaster will.'

It took several hours to sort out a replacement for the ransacked jeep. Declining Malloni's offer of a *colazione inglese*, an English breakfast – by which he actually meant, James knew from experience, yet another tin of 'Meat and Vegetables', but this time burnt into a crisp, blackened pancake in a frying pan rather than simply warmed through in a pot – James took the motorbike and went to the elegant house in Vomero where he had interviewed Signorina di Catalita-Gosta and her father.

The door was unlocked, so he stepped inside. It was very quiet. Silently, James went into the room where the interview had taken place. It was rather barer than it had been. The impressive paintings, the heavy furniture, the antiques – all had gone, replaced by newer, showier pieces of art deco. A man's coat lay sprawled across one of the chairs. Behind a door at the far side of the room, James heard someone moving.

He went to the door and pulled it open. On the floor, a scrawny male bottom rose and fell rhythmically between the M of a woman's legs. 'I'm so sorry,' James exclaimed, stepping backwards. And then he froze. At the sound of his voice, both the man and the woman had looked up at him. The man who was making energetic love to Emilia di Catalita-Gosta was none other than her own father.

'We appear to be having,' Major Heathcote said slowly, 'an epidemic of miracles.' He turned his attention back to the report in his hand, paus-ing occasionally to look up at James and scowl.

James already knew the report's contents. What he had failed to anticipate in the Duomo was that there were many other priests in Naples, all equally hungry. As a result, all over the city, crucifixes were now bleeding, sweating, weeping, growing their hair, losing their hair, grinding their teeth, or in various other ways animating themselves, to the delight and enrichment of the priests who attended them. In the church of Sant' Agnello our Lord had been engaging in lively conversation with a statue of the Virgin Mary, a fact independently confirmed by several news reporters. In Santa Maria del Carmine he had to be shaved regularly by the royal barber, so thick was his stubble, while in San Gaudiso he had taken to winking at pretty girls. Meanwhile, the blood of the city's saints had taken on a whole range of properties hitherto unknown to science. One lady's was liquefying at precisely ten o'clock every Tuesday, while San Giovanni's bubbled away obligingly whenever it heard Holy Scripture.

At last Major Heathcote put down the report. 'But I'm sure you can explain all this,' he said with ominous mildness.

'Sir,' James said awkwardly. 'The Italians seem to believe there's some kind of great disaster on the way. The priests are simply taking advantage of their credulity. In the case of the Duomo, it didn't seem appropriate to intervene in what was clearly an internal Italian affair.'

'Well, quite,' the major said reasonably. 'The fact that the civilian population has now been whipped up into a state of hysterical delirium because they think the Allies are going to bring down some kind of unspecified catastrophe is clearly not something that causes *you* any concern.'

'Sir,' James began again.

'Don't interrupt me.' The major banged the table in a sudden explosion of rage. 'Some people are saying the Germans are going to come back and raze the city to the ground – did you know that? Others are openly talking about a return to fascism. Meanwhile the black market is out of control, the only people who can't buy penicillin freely on the Via Forcella – thanks to you – are our own army medics, the streets are full of syphilitic girls spreading disease to our soldiers, the Americans are complaining that FSS owe them a jeep, and – oh yes.' He picked up another report. 'On your approval, one of General Clark's favourite staff officers has somehow got himself married to the mistress of a former high-ranking fascist.' He glared at James. 'Have you any comment to make about *that*?'

'I thought the man in question was Miss Catalita-Gosta's father, sir.'

'Did he *say* he was?'

'Now that I think back, sir, he never actually said it. But he deliberately gave me that impression. He said things such as, er, it would have meant a lot to Emilia's dead mother if she and the major could get married quickly. And they'd borrowed pieces of antique furniture to make it look like a family home, rather than a love nest.'

'And you *fell* for it?' Major Heathcote demanded incredulously.

There was nothing James could say.

'The officer in question,' the major said, 'is – was – integrally involved with preparations for the forthcoming sea landings, about which we would naturally prefer the Germans to hear as little as possible. He's had to be sent on an extended honeymoon, without his new bride, while someone clears this mess up.'

'I'm very sorry, sir.'

'Captain Gould,' the major said heavily, 'the only thing that is preventing me from sending you to the front line immediately is the knowledge that they need decent soldiers up there, not gutless incompetents.' He sighed. 'I wish to God I'd never lost Jackson. Anyway, these are your orders. You will get a grip on the civilian population of this city, and use whatever means necessary to stop this shambles. You will impose the regulations and requirements of the Allied Military Government without exception or favour. Do you understand?'

'Yes, sir.'

'Then get out of here. And send in Second Lieutenant Vincenzo.'

Sixteen

After his carpeting by Major Heathcote James was left in absolutely no doubt what was required of him, and he carried out his orders scrupulously. Troops were brought in each day to clear the Via Forcella of contraband. Miracles of all kind were ruthlessly suppressed, usually by the simple expedient Eric had proposed in the Duomo, namely producing a gun and waving it threateningly at the nearest clergyman. More stubborn manifestations of the miraculous sometimes required an arrest, and it was remarkable how often a statue that had been chatting, winking, sweating and so on became quite docile as soon as its earthly guardians were in jail. Meanwhile, a series of raids closing bars, brothels, restaurants and other unauthorised premises removed the black marketeers' main outlets, and brought an end to the carnival atmosphere that had become such a feature of occupied Naples.

James himself led the raid that shut down Zi' Teresa's. He felt a pang of guilt when he saw the reproach in the eyes of Angelo, the maître d', but he forced himself to be businesslike.

'Here,' he told him, handing over a proclamation in English and Italian. 'You must put this on your door.'

Angelo barely glanced at it. 'This is a sad day.'

'An unfortunate necessity.'

'May I ask how long we must be closed for?'

'I suppose until the end of the occupation.'

'Then I congratulate you, Captain Gould. In all these years of war, Zi' Teresa's has never closed, not once. You have done what the fascists, the Germans and the Allied bombers all failed to do. You have made me shut my doors to the people of Naples.'

'I'm sorry if it causes you any hardship,' James said stiffly.

'This isn't about profit,' Angelo said quietly. 'This is about our pride.'

Soldiers with bayonets were hidden in the back of every supply truck, with orders to chop down on the hands of anyone who tried to pilfer Allied goods. For three days the hospital was full of *scugnizzi* who had lost their fingers, before the urchins cottoned on that truck-robbing was no longer a good idea. Meanwhile, the penalty for prostitution or trading in stolen property was raised to ten years' imprisonment. Notices on the roads into the city warned of the prevalence of venereal disease, and James personally delivered lectures on the symptoms and dangers of syphilis to audiences of exhausted soldiers just back from the front line. He quickly found that emphasising the number of syphilitic prostitutes in Naples simply made his audiences cheer approvingly, but that a few horrific slides of diseased male members, provided by a contact in the medical corps, silenced even the most battle-hardened GI.

To a certain extent, all this was effective. The visible signs of decadence and corruption, always so cheerfully on display in Naples, vanished almost overnight. Streets that had been filled with troops on leave, ducking in and out of the bars while they made their choice among the local women, were now drabber, quieter places. Major Heathcote even went so far as to call James and Eric into his office to congratulate them.

'I'm not saying you've done a good job, mind you,' he said pointedly. 'But at least this time you haven't fucked up.'

However, the new regime was not actually as successful as it seemed. For one thing, James knew that the black market, although driven underground, had barely been inconvenienced. His informant Dr Scottera told him with some pleasure that all James had succeeded in doing to the trade in penicillin was to raise the black market price by half. This meant that those who wished to obtain it had to engage in even more illegal activity in order to raise the necessary funds. Now that the brothels were off-limits, front-line troops, instead of peeling off quietly in ones or twos to find women as they had done previously, spent their leave in noisy, drunken groups, often releasing their pent-up testosterone in fights. Nor had there been much effect on the epidemic of sexually transmitted diseases. Despite the lectures, the Allies actually had more soldiers laid up with venereal disease than with battle wounds.

James was still working his way through the backlog of wedding vettings, but the work was made faster now that he had adopted a policy of turning all the applicants down unless there was a glaring reason not to.

'And so far,' he told Eric, 'I haven't found one. Basically, you now have to be a nun to marry a British soldier.'

Eric screwed up his face. 'How would that work, exactly?'

'Figuratively speaking.'

Eric sighed. 'You know, James, I don't think I like this.'

'Nor do I. But orders are orders.'

Violetta Cartenza, aged nineteen, was recommended for refusal on the basis of 'sloppy housekeeping'. Serena Tivoloni, aged twenty, was 'overly pert'. Rosetta Marli, twenty-four, was 'incapable of sitting still'. Natalia Monfredo, nineteen, was 'far too superstitious'. Martina Fontanelle sat demurely in front of him, answering his questions, but all the time an envelope stuffed with money sat on the table, apparently ignored by both of them. He left it there when he got up, and wrote on her file the single word 'corrupt'.

Silvana Settimo, aged twenty, told James calmly and immediately that she was still a virgin. It was a trump card. If true, he could hardly claim that she was of bad character, let alone a prostitute. But something about her wide-eyed innocence rang a warning bell. He told her he would need to make some enquiries and went to see her fiancé, a cheery bombardier from London, who confirmed that they hadn't slept together.

'We both want to wait until we're married,' he told James. 'Some of the other blokes think I'm mad not to sample the goods before, so to speak, but I know my mum wouldn't approve. Call me old fashioned, but that's the way I am, and Silvana's just the same.'

Still concerned, James sought out the medical officer who had provided the slides for his troop lectures.

'Is it possible to fake virginity?'

'Well enough to fool a husband on his wedding night, or well enough to fool a doctor?'

'Both.'

The doctor considered. 'The former, possibly. What is it that's bothering you about her?'

'I'm not sure.' He thought back to his own awkward half-conversations with Jane, and then the sudden frankness of her letter. 'I suppose,' he said slowly, 'it's because she wasn't particularly embarrassed.'

'Well, I'll happily take a look at her if you'd like me to.'

Silvana agreed to the medical examination with good grace, and for a while James began to think he must have been wrong. But after the examination the doctor called him in.

'There's her virginity,' he said, handing James a steel dish containing a small blob of waxy material about the size of a chestnut.

'Are you serious?'

'Watch.' The doctor took a scalpel and cut into the object. After a little resistance there was a sudden gush of dark blood.

'Candlewax, most probably,' the doctor suggested. 'Mixed with oil to soften it, and then moulded into the right shape.'

'Is the blood real?'

'Can't be, or it would have clotted. I guess it can't be too hard to fake blood, though.'

'Oh, they're good at that here,' James assured him, thinking of the priests and their relics. 'There's quite a market for it. I wonder if it bubbles whenever she hears someone read the Bible, like San Giovanni's?'

'Well, wherever she got it, I'm sure it didn't come cheap.'

With Zi' Teresa's and all the other restaurants closed, there was now no respite for James from Malloni's cooking, which in turn meant there was no respite from tinned 'Meat and Vegetables'.

'I say, Malloni, are you quite sure you're a cook?' Horris asked. He was a recent addition to the section, Major Heathcote having decided that James had earned the right to some assistance.

'Of course. I was born with a knife in my hand,' Malloni said darkly. Which, James reflected later, was not really much of an answer.

The closure of the restaurants had been particularly hard on Jumbo Jeffries. Deprived of his high-fish diet, he was now dependent for his super-charged libido on lucky charms, and each time James saw him he seemed to be bedecked with yet another religious necklace, amulet or brooch, pressed on him by an impatient Elena. He hinted bleakly to James that he was not very keen about some of the demands being made of him of late.

'They do things English girls would never dream of doing,' he confided. 'Some of it can be a real eye-opener, I can tell you. But then, dammit if you aren't expected to turn around and do the same sort of thing back to them.'

James made what he hoped were sympathetic noises.

'The thing is,' Jumbo said wistfully, 'Elena seems to have so much more time on her hands now. They've shut down the school where she teaches or something. At least when she was working it tired her out. Now she's positively bursting with vim.'

'If you've had enough of it,' James suggested, 'you could always give her the push.'

Jumbo stroked his moustache with a faraway look in his eye. 'Easier said than done, old man. Easier said than done.'

They reached an understanding that on those rare occasions when Malloni was able to supplement their diet with tins of corned beef, Jumbo was to have extra helpings, since it was now firmly established throughout Naples that this particular dish was an aphrodisiac. On these evenings Jumbo sat alone, eating his food with an expression of fixed determination, hurrying off immediately afterwards so as to be with his lover when the full force of the meal took effect.

One night he took James aside on his way out. 'Gould. How do I say, "I really think that's gone far enough, now"?'

'Something like – *Penso che dovremo fermarmi adesso.*'

'And how about, "I don't mind watching, but I'd rather not join in"?'

'*Non mi dispiace guardare ma preferisco non partecipare.*'

'Thanks.' He nodded, and straightened his shoulders before marching out into the night. It seemed to James that Jumbo could hardly have looked more daunted if he had been entering enemy-occupied territory on one of his secret missions.

Despite the occasional setback, however, James was able to tell himself that he had at last got his district under a semblance of control. The back-log of paperwork he had inherited from his predecessor had been reduced to manageable proportions. The biscuit tin in the cupboard, once stuffed with small-denomination notes for the purposes of bribery and corruption, now contained only a collection of sharpened pencils. There was an appointments book, which Carlo and Enrico still did their best to ignore. He had even managed to obtain a single grey metal filing cabinet, of which he was secretly rather proud. Despite his limited resources, and the difficult conditions in which he had to work, James had been a success.

And yet as each day passed he felt increasingly that what he had been working so hard to achieve had not, in the end, been worth the effort. Like a teacher struggling to control a class of unruly schoolchildren, who managed to get their attention only to discover that he had nothing to say, James found himself at a bit of a loss. Stamping down on the black market had not made the ordinary Italian's life any worse, but neither had it made it much better. Banning a few servicemen from marrying had not produced any great breakthrough at the front. He was conscious of feeling restless, almost bored. It was crazy: he often worked fourteen hours a day, so he couldn't be bored, not in the usual sense. But when he passed a lemon tree in blossom, or caught the scent of some unfamiliar, exotic herb wafting through an open window, or heard a snatch of opera being sung behind a door, or even just when a shaft of Neapolitan sunlight suddenly fell across him as he worked, warming up his skin, he was aware of a strange sensation, like a sharp pang of hunger. Perhaps it *was* just hunger, he thought: Malloni's unvarying diet of tinned rations was so monotonous that he was often unable to bring himself to eat. Not that he would have dreamt of complaining. Compared with the sacrifices so many others were making just then, his life was ridiculously cushy. It didn't do to think about what you might be missing, not when there was a war on.

Seventeen

The next time Alberto came to Fiscino he brought a chicken, which he asked Livia to cook for him.

'It's not a young one,' he said, holding it by the neck and regarding it critically as it flapped and wriggled in his grasp. 'Or particularly plump. But you know what they say: *gallina vecchia fa buon brodo*. The older the chicken, the better the broth.' He pulled the chicken's neck to snap it before handing it to her with a bow.

She had not eaten since the last of the loaf was finished, and her mouth watered as the bird bubbled in the stockpot with an onion, celery and some carrots that Alberto had also brought. 'Will you eat with me?' he asked her.

'I can't. I'm the cook.'

'You don't have any other customers.' He laid two places on her kitchen table. 'It's a good chicken,' he said persuasively.

She went to stand over by the stove. 'Even so.'

When the broth was made, he watched as she took the bird out of the pan and placed it on a dish. The broth she served to him just as it came out of the stockpot, thickened only with a little pasta.

'Such a simple dish,' he said, sucking it down in great spoonfuls. 'Yet so difficult to cook well. It's wonderful, Livia.'

She couldn't help being pleased. 'Thank you.'

'Won't you try some?'

'No.' She had already decided that she would eat later, from the left-overs. Even Alberto, surely, could not devour a whole saucepan of broth, not in these days when many people had not tasted meat for a year, and a chicken such as this could feed a whole family for weeks.

'Suit yourself.' He went back to the broth. 'It really is very good.'

She could see that the soup was that wonderful grey colour that comes from a well-boiled chicken, speckled here and there with golden morsels of fat. She was by now dizzy with hunger, and if she had not had the stove to lean against she might have fallen. She watched as he drained every drop.

'And now,' he said, reaching for the chicken, 'for the *secondo.*'

He broke it open with his thick fingers, deftly easing the breast meat away from the bone, twisting off the legs and thighs with well-practised movements until the bird lay dismembered on the serving dish. 'Please,' he said, indicating the other place at the table.

'I can't,' she said again, but as the aroma of cooked chicken flesh filled the air, she felt weak again, and surely when her legs were so wobbly it was no great crime to allow herself to flop into a chair. Alberto pushed a long sliver of breast meat into his mouth, and chewed it with an expression of rapture. Then he picked out a smaller piece and held it towards her. She started to reach for it, but then she felt his other hand on her arm, gently pushing it back towards the table. She understood what he wanted now, and obediently opened her mouth as he put the piece of chicken to it.

She closed her eyes. It was easier that way. She could feel his thick fingers, slick with chicken grease, pushing against her lips, but all she could taste was that chicken, the rich, thick meaty flavour of it, filling her mouth and her mind, blotting out everything else. Then it was gone, and she could not help it – she had opened her mouth for more, the way a baby bird opens its beak to be fed. She felt two thick fingers pushing into her mouth, and she found she was sucking the chicken grease off them eagerly, desperate for every last morsel.

When he pulled his fingers away she opened her eyes, ashamed of what she had just done. But there was more chicken in his hand now – the *sella*, saddle, two tiny pieces of dark flesh from the underneath of the bird, just behind the wings: the best part of the meat. Again she closed her eyes, and again she felt his fingers pushing into her mouth until she had licked them clean.

She heard his voice in her ear. 'When you asked me, last time, why it had to be you,' he said quietly, 'I told you a lie. It wasn't just that I can't afford to be laughed at. It's because I love you.'

It was easier to keep her eyes shut, to blot out what was happening, what she was hearing. She said nothing, and after a little while another sliver of chicken was pushed between her lips.

*

After he had gone she felt sick. But that evening she went to a corner of the kitchen, where she had carefully collected all the chicken's blood into a saucepan.

'I've had an idea,' she said to Marisa. 'What about the tank?'

'Which tank?'

'The one that broke down after you made a spell against the *tedesco* soldier. If we could get it to work, we could use it instead of a tractor.'

Marisa considered. 'I would need some cock's blood.'

Livia held up her saucepan. 'How about a very old cooking hen?'

'Possibly. But, Livia, neither of us knows how to drive a tank.'

'So?' Livia shrugged. 'It can't be that difficult. Soldiers do it, and look how stupid most of them are.'

That afternoon they went up to the field behind the village where the German tank had broken down. Marisa poured a foul-smelling concoction into the fuel reservoir from a bottle she had brought with her. Then she laid her hands on the tank's outer plates.

'Try it now,' she said.

Livia climbed inside. It was very dark – the only light came from a few slits in the armour. The interior smelled of engine oil, rank male sweat and another, smokier smell that she realised must be cordite.

She sat in the driver's seat and looked at the controls. They seemed simple enough. On either side of her were two large levers, which presumably controlled the two tracks. In front of the driver's seat a tiny eye-slit showed a very limited view of the way ahead. On her right were a number of other levers and switches whose function she couldn't work out. A black button looked as if it might be the starter motor. She pressed it. Nothing happened. She tried pushing all the other levers around to different positions, then tried again. This time the whole tank shook – she thought for a moment she had somehow fired the gun, then she realised it was just the engine catching, right under her feet. The interior filled with dense black smoke. She pushed at the levers, and the machine lurched forwards.

Eighteen

James was by now accustomed to excitable officers ringing with wild reports of counter-invasions and other security threats, so when a captain from Sant' Anastasia phoned to say that there had been sightings of a German tank in the area around Boscotrecase, he remembered Jackson's warnings and said, 'Don't worry, that rumour's been looked into, and there's nothing in it.'

'Well, I don't know how hard you looked,' the captain's disembodied voice said, 'but the man who reported it to me saw combat in Africa. He's not given to exaggeration, and what's more he's familiar with German tanks. Says he saw the outline of a panzer quite clearly, driving along above Cappella Nuova.'

James checked a map. Cappella Nuova was on the slopes of Vesuvius, only a few miles from the Allied airfield at Terzigno. If there really was a division of panzers holed up in the area, they could do a lot of damage if they decided to attack.

He phoned Major Heathcote and explained the situation. 'I think we'd better phone the airfield and put them on an alert, sir,' he said. 'And perhaps a few of our own tanks should go and take a look.'

'Tanks? Where on earth do you suppose I'm going to get tanks from?' the major snapped. 'Every piece of armour we've got is up at Cassino. You'll have to do a recce yourself, and if there's really anything in it, call in air support.'

'Er – isn't that more a job for the infantry, sir? Or at least someone with anti-tank weapons?'

'Take a few *carabinieri*. And if anyone has to get blown up, try to make sure it's you rather than them.'

Carlo and Enrico perked up visibly at the thought of an excursion.

The following morning they turned up with half a dozen of their friends, once more dressed in their best Capone-movie outfits – bow ties, spats, boaters and waistcoats. Once again the issuing of tommy guns caused them all to start posing gleefully, and there were even some flash photographs being taken until James called them all to order.

'No heroics,' he told them. 'If we do see anything, we're calling in the air force. Absolutely no one is to fire his weapon unless I give the order, and if at all possible we'll observe from a distance without being seen ourselves.'

It was the first time James had been out to Vesuvius. It was not apparent, from the other side of the bay, just how vast the volcano was – not a single mountain at all, but a whole series of foothills and escarpments that suddenly resolved themselves into the gargantuan twin peaks of Monte Somma and Monte Conna, the volcano proper. The smoke that perpetually hung over its tip, which in Naples had seemed so delicate and ethereal, now loomed menacingly over their heads. It looked, James thought, like the smouldering of an old fire that refused to go out.

Driving in convoy – James had brought the motorbike, rather than travel in the jeeps with the gun-toting Italians – he saw a battered sign that indicated they were passing the ruins of Pompeii. He made a mental note to come back and explore them sometime.

As they began to wind their way up the mountain, great tongues of cooled lava scarred the landscape, some of them shiny as if they were made of molten black glass. Yet despite this there were more than a dozen villages and towns scattered across the lower slopes – a triumph, James supposed, of optimism over forward planning. Surely Pompeii was all the reminder one needed of the folly of building here?

All morning they criss-crossed the slopes, occasionally stopping to question the villagers. In San Sebastiano he was shown where the lava from the 1923 eruption had broken into two streams and flowed right around the town – a miracle, according to the man who showed this to him, worked by a wooden statue of Saint Sebastian, which the white-hot lava had been unable to burn. The same statue, slightly scorched, now stood in the church just a few hundred yards from the lava's edge, where it had not been fixed to the wall in case the saint was ever needed at short notice in the future. James asked if any tanks had been seen in the vicinity, and the man shrugged. 'They are hiding in the volcano itself,' he said fatalistically. 'Everyone knows that. One day they will come out again and retake Naples.' It sounded to James more like a reworking of some old folk myth than anything based on actual observation.

On the far side of the mountain, though, sightings became more reliable. A shepherd had seen a tank travelling at speed down a country lane just two days earlier. Several other people claimed to have seen a panzer in the fields above Boscotrecase. 'Near Fiscino,' seemed to be the general consensus, and as the afternoon drew to a close that little village seemed a logical place to head towards.

They were still riding in convoy, so that James's view was mostly blocked by the forward jeep. It was only when it suddenly veered off the road and screeched to a halt that he realised something was wrong. He looked up, to his left. Yes, there was a panzer, the swastika on its side quite visible. After so long chasing it, he was almost relieved – it had started to take on the insubstantiality of a mythical beast, and at least he now knew the threat was real. It was in a field about fifty yards above him, bumping slightly as it churned towards them. Already the *carabinieri* were piling out of the back of the jeep, clutching their tommy guns.

'Remember the plan,' he shouted. 'We'll fall back and call for air support.' No one paid him the slightest attention as they hurried towards the tank, the guns at their hips spraying shots in all directions. Sparks flew from the panzer's body as bullets pinged off metal. James felt a sudden sharp pain in his left shoulder. 'Bugger,' he said, with feeling. A ricochet had just winged him. He felt the wound gingerly. Luckily it seemed to be nothing serious. He raised his voice. 'No! Fall back!'

This time, the *carabinieri* were only too happy to oblige. Having realised their bullets were useless against the tank's armoured sides, they put as much enthusiasm into a pell-mell retreat back to the apparent safety of the jeep as they had into their previous attack. James became acutely aware that he was the only person still standing exposed in the tank's path.

The tank bumped over a slight rise in the ground and skewed onto the road, demolishing part of a wall in the process. The gun appeared to turn in his direction – or was it just the effect of the uneven ground, jolting the barrel? Conscious that the *carabinieri* were all watching him, James took out his pistol. 'Stop!' he shouted. He realised that, even if they could hear him above the noise of the engine, this was unlikely to mean very much to a panzer crew. '*Halte!*' he added for good measure, raising his free hand in the air, palm forward.

The tank did not halt. It was weaving erratically as it lurched towards

115

him, presumably as some kind of anti-tank-missile evasion procedure. If he continued to stand where he was, it was simply going to run him over.

At the last moment the tank came to a standstill. The barrel of its enormous gun dropped, pointing directly at him. He felt an irrational surge of anger. He was going to die a virgin, a long way from home, and all because the bloody Italians hadn't stuck to the bloody plan.

The hatch opened and a face appeared. James could see that although it was streaked with oil it was a rather pleasing face, all big eyes, delicate cheekbones and dark eyebrows. At the moment, however, it was scowling fiercely.

'What in the name of all the saints are you doing, standing in the middle of the road like that?' the face yelled in Italian. 'I could have killed you, you stupid fool.'

'I ordered you to stop,' he pointed out.

'Why should I stop? *You* could easily have got out of *my* way.'

The woman put her hands on the top of the tank and pulled herself out of the hatch, revealing a length of slender brown leg. There was a collective intake of breath from the *carabinieri*. As she slid down over the tank's side to the ground, some of the quicker ones leapt forward to offer her a hand. Slightly bemused, James said, 'Is this your tank?'

'Well, obviously not originally,' she retorted. The *carabinieri*, their previous terror now apparently forgotten, laughed. The one who had helped her down seemed to be reluctant to let go of her hand, until she turned to him with a dazzling smile and a gracious, '*Grazie mille.*'

'So it's stolen,' James persisted.

She pulled her hair, which was long, glossy and very black, out of her collar, where she had tucked it out of the way. 'So what?'

'I'm afraid you can't keep it.'

The young woman looked from the tank to James and raised an eyebrow. 'You want me to find some Germans and give it back?' she said incredulously. The *carabinieri* chuckled delightedly.

'You need to give it to *us*.'

'But then *you* would have stolen it.' The *carabinieri* nodded as one man, and looked at James to see how he would respond.

'We're sort of allowed to,' he pointed out. 'As the winning side.'

She considered this. 'Very well,' she said. 'I'll sell it to you. Make me an offer.'

'The penalty for being caught in possession of military weapons is ten years' imprisonment.'

'It is?' She looked astonished. 'Oh. But I don't have any military weapons.'

'Madam,' James said, 'you were driving a tank.'

She made a dismissive gesture. 'So?'

James looked pointedly at the four-inch gun barrel above his head.

'Oh, that,' she said, appearing to notice it for the first time. 'There happens to be a gun attached to it, certainly, but that's nothing to do with me. As far as I'm concerned, it's a tractor. Look.' She pointed to the rear of the tank where, James now saw, some kind of primitive hoeing device had been fastened.

'May I ask whether you have a permit to run a vehicle?'

The woman seemed to be about to answer this question when she suddenly noticed his shoulder. 'You're wounded.'

'May I just ask—'

'You're bleeding.'

He looked. It was true. In the adrenaline of the moment, he hadn't noticed that his shoulder was becoming soaked with blood. 'I'm all right,' he said. But the young woman had turned away and was berating the *carabinieri* for standing there doing nothing while their captain was bleeding to death. Did they have bandages? No? Then he must be carried to her house, fortunately just around the next corner, where her sister the *maga* would dress it at once. Look, the captain was swaying, he must be faint. He should sit down and get his head between his knees while a stretcher was fetched.

Suddenly James found himself being ministered to by half a dozen *carabinieri*, working far more efficiently under the young woman's instructions than they had ever done for him, although he would have felt safer if they had put their tommy guns down before forcing him to the ground and pushing his head between his knees. From one of the jeeps a stretcher was produced. He was lifted onto it as delicately as if he were a baby, and then carried with infinite care over the rough ground.

He was placed on a kitchen table while another young woman, with similar features to the first and almost as pretty, was fetched to look at the wound. Before James quite knew what was happening both girls were peeling off his shirt and examining his shoulder, the younger one making exclamations of concern. His wound was washed, and the younger woman pressed all around it with firm, cool fingers. She spoke to her sister in rapid dialect, and the older girl leant over him and offered him her hand. 'Squeeze this,' she instructed. As he squeezed he felt the hard band of her wedding ring.

'I think it may be sprained as well,' the younger one said. She left the room. James was left on his back, staring up at the mass of fragrant black hair that tumbled over the tank driver's forehead. He realised he was still squeezing her hand. 'Sorry,' he said, withdrawing it.

'What's your name?' she asked.

'Captain Gould. James Gould.'

'Chames Ghoul?'

'James *Gould*.'

'Jems Goot?'

'Near enough.' Despite himself, he suddenly felt rather cheerful. He had thought he was about to be blasted to smithereens by a tank gun, and now here he was being ministered to by two of the prettiest girls he had ever met. It was the sort of thing that could only have happened in Italy.

The younger sister returned with two small jars. 'Stay still,' she told him. Reaching carefully into the first one, she took out a bee. The insect appeared to be tame, or perhaps it was just used to her: it walked over her fingers as unconcerned as a ladybird. 'This will only hurt a little,' she said. She held the bee to his shoulder, and James felt a sudden sharp pain as it stung him.

'What in God's name—' he began, trying to get up.

'It will help the cut heal.' From the second jar she spooned a small amount of what looked like honey, which she dabbed on the edges of the wound. 'This too.'

It was nonsense, of course, but he supposed they were only trying to help. And her fingers were really very deft, massaging away the pain . . . He lay back and closed his eyes.

When he opened them again, his shirt was being cut up to make band-ages. 'Thank you,' he said. 'You're very kind.'

'It's not kindness,' the older sister said matter-of-factly. 'We don't want to go to prison, that's all.'

'And I thought you were doing it out of the goodness of your hearts,' he said drily.

'Marisa thinks that one of us should flirt with you, just in case. She thinks it should be me,' she added, 'because you like me better.'

How on earth did she know that? 'I hope you told her you're not that kind of girl,' he muttered.

She turned to look down at him. Her eyes, he noticed, were deep green in colour, and they regarded him with a sudden flash of what looked remarkably like contempt. 'No,' she said. 'I told her that I would rather die than flirt with a British officer.'

The younger girl began to wind the bandage around his upper arm.

'I'm very glad to hear it,' James said, confused by the sudden bitterness in her voice.

But for once, he wasn't completely sure that he was.

By the time the wound was dressed, and a sling rigged up, the pain in his shoulder had turned into a fuzzy warmth. Perhaps the bee sting had helped after all, James thought: he must ask his medical friend if there was anything in it.

A plate of small, round, white objects was placed in front of him, together with a fork. 'Eat,' he was commanded. He pushed the fork into one of the objects. It was as soft as a poached egg and, when he punctured it, oozed what appeared to be ivory-coloured cream. He tried some. Richness flooded his mouth. The taste was fresh, almost like chewing grass, but filling and slightly sweet.

'Gosh,' he said. 'What is this?'

'*Burrata*. We make it ourselves.'

It was not a word he knew. He said firmly, 'I'm afraid I'll need some more details about this tank. How did you come by it in the first place?'

'Marisa put a spell on it.'

James's heart sank. He could imagine Major Heathcote's reaction if he put that in his report.

He listened as Marisa and Livia explained the story of the widow Esmerelda and the spell that was put on the tank in retribution for her death. It took a while, and was somewhat confused, owing to the girls' habit of talking over each other. He stroked his chin. It was a more complex situation than he had first assumed, because the tank had been taken directly from the Germans, and was thus technically not stolen, but captured . . . . . . 'Let me think about this,' he said. 'But in the meantime I'll have to impound the tank. And you'll have to come with us, I'm afraid,' he added to Livia.

'Where to?'

'The military compound in Naples.'

'There may be a problem with that.'

'Oh? Why?'

'That tank runs on my father's grappa. While you're sitting here chatting, your men outside are drinking all the fuel.'

James went to stop the *carabinieri*, who as Livia had said were making hefty inroads into the bottles of pungent, colourless alcohol the girls had been using to run the tank. It was only then that he realised that the house, although no different in appearance to any of the other houses in the village, doubled as a bar and restaurant. 'And I'm afraid you'll have to close this place,' he told the two sisters. 'All places of entertainment are off limits until further notice.'

'By whose stupid order?' Livia demanded.

'Mine, actually.'

'But we live here.'

'Well, you'll have to close the kitchen and dining room.'

'But it's *our* kitchen. And our dining room.'

James scratched his head. Rules which had seemed straightforward when drawn up in Naples seemed rather more complicated here. 'You'll just have to turn your customers away,' he suggested.

'We don't have any customers. Apart from your *carabinieri*.'

This was clearly going to be one of those circular conversations at which Italians excelled. 'In that case you can stay open,' he said, 'until you have some customers, at which point you will have to close. Is that fair?'

The girls reluctantly agreed that this was acceptable, so long as they were recompensed for the grappa. There was a brief negotiation, which somehow resulted in James agreeing to pay them an extortionate amount, and Livia went off to get some things.

Upstairs she took Marisa and her father aside. 'Don't worry about me,' she said. 'I'll be fine. But since they're taking me to Naples, I think I should stay there.'

'Why?' Nino asked, aghast.

'While I'm here, Alberto will never leave us alone. If I go, perhaps things will be better. There's enough food for the two of you, if the neighbours help out.'

'But how will you survive?'

'I'll go to Enzo's family and get work in the factory. His mother won't let me starve.' Fighting back tears, she said, 'Really, it's for the best. I don't want Alberto to win any more than you do, but what choice do we have? You know as well as I do that no one here can stand up to him.'

Marisa hugged her. 'All right. Go, if you think you have to. But come back to us as soon as you can.'

Nino said, 'I don't like to think of you getting a lift from soldiers.'

'I'll be careful. Besides, if this officer was going to try anything it would have been before, when he could have threatened us with prison about the tank.'

'Livia's right,' Marisa said. 'He's not like the officer who took our food.'

'A soldier is still a soldier,' Nino said. 'Leave here with him if you must, but don't give him any encouragement.'

'Of course I won't. The only difficulty will be forcing myself to be polite to him.'

There was almost a fight among the policemen for the honour of helping Livia up into the back of the jeep, but as it turned out, none of the *carabinieri* knew how to drive the tank. Livia tried to teach one of them, but he kept crashing it into the side of the road. James suspected that he was simply overcome by the experience of being confined in a very small space with Livia. When they finally left for the military compound it was in a convoy, with Livia driving the tank, James standing to attention in the command hatch, and the other vehicles bringing up the rear.

As they drove down the foothills of Vesuvius, James was conscious of an unfamiliar sensation. He was enjoying himself. He was alive; he was commanding a German tank; the scenery was beautiful, the sea air was warm and salty on his face, and the scent of ilex trees was filling his nostrils. And the girl who crouched down in the driving seat, her thick black hair billowing behind her – there was definitely something about her that was contributing to this feeling of well-being. Quite apart from anything else, it was such a pleasant novelty to meet an Italian girl who wasn't trying to get one into bed.

'So you see,' James explained to Major Heathcote on the telephone, 'this woman and her fellow partisans took part in a local resistance operation. The partisans captured this tank, but there was no fuel to drive it. Then, after the Germans had left, they hit on the idea of refuelling it with grappa, and that's when the tank was spotted, as they tried to deliver it to the Allies.'

None of this was strictly a lie, but neither was it strictly true. It was, he told himself, simply a matter of making sure that busy people such as the CO didn't spend more time than they needed to on things that really weren't all that important.

'These partisans,' the CO said thoughtfully. 'What are they known as?'

'Er – the Pertini band, I believe, sir.'

'Not communists, are they?'

James thought of those negotiations over the grappa. 'No, sir. From what I've seen of them, they are most definitely democratic capitalists.'

'Good. Tell 'em we're very grateful for their gallant efforts, et cetera, and send them on their way.'

*

121

By the time James found someone prepared to take receipt of an operational German panzer it was late. Livia was still surrounded by a mass of attentive Italians, but she was yawning, and she had little choice but to accept James's offer of a lift.

With one of his arms in a sling, and the back of the bike weighed down by Livia's bag, they made unsteady progress on the Matchless as they set off from the compound. 'Sorry about that,' he called over his shoulder as he hit a pothole.

She didn't answer. After a couple of other attempts at small talk met a similar reaction, he gave up and concentrated on driving. After a while he felt her head rest against his back. The contact was rather agreeable, and for a moment he wondered if she was showing some interest in him after all. Then he realised that she had simply fallen asleep, curled up against his back as lightly as a cat.

Naples was quiet, illuminated by a huge moon, and as he steered his way carefully through the cobbled streets James felt a pang of affection for the place; so unpredictable, so maddening, yet capable of springing surprises like putting a sleeping girl on your motorbike in the middle of the night, and in the middle of a war to boot.

In fact, Naples was not completely quiet that night. Behind the blackout curtains at Zi' Teresa's, the closed-down restaurant was the venue for a meeting of the disaffected.

Angelo, who had called the meeting, was there, as was the beautiful glass-eyed whore Elena Marlona. Amongst the other women in the room were several others James would have recognised: Algisa Fiore, Violetta Cartenza, the born-again virgin Silvana Settimo, Serena Tivoloni . . . The room was filled with the flower of Neapolitan womanhood, and the flower of Neapolitan womanhood was not happy.

'How can we work if the brothels are shut?' Algisa Fiore demanded. 'It's ridiculous. We have to operate from home, or slip out onto the streets when no one's looking.'

'It's worse for us,' a middle-aged man who ran one of the city's oldest pizzerias pointed out. 'At least you carry the tools of your trade around with you. Me, I can't do anything without my oven.'

'For myself,' Elena said, looking around haughtily with her one good eye, 'the closure of the brothels makes little difference. I was the best whore in Naples before the war, and I'll be the best whore in Naples after the war is over. But this ban on marrying is a pain. The market's getting clogged up with too many amateurs.'

'It's all down to this Englishman, Gould,' someone said. 'Surely we can do something?'

'We could have him killed,' a villainous-looking pimp suggested. 'I'll do it myself, for a small consideration.'

'A waste of time,' Angelo said. 'They'll just replace him with someone else. And I know the British: if their man is murdered, they'll clamp down even harder.'

'Then he must be seduced.'

'I tried that,' Algisa Fiore said gloomily. '*Niente.*'

'Or bribed.'

'He didn't even open the envelope,' Martina Fontanelle said.

'Perhaps he likes little girls, like Jackson. Or boys. There's always something that will corrupt a man.'

'Not this one,' Angelo said. 'He even pays for his own dinner. But come to think of it . . .'

'What?'

'There is something that he likes. Food.' Angelo looked thoughtful. 'Though I think he may not even have realised it himself.'

'Hardly surprising, if his cook is Ciro Malloni.' Those who knew Malloni chuckled.

'Malloni is there for a reason,' Angelo said. 'He works for Vito Genovese. But I hear the Genovese family aren't too happy about these restrictions either . . . Leave it with me. I'll think of something.'

PART THREE

'In pursuit of certain lusty gratifications of the palate, no ingredient can take you further than beans.'

Marcella Hazan, *Marcella's Kitchen*

'The humble bean (fagioli) for generations scorned by everybody but the lowest classes has risen to a delicacy which can only be afforded by the rich at 150 lire per kilo as compared with a lira or less in normal times.'

Memo, Public Health Dept, AMG Region 3, 1943

Nineteen

Livia woke up as they reached the harbour. 'You can drop me here,' she said, tapping him on the back. He pulled up, and watched as she untied her bag from the pannier.

'Perhaps I'll see you again,' he said tentatively.

'Perhaps,' she said, in a voice that suggested she rather hoped not. She reached up into her hair and with her fingers combed out some tangles from the journey. 'Thank you for the lift.' She picked up her bag and walked away without another word.

'Will you be all right?' he called after her. She didn't reply. He supposed she was still upset about having the tank confiscated. But really, she could hardly have expected him to let her keep it. In fact, when he looked back at the afternoon's events it seemed to him he had gone out of his way to be reasonable. So why was she persisting in being so very ungrateful? And why was he so exasperated that she was?

For a moment he almost went after her. Then, with a sigh, he turned the bike in the direction of the Palazzo Satriano.

Livia had intended to walk the rest of the way. She had not realised, though, how much of a battering Naples had taken since she was last here. Picking her way through the dark streets was a precarious business. Worse, when she got to the street in which Enzo's family lived, she saw that there was only a huge gap where their house had once stood.

'Excuse me,' she said, stopping a woman who was entering a nearby doorway. 'Can you tell me where the Telli family are now?'

The woman crossed herself. 'In heaven, God willing. They were all killed in an air raid.'

Livia stared at the mass of rubble, shocked. Of course, people were

127

dying in the raids all the time, but this was different. It occurred to her that if she hadn't gone back to Fiscino, she would almost certainly have been with the rest of the Telli family when they were killed.

'It was after little Enzo died in Russia,' the woman added. 'His family got the letter, and that's when they stopped going to the shelters. His mother said that if God took her to join him, she wouldn't complain.'

Poor Quartilla, Livia thought. She had been a tough mother-in-law, but she had adored her son.

'You look upset,' the woman commented. 'Did you know the family well?'

'I was married to Enzo,' Livia managed to say.

'*Ai, ai.* Everyone knows someone who's lost a family,' the woman said. 'Me, I lost all my brothers. I thank God I don't have any sons, or they would have gone too.' She looked at Livia sympathetically. 'You've had a bad shock. I'd give you some food, but I don't have any.' She threw up her hands. 'This war. When will it ever end?'

With the last of her money she rented a room in a shabby boarding house near the port, and the next morning she went to the munitions factory to see if they had any work. But the munitions factory was gone too. An old man who was picking through the rubble for scrap told her that it had been destroyed by the Germans before they left. He thought the hospital the was taking on cleaners, so she walked two miles across Naples to the Ospedale dei Pelligrini, only to discover that the jobs had been filled days ago. 'You could try the big hotels on Via Partenope,' the hospital administrator suggested. 'They've reopened now for Allied officers, and one supposes they must have chambermaids.' Livia knew it was a long shot, but she walked all the way back to Via Partenope anyway.

The concierge at the first hotel where she asked for work was brutally dismissive. 'As a chambermaid, or a whore?' he asked. 'Not that it matters. I've got no vacancies for either.' It was the same everywhere she went. After a while she tried going directly to the hotel kitchens, reasoning that her skills as a cook must surely be in demand somewhere, but here too the message was identical: we have all the cooks we need, and more.

On the Corso Garibaldi she saw a girl gratefully accepting a tin of rations from two Canadian soldiers, before slipping off with them into a stairwell. However bad things had become in Fiscino, she realised, here they were much worse, worse than she'd ever imagined.

She returned to her room that evening exhausted. She hadn't eaten all day, but she was so tired that even her hunger couldn't prevent her from sleeping.

The next day there was more of the same. She was told there was definitely a job going unloading pallets in the harbour, but when she got there, the line of applicants stretched for three hundred yards and fights had already broken out over places in the queue. She went back to trudging round kitchens. In many places her knock was not even answered: the restaurants were boarded up and silent, closed by the crackdown on black marketeering.

She stopped for a rest on a doorstep, and a pretty girl her own age waved to her from across the street. Grateful for some human contact, Livia waved back, only to realise from the other girl's scowl that she wasn't actually waving, but gesticulating for Livia to get out of the doorway. '*Vai via!*' the girl screeched. 'Scram! That's where I work, you little thief. Find your own place, or my brother will knife you.'

Despite his inexperience, James was not completely ignorant of sexual matters. At school there had been a dissection of the reproductive organs of a frog, which left him with the impression that sex was probably not for the squeamish, and a veiled talk from his housemaster in which the words 'spiritual hygiene', 'self-control' and 'bodily purity' had featured heavily, which left him with the impression that a tendency to self-abuse would ruin him for marriage. Eventually one of the other boys had got hold of a copy of Richard Burton's notorious translation of the *Kama Sutra*, but despite the eagerness with which they devoured its pages, that too tended to mystify rather than elucidate. 'Man is divided into three classes,' Burton explained breezily, 'the hare man, the bull man, and the horse man, according to the size of his *lingam*. Woman also, according to the depth of her *yoni*, is either a female deer, a mare, or a female elephant. There are thus three equal unions between persons of corresponding dimensions, and there are six unequal unions, when the dimensions do not correspond, or nine in all, as the following table shows:

EQUAL		UNEQUAL	
MEN	WOMEN	MEN	WOMEN
Hare	Deer	Hare	Mare
Bull	Mare	Hare	Elephant
Horse	Elephant	Bull	Deer
		Bull	Elephant
		Horse	Deer
		Horse	Mare

'Amongst all these, equal unions are the best, those of a superlative degree, i.e. the highest and the lowest, are the worst, and the rest are middling, and with them the high are better than the low.'

This seemed to James even more worrying than the talk from his housemaster had been. How was one meant to know if one was a bull or a horse? More to the point, how was one to know whether one's intended wife was a deer or a mare? Even supposing she knew herself, which seemed unlikely, you could hardly come right out and ask her. And what happened if, through simple ignorance, a horse married a mare (a natural enough occurrence, one would think, but a union which Burton specifically advised against) and the two parties thus found themselves inadvertently mismatched for an entire lifetime? On a statistical basis, in fact, since there were more unequal combinations than equal ones, it seemed you were more likely to have a disaster on your hands than not.

Nor, despite an impressive list of sexual positions and embellishments, did one learn very much from the *Kama Sutra* about the act itself, owing to the difficulty of visualising Burton's rather vague descriptions. 'When she raises her thighs and keeps them wide apart and engages in congress, it is called the "Yawning Position",' Burton wrote. 'When she places her thighs with her legs doubled on them upon her sides, and thus engages in congress, it is called the "Position of Indrani" and this is learnt only by practice.' James could just about picture what she was doing with her legs, but where was the man while all this was going on – on top? Underneath? Watching? And what exactly were the dangers of attempting the 'Position of Indrani' without practice?

'Auparishtaka, or mouth congress,' Burton warned, 'should never be done by a learned Brahman, by a minister that carries on the business of a state, or by a man of good reputation, because though the practice is allowed by the Shastras, there is no reason why it should be carried on, and need only be practised in particular cases.' These 'particular cases' might include 'unchaste and wanton women, female attendants and serving maids,' who were apparently expert in a technique called 'Sucking the mango stone'. As James had never come across a mango, let alone a wanton woman, this information was not much use either.

One thing he remained particularly unclear about was just what a woman got out of sex. Even Burton, usually so dogmatic in his obscurity, seemed unsure on this subject. 'Females do not emit as males do,' he wrote. 'The males simply remove their desire, while the females, from their consciousness of desire, feel a certain kind of pleasure, which gives them satisfaction, but it is impossible for them to tell you what kind of pleasure they feel.' Amongst the few friends James was able to discuss the matter with, opinion was divided. Was sex for a woman simply a duty, or was there actual pleasure involved? A boy who had been carrying on an affair with a serving maid – one of Burton's 'wanton women' – claimed that they did, but it was generally held that he was being spun a line, and that whilst men desired women for their bodies as well as their minds, a woman's desire was principally for the admiration of a man.

After he met Jane, and marriage seemed a real possibility, James had taken the bull by the horns and visited a small bookshop on the Charing Cross Road, where he purchased a slim volume entitled *Married Love*. The man who sold it to him had, it seemed to James, given him a faint smirk as he wrapped it up in brown paper, and it was not until he was completely alone and sure of being undisturbed that he had dared to open it.

> It has become a tradition of our social life that the ignorance of woman about her own body and that of her future husband is a flower-like innocence . . .

the author wrote,

> and to such an extreme is this sometimes pushed, that not seldom is a girl married unaware that married life will bring her into physical relations with her husband fundamentally different from those with her brother. When she discovers the true nature of his body, and learns the part she has to play as a wife, she may refuse utterly to agree to her husband's wishes. I know one pair of which the husband, chivalrous and loving, had to wait years before his bride recovered from the shock of the discovery of the meaning of marriage and was able to allow him a natural relation. There have been not a few brides whom the horror of the first night of marriage with a man less considerate has driven to suicide or insanity.

James had read on with his heart in his mouth. This was exactly the sort of thing he was afraid of.

> Those who are shocked at the publication of such a book as this on the ground that it gives material for impure minds to sport with, need only reflect that such material is already amply provided in certain comic papers, in hosts of inferior novels, too often on the stage and film, and

131

presented thus in coarse and demoralising guise. It can do nothing but good to such minds to meet the facts they are already so familiar with in a totally new light.

And shed new light it did. True, the author, a woman scientist named Dr Stopes, had much to say about her own discovery of certain fundamental principles governing female responses ('We have studied the wave-lengths of water, of sound, of light; but when will the sons and daughters of men study the sex-tide in woman and learn the Laws of her Periodicity of Recurrence of Desire?') But on one subject she was quite clear, and that was that women were capable of enjoying married relations:

> By the majority of 'nice' people a woman is supposed to have no spontaneous sex-impulses. By this I do not mean a sentimental 'falling in love,' but a physical, physiological state of stimulation which arises spontaneously and quite apart from any particular man. So widespread in our country is the view that it is only depraved women who have such feelings (especially before marriage) that most women would rather die than own that they *do* at times feel a physical yearning indescribable, but as profound as hunger for food.

> It is true that in our northern climate women are on the whole naturally less persistently stirred than southerners; and it is further true that with the delaying of maturity, due to our ever-lengthening youth, it often happens that a woman is approaching or even past thirty years before she is awake to the existence of the profoundest calls of her nature.

Nor did Dr Stopes shirk from explaining how this stirring could come about:

> Woman has at the surface a small vestigial organ called the clitoris, which corresponds morphologically to the man's penis, and which, like it, is extremely sensitive to touch-sensations. This little crest, which lies anteriorly between the inner lips round the vagina, enlarges when the woman is really tumescent, and by the stimulation of movement it is intensely roused and transmits this stimulus to every nerve in her body. But even after a woman's dormant sex-feeling is aroused and all the complex reactions of her being have been set in motion, it may even take as much as from ten to twenty minutes of actual physical union to consummate her feeling, while two or three minutes often completes the

132

union for a man who is ignorant of the need to control his reactions so that both may experience the added benefit of a mutual crisis to love . . .

> This mutual orgasm is extremely important, but in many cases the man's climax comes so swiftly that the woman's reactions are not nearly ready, and she is left without it.

A woman's orgasm, Dr Stopes explained briskly, particularly 'a really complete and muscularly energetic orgasm', was necessary to her health, her nerves, her sleep, and even her ability to conceive. A dutiful husband would, through self-control, ensure his wife's pleasure even before his own, although many, even most, neglected to do so.

> But as things are to-day it is scarcely an exaggeration to say that the majority of wives are left wakeful and nerve-racked to watch with tender motherly brooding, or with bitter and jealous envy, the slumbers of the men who, through ignorance and carelessness, have neglected to see that they too had the necessary resolution of nervous tension.

James had immediately resolved never to leave Jane either wakeful or nerve-racked. But on one subject Dr Stopes was just as firm as his housemaster: the exercise of these duties was a matter to be left until after marriage:

> However much he may conceal it under assumed cynicism, worldliness, or self-seeking, the heart of every young man yearns with a great longing for the fulfilment of the beautiful dream of a life-long union with a mate. Each heart knows instinctively that it is only a mate who can give full comprehension of all the potential greatness in the soul.
>
> It may be that after years of fighting with his hot young blood a man has given up and gone now and again for relief to prostitutes, and then later in life has met the woman who is his mate, and whom, after remorse for his soiled past, and after winning her forgiveness for it, he marries. Then, unwittingly, he may make the wife suffer either by interpreting her in the light of the other women or perhaps (though this happens less frequently) by setting her absolutely apart from them.

As for what his housemaster had referred to as 'spiritual hygiene', Dr Stopes was also of the opinion that abstinence was the correct path, although her reasons were more scientific:

The analysis of the chemical nature of the ejaculated fluid reveals among other things a remarkably high percentage of calcium and phosphoric acid – both precious substances in our organisation. It is therefore the greatest mistake to imagine that the semen is something to be got rid of *frequently* – all the vital energy and nerve-force involved in its ejaculation and the precious chemical substances which go to its composition can be better utilised by being transformed into other creative work.

James was utterly converted, and from then on he had resolved, firstly, to keep his baser lusts, along with all the potential greatness in his soul, to himself, at least until his wedding night; secondly, to keep away from prostitutes; and thirdly, to reserve his own stores of calcium and phosphoric acid for his work. Since Jane had broken off their engagement the first had been pretty much assured, and the second held little attraction in any case, but the third had not been easy, particularly now that he was subject to the stirring influence of a southern climate himself. He had tried to steer clear of seafood, as per Jackson's instructions, but sunlight was harder to avoid, and there had been one or two occasions when his work at the FSS had been somewhat calcium-deficient. He had noticed, however, that Dr Stopes and his old housemaster seemed to be wrong about one thing. Far from turning him into a raving sex-fiend, his occasional lapses actually seemed to have the opposite effect, making his baser thoughts temporarily less pressing, whilst it was when he was apparently being virtuous that he was more troubled by thoughts of women.

And at the moment he was extremely troubled by thoughts of women. Or, to be more precise, by thoughts of one woman in particular. When a naked arm reached into his mind and beckoned alluringly to him, or when a dress slipped off a shoulder, or a shadow brushed past him, the face it belonged to – the mischievous face, its eyes a bold mixture of challenge and haughtiness – was that of Livia Pertini.

She would steal up on him at the most inopportune moments. He could be conducting an interview or writing a report: one moment his mind would be on his work, the next, a sort of cold, melting feeling in the base of his spine would herald an almost physical shock as Livia pressed her lips against his. He could imagine the cool skin of her cheek, the warm softness of her ears, the tiny pulse at the base of her neck . . . Most disturbingly of all, his body reacted quite physically to these visitations. More than once he had to quickly cover his lap with a file, before whoever he was vetting thought that it was she who was causing him this discomfort.

*

134

His arm was giving him no trouble, but he thought it prudent to get it examined by a medic.

'It's a good dressing,' the doctor commented as he unwound Marisa's bandage. He peered at the wound. 'And no sign of infection. What did you say this girl put on it?'

'Honey,' James confirmed. 'And she got one of the bees to sting me. It couldn't really have helped, could it?'

The doctor shrugged. 'It's an odd thing, but when I was in Nepal I heard of healers there using the same remedy. Perhaps there's something in it after all.' He redressed the wound. 'Either way, you've been lucky. I've only got a single crate of penicillin left, and my orders are to reserve it for combat casualties. If you'd got an infection, you'd probably have lost your arm. Is there anything else you wanted to ask me about?'

'Actually, there is.' James explained about his problem. 'I wondered if I might have a touch of malaria or something,' he concluded.

'Hmm. Stick your tongue out?'

James complied. 'Looks healthy enough to me,' the doctor said. 'My advice is to drink plenty of tea. It won't reduce your urges, but in my experience it's hard to contemplate doing anything really beastly while drinking a nice cup of tea.'

Twenty

It was late when Livia finally tried the kitchen of Zi' Teresa's. Even though the restaurant was shrouded with blackout blinds, it was clear that it was shut, and she was really only knocking because she was too tired and hungry to do anything else.

To her surprise, though, the door opened a crack, and a man's face peered out. 'Yes?'

Livia repeated her litany. 'Please, I'm looking for a job.'

'Go away. We're closed, we have no work.' Angelo regarded the girl in front of him for a moment. She was swaying on her feet, and her eyes had a blank, unfocused expression. Softening, he said 'Have you eaten today?'

Livia shook her head.

'Perhaps I can find you something,' he muttered, holding the door open. 'Come in. But only for a minute, mind.'

He gave her some cold beans and watched her as she devoured them. 'What kind of work are you looking for?' he asked.

'I'm a cook. My family run the *osteria* at Fiscino, but there are no customers any more, and no food to cook with.'

'Ah, so that's who you are.' Angelo nodded. 'I ate at your *osteria* once. It was a few years ago, but I can remember the food as if it were yesterday. Do you still make that wonderful *burrata*?'

'Yes, but now we can't get it to the market.'

She explained about the impounded tank, and the closing of her own restaurant.

'Ah. So you've met Captain Gould.'

She sighed. 'Yes, I've met him.'

'That young man,' Angelo said, 'is not nearly as fierce as he seems. But I'm afraid you did the wrong thing coming to Naples. You'd be better off going back to Fiscino and finding someone to look after you until this is all over.'

Livia shuddered. 'There's someone who offered. But I'm not going to do that. There must be someone in Naples who needs a cook.'

Just then Angelo was struck by an idea. 'Actually,' he said, 'there is one person.' He nodded thoughtfully. The more he considered his idea, the better it seemed. 'Livia, I might just be able to get you some work after all.'

'She's as sweet as bread,' he told Elena. 'A real country girl – honest, hardworking, passionate, and pretty with it. And she knows how to cook – not fancy stuff, but proper country cooking. I had her make me some *pasta e fagioli*, and it was the best I've ever had.'

'So you want her to seduce him?' Elena asked sceptically. 'I thought that had been tried before.'

'No.' Angelo shook his head. 'She's not like that, and in any case, it isn't necessary. *Panza cuntenti, cori clementi: panza dijuna, nenti priduna.** At the end of the day, sex is only sex. A man can be sleeping with the most beautiful woman in the world, but when he gets up from her bed he's still exactly the same person he was before. But a man who has eaten well – he's at peace with the world, he's happy, and more importantly, he wants other people to be happy. He looks at young lovers, and thinks how nice it would be if they could get married. He thinks about war, and it occurs to him that really peace is much nicer. He stops worrying about proclamations and paperwork, and lets people get on with their own business without interfering. In short, he starts to become a more generous, civilised human being. You follow?'

Elena shrugged. 'And she's happy to do it?'

'Not very,' Angelo admitted. 'Her family have suffered at the hands of the Allies, and she took a little convincing.' This was an understatement: it had taken all his powers of persuasion to get Livia to con- sider working for the British officer, and in the end he had only succeeded because she realised that it was the only job she was likely to be offered. 'But I'm sure it will work out,' he said, more optimistically than he felt.

'We'll see,' Elena said. 'If it doesn't, we could always try seducing him again.'

*

* A contented stomach, a forgiving heart: but a hungry stomach pardons no one.

137

'Arrested?' James said, perplexed. 'But what on earth can Malloni have been arrested for?'

'Stealing Allied Government property,' Carlo explained. 'Your rations. It turns out he was taking all the good stuff and selling it up on the Via Forcella, leaving you with what he couldn't unload.'

'Good Lord. Though I have to say, I'm not completely surprised. There was always something a little unlikely about Malloni. I suppose this means we'll have to find a new cook?'

'I have already taken the liberty of advertising.'

'Shouldn't be too hard, presumably? Naples must be full of people desperate for jobs.'

'Exactly. I have spread the word that interviews will take place from ten o'clock tomorrow morning.'

'*Grazie tante*, Carlo. I'm very grateful.'

The next morning James woke up early. He sniffed the air. An unfamiliar aroma was wafting into his bedroom. He sniffed again. That was it: it was the smell of fresh bread, and it was quite delicious. His stomach groaned involuntarily as he pulled on his uniform.

Going into the kitchen, he saw the back of a woman's head peering into one of his cupboards. For a moment he thought it was Livia Pertini, which was ridiculous. Then she turned around, and he realised it *was* her. 'What on earth are you doing here?' he said, astonished.

'I'm your new cook,' she said.

'Oh.' He rubbed his head, trying to resist the temptation to grin inanely at her. 'I'm afraid you're early. The interviews aren't until ten o'clock.'

'Well, why don't I make you breakfast, and you can interview me afterwards?'

'Um.' James had a vague idea that there was something slightly improper about this, but he couldn't think exactly what it was. And it was really very nice to see her. 'I suppose that's all right.'

'What is this?' she asked, showing him the tin of 'Meat and Vegetables' in her hand.

'Oh, that. It's a kind of . . .' he struggled to find the Italian word. '*Stufato*, I suppose. A stew.'

'Is it good?'

'It's absolutely horrible.'

She put the tin back in the cupboard. 'Then why do you have so much of it?'

'It's a long story.'

'Anyway,' she said, 'I managed to swap some with the woman upstairs for bread and fresh goat's milk, and I have pastries and mozzarella cheese and some oranges. How does that sound?'

'It sounds rather nice,' he admitted.

'Where's your tablecloth?'

'We don't usually bother with a tablecloth for breakfast,' he said. 'As a matter of fact, we don't usually bother with a table.'

'No wonder you get indigestion.'

'As a matter of fact, I don't.'

'Of course you do,' she said, with an air of finality that brooked no argument. 'Presumably you must have a clean sheet somewhere?'

'I suppose I—'

'Could you get it, please?'

When he returned with the sheet, he found that she had picked some blossom from the lemon tree in the courtyard and stuck it in a vase. She laid the sheet over the table and pointed to a seat. '*Prego.*'

'Aren't you going to eat?'

'Maybe later. Go on, sit.'

He sat. He had to admit, it all looked rather splendid. The bread was on a wooden cutting board, and the milk was in a little pottery jug, with the vase of lemon blossom next to it. Livia placed a ball of wet newspaper on the table, and proceeded to unwrap it. 'What's that?' he asked.

'Mozzarella cheese, of course. It's like the *burrata* you had before, but different.'

'It's soft,' he said, pushing his fork into the piece she passed him.

'You've never eaten mozzarella?' she said incredulously.

'In England we only have three cheeses,' he explained. 'Cheddar, Stilton and Wensleydale.'

'Now you're making fun of me,' she sniffed.

'Not at all.' He put some of the milky white cheese into his mouth. 'Oh,' he said. 'That's rather good, isn't it?' It was so soft it melted in his mouth, but the taste was explosive – creamy, and cuddy, and faintly tart all at once.

The door opened and Horris walked in. 'I say, something smells good.' He looked at the table. 'What's all this?'

'It's breakfast,' James explained.

'Excellent.' Horris pulled up a chair.

There was a knock at the door and Jumbo Jeffries stuck his head around it. His eyes were bloodshot and surrounded with dark pouches, but he brightened when he saw the table.

'Are those oranges?'

'I believe they are.'

'Oranges,' Jumbo said authoritatively, 'are just the thing for a flagging constitution.' He pulled up another chair. Within a few minutes another four or five officers had also joined them.

Livia put a plate of pastries on the table. James had never seen anything so ridiculous. Each one was as intricate and ornate as a girl's bonnet, with various decorations of candied lemon, custard, and marzipan flowers. He picked one up suspiciously and bit into it.

He had to admit, it tasted a lot better than it looked. Next to him, Horris was on his second, and the others were fast catching up. Soon James was looking at a table that had been cleared of everything but a few crumbs.

'I'll make sure there's more tomorrow,' Livia said.

'If you get the job,' James pointed out.

'The extraordinary thing is,' he told Livia at eleven-thirty, 'you seem to be the only applicant. Or at least, the only one who's shown up.'

She shrugged. 'You're obviously a very unpopular employer.'

'I suppose we ought to re-advertise. I mean, I can't really give the job to the first person who knocks on the door, can I?'

'How many cooks do you need?'

'Just one.'

'So how many applicants do you need?'

'Well – one, I suppose.'

'There you are, then.'

'But how do I know your cooking is up to scratch?'

'If there wasn't a war on,' Livia said, 'I would take great exception to that remark. But since times are hard, why don't I cook you lunch, and you can keep me on if you like it?'

Lunch for the British personnel was usually another quick bite taken at their desks, but even before Livia started going around the apartment looking for more sheets to use as tablecloths James realised she was unlikely to find that an acceptable arrangement. All morning a succession of extraordinary smells emanated from the kitchen, although since Livia absolutely forbade access it was impossible to know what was causing them.

Halfway through the morning a thought occurred to James, and he went to knock on the kitchen door. When Livia opened it, he said, 'There is just one thing, Mrs Pertini. I hope it's not too late to say this: we none of us eat garlic.'

She looked at him as if he were quite mad. 'Well, of course. No one *eats* garlic. It's not a vegetable.'

'No, I mean – none of us eats garlic *at all*. In our food. We don't want to smell afterwards, you see.'

She opened her eyes very wide. 'Is there anything else you don't like? Parsley, perhaps, or oregano?'

'I should imagine herbs would be all right – in moderation, of course. And so long as it's herbs, rather than spices. That red pepper you eat here—'

'*Peperoncino*?'

'That's the one. We don't like that.'

She opened her mouth and then closed it again. 'Is that all?'

'Well, while we're on the subject, potatoes are preferable to pasta – we're not quite as keen as you Italians on the old *maccheroni*. But you'll find we're pretty easy going. Plenty of meat, properly cooked through, tomatoes preferably not cooked at all, bread, gravy when you can stretch to it . . . If you can get hold of some butter, that would be champion. And, er, a light touch with the olive oil.'

Livia nodded thoughtfully. Then she shut the door without comment.

Just before noon she came into the big room that they used as their main office. 'We can't eat in that kitchen,' she said. 'It's not big enough.' She looked at the vast dining table. 'This will do. Can you clear those papers off, please?'

'I'm afraid not,' James explained. 'This is our work.'

'It'll still be your work later. Lunch will be in fifteen minutes.'

In fact, it was half an hour before lunch arrived. Livia insisted that everyone had to be seated before she served the food – 'The people wait for the pasta, not the pasta for the people,' she said firmly. She also ensured that the table itself held a jug of water, a phial of oil, a dish of salt, and a vase of fresh blossom. Once again James was struck by the efficient way she organised everyone to do exactly what she wanted. By the time the moment arrived, every British officer in the building was waiting to see what Livia would serve.

The door opened and she entered. She was bearing an enormous dish of steaming *fettuccine*, tossed in a sauce made with tomatoes, olive oil, chopped onion, celery and garlic, and decorated with freshly torn basil leaves. So much, James thought, for his suggestions. But perhaps Livia had been limited by what had been available.

As she filled each bowl, she grated a little hard cheese and some pepper over it. 'You're quite sure none of this food came from the black market?' James asked, eyeing the cheese warily.

'Of course not. I swapped it for your rations,' Livia said. This was the truth, although she did not mention that the person she had swapped with had been the maître d' of Zi' Teresa's.

Plunging his fork into the pasta, James twisted it until he had, with some difficulty, managed to get some of the wriggling, slippery mass to stay on the tines. Then he placed it in his mouth.

It was extraordinary. He had never tasted anything like it – certainly not in the long years of rationing, but not even before that, in a decade of eating grey, tasteless boarding-school food, or even for that matter his mother's dry Sunday roasts, with their accompanying soggy potatoes and overcooked vegetables. Come to that, he had never in his life eaten pepper that was freshly ground, nor cheese that coated one's food like this in a thick white snowfall . . . The long silence as the other men around the table concentrated on their food suggested that they, too, were experiencing similar epiphanies.

It was hard to get the *fettuccine* to stay on one's fork: by the time it was in your mouth, stray ribbons of pasta were drooping out. After a little experimentation, James realised it was easier to suck it in than to bite it off, and made for a more filling mouthful as well. He looked across at Horris. He was slurping cross-eyed at a long ribbon of *fettuccine* that hung from his lips, like a snake slithering at its own tongue. Only Jeffries was coping with the slippery lengths of pasta with anything like competence. But none of them seemed inclined to stop eating until every last morsel had been cleared from their bowls.

At last Horris pushed his chair back and said, 'That was rather different from what old Malloni gave us.'

'I'm absolutely stuffed,' Walters ventured.

'Me too,' Horris agreed. 'Oh well, back to work.' He started to get to his feet.

The door opened and Livia entered, holding a dish even larger than the one in which she had served the pasta.

'The *secondo*,' she said, putting the dish on the table. 'There aren't enough plates, unfortunately, so you'll have to use the same ones.'

'What's this?' Horris asked.

'*Melanzana alla parmigiana*. It's a typical Neapolitan dish.'

There was a short silence. Walters said, 'Well, I don't want to give offence. I'll just have a taste.' As he spooned some onto his plate the smell of aubergine, baked in layers with tomato, garlic and herbs and topped with grilled cheese, filled the room.

'I say,' Horris said, looking at the way Walters kept on spooning more onto his plate. 'Leave some for the rest of us.'

Livia placed two jugs of red wine on the table. '*Nun c'è tavola senza vinu*,' she said reprovingly. 'It isn't a table without wine.' James opened his mouth to protest, but thought better of it.

He dipped his fork into the layers of aubergine and cheese. Moments later, it seemed to detonate in his mouth. The pasta, he now realised, had simply been a curtain raiser, carbohydrate to take the edge off his hunger, but this new dish was something else, teasing his appetite awake again, the intensity of its flavours bringing to life taste buds he had never even known existed. The cheese tasted so completely of cheese, the aubergine so rich and earthy, almost smoky; the herbs so full of flavour, requiring only a mouthful of wine to finish them off . . . He paused reverently and drank, then dug again with his fork.

The *secondo* was followed by a simple dessert of sliced pears baked with honey and rosemary. The flesh of the fruit looked as crisp and white as something Michelangelo might have carved with, but when he touched his spoon to it, it turned out to be as meltingly soft as ice cream. Putting it in his mouth, he was at first aware only of a wonderful, unfamiliar taste, a cascade of flavours which gradually broke itself down into its constituent parts. There was the sweetness of the honey, along with a faint floral scent from the abundant Vesuviani blossom on which the bees had fed. Then came the heady, sunshine-filled fragrance of the herbs, and only after that, the sharp tang of the fruit itself.

By the time the pears were eaten, both jugs of wine had been emptied too.

Twenty-one

After lunch James went to the kitchen, and found Livia elbow-deep in a pile of dirty dishes.

'Here, let me help you with those,' he offered.

In Livia's experience, there was only one reason why good-looking young men offered to help in the kitchen, and it had nothing to do with being helpful. 'I'm fine, thank you,' she said in a voice intended to extinguish any thoughts of flirtation.

'Well, let me dry them for you, at least.' He reached for a towel. 'That lunch was absolutely marvellous,' he said with feeling.

To Livia, who was used to having her cooking receive much more effusive compliments than this, his reaction sounded half-hearted, almost insultingly so. Since she knew that the dishes she had produced had been excellent, she suspected that the British officer's reticence was a simple negotiating tactic, and she waited cautiously to see what his ploy was going to be.

'I've just had a word with the others,' James said, 'and we'd all be delighted if you'd take the job.'

She shrugged, waiting for the catch.

'If that's still acceptable to you?' It occurred to him she might be holding back because they had not yet negotiated her wages or accommodation. 'Of course, we'll need to sort out your sleeping arrangements,' he said. 'And I'm sure you'll want to talk about money.'

Aha, Livia thought. So that's it. He wants me to be his whore as well as his cook, just like Alberto. She glared at him.

'How much were you thinking of?' he prompted.

'Whatever you try to offer me,' she said curtly, 'it will be an insult.'

144

'Well, quite,' he agreed. 'But some idea of what you would accept would be useful.'

'I will never do it for money.'

'I can see that,' he agreed, completely mystified. Presumably she meant that she was some kind of artist. He had heard that cooks could be temperamental that way.

'So long as that's clear.'

'Absolutely. I'll just – er – how about if you get the same as Malloni? Not that his cooking was a patch on yours, of course,' he said quickly. 'And you can have his old room upstairs, if that's acceptable.'

'Malloni?' she said. She had just realised that this conversation was, in all probability, not about what she thought it was about. 'Well, I suppose that would be all right,' she conceded.

As James sat at his desk afterwards, trying to make sense of a long and largely irrelevant Bureau briefing on some new problem that had sprung up, he felt his eyelids start to droop.

'Aren't you taking a siesta?'

He looked up. It was Livia, standing at the door.

'We don't really do siestas,' he explained. 'It's not really a British thing.'

'But how do you digest your food?'

James shrugged. Digestion, he was coming to realise, was one of Livia's self-appointed areas of expertise. 'We just – work through it, I suppose.'

'Ridiculous,' Livia said decisively. 'You'll never win the war that way.' Then she was gone.

James decided it would be churlish to point out that taking siestas had not, in fact, helped the Italian army win anything very much. Besides, he really was feeling rather sleepy. Perhaps, he thought, a very brief nap might not be a bad idea. When in Rome, and so on . . .

As he stumbled to his bed there was another thought struggling to articulate itself in his mind, something to do with the fact that the Allies were not actually in Rome, and that was the whole problem with the war at the moment. But by the time he had managed to clarify this to himself, he was already asleep.

He woke feeling refreshed, and went to get himself a glass of water from the kitchen. Livia was chopping a big pile of courgettes.

'You were quite right,' he told her. 'My digestion is suitably grateful.'

She shrugged. 'Of course.'

'What about you? Did you get any rest?'

She shook her head. 'Too much to do. It will be supper soon.'

'But you must have terrible indigestion,' he said. 'Let me get you something for it.'

She glanced at him suspiciously. 'It's all right,' he assured her. 'I'm only . . .' What was the Italian for ribbing? Now that he thought about it, ribbing wasn't really something the Italians did. They were either laughing or crying, shouting or silent: there was nothing in between. 'I was taking you for a *giro*, a little ride,' he explained.

She sniffed. 'Well, don't.'

'Better get used to it. It's how the British flirt, I'm afraid.' She gave him a wary look. Instantly he felt a fool. The woman was married, and he was her employer. 'Not that I'm flirting with *you*, of course,' he said. 'I do apologise.'

She carried more courgettes over to the chopping board. 'Do you have a girlfriend, Captain Gole?' she asked pointedly.

He hesitated. A part of him wanted to be honest with her, but the deception had become so habitual that he heard his own voice saying, 'Yes, as it happens.'

'Is she pretty?'

'Well – fairly.'

'Fairly?' Her eyebrows went up. 'Is that what you tell her, that she's *fairly* pretty?'

'Well—'

'And are you going to marry her?'

'I suppose we'll have to wait and see.'

'If you're not sure,' Livia said, 'you won't marry her.' She stopped chopping for a moment. 'I knew the first time Enzo kissed me that I would marry him.' A faint smile played across her face.

James felt a pang of envy. Of course, he told himself, it was a wonderful thing that she was so devoted to her husband. And it was fortuitous, too: it meant there was absolutely no chance that he would make a fool of himself with her. All the same, as he studied her profile as she bent over the chopping board, and the way her delicate hands sliced and chopped in a surprisingly energetic blur, he could not help regretting that the only woman he had met in Italy who so completely delighted him was already spoken for.

'Let me help you with those,' he said, indicating the pile of vegetables.

'Don't you have work to do?'

'The work can wait,' he said, picking up a knife. 'Show me what to do.'

Now he will make a pass at me, Livia thought to herself as they chopped courgettes. The way he kept glancing at her when he thought she wouldn't notice, coupled with his evident reluctance to discuss his marital status, all added up to only one thing. Well, let him, she thought, as she viciously chopped a courgette in a blur of sharp steel. I'll show him. Mentally, she rehearsed a battery of Neapolitan put-downs, most of them involving the British captain's sister, his mother, and his own inadequacies as a man. The prospect of withering his ardour with a good blast of invective was a deeply satisfying one, and she was soon keenly looking forward to the confrontation.

Unfortunately for her state of mind, James did not make a pass at her. Nor did he venture so much as a suggestive remark. All in all, he was infuriatingly respectful, and by the time supper was served she was ready to murder him.

Twenty-two

After a couple of days, James spotted something strange about the food they were eating.

'It's an odd thing,' he remarked to Jumbo, 'but every single meal seems to contain at least one dish that's red, green and white. Yesterday it was that wonderful salad – tomatoes, basil, and that white mozzarella stuff. Today it was some sort of herby green paste on white pasta, with tomatoes on the side.'

Jumbo screwed up his face. 'What's so odd about that?'

'They're the colours of the Italian flag.'

'So they are.' Jumbo thought some more. 'Probably a coincidence, though. After all, they eat a lot of tomatoes, so the red's there from the start.'

'Probably,' James agreed.

But later that afternoon he made an excuse to drop by the kitchen, and peer over Livia's shoulder at what she was preparing for dinner. 'What are these?' he asked casually.

'*Pomodori ripieni con formaggio caprino ed erba cipollina,*' she said tersely. 'Tomatoes stuffed with goat's cheese and chives.'

Ignoring the fact that his mouth was watering, he said, 'They're the same colours as your flag.'

Livia affected to notice this for the first time. 'So they are. How strange.'

'As was one of the dishes at lunch. In fact, every meal you've cooked us has had something similar.'

Livia, who hadn't reckoned on her employers spotting her small gesture of defiance, decided that the best form of defence was attack. 'Well, there's hardly any choice in the markets at the moment, thanks to your ridiculous restrictions. And what little there is goes for outrageous prices. The only people who can afford to eat properly now are foreign soldiers, and their whores of course. You've turned us into a city of beggars and thieves and prostitutes, and I'd like to know what you're going to do about it.'

James blinked. 'We are doing our best to protect the civilian population.'

'Well, you're not doing a very good job of it.'

To her surprise he said helplessly, 'I know. We're letting you people down. But it's an impossible task, and there are so few of us to do it.'

'Huh,' she said, turning away. Captain Gould was probably not such a bad person after all, she decided, but on the other hand there was no point in letting him know that.

Gina Tesalli was pregnant. A crescent of taut brown belly peeked out between her skirt and the thin white shirt she was wearing. She put her hands on the bulge protectively and smiled at him.

'It's Corporal Taylor's, there's no doubt about it,' she said. 'I've never had another boyfriend.'

James scratched his head. Gina was proving a hard one to turn down. Before the war she had been a student at the university. Now she lived with her family, or at least the female members of it, her four brothers and father all having been conscripted by the Germans. They were good, middle-class people, although struggling in these times like everyone else.

If James refused to give Gina permission to marry, an Englishman's child would be born out of wedlock. But if he gave her permission on those same grounds, he knew exactly what would happen – as soon as the girls of Naples realised that all they had to do to secure a wedding was to get themselves pregnant, all birth control would be thrown to the winds. The spread of syphilis and gonorrhoea, already at epidemic rates, would multiply overnight, and on top of that there would be tens, if not hundreds, of babies born for no better reason than to guarantee their mothers a ticket on the promised war brides' ships to England.

It was a complicated problem, and one which his orders seemed completely inadequate for dealing with. Between the conflicting demands of a well-intentioned, perfectly sensible policy on the one hand and the happiness of three human beings on the other, he faltered.

He told Gina he would have to make some further enquiries before he wrote his report. It was a lie – he was going to leave her case to one side for the moment, in the hope that a solution would eventually turn up.

'Of course,' Gina said, clearly trying not to sound disappointed. 'Our baby won't be born until the summer. There's plenty of time.'

Twenty-three

The hour before lunch had become James's favourite time of the day. It was the time when just enough work had been done to feel virtuous, but not so much as to induce fatigue. There was the anticipation of a wonderful meal, to be followed by a refreshing nap. Best of all, there was the sound of Livia bustling around the kitchen as she cooked.

This was itself an operatic performance, divided into five separate acts. First, there was a prelude, as she returned from the market with her purchases and went through each item, telling anyone within earshot – which, since her voice had considerable powers of projection, meant pretty much everyone in the apartment – what its particular qualities and defects were, how long she had queued for, how much the thieving stall-holder had tried to charge her for it, and that it was in any case not a patch on the produce available in her home village before the war. Then came the preparation of pasta. This generally involved less speech, since Livia was now concentrating, but if anything was even noisier. Livia made pasta the traditional way, adding eggs to flour and combining them into a smooth, hard ball of dough, which then had to be pummelled by hand for almost ten minutes until the texture was light and airy. Livia's slight frame might not look as if it was built for pummelling, but like a scrawny tennis player who compensates for a lack of muscle by grunting, she produced a range of expressive noises as she pounded the dough two-fisted, which left no doubt as to the sheer physical effort required. This might be followed by a brief *intermezzo*, a conversation with Carlo or Enrico about what was for lunch, or what the weather was like today, or what the latest rumours were in the market. However casual these conversations, they always sounded to James like fierce arguments, owing to the natural volubility of the participants. There then followed a quieter period, in which meat was

151

prepared and vegetables chopped – a dramatic drum roll of knife blades clicking on marble. Water hissed into saucepans: lids began to rattle; delicious smells rippled outwards from the kitchen, suffusing the whole apartment with the odours of cooking tomatoes, fresh basil and oregano. Finally, Livia would look into his office and inform him that it was time to stop work. As if by magic, the big table would be cleared of papers and transformed with oil, vinegar, bread, and jugs of flowers and wine. People would gather: bread would be broken: the contented silence of the well-fed would alternate with the murmur of conversation.

Livia's manner towards him could still hardly be described as friendly. But after the coquettishness and flirtation he had become accustomed to in his wedding interviews, it was still something of a relief to spend time with someone who was absolutely not trying to seduce him. And if her attitude sometimes bordered on the downright hostile, he found that for some reason it only made him want to laugh. There was something completely delightful about her glares and stares: so much so that on occasion he even found himself teasing her, just a little, for the simple pleasure of provoking them.

He was too unfamiliar with these symptoms to recognise them himself, but there was absolutely no doubt that James Gould was falling in love.

He was working at his desk one evening when he noticed that the glass of water he had by his left hand was behaving in a curious way. A series of concentric circles, pulsing inwards from the rim, rippled across its surface. He studied it, fascinated, then carried it into the kitchen. 'Livia,' he asked, setting it down, 'do you know why it does this?'

She glanced at it. 'An earthquake,' she decided. 'Just a little one. We get them all the time here, particularly when it gets warmer.'

He put his fingers to the wall. He could feel something now, a tiny vibration that hummed through the old stones of the building. But it was getting stronger, he was sure of it. It couldn't be an earthquake, surely? An earthquake would come and then go again, not build to a solid, thrumming hum like this.

'Don't worry,' she said casually. 'These buildings are very strong. They're designed for it.'

Outside, the air raid sirens went off. 'It's not a ruddy earthquake,' he said, 'it's a raid. We should get to the shelters.'

She indicated the pan. 'I can't, or this will be ruined, and I queued over an hour for it. You go ahead.'

'I'll wait with you,' he said. He looked out of the window. He could see the German planes now, wave after wave of pencil-slim Junkers 88s. They were coming in from the north, very high, to avoid the guns on the warships in the bay.

'Keep away from the windows, then,' she said grudgingly. 'If the glass goes you'll be cut to pieces.'

He stepped back. A loud boom cut through the noise of the sirens.

'And it's better if the windows are open. That way the pressure won't shatter the glass.' She caught his look. 'We've had raids before.'

He pulled the windows open and went to stand in the doorway, his back against the frame. 'They're bombing the castle,' he said, listening to the explosions. This must be the Germans' response to the big push in the north.

Suddenly, there was a deafening bang which seemed to lift the whole building, followed by the sound of cracking stone.

'That was close.' She was still chopping courgettes.

'Will you come here,' he snapped, pulling her into the doorway. She looked faintly surprised. 'The lintel,' he explained. 'Strongest part of the room.' He had his arm around her, but he had no intention of letting go now.

'Are we dancing a waltz, Captain Gull?' she said, looking pointedly at his arm. But she did not push him away.

Then there was another bang, even closer. He felt the ground heave under his feet, as if the building were a ship riding a sudden swell. Livia gasped, and he pulled her further under the lintel. 'Fuck,' he said, with feeling. They were right in the thick of it, and there was absolutely nothing they could do except wait. If they tried to reach a shelter now, they could be caught in the open.

They were so close he could feel the pounding of her heart. Then the loudest explosion so far slammed the wall into their backs. He felt his ears pop. 'That was next door,' he said. If they were going to be hit, it would be soon, while the smoke from the building next to them was there to guide the next wave of bombers. But all he could think about was how wonderful it was to be this close to her, breathing in the heady rosemary aroma of her hair, feeling her fragile shoulders moving under his hand. Is this what it would feel like, he thought, if they were lovers? He wondered if he dared kiss her, and he suddenly experienced a kind of delicious, dizzying terror that had nothing at all to do with German bombs.

You mustn't kiss her, he told himself. Of course you mustn't.

He felt something hard in his breast pocket, and took it out. It was the little piece of saint's bone the priest had pressed on him in the cathedral. He had almost forgotten it was there. 'What's that?' she asked.

'Just a lucky charm someone gave me.' He put it back. 'Livia?'

'Yes?'

'Can I ask you a question?'

'You just did, Captain Goot, so you might as well ask another.'

'If you died right now, is there anything you would regret?'

She thought about it. 'No,' she decided. 'And you?'

There were so many things, and none of them could be spoken out loud. But he was intoxicated with her presence. Once when he was at school there had been a competition to see who could jump off the highest branch of a tree into the river. They had dared each other to go higher, and then higher, and then higher still. He still remembered the extraordinary exhilaration of it – that mixture of fear and abandon. He felt the same way now. 'Well, I won't regret this,' he said. 'It's been the best ten minutes of the best afternoon of my entire ruddy war. Though I would regret not having taken the opportunity to kiss you.'

He leaned towards her. He was aware of her eyes flashing, and her foot stamped hard on the floor. Her lips were moving, and he realised she must be shouting, cursing him. But he could not hear the words. At that moment, the air was sucked from the room and an enormous explosion buffeted him around the head. His kiss, cut off a moment before their lips touched, turned into a clumsy embrace as he stumbled against her. A high-pitched whining filled his ears – concussion, he supposed. Dust poured through the doorway. Dimly, through the muffled aftermath, he heard a rattling sound as dozens of roof slates clattered into the court-yard, where they smashed on the flagstones one by one.

The explosion had caved in one wall of the Americans' HQ. James immediately offered his own floor as temporary accommodation. It was the least he could do, and besides, he could hardly claim he was short of space.

Like a colony of ants moving nest, the CIC operation disgorged itself from the ground floor. Trunks of papers and crates of equipment were ferried up the stairs by purposeful, bustling orderlies. Desks, chairs, type-writers, document cabinets and endless lengths of telephone cable all moved themselves into the various nooks and crannies of James's offices. Within a couple of hours the move was complete.

There was another problem, however. The Americans' mess was

temporarily unusable. A couple of roof beams had fallen in, and they needed to make alternative arrangements.

'Only for a few days,' Eric told James. 'And if your charming cook could see her way clear to helping us out as well . . .'

'There's far too many of you,' James said firmly. 'Can't you eat field rations?'

'Is there a problem?' Livia's voice said behind him.

He turned. 'These people were asking if they could eat with us. I said it was too many.'

He could not meet her eye. After the all-clear sounded he had made an excuse about inspecting the damage, and had hurried away before she could see how ashamed he was.

'It's how many – about thirty people?' She shrugged. 'I used to cook for that many every day at the *osteria*.'

'As you wish,' he said stiffly. 'But is there enough food?'

'I'm sure I'll manage,' she said. 'And we can eat outside, in the courtyard. There's more room down there.'

'You'll need some help with serving, at least.'

'I can get some people in. There'll be no problem.' Angelo would know where to find temporary waitresses.

Eric bowed. '*La quinta forza armata è molto grata, Signora*. The Fifth Army is extremely grateful.' His Italian, James noted, was really getting quite good.

Livia, to her surprise, was enjoying herself. She might dislike the Allies on principle, but she had to admit that, taken as individuals, they were fairly easy to get along with. They were somewhat passionless, of course, and completely obsessed with their work, but after a lifetime of having to pretend that you hadn't heard what men were muttering at you as you passed them in the street and being groped at the slightest opportunity, it was rather nice to be able to relax in the company of these shy, quiet, well-mannered foreigners.

And above all, she was cooking again. She had not realised how important it was to her. For four years she had been cobbling together odds and ends, just in order to put on the table something that resembled food. But now, thanks to Angelo and his black market contacts, she was cooking with real ingredients, and in the sort of quantities she had previously only dreamed of. A whole fresh tuna, a wicker basket of San Marzano tomatoes, a crate of anchovies, great handfuls of parsley . . . Dozens of new potatoes, still encrusted with the black volcanic earth of

Campania, their flesh golden as egg yolks . . . A pale wheel of parmesan, big as a truck tyre . . . A sack full of blood-red watermelons . . . An armful of mint, its leaves so dark green they were almost black . . . All afternoon and all evening she chopped and baked, and by the time darkness fell she had pulled together a feast that even she was proud of.

For many of the Americans, the air raid was the first they had experienced. That night there was an extra brightness in their chatter, and more wine was consumed than normal. And there was a kind of gaiety too in the setting, in eating on temporary tables in the courtyard under the lemon tree and the stars, with broken roof tiles still crunching underfoot. There were no candles, but someone had found a few kerosene lamps, and they made a bonfire out of broken roof beams. Angelo had supplied Livia with wine as well as food, all of which was served to the soldiers by half a dozen of the prettiest girls the maître d' could locate at such short notice.

'I'm sure I just saw Silvana Settimo,' James told Eric as he watched yet another jug of wine pass him on the way to a table.

'Who's she?'

'A girl I vetted. She was pretending to be a virgin at the time.' His head turned as another strikingly beautiful Italian placed a bowl of pasta nearby. 'And that's definitely Algisa Fiore. The last time I saw her she didn't have any clothes on.'

'What an interesting life you lead, James.'

'But they're all prostitutes.'

'You know, we should probably keep that information to ourselves,' Eric suggested. 'Otherwise it's going to be mayhem around here later on.'

The food, of course, was amazing. Livia had surpassed herself. Selfishly, James found himself hoping that the Americans would not realise just how good it was, since he had absolutely no wish to share Livia's skills on a permanent basis. But from the noises of appreciation all around him, he realised that it was going to be impossible to keep her talents a secret.

After the meal was eaten, it was inevitable that there was going to be dancing. Eric picked up his clarinet, various other soldiers found instruments of one sort or another, and an impromptu jazz band struck up. Soon the Americans were enthusiastically showing the waitresses how to do-wop and jitterbug.

James took the opportunity to go and speak to Livia. 'Mrs Pertini,' he said formally, 'I want to apologise for my behaviour earlier.'

'What do you mean?'

'What I said to you during the raid.'

'What did you say?' she asked curiously.

He hesitated. 'You didn't hear?'

'I heard the bomb falling. And I shouted at you to get down, but I couldn't hear what you were saying.'

'I was saying,' he paused. 'I was talking nonsense. Must have been a bit rattled by those bombs. Anyway, I do apologise.'

'That's all right,' she said, giving him a strange look. Then one of the Americans approached her, asking for a dance, and she was taken away from him.

Five minutes later she was back, a little out of breath, her face flushed with pleasure at the exertion and all the compliments she had received for her cooking. On an impulse she said, 'Captain Gute, aren't you going to dance with me?'

'Very well,' he said. 'But it will have to be a proper dance, not this jive nonsense.'

'I'm sure that everything you do is proper,' she said with a sigh.

'I was referring,' he said, standing up and leading her onto the dance floor, 'to the foxtrot, king of dances.'

Livia did not know how to dance the foxtrot, and said so.

'Then it's fortunate that I do. Just follow my lead.' He interleaved the fingers of his left hand with her right, placed his other hand on her shoulder, and gently but firmly propelled her into the promenade position. 'Slow – slow – quick – quick,' he instructed. 'Really, it couldn't be simpler.'

'So I see,' she said, fitting her movements to his.

'And now we turn . . .' He twisted into the conversation step, bringing their hips into momentary contact.

'Captain Ghoul,' she said, surprised, 'you are a very good dancer.'

'I know,' he said, easing her into a box turn. 'And quick . . . And slow.'

She studied her own left hand, where it rested on James's shoulder. It was, she noticed, a rather firm, rugged shoulder. She remembered what he had looked like with his shirt off, when her sister was dressing his cut, and she found herself wondering whether, if she were to slide the hand down a little, she would discover that his upper arm, under his uniform, was just as hard as his shoulder. She didn't, of course, but she met his eye and relaxed perceptibly into the movements of the dance.

For his part, James had suddenly become acutely aware of how close

157

she was. Her glossy black hair, as she twisted this way and that, released more enticing waves of rosemary. Her hand and back, where he was touching her, seemed as fragile as birds' wings, and her huge eyes were for the first time in their acquaintance regarding him with what might almost be considered a smile. He felt a sudden tension in his trousers, and was obliged to quickly introduce several more hip turns in order that Livia remained unaware of it.

What am I doing? Livia thought. These are the people who killed my husband. These are the people who killed Pupetta.

She was rather ashamed to realise that, in her mind, the two deaths were almost of equal significance. But after all, she had been present when Pupetta had been shot, whereas poor Enzo had been gone for almost four years when he died – four times longer, in fact, than he and Livia had ever been together.

But why, she asked herself, am I enjoying this so much? It's only a dance, and not a very interesting one at that.

For both partners, it was both a relief and a disappointment when the music came to an end.

He led her back to the table, and an uncomfortable silence fell between them. Occasionally she glanced at him, hoping that he would say something, and occasionally he glanced at her, and seemed about to speak. But he remained tongue-tied, and for once, her Neapolitan volubility seemed to have deserted her as well.

Eventually she jumped to her feet. 'I'll show you how to dance the *tarantella*, if you like,' she said.

James, who was still suffering from intermittent amplifications below the waist, shook his head. 'That's very kind, but I'd better not. I'm all danced out.'

'But it's how we Italians flirt,' she said mischievously. She stepped away from him, raising her arms above her head and spreading her fingers, then fluidly spun on her heels into the space beside the fire.

Just for a moment, he was tempted. 'All the same,' he said, 'I think I'll sit this one out.'

She shrugged. 'Carlo?' Instantly Carlo was in front of her, his shoulders squared as he began to move his body in time with hers. Enrico took a guitar from one of the Americans and strummed it meditatively.

'In most Italian dances,' Livia said over her shoulder to James, 'the man pursues the woman. But in the *tarantella* it is the woman who is possessed by passion. So the man stays where he is, and the woman approaches him.' Enrico's fingers moved more fluently over the strings of the guitar, picking up the pace, as Livia danced sinuously towards Carlo. 'But then she changes her mind. She doesn't need him after all, she's happy on her own.' Abruptly she twisted away.

Everyone was watching her now, the other dancers pulling back to give her room. As she spun this way and that, the folds of her skirt spun with her. 'Then she realises she misses him. So she returns. But she doesn't want him to touch her. Just when he thinks he has her, she slips away again.' She closed her eyes, twisting her hips lithely, pirouetting around Carlo's barely moving body. The tempo of the guitar increased still further. 'Now she is overcome. She is crazy about him, she is possessed, her whole body is on fire,' she called. 'So at last, she lets him come to her.' She spread her arms either side of Carlo's. Her shoulders were still, as if the two of them were embracing, but her hips still writhed with the fluid, pulsating rhythm of the dance. With a final shout, the music ended. It was the most erotic thing James had ever witnessed. Next to this sensual, potent ritual of desire, the jitterbug and the do-wop looked like mere gymnastics.

The men at the tables were on their feet, clapping and shouting their appreciation. Enrico started another tune, and the servicemen pulled the Italian waitresses into the circle of firelight and started enthusiastically copying what they had just seen.

Livia walked out of the ring of firelight. James stood up, hoping that she would come back and talk to him. She caught his eye and smiled. But then another man in uniform had intercepted her; was speaking to her; was leading her to a quiet table away from the firelight and the lamps. She cast James a rueful look, as if to say that he had had his chance and not taken it. He turned away, but not before he saw that the man who was so keen to have her company was Eric.

Twenty-four

The applicant's name was Vittoria Forsese, and she was demurely dressed in a black frock. Her first husband, she said, had died fighting in Greece. But now, a year later, she had been lucky enough to meet another man who cared for her, a corporal in the Engineers.

James could see why her fiancé had been attracted to her. She was extremely pretty and completely charming.

'And what have you been living off?' he asked, his pen poised over his notebook.

There was just the faintest of pauses. 'Savings.'

'Which bank do you have your savings in?'

Another pause. 'The Banco di Napoli.'

Something about that name rang a bell. 'Wasn't that the bank the Germans raided?'

'Yes. To pay for their war. They stole everything.'

'So how have you been supporting yourself since then?'

'My neighbours give me food sometimes,' she said hesitantly.

'Can you tell me their names?'

Another pause. 'Sometimes it's one neighbour, sometimes another.'

'Is there anyone who can vouch for you? I must have a name, you see, and follow it up.'

'I don't remember,' she muttered.

'You don't remember your neighbours' names?'

She shrugged miserably.

He glanced around the little apartment. It was spotlessly clean, and hardly opulent. But there were the usual telltale signs – a lipstick in the bedroom, a small jar of olive oil in the kitchen, a pair of shoes with leather soles instead of wood. 'The money comes from soldiers, doesn't it?' he said gently. She did not answer, but a tear rolled silently down one side of her face.

He considered what to do next. She was beautiful; she seemed hard-working, loyal and sweet-natured. And she had had the ridiculous good fortune to meet someone she loved who loved her.

He hesitated, his pen still hovering over his notebook. Then, abruptly, he came to a decision. Closing the notebook with a snap, he got to his feet and held out his hand.

'You must be very fortunate in your neighbours,' he said. 'Not to mention your fiancé. Congratulations, Vittoria. I can see no reason why you shouldn't be married as soon as possible.'

As he walked away from her apartment, her tears of gratitude still damp on his cheeks, he stopped and took a deep breath. Naples was going about its business, much as it always did. The sun was shining. High above his head, two unseen housewives were arguing across the narrow gap which separated their apartments. On the street, two old men stopped and greeted each other with a kiss. In a shady doorway, a plump baby sat on its mother's lap and surveyed its surroundings regally, as if from a throne, gravely accepting the salutations and tickles of passers-by. From somewhere the smell of tomatoes simmering with parsley and garlic wafted majestically down the street, mingling with the dusty scent of hot stone. The baby's mother smiled shyly at James, and he tipped his hat to her in response.

Yes, he thought, Vittoria Forsese was indeed fortunate in her neighbours. As they all were, in this extraordinary city.

Twenty-five

More and more often, James found himself making excuses to hang around the kitchen.

'Don't you have a war to fight?' Livia asked him once.

'I don't really do fighting,' he explained. 'I'm not fierce enough.'

'I think you're very fierce.'

'Really?' He felt ridiculously pleased.

'When you pointed your gun at my tank, I was scared.'

'Not half as scared as I was,' he assured her. He gestured towards the tomatoes she was peeling. 'Let me help with those.'

'If you like.'

He loved to watch her slim fingers turning the vegetables this way and that, twisting the flesh out of the bursting skins, and to try to copy what she was doing.

'Tell me more about this girl of yours,' she said as they worked.

He glanced at her. The temptation to fantasise was irresistible. 'Well,' he said, 'she's quite small, and rather skinny. And she has dark hair. She teases me a lot. And she's rather . . . imperious. She likes to boss people around.'

'She sounds a little bit like me. Not the bossy bit, of course. But what she looks like.'

'Yes,' he said. 'Yes, I suppose she is a little bit like you. That hadn't occurred to me.'

'Perhaps, if you'd never met her, you would have liked me instead. Wouldn't that be funny?'

'Livia,' he said.

'Yes?'

'Nothing.'

162

They worked in silence for a few moments.

'Captain Gud?'

'Please,' he said, 'I'd much rather you called me James.'

'Joms?'

He smiled. 'Yes?'

'What's a "pot"?'

'It's a pan. Like that.' He indicated the saucepan on the stove.

'That's what I thought.' She put another handful of tomatoes into the saucepan. 'So how can I be a pot?'

'Who says you are?'

'Eric. He says I'm a sexy pot.'

'Does he?' he heard his own voice say. 'And when was this?'

'This morning. Did I tell you? He's teaching me to speak English.'

Well, he didn't waste any time, James thought. Bloody Yanks. Oversexed and over here, as the saying went.

'He's taught me three phrases,' she said proudly. 'Would you like to hear them?'

'I think I'd better,' he muttered.

She stopped chopping, the better to concentrate on what she was saying. 'Eylo, Jimms. Mare nem ees Livia. Ay lick ver' much to cock.' She looked at him triumphantly.

'Cook.'

'That's what I said. "Cook."'

'No, "cook". You said "cock."'

'So?'

'In English it's a rude word.'

Her eyes widened. 'Yes? What does it mean?'

'It means – well, a man's parts. Like *cazzo*.'

'Now I've embarrassed you.'

'Not at all.'

'I hope you're not this shy with your girl,' she said mischievously.

'As a matter of fact,' he said tersely, spearing a tomato with his knife, 'I am.'

Livia had finally realised why James was behaving in such an odd manner. The way he veered back and forth between friendliness and pomposity, the blushing whenever anything sexual was mentioned, the absence of any attempt to grope her, the hanging around in the kitchen chatting, the obvious nonsense about the imaginary girlfriend whom he couldn't even describe properly, the ridiculous formality, and the fact that he was such a good dancer, all pointed to a very obvious explanation. Captain Gould was a *finocchio*, a piece of fennel; in other words, homosexual.

Livia's reaction to her own brainwave was interesting. First of all, she clapped her hands together, delighted at her own cleverness. Of course! Why hadn't she realised sooner? It really did explain everything. She had no personal objection to homosexuals – there had been a boy in the village who had always preferred the company of the girls, trying their lipsticks and putting ribbons in his hair, and after she was married and moved to Naples she had known several young men who went with tourists for money. She had noticed that they too often found it easier to befriend women than their own sex, which explained her own growing friendship with the captain.

Her second reaction was a sense of disappointment. This took her by surprise, somewhat, and she spent a little time working out why it should be so. It surely wasn't that she was interested in the captain for herself. No, she decided; it was just that homosexuals were by and large sad, unhappy people, doomed to live unfulfilled lives, and since she quite liked the captain, she decided to show him that she, for one, did not mind what his sexuality was, by being as pleasant to him as possible.

Once she had settled this in her own mind she felt much better, and the sense of disappointment she had felt was lessened by the new anticipation of having him as her friend.

James went to find Eric, but found his way barred by an orderly. 'Restricted area, sir. CIC only.'

'Don't be ridiculous. I work here.'

'It's for security reasons.'

'We're on the same side, for God's sake.' He tried to push past, but the orderly – who was in fact, James now saw, standing here for exactly this purpose, as a kind of sentry – was equally insistent.

'James.' It was Eric, hurrying out as soon as he saw who it was. 'What's up, buddy?'

'I can't get into my own offices, for one thing.'

'It's just a temporary precaution,' Eric soothed him. 'There are a few sensitive files lying around, that's all.'

'So sensitive you can't show them to your allies?'

Eric shrugged. 'Bureaucracy. You know how it is, James – someone gets upset about something, an order's issued, we're the poor dopes who have to see it through. But what's bugging you?'

164

He had taken James by the arm and led him into another room. James said pointedly, 'Mrs Pertini.'

Eric raised an eyebrow. 'The beautiful Livia? What's the problem?'

'You've been teaching her English. Or rather,' he said sarcastically, 'American, which is not quite the same thing.'

Eric ignored the insult. 'Between you and me, James, I hope to teach her a great deal more than that,' he said with a grin. 'But so what?'

'You called her a sexpot.'

Eric laughed.

'It's hardly a proper way to behave,' James snapped. 'The clue is in the name, Eric. *Mrs* Pertini? She's married.'

'But her husband's dead,' Eric pointed out. He saw James's expression. 'You didn't know? He got himself killed in Russia, fighting for the Germans.'

'Oh,' James said.

'Although at that point she hadn't seen him for four years. As you'd know yourself if you'd taken the trouble to have her vetted.'

It was true: he had given her the job without knowing anything about her.

'She could have been a German spy, James,' Eric said, enjoying his discomfort. 'And that story in her file about being a member of a partisan group rang several alarm bells.'

'Livia has a file?'

'Oh, everyone has a file,' Eric said vaguely. He clapped James on the back. 'So now that your chivalrous Brit instincts have been reassured, presumably it's OK for me to give the lady language lessons? After all, it's not as if you're in the running.' His eyes narrowed. 'Unless it's something rather less chivalrous you had in mind for yourself?'

'Of course not,' James said stiffly.

'Well, there you are, then. Keep yourself pure for – what was her name?'

'What? Oh. Er, Jane.'

'Keep yourself pure for Jane.'

He strode back to his desk, pointedly ignoring the sentry who still stood guard outside the Americans' rooms. A great feeling of elation was sweeping over him. Livia wasn't married. All he had to do now was to remove the small impediment of his imaginary engagement to Jane, and then he would be able to court her – and the sooner the better, given that Eric had clearly stolen a march on him.

Disposing of Jane was easy. Men got letters from home jilting them all the time. No: even better than a jilting, he thought, would be a tragic bereavement. He could announce Jane blown to smithereens by a doodle-bug, or mown down by a Messerschmitt's cannon. The blackout provided plenty of good opportunities for a fatal accident: motor cars without headlights, sharing the dark streets with pedestrians without torches, had caused so many casualties that another one wouldn't be a problem. Or perhaps something more noble was in order. Jane could have para-chuted into France on a hush-hush mission and been captured by the Nazis . . . He was just mulling over the possibilities when, like a thunder-bolt, an appalling thought struck him. He was the wedding officer.

He remembered what Jackson had said on James's first evening in Naples. *Got to set the right example.* He could imagine only too well what Major Heathcote would say if James himself applied for permission to marry an Italian girl.

Of course, there were officers who carried on relationships with Italians without necessarily intending to marry them. But that was quite differ-ent from courting a woman in the full knowledge that marriage was impossible. And he suspected that in any case the laxity shown to other officers might not apply to someone in his position. The high command could hardly approve of the wedding officer openly flaunting just the sort of relationship he was meant to be discouraging.

As he sat there, miserably weighing up the options, the door opened and Livia came in, bearing a glass of freshly squeezed lemon juice.

'Good morning,' she said brightly. 'It's so hot, I brought you a drink.'

'Oh. Thank you.'

He took the glass from her and drank. It was good, the lemon natu-rally sweet and refreshing. He noticed that Livia was lingering, evidently eager to chat. Over the last few days she had definitely started to find him more agreeable. Previously, this observation would have sent him into a spiral of jubilation. Now, it only served to deepen his misery.

'How are you?' he asked glumly.

'Me? Oh, I'm well. Do you know,' she said casually, 'it's occurred to me that I have plenty of friends in Naples. *Male* friends. You really ought to meet some of them. There's Dario, for example. I think you'd like him.'

He raised his hands from the desk and let them fall again. 'Livia, I don't have time to meet your friends. I've got too much work to do.'

'But you should make time to have some fun. Dario's nice. You'd have a lot in common. And –' she paused significantly – 'he has a lot of friends like him.'

He saw what was happening now: this friend of hers had asked her if she could use her contacts with the Allies to get him some kind of employment as an informant. Normally he refused such requests, but this was Livia . . . 'Perhaps I could meet him one evening,' he suggested wearily. 'But you'd better warn him, it'll have to be a quick one. I'm not really looking for anyone permanent at the moment.'

'But if the right person happens to come along . . .'

'And I don't pay,' he warned her. 'Not unless it's something really special.'

'Of course not,' she said, a little uncomfortable at the frankness of this conversation. 'I don't think that would worry Dario, although I happen to know he's taken money for it in the past.'

'That was probably for a different position,' he explained.

Livia – who after all was a country girl, and had thought herself unshockable – was shocked. She retired to the kitchen, her cheeks burning.

James sighed. Involuntarily he watched her as she walked to his door, with that hint of sway in her hips that all Italian girls seemed to have, and then the final toss of a length of black hair over the shoulder as she left the room . . . It's no use, he thought. I'm in love. I'm in love with Livia Pertini.

It was rotten luck, but there was only one solution. He couldn't go out with her, so he would just have to keep his feelings hidden, in the hope, first, that he wouldn't make a complete ass of himself, and second that he wouldn't cause Livia any unnecessary embarrassment.

Twenty-six

James found himself increasingly curious as to why CIC were reluctant to let him into their offices.

The Americans' offices were next door to his own bedroom. One night, he waited until everyone was asleep and climbed onto the ledge of one of the huge windows. A brief nerve-wrenching scramble from one window to another, and he was inside their inner sanctum.

The place was full of documents. Everywhere he looked, there were boxes of files. He rifled through them until he found one marked 'Top secret – CIC only'. It contained a single folder. This must be it, he thought. It was marked 'Operation Gladio'. He opened it and scanned the first page.

Background

After the war, the political situation in southern Italy is likely to be troubled. The British support the automatic restoration of the monarchy. However, this is by no means the only possible outcome. In the south, some wealthy individuals are agitating for an independent 'Kingdom of Naples'. The communists, who have the support of the majority of the poor, are content to let these fantasists exhaust themselves, and will attempt a Stalinist revolution as soon as the Allies withdraw, linking up with workers' movements in Greece and Yugoslavia in order to create a Europe-wide superstate stretching from Moscow to Milan.

At the present time, the only alternative to communist takeover in Italy is probably the remnants of Mussolini's fascists, who are more than willing to deal with the communists if they are given the means to do so.

The third most powerful grouping in southern Italy is the Mafia, known locally as the camorra. They have no political allegiance, but are vehemently opposed to the communists, probably because they sense that the communists would make life more difficult for them than most of the alternatives.

The most unpredictable element in this are the partisans, many of whom are presently fighting the Germans in well-organised, effective groups run on communist lines . . .

There was much more in a similar vein. It made no sense to James at all. Why were the Americans worrying about what happened after the war, when they couldn't even get a grip on the black marketeering and corruption that was going on right under their noses? And what on earth was so secret about a fairly obvious assessment of the political situation in southern Italy?

He was replacing the folder when he his eye was caught by a small book on one of the tables. He picked it up. It was an Italian phrase book he had seen being sold in the street markets, entitled *What Is Sufficient to Speak in Italian – the Small Modern Polyglot*. There was a marker, and he opened it at a section headed 'Greeting the Ladies.'

'Good morning, madam. How beautiful you are. Have you a bridegroom? Indeed, you have made me very agreeable,' he read. He smiled. Perhaps he had nothing to fear from Eric after all. He put the book down, and exited the way he had come in.

Twenty-seven

Spring had arrived, as hot as an English summer. You could tell which men had recently been at the front line by their sunburn, and the municipal gardens along the seafront were filled with hawkers selling food and drink – freshly squeezed lemon juice into which a teaspoon of bicarbonate was stirred to make it froth, which the soldiers had discovered made an excellent hangover cure; *spasso*, a mixture of sunflower seeds and other nuts, and *pastiera*, a cake made from grain and honey. The people of Naples did not look so gaunt now. The Allied Military Government had finally opened up the food markets again, and fresh produce began to pour into the city: still expensive, but full of nutrition and vitamins. Now when James took a siesta he had to close the shutters of his bedroom against the heat of the midday sun, and even in his office he worked in shirtsleeves.

His feelings for Livia might be hidden, but they were no less intense for that. Every time he heard her in the kitchen, singing, his heart soared with her voice: every time she put a plate of food in front of him, his passion fed on the sight of her slender hand, just as ravenously as his mouth devoured her cooking. When she brushed past him, it was as if her light summer dresses were made of stone, so acutely did he feel the slightest touch. When she smiled, he felt as if he would burst with pleasure: when she frowned, he ached with the urge to put his arms around her and talk nonsense until she smiled again. At night she floated to his bed and inhabited a bolster: when he gave free rein to his most feverish imaginings, he could almost have sworn that she kissed him back, urging her feather-filled body against his with little cries of pleasure. After these fantasies had reached their natural conclusion he felt filled with self-disgust, imagining how appalled Livia would be if she knew that he was borrowing her body in this way for selfish sexual release. But by morning he would once again be in a frenzy of unfulfilled passion, like a very ripe apple that only needs the slightest touch to send it plummeting from the tree.

With the black market apparently under control at last, he was no longer so busy. But every moment not spent with Livia was a moment wasted. He spent hours sitting at his desk trying to think of reasons to go and talk to her. Bloody Eric, of course, had ample opportunities with his English lessons, while he had to make do with everyday chat. But there were only so many times each morning one could wander into the kitchen and ask casually, 'What's for lunch?', whilst the weather, always such a good conversational opener at home, was not quite so obliging here in Naples, since the phrase 'Hot today, isn't it?' could only ever be answered with an affirmative.

Then he had an inspiration.

The next time they were alone together, he asked Livia if she would teach him to cook.

She stopped what she was doing, taken aback. 'That's a big thing, to learn how to cook,' she said warily.

'Not everything you know, of course,' he assured her. 'Just the easy stuff.'

She considered. In Naples, there were very few men who cooked. In fact, there was no Neapolitan word for 'chef', it being assumed that all cooking was done by enthusiastic amateurs. But James, after all, was a *finocchio*, and given to womanly pleasures.

'Well,' she said, seeming to come to a decision. 'I'll show you a few things, and we'll see what kind of pupil you are. How does that sound?'

When James was doing his basic training, back in England, there had been a sergeant major who delighted in terrorising the young officer cadets. On the first morning he lined them up in the freezing dawn. 'I will address you as "sir,"' he informed them menacingly, 'and you will address me as "sir". The difference is that you will mean it.' His favourite technique involved shouting instructions at them so rapidly and at such deafening volume that it was almost possible not to become confused, thus inciting their tormentor to unleash ever more voluble streams of invective.

James was reminded of this sergeant the moment he started trying to learn the basics of cooking from Livia.

171

'We'll begin at the beginning,' she said, chopping some ingredients together on a board, her knife a blur. 'This is a *battuto*. Parsley, lard, onion. It's the base for most of our sauces. And garlic, of course. But we add that later, or the onions will overcook. Only a lazy cook puts the garlic in at the same time as everything else. Here, you try. No, not like that. Chop the parsley into small pieces, like I told you.'

'Actually, you didn't mention—'

'And then you must simmer them in some oil. That's a *soffrito*,' she said. '*Battere, soffriggere, insaporire*. One, two, three. What are you doing? You don't stir the onions until they've had a chance to cook. Don't forget the oil. That pan's too hot; it will burn the onions in a moment. Don't cut the garlic, crush it. Ay, ay, ay, now your pan is burning.'

'This is too difficult,' he sighed, taking the burning pan off the heat.

'Nonsense. You just need to listen more and talk less.'

The problem, he realised, was that she herself had never actually learned to cook – she had simply assimilated it, along with speaking and walking. For her to teach him what she knew was as hard as explaining how to breathe. Eventually they agreed that she would carry on doing what she usually did, and he would try to copy her, asking questions when there was something he didn't understand.

The next morning he accompanied her to the market. 'The first thing you have to understand is that in Italy we don't cook dishes, we cook ingredients,' she said. 'First, we decide what looks good, and then we buy the other things we need to go with it.'

'So what are we looking out for today?'

She shrugged. 'Who knows? Perhaps some fish. Tomatoes. Vegetables, of course.' She picked up a courgette from a basket and bent it in her hands. 'This was picked yesterday, which is why it's a little limp.' The courgette snapped, and she tossed the two pieces back into the basket dismissively. The stallholder bellowed at her, protesting that his cour-gettes were the freshest in the market and who was going to pay for the one she had just ruined? Ignoring him, Livia plunged into a melee of shouting Neapolitans around a fish stall, jabbing with her elbows until she had inserted herself into the very thick of the throng and emerging triumphantly with a slab of swordfish the size of a tree trunk.

'On the other hand,' she told him, 'if you see something really good, you have to be prepared to fight for it. Now we need some peppers, to make a salsa.'

*

A little further on she managed to find some courgettes she was happy with, and back in the kitchen he watched as she sorted them into two piles, one of wrist-thick vegetables with veined orange flowers at the end, the other of star-shaped open flowers.

'These are pretty,' he remarked, picking up one of the blooms.

'They taste good, too.'

'You eat the flowers?' he said, surprised.

'Of course. We'll have them stuffed with mozzarella, then dipped in a little batter and fried. But only the male flowers. The female ones are too soft.'

'I hadn't realised,' he said, taking one and tucking it behind her ear, 'that flowers could be male and female. Let alone edible.'

'Everything is male and female. And everything is edible. You just need to remember to cook them differently.'

'In England we say, what's sauce for the goose is sauce for the gander.'

'How very stupid. A goose has a light taste, so you would cook it in a gentle white wine sauce, perhaps with a little tarragon or oregano. But a gander has a strong, gamey flavour. It needs rich tastes: red wine, per- haps, or mushrooms. It's the same with a *gallina*, a hen, and a *pollastrello*, a cock. ' She glanced sideways at him. 'If the English try to cook a *pollastrello* and a *gallina* the same way, it explains a lot.'

'Such as?' he asked, curious. But she was busy with her cooking, and only rolled her eyes at him as if the answer were too obvious to mention.

Later he watched as she took one of the delicate, velvety blossoms and dipped it quickly in a bath of batter. She held it for a moment above the bowl, allowing the excess to drip away, then transferred it to a large pan of hot oil, where it bubbled and spun. She added another, and another, and moments later, the first batch was cooked, lifted out with a slatted spoon and transferred to a piece of newspaper to soak up the oil. She threw some salt over them, then picked one up and bit it with a critical expression on her face. Evidently it met with her approval, because she nodded and held it out to him.

'Taste. Go on, they're best when they're hot like this.'

He held her wrist to steady it. The batter had cooked to a translucent crust, crunchy and brittle as the most delicate pastry. Inside, the flower had softened, an insubstantial mouthful of fragrance that dissolved to nothing in his mouth.

She was watching him, waiting for his reaction, but all he could think

173

was that he was holding her wrist, and her beautiful lips were only inches away from his, dabbed with fragments of that fragrant batter, just as his own were. He put out his tongue and licked the fragments up, tasting them, knowing that this was how she would taste if he kissed her now.

'Wonderful,' he agreed, reluctantly letting go of her hand. 'It's absolutely wonderful.'

Twenty-eight

Livia and James stroll back from the market together in the pleasant warmth of a Naples morning, their arms laden with produce. In James's hand is a huge tomato, as big as a grapefruit and as red as a Neapolitan sunset.

'Again,' he says.

'To-mayto.'

'Tom*ar*to,' he corrects. 'And this –' he delves into a bag and holds up an aubergine – 'is an "au-ber-gine".'

She frowns. 'Eric says it is called a "aygplent".'

'Well, that's just silly,' he points out. 'How can it be an eggplant? A *melanzana* is nothing like an egg.'

She considers. 'Au-ber-gine.'

'Exactly,' he says, a note of quiet satisfaction in his voice. One nil to the Brits.

A little further on they come to a stall James has never seen before. It is festooned with tiny cages, and in each cage there is a bird. The song of thrushes, nightingales and robins fills the air, and for a moment he is transported back to England, and the sound of a spring dawn chorus.

'I don't understand. Are these being sold as pets?' he asks Livia.

'Pets?' She laughs. 'No, not pets. Pies.'

He makes a face. 'You eat robins?'

'Of course. People here will eat anything. Although personally, I never see the point of eating nightingales. The song is better than the meat, and there's much more of it, too. What are you doing?'

Impulsively, James has pulled a pile of lire from his pocket, thrust it into the stallholder's hands, and is pulling open the cages. Wings flutter

175

around his head as the tiny birds wheel and scatter to freedom. The stall-holder launches into an operatic denunciation of the madman's behaviour, and even Livia looks taken aback.

'Captain Goal,' she says, 'you are even stranger than you appear to be.'

'I don't care. There are enough pies in the world already, and not nearly enough robins.'

She shrugs. 'OK.'

He stops. 'What?'

'I said OK. Why?'

'Nothing.'

All day he listens to her carefully, noticing how often she uses the expression 'OK'. Admittedly, it does not sound much like 'OK', since Livia pronounces it 'au-*kaya*', with the emphasis on the second of her three syllables. In addition, she tends to use it as a form of expletive, meeting any request when she is busy with an indignant toss of her head and a yelled 'Au-*kaya*! Au-*kaya*! A'mm *doing*!'

The American inflection is almost imperceptible, but every time he hears it James experiences a sharp stab of jealousy.

'The thing is,' he confides to Jumbo, 'I'm in love with her.'

'When you say you're in love with her – how can you be so sure?'

'I think about her every minute of every day. When I'm sitting at my desk I have long, imaginary conversations with her. Then, when I'm with her, I talk utter nonsense. I find myself doing stupid things in the hope of impressing her. Sometimes I find myself doing stupid things even when I'm not with her, in the hope of becoming more worthy of her. I'm learning to cook because of her. I lie in bed dreaming of Livia in a white wedding dress, walking down the aisle of the church in my parents' vil-lage. Then I imagine taking off her wedding dress, and finding her naked under it, and throwing her onto a big double bed—'

'Yes, I see,' Jumbo said quickly. 'That does sound as if you might be, ah, becoming quite attached to her. Either that, or you're getting a touch of malaria.'

Twenty-nine

'I need to go home,' Livia announced one evening. 'I have to get some more cheese, and to see that my sister and my father are all right.'

'I'll give you a lift on the bike, if you like,' James said, trying not to sound too eager. 'And, er, Amalfi's meant to be lovely, isn't it? We could make a day trip of it.'

'Thank you,' she said. 'That would be very nice.'

She likes me, he thought, dazed with happiness. She *must* like me. We're going on a trip.

It was another hot day, and the sun-drenched countryside wafted wave after wave of scents at them as they headed towards Vesuvius – orange blossom, myrtle, flowering thyme, and the peculiar smell of baked, dusty roads. There were potholes everywhere, and James deliberately steered round them at the very last moment for the simple pleasure of feeling Livia's hands tighten around his waist. Perhaps this was why Italians drove so badly, he thought: it was all part of the game to them. He swerved abruptly round a particularly deep bomb crater, and she pinched him.

'Ow,' he protested happily.

'Drive properly,' she said into his ear.

'Like an Englishman, you mean?' But he slowed down a little.

She said thoughtfully in English, 'Wheech es dhe pletforum for dhe Roma tren, pliss?'

Eric had lent her *The Small Modern Polyglot*, which she was using to learn English by a process of backwards deduction. It lacked, of course, any kind of phonetic instructions for the English half of the conversation, and in order to have her pronunciation corrected she would regularly break into a sort of question-and-answer routine that was only tangentially relevant to the circumstances.

'The platform for the Rome train is over there,' he shouted helpfully, gesturing at the sparkling sea.

'Pliss ken u hep mey weeth mey luggy edge?'

'I would be delighted to help with your luggage.'

'U ken nurt be urn dhe plate form unless u hev burt a tea kit,' she said sternly.

'Then I'll buy a ticket,' he yelled happily. 'I'll buy a ruddy handful.'

They passed a sign to Pompeii. It was a few miles out of their way, but he asked if she minded him taking a look.

They followed the road towards Torre Annunziata, where another, smaller sign prompted them to turn up a narrow track that led towards a cluster of ramshackle buildings. But these were modern: the Roman town was immediately behind them, over a slight rise; imperfectly excavated, but even after two millennia more solid-looking than its modern counterpart.

James switched off the engine. There was no one about. A dog scratched its hindquarters energetically in the dust.

'Have you been here before?' he asked.

'No,' she said, looking around. 'It was only in the last ten years, under Mussolini, that they dug this out.'

It was the sheer scale of the place which staggered. He hadn't expected it to be so large – a whole town, abruptly obliterated by the mountain at its back. The forum, the large buildings that were obviously municipal offices, the private houses that presented only a doorway to the street but opened into large column-lined courtyards – it was not so very different in layout from any of the other Italian towns he had visited, with a forum instead of a piazza and temples instead of churches.

Here and there they came across casts of the inhabitants. Even after so long, you could still sense the terror and despair in their postures. One had been frozen in the act of holding something to his face, presumably a piece of cloth to breathe through. Another had blundered into a wall, lying down to die with his arms curled over his head as if to ward off blows raining from the sky. Yet another had tried to shield his companion from whatever was happening, and had died with his arms curled protectively around her.

'*Eh, signori.*'

The croaking voice belonged to a very old man, evidently some kind of guardian, who was calling to them from a doorway. He had a speech impediment, but he managed to communicate that for a small fee he could show the two of them around the excavations. James was disinclined to have company. He tipped the man a few lire and said that they would prefer to look round on their own, at which the old man grinned slyly and gestured for them to follow him.

'He wants to show us something,' Livia said. 'We'd better go, or he won't leave us alone.'

They passed another plastercast – a body crouched in a doorway, carrying a shapeless sack of possessions. The old man cackled, and muttered something in his odd, stunted speech, gesturing at the heavens. James caught the Italian for 'sky' and 'coming back'. He understood what the man was trying to say: these inhabitants had been killed not in the act of fleeing, but because they tried to return. They must have thought the worst was over, only for the mountain to have suddenly moved into another phase of the eruption, even deadlier than before. But this was not what the old man was pressing them to see. He was scuttling towards a small building in a side street.

'*Prego, signori,*' he said, unlocking a padlock and ushering them inside with a flourish, '*di lupanare.*'

James looked quizzically at Livia, but she seemed as mystified as he was. The old man winked extravagantly at James and withdrew. Livia looked at the walls, and laughed.

The frescoes were faded, but it was not hard to see what they represented. On every side, men and women were copulating in a dozen different ways. There were women on top, women underneath, women applying male genitalia to their mouths as casually as if they were lipsticks, women lying with women, even a group of both sexes engaged in what appeared to be some kind of mutual flagellation.

'It's a brothel,' Livia exclaimed. 'These must have been all the services you could get.'

James understood now – the old man had thought he was being bribed to show them the pornography. 'How ghastly,' he said. 'Livia, I'm so sorry.'

'Oh, I don't know,' Livia said thoughtfully. 'That one looks quite interesting.' He couldn't help but glance at what she was looking at, and immediately found himself blushing. She laughed again.

'If all Englishmen were like you,' she said, putting her arm through his, 'there soon wouldn't be any Englishmen left.'

'I'm glad I amuse you,' he said stiffly.

'I think it's nice,' she said as they walked to the door. 'It makes me feel safe.'

'Safe,' he repeated. 'Well, that's great. I'm safe and I'm nice. Just what every soldier aspires to be.'

'There are worse things,' she said, her mood suddenly sombre. For a moment she seemed lost in her thoughts, and he guessed she was thinking about what had happened to her husband.

They left Pompeii and drove up the winding roads towards Fiscino. Occasionally James found himself glancing up at the summit of the volcano. The plume of smoke was leaning out to sea today, like a quill propped in an enormous inkpot. It would have looked much the same in the days before it destroyed Pompeii, he thought: there couldn't have been much in the way of warning, or the inhabitants wouldn't have stayed.

'Don't you ever think about it going up again?' he said.

'Of course.'

'Doesn't that make you want to leave?'

'No,' she said seriously. 'It makes me live each day as if it were another life. Because one life lived here is worth ten lived anywhere else.' She tightened her arms around him, and for an instant he felt it too: a sense that they, and the mountain, and even this war, were all just part of some bigger pattern, some mysterious power that had somehow brought them both to this moment.

When they got to Fiscino, Marisa and Nino greeted Livia with cries of delight. With James they were more guarded, which he thought was only natural, although it seemed to him that there was suspicion in the glances which Livia's father shot at him from under his craggy eyebrows.

'He thinks you might be my boyfriend,' Livia whispered as they were led to the kitchen to inspect the mozzarella from that morning's milk. 'Don't worry, I'll tell him you're not, although I won't explain why. He's quite old fashioned.'

'Fine,' James said, mystified.

A huge piece of mozzarella, so fresh and moist it still seemed to be oozing milk, was passed to him on a fork, and everyone watched expectantly while he sampled it. He made appreciative noises – which wasn't hard; the cheese was absolutely delicious. Livia, though, was more critical, and cross-questioned her father at length about the state of the pasture. Then she took James to say hello to Priscilla. When the buffalo saw who had come to visit her she snorted with delight and hurried over to the gate, nudging her massive black nose under Livia's arm, hoping for a handful of hay.

'We used to have two of these,' Livia explained as she scratched Priscilla's forehead. 'The poor thing gets lonely on her own.'

'What happened to the other one?'

Livia looked at him with a sudden frown that echoed her father's expression earlier. 'Some soldiers shot her.'

'You mean the Germans?'

She laughed sarcastically. 'Because obviously, nothing bad is ever done by Allied soldiers? No, the Germans did many terrible things when they were here, but they never shot our *bufale*. It took Allied troops to do that.'

'When? How did this happen?'

She found herself telling him an edited version of Pupetta's death – how the soldiers had been tipped off by a neighbour who bore her a grudge because Livia didn't like him, and how they had taken everything, all the food the Pertinis had, before opening fire on Pupetta. By the time she was halfway through she had to stop because she was crying.

James found himself wanting quite desperately to take her in his arms and kiss her. It was a very different feeling from the time when he'd tried to kiss her during the air raid. That had been excitement and desire: this was horror, and the wish to comfort, but the compulsion was if anything even stronger. He reached forward and slipped his arm round her shoulder, and then, because she so clearly needed the reassurance his arms could give her, and because in her misery she buried her face in his chest, he put both arms round her and hugged her properly. She wiped her eyes against his shirt, and lifted her face to his.

'And then they threw me in their truck,' she said. 'Pupetta was lying there, and I had to fight off those animals. And then the officer – the officer—'

'The officer what?'

'The officer tried to give my father money for me,' she said quietly.

James let her go. He was horrified, but more than that, he felt tainted by association. No wonder the Italians resented their liberators, he thought, if this was how they behaved. The fact that it was an officer who had done this only made it worse.

'Livia,' he said grimly, 'I'm so sorry.'

'Why? You weren't there.'

'I'm sorry about what happened. More than that – I'm appalled. But look – we can trace him. Did you notice any regimental markings on his uniform? Or a number on the lorry? I'll make sure the brute's court martialled for what he did.'

It was the first time she had seen him really angry, and she secretly found it rather impressive. 'Court martialled for what?' she pointed out. 'We were the ones breaking the law, not him. According to the military government's rules, what we were doing was hoarding, and that's a crime. If you're a soldier, you can proposition as many women as you like.' She shot him a glance. 'Or men, for that matter.'

'It's one thing to offer a prostitute money. But to offer money to a respectable girl. . .'

'Often there's not much difference, these days.'

'Of course there is,' he said hotly. But he was revisited by a thought which had struck him when she had laughed at the paintings in the *lupare* – and before that, even, when he first read *Married Love*: that all his received notions of what constituted respectability in a woman might be too simplistic for the times he was living in.

Livia kissed Priscilla's forehead, hugged her massive neck and said goodbye to her. As they walked back towards the house she said, 'Would you take me out to lunch, Shames?'

'Of course. I was assuming we'd stop somewhere.'

'I wouldn't ask, but my father and Marisa will want us to stay and eat with them. However much they tell us they've got plenty to eat, you must refuse. The truth is there's almost nothing here – I looked in the cupboards earlier. I'm going to give them the money I've earned working for you, but prices are so ridiculous now that it won't buy them very much.'

Livia was right – her family begged them to stay and eat, but James made up some excuse about a meeting he needed to be at, and instead of lunch they accepted a glass of Nino's *limoncello*. James saw the wistful way Livia looked around her before she left and realised that this was hard for her. In some ways, Naples was as alien to her as it was to him. It must be wonderful, he thought, to love a place as much as she clearly loved it here. Nowhere that he had ever lived had inspired such affection in him. For him, home was simply where you went when you weren't away at school.

There was a protracted Italian farewell, with many embraces and protestations of love. This included a long and elaborate series of kisses from Nino for James. After he had got over the shock of having another man's stubble rasping his cheek, an intriguingly scratchy sensation – surely his own cheek couldn't be so rough, he thought – it was strangely pleasant to be clasped to another man's breast like this, both daringly bohemian and childishly comforting.

When he had started the Matchless Livia climbed on the back, and Nino and Marisa festooned the handlebars with canvas bags full of *mozzarelle*, packed in water to keep them fresh. The liquid dribbled over James's legs as they set off again, the extra weight conspiring with the *limoncello* to make the steering decidedly erratic.

Once on the coast road he turned south, towards Sorrento and Amalfi. This side of Vesuvius was wooded and craggy, the sea often hundreds of feet below them as the road twisted up the side of sheer cliffs and revealed a succession of vertiginous vistas. Different smells filled his nostrils now: the salty tang of the sea, mixed with the fragrant, tropical scent of the citrus groves that lined the shore side of the road for mile after mile.

'Ay assed fur a dubble rume weeth ay beth,' Livia told him airily as they puttered along.

'A double room with a bath is not available.' For a moment he entertained a delicious fantasy that he really could book the two of them into a hotel in Sorrento.

'But ey hev a razor fashion.'

'A reservation.'

'That's what I said.'

'I have a reservation. *Ho prenotato una stanza.*'

'You really must do something about your accent, Chems. It's terrible. Like a Tuscan's.'

On the coast road near Sorrento they found a tiny restaurant. There was no menu, but the owner brought out plates of tiny sand eels fried in batter and soused in lemon juice, some things Livia said were called *noci di mare*, a couple of sea urchins and a plate of oysters.

Livia picked up an oyster and sniffed it. 'No smell,' she said approvingly. 'That's how you can tell it's fresh.' She took the lemon the owner had provided and expertly squeezed a few drops onto one before handing it to him. 'Have you eaten oysters before, Yames?'

'I don't believe I have,' he said dubiously, inspecting a grey-white puddle of flesh nestled in its shell amidst a little slimy-looking liquid.

'You'd know if you had. They say you never forget your first time,' she said mischievously. 'Like making love.'

He took a deep breath. 'Actually,' he said, 'I wouldn't know much about that either.'

183

She smiled. 'I know.'

He glanced at her. 'You could tell?' He hadn't realised his inexperience was so apparent.

'Of course. A woman has an instinct about these things.' She was busy sorting out the next biggest and juiciest oyster for herself. She clanked the shell lightly against his, as if they were drinking a toast. 'It doesn't bother me, really. *Cincin.*'

'*Cincin.*' They tipped the shells against their lips in unison.

It was salty, it was sweet, it was fishy, it was liquor, it was like a deep breath of seaweedy air and a mouthful of sea spray all at once. He bit once, involuntarily, and felt the flavours in his mouth swell and burst like a wave. Before he knew what he had done he had swallowed, and then there was another sensation, another flavour, as the soft shapeless mass wriggled past the back of his throat, leaving a faint, cool aftertaste of brine.

He felt a sudden sense that nothing would be the same again. Eve in her garden had bitten an apple. James had eaten an oyster, sitting outside a tiny restaurant overlooking the sea by Sorrento. His undernourished heart swelled in the Italian sunshine like a ripening fig, and he laughed out loud. With a great flood of gratitude he realised that he was having the time of his life.

'Another?' She handed him one, and took another for herself. This time he watched her as she swallowed hers – the way her eyes closed as she slipped it into her mouth, the tightening of her cheeks as she bit it, the twitch of her throat as she swallowed, and then the slow opening of her eyes again, as if she were reluctantly coming awake from a delicious dream.

The restaurant owner brought them wine, pale and golden and cool. There were just four oysters each, and when they were all gone they turned their attention to the *cecinella*. After the soft shapeless texture of the oysters these were almost the opposite: hard, crunchy skeletons whose flavour was all on the outside, a crisp bite of garlic and chilli that dissolved to nothing in your mouth. The sea urchins were another taste again, salty and exotic and rich. It was hard to believe that he had once thought they could be an austerity measure. After that they were brought without being asked a dish of baby octopus, cooked with tomatoes and wine mixed with the rich, gamey ink of a squid.

For dessert the owner brought them two peaches. Their skins were wrinkled and almost bruised, but the flesh, when James cut into it with his knife, was unspoiled and pefectly ripe, so dark it was almost black. He was

184

about to put a slice into his mouth when Livia stopped him.

'Not like that. This is how we eat peaches here.'

She cut a chunk from the peach into her wine, then held the glass to his lips. He took it, tipping the wine and fruit together into his mouth. It was a delicious, sensual cascade of sensations, the sweet wine and the sweet peach rolling around his mouth before finally, he had to bite it, releasing the fruit's sugary juices. It was like the oyster all over again, a completely undreamt-of experience, and one that he found stirringly sexual, in some strange way that he couldn't have defined.

After lunch they continued along the coast, the road skirting the green clear waters of the bay. It was hot now, and the combination of sun and moving air was burning them.

'I want to swim,' Livia said. She pointed. 'I think we can get down to the sea that way.'

He turned onto the track she had indicated, which led through a grove of lemon trees down to a rocky beach. A goat, seeing them approach, shook its head and scrambled effortlessly away.

James turned off the engine. The sea was the colour of a field of lavender, and so clear you could see every rock and seashell on the bottom. Apart from the yelling of crickets, and the faint soughing of the water as it sucked gently at the pebbles, everything was very still. The Matchless ticked and creaked quietly as it cooled. For a moment he felt a pang of guilt that a scene so perfectly beautiful could exist for his personal pleasure in the midst of a whole continent at war.

'We can undress over there,' Livia said, indicating a group of rocks.

The rocks were fifteen feet from the water. 'You go in first, if you want,' he offered. 'I won't look.'

But he did. He couldn't help it – he heard the sound of her bare feet as she ran to the sea, and then a splash and a shriek, and he looked up just in time to see a brown flash of nearly naked Livia, wearing only her drawers, plunging headlong into the water. After a moment she surfaced, pushing wet hair out of her eyes.

'Aren't you coming?' she called.

'Just a moment.' Behind the rock he took a series of deep breaths before he climbed out of his uniform and ran, as quickly as he could, into the mercifully icy water.

Afterwards they lay in the shade of a lemon tree, looking up at the sunlight flickering through the branches.

185

'My father eats lemons straight from the tree,' Livia said idly. 'Even the skin.'

'Aren't they bitter?'

'Not when they're warm from the sun.' She reached up and plucked one to show him. 'This is a good lemon. We have a saying: The thicker the skin, the sweeter the juice.' Experimentally she took a bite, and nodded. 'It's good.' She held the fruit towards his mouth.

He steadied her hand and tried it. She was right: it was sweet, as sweet as lemonade.

She took another mouthful herself and grimaced. 'Pip,' she said, spitting it into her hand. She smiled at him, and in that moment all his delusions of self-restraint evaporated. He took her head in his hands and desperately pressed his lips against hers. Her mouth was sweet and bitter, a faint saltiness mingling with the sharp tang of lemon. He felt the hard edges of her teeth against his tongue – the pips in the fruit of her mouth – before she pulled away.

'Jamus!' she exclaimed.

'Come here,' he gasped. He kissed her again. After a moment's hesitation, he felt her lips parting as she kissed him back.

There were so many unfamiliar textures – her tongue, now slippery and yielding, now hard and pointed and darting between his own lips; the ridged vault of her palate; the delicate bones of her back, and the muscles in her neck, as they pulsed beneath his fingers.

After a while she pulled free, a puzzled expression on her face. 'So you're not a fennel after all?'

'What?' he asked, perplexed.

'A fennel. You know, a *finocchio*. A *ricchione*.'

'A big ear?' he said, his confusion mounting.

'I guess not,' she said. Then she laughed. 'I'd never have swum – I didn't realise—' He kissed her again. She responded more hungrily this time, and he felt so happy it was as if he were falling.

She pulled away again, and this time her eyes had narrowed. 'So that was just a trick, was it, pretending to be a *culattina*?'

'Livia . . . I never pretended to be a *culattina*. Whatever a *culattina* is.'

'Yes, you did,' she reminded him. 'When we ate the oysters.'

'I told you that I wasn't experienced,' he said. 'Where's this . . . other thing come from?'

'Ah,' she said. She was beginning to realise that her feminine intuition might have been struggling with the translation from British body language to Italian. But the more she thought about that, the more a faint

186

but persistent sense of disappointment that had been constantly present ever since she accepted the job at the Palazzo Satriano seemed to lift, leaving behind it only a pleasant feeling that being kissed by James was rather nice.

She leaned forward to be kissed again, and he quickly obliged. 'You don't kiss like somebody inexperienced,' she commented.

'I'm a fast learner.' This time he went more slowly, kissing the tip of her adorable nose, and the lobes of her ears, and the delicate skin around her eyes before he came back to her lips.

But – he could have kicked himself – it was he who broke the spell. Pulling away, he said, 'What about Eric?'

Livia's expression darkened. 'What about him?'

'Do you kiss him too?'

'You've only just kissed me,' she said, 'and already you want to own me?'

'I just need to know where I stand.'

'I like you both,' she said simply. 'I didn't mean to kiss you, though I'm not sorry I did. But it doesn't mean anything.'

'Of course not,' he said, disappointed. He tried to kiss her again, but she turned her head away. He had changed the mood.

'Can I hold you?' he asked, realising that she wasn't going to change her mind.

'If you like.'

She settled herself against him. They were silent for a few minutes. 'You have a lot of self-control,' she said at last. 'That's a good thing. But I don't think you understand women that well.'

He turned this remark over in his mind, wondering what the best response to it might be. Was she telling him that he must be more of a man, that he should be more forceful? Or was she telling him the opposite – that he had ruined his chances by being too presumptuous? Or was she simply saying that he had ruined a perfectly good kiss by questioning it?

He was still wondering what to say when he realised that Livia, at least, wasn't torturing herself with questions. She was fast asleep.

When they finally returned home on the motorbike, Livia dozed on the back, her head nestled between his shoulder blades.

James rounded the last bend in the coast road and suddenly, across the bay, there was the city again, with the hills at its back, shining in the late afternoon sunlight. Livia stirred, saw where they were, and slid her arms round him again.

'Do you lick nipples, Gems?' she said sleepily into his ear.

'I lick – I like Naples very much.'

'Eye mm gled. Ees a booty'fuel city.'

That night, Livia announced that she needed a wood-burning oven if she was to do justice to the ingredients they had brought back from Vesuvius. After some thought, she had realised that James already possessed the perfect article – the *schedario*, his grey filing cabinet.

'We'll put the wood in the bottom drawer,' she explained. 'Then the middle drawer will become a very hot oven, where we can make pizza and roast meat. The top drawer will be a little cooler, for vegetables and mozzarella.'

'The flaw in your plan,' James pointed out, 'is that the *schedario* is already full of *archivi*, files.'

'But you can put the files somewhere else,' she said persuasively.

Strictly speaking this was true, he supposed. After all, they had managed perfectly well without a filing cabinet before.

For dinner they ate wood-roasted pizza with a sauce of fresh tomatoes and mozzarella, decorated only with salt, oil and basil. He had never eaten anything so simple, or so delicious. But when he finally went to bed it was another taste he dreamt of, the taste of some all-too-brief kisses in a lemon grove above Sorrento.

Thirty

'You see,' James explained, 'love isn't just something you *feel*. Love is something you *become*. It's like – going to a new country, and realising that you never particularly liked the place you left behind. It's like a sort of tingling and – oh, I don't know – when she smiles I just want to start clapping or something. Look, I'd better shut up, I seem to be talking the most awful nonsense.'

The girl, who was called Addolorata, put her hands together and smiled. 'No, that's exactly right!' she exclaimed. 'That's just how I feel about Magnus, too.'

'Magnus is a lucky chap,' James said. He realised that he had not, in fact, asked Addolorata very many questions so far about her fiancé, or her financial situation. It seemed inconceivable, however, that he should turn her application down, given the splendid way they were getting on. 'Look,' he suggested, 'I've got to write this report, but it'll probably help you a bit if I tell you first what the best answers to my questions are. For example, if I were to ask you what you've been living off . . .'

'An uncle sends me money,' Addolorata said quickly.

'. . . you might turn out to have stolen some money from a German. No Germans around now to check with, you see. Uncles have a tiresome habit of being contactable.'

'That's what I meant – I stole it from a German.'

'Excellent,' he said, beaming at her. 'I think this is going to go rather well.'

Later, as he typed up his report, Livia stuck her head round his office door. 'What are you doing?' she asked.

'Marrying someone.'

189

'Who's the lucky girl?'

'Addolorata Origo. It's not me who's marrying her, actually, it's a captain in the Highlanders. I'm just helping.'

'Well, if you're not going to be long, I thought we might go for a walk,' she said casually, producing a bonnet he had not seen before. 'It's sort of traditional at this time of the evening.'

He had seen the young couples strolling arm in arm down the Via Roma, and he knew putting yourself on display like this was an integral part of Italian courtship.

'Livia,' he said, his heart suddenly heavy, 'I'm afraid a walk's not going to be possible.'

'If you're too busy tonight, then perhaps tomorrow.'

'Tomorrow night won't be a good time either. Or any night.' He took a deep breath. 'I'm terribly sorry, Livia. The wedding officer simply can't be seen to have an Italian girlfriend.'

He saw her thunderstruck expression. 'I should have told you earlier,' he said lamely.

Her foot, he noticed, had started tapping rather dangerously. 'Are you ashamed of me?' she demanded.

'It isn't that. It's my position—'

The slam of the door closing left him in no doubt what her feelings about his position were.

He pulled the report out of the typewriter and read it through. It was, he realised, utter nonsense. With a sigh he screwed it up into a ball, tossed it at the bin, and started over again.

He hoped that by dinner she might have cooled down, but from the hostile stare she gave him he saw it was not the case. His plate was banged down on the table in front of him, and it seemed to him that he was given a far smaller helping than anyone else. To make matters worse, after dinner she seemed to make a beeline for Eric's table, where she laughed uproariously at everything he said. After twenty minutes of this, James could bear it no longer. He got up, kicked the table leg savagely for want of anything better to kick, and went up to bed.

The next morning he awoke before dawn and went to the market. Going from stall to stall he showed the stallholders a large pile of lire and made some discreet enquiries. Eventually, someone indicated that he might be able to supply what James was after. He was made to wait for half an hour, and then the man came back with a small paper bag.

190

'Here,' he said, passing it over. 'There's an eighth of a pound in there.'

James opened the bag and checked the contents. The smell, charred and dark and rich, filled his nostrils. The twenty or so coffee beans were like tiny black pearls.

A little further on he found someone selling freshly baked *sfogliatelle* – tiny pastries filled with ricotta, candied lemon zest and cinnamon, like the ones which Livia served for breakfast. A large bag of oranges and some fresh goat's milk, and his shopping expedition was complete.

Taking his purchases back to the apartment, he had just managed to lay the table with a cloth, flowers and china, and to press some juice from the oranges, when Livia emerged, yawning, from her sleeping quarters. After a moment she stopped and sniffed the air suspiciously.

'It's not Nescafé,' he said. 'It's real.'

Her eyes widened. '*Real* coffee?'

'I may not be able to cook, but I *do* know how to make a breakfast.'

'Oh James – that's wonderful.' Then she remembered she was cross with him. 'If a little desperate.'

He began to make the coffee. Livia was instantly at his shoulder, eagerly proffering advice, lest through his incompetence the precious beans be ruined.

'It's all right,' he said, 'I know what I'm doing.'

'Of course,' she said. 'Have you warmed the cups? You'll need to. And how are you grinding the coffee? Not like that, you need to crush the beans more finely. No, let the water cool a little first—' She grabbed the coffee jug and the beans from him, but she was so excited he couldn't take offence.

When she had poured them both a tiny cup of dense black liquid, so strong it not only had the consistency of engine oil but also a faint sheen of coffee oil on the surface, they both took a bite of a *sfogliatella*, and drank.

'That is two firsts for me,' she said at last. 'The first coffee I've had since the start of the war, and the first time anyone has ever made me a meal. Thank you, James.'

'No one ever made you a meal before?'

She shook her head. 'I always wanted to do everything myself.'

'One day,' he said, sipping his coffee – she had drunk hers in three ecstatic gulps, he noticed, 'I will cook us both dinner. Just for the two of us.'

She took a sudden interest in the bottom of her coffee cup. 'So you think you might want to step out with me after all?'

'I want to be with you more than anything else in the world. But,

Livia, I'm going to have to be clear about this. I can't be seen with you in public. I can't acknowledge you as my girl. I can't even let the other officers know how I feel about you, because the CO might find out, and then I think I'd get the sack and be transferred back to Africa. I know it's not ideal, but it's all I can offer.'

'And, of course, you can't ever marry me,' she said quietly.

He shook his head.

'Where I come from that's quite a big thing, to court someone you've got no intention of marrying. If my father knew . . .'

'The war won't last for ever.'

'It's lasted four years already. Who knows how much longer it will go on for?' She smiled ruefully. 'Besides, when the war is over you'll go home. You'll have had enough of me by then.'

'I will never have had enough of you.'

'Hmmm,' she said. 'Well, I'll think about it.'

And with that he had to be content.

But the cooking lessons, at least, were resumed. James gave Livia much amusement by going out and buying himself a pair of kitchen scales. Thereafter, as he watched her cook, he would cross-question her about the quantities she was cooking with.

'How many aubergines are you using per person?'

A shrug. 'One or two. It depends how big they are.'

'On how big the aubergines are?'

She rolled her eyes. 'No, stupid, how big the person is.'

'How long do you cook them for?'

Another shrug. 'Until they're done.'

'Well, how much breadcrumb do you use?'

'Enough to fill the aubergines.'

'Livia,' he said, exasperated, 'how are you going to teach me to cook if you won't tell me the amounts?'

'But I don't *know* the amounts.'

'There must have been a time when you at least weighed your ingredients.'

'I don't see how, since my mother didn't own a pair of scales either.'

He tried a different tack. 'Suppose someone gave you a recipe – wouldn't you want to be able to follow their instructions properly?'

Livia laughed scornfully. 'If someone were prepared to give away a recipe, it obviously wouldn't be much good.'

*

In one of the many bookshops on the Via Maddaloni, he found an old book of recipes and took it back to show her.

'You see?' he said triumphantly. 'Recipes. They do exist.'

Livia turned some of the pages, a frown on her face. 'These are very poor,' she announced.

'How do you know if you haven't tried them?'

'They're the wrong amounts. And sometimes in the wrong order.'

'But how do you know, if you can't tell *me* what the right amounts are?'

She shrugged. 'I just do.'

He sighed. 'I'll tell you what. Next time you cook, will you use the scales to measure what you put in, and write it down, just like they do in the book? Then I'll be able to copy you.'

'If I have to.'

After she had cooked *melanzane farcite* he found a note scrawled on the back of an army Bureau bulletin. It was heavily stained with oil and onions, and it read:

Aubergines – a few
Tomatoes – twice as many as the aubergines
Oil – q b
Onion – 1 or more depending on size
Almonds – q b
Breadcrumbs – q b

'What's this?' he asked.

She seemed surprised. 'It's the recipe, like you asked me.'

'Livia, it's a *list*.'

'There's a difference?'

'Well, what does this q b mean?'

'*Quanto basta*. Whatever is enough.'

He gave up, and the next day the scales had vanished from the kitchen.

Her preferred way of teaching involved sharing her mother's favourite kitchen sayings. Livia was quite happy to tell him, for example, that *quattr' omini ci vonnu pre fari 'na bona 'nzalata: un pazzu, un saviu, un avaru, e un sfragaru* – it takes four men to make a salad: a madman, a scholar, a miser and a spendthrift.

'Meaning what, exactly?' James asked, mystified.

'Meaning that you need a madman to mix it – *so*,' she said, shaking the ingredients vigorously together with her fingers, 'but a scholar to measure out the salt – one pinch. Then you need a miser for the vinegar.' She added a few tiny drops of vinegar. 'But with the oil, you want a spendthrift, because of course you cannot be too generous with good oil.'

He learnt, too, that *sparaci e funci svrigògnanu cocu*, asparagus and mushrooms teach a cook humility; that you should favour *latti di crapa, ricotta di pecura e tumazzu di vacca*, milk from the goat, ricotta from the sheep and cheese from the cow; and that *cci voli sorti, cci voli furtuna sinu a lu stissu frijiri l'ova*, it takes both luck and good fortune just to fry eggs. Some of this made sense and some of it did not, but it was all worth it for the pleasure of her company.

Other aspects of her cooking lessons were even more mysterious. When he asked her why she put a cork in the pot whenever she boiled seafood, she muttered something darkly which he could not quite catch. On closer questioning, it turned out that the cork would ward off *malocchio*, the evil eye. Similarly, to eat cucumbers in August, or melons in October, brought bad luck as well as fever. To spill wine was good luck, but the pieces of a broken mirror had to be carefully gathered up and submerged in running water. Once, he found her counting the seeds in a lemon: when he asked her what she was doing, she told him that she was counting how many children she would have. She had an absolute horror of silverware left uncrossed on an empty plate, and when she bought a lottery ticket from the hunchback who patrolled the municipal gardens every day with a great placard of fluttering tickets hanging around his neck, she stroked his hump for luck. However, she would never buy a ticket, or undertake any other venture requiring good fortune, on a Tuesday or a Friday, since it was well known that *ne di venere ne di marte non si sposa ne si parte!* – you should not marry, travel, or do something new on those days of the week.

It was all nonsense, but then, he reflected, he himself had never got around to throwing away that piece of bone the priest had given him in the Duomo.

He wanted to talk to her properly about her husband, and he chose his moment carefully, waiting until dinner was over and the other officers were busy with their game of *scopa*.

'I know I can't ever replace Enzo,' he said. 'And I promise I won't ever try to.'

'Actually, it isn't like that,' she said thoughtfully. '"Replace" . . . that

194

suggests men are interchangeable, like lightbulbs. But people, I think, are more like recipes.'

'Livia,' he said, mystified, 'I really, really want to understand what you're saying right now. But I don't.'

She was surprised: to her this was obvious. 'When you change a lightbulb, of course you need the same sort of bulb to replace it with. But recipes are the opposite. Remember when we went to the market, and we chose the swordfish? Well, on another day, I might have chosen tuna instead. But they would have ended up as two different dishes, with completely different ingredients. In a tuna recipe, you can't replace the tuna with swordfish, and vice versa. So if what you have is swordfish, you choose a different recipe. Both good, but different.'

'So Enzo was tuna?' he said, understanding now.

'No, Enzo was swordfish. You're tuna.'

'Oh,' he said, slightly crestfallen. 'Can't I be swordfish? I don't like tuna.'

She laughed. 'Sometimes, you are just the smallest bit like him. He would have hated being told he was a tuna, too. He was a sweet boy,' she said, tears springing to her eyes at the thought of him, 'but a bit vain, and not as clever as you are.'

He said nothing, putting his arm around her as she cried for a little while.

'Thank you,' she said, drying her eyes on his sleeve. 'You see? I told you you were clever. You let me cry, whereas Enzo would have been furious if he'd seen me crying over someone else.'

In the market, she showed him how to choose oil. 'There's *extra vergine*, *sopraffino vergine*, *fino virgine* and *vergine*,' she explained.

'And extra virgin is good?'

'Of course. The more virgin the better.' There was just the merest hint of mischief in her voice. 'Much sweeter. And you know what? They say that the very first pressing is the sweetest one of all.'

Sometimes as they cooked he would kiss her, and their kisses would be flavoured by whatever it was she was cooking with – the astringent echo of a mint leaf, or the slow spreading warmth of oregano. But although he was certain that she enjoyed these embraces, sooner or later she would push him away. 'You can't fry fish in water,' she would mutter enigmatically, or '*Lu cunzatu quantu basta, cchiù si conza, cchiù si guasta*. Too much seasoning is more than enough.'

Thirty-one

'As you know,' Major Heathcote was saying, 'it is the responsibility of A-force to come up with initiatives to destabilise the Germans' hold on northern Italy.'

James nodded. He still wasn't quite sure why the CO had asked to see him, although he was relieved that for once it seemed not to be to bawl him out.

'And as you are also aware,' the major said slowly, 'with penicillin in such short supply, the spread of syphilis has been a big problem for our medical chaps. The Germans, on the other hand, don't seem to be nearly so troubled by it.'

James nodded again.

'A-force have a plan.' The major sighed. 'A sort of two birds, one stone scenario. The idea is that we round up women with syphilis and then ship them up north, behind the lines. Where, one presumes, they will spread their diseases amongst the German soldiers rather than our own. Apparently something similar has already been tried in France.'

James found it hard to believe what he was hearing. Even by the dark standards of A-force this sounded ill-conceived. 'But isn't that rather – well, unethical? Using civilians to do our dirty work for us. And women, at that – sick women?'

'Oh, for God's sake,' the major said irritably. 'Is razing cities to the ground with incendiary bombs ethical? Is flooding each other's countries with pornography and black propaganda ethical? It's a total war, Gould. That means we fight with every weapon at our disposal.'

James said nothing.

'No, it probably isn't ethical,' the major muttered. 'Personally, I think it's a damn poor business. But it's been approved at the very highest level. Your job is simply to arrange the detention of some suitable women.'

'*Rastrellamenti*,' James said.

'What's that?'

'That's what the Italians called the German round-ups – *rastrella-menti*. They probably never expected to find their liberators doing exactly the same thing.' A further thought struck him. 'When we find these girls, presumably we're not going to give them medical attention for their condition?'

'It would rather defeat the object if we did.'

'Even if they ask for it?'

The major hesitated. Denial of medical attention was a breach of the Geneva Convention. 'We'll just have to hope they don't ask. And technically, I suppose they aren't exactly combatants.'

'And how are the women to be selected?'

'From among those with records of prostitution, presumably.'

'But that could mean we include the fiancées of some of our own soldiers. Women who haven't married only because we won't allow them to.'

'We can hardly show special favours to those who we've already decided are unfit to marry our troops,' the major pointed out. 'Really, Gould. I think you're failing to focus on the big picture.'

'It's only when one focuses on the small picture,' James said, 'that the full horror of this scheme becomes apparent.'

The major looked at him sharply. 'I hope you're not suggesting you won't carry out your orders?'

'No, sir.'

'I'm very glad to hear it.' The major waved him away. 'Dismiss.'

They sat on the roof of the Palazzo Satriano, amongst the chimney stacks and the broken red roof tiles, as the sun set over the bay. Livia was plucking a pigeon. James nestled a tommy gun in his lap. Occasionally, when further pigeons landed on the rooftop, he would fire off a few shots in their direction. If he was successful, the bird got added to the pile at Livia's feet.

'I vould layk tu seets een dhe frond ro,' she said thoughtfully.

He grunted.

'Can iu tail may, vat time ees dhe intarval, pliss?' She switched to Italian. 'What's the matter, Giacomo?'

'Nothing.'

197

'You know,' she said, 'English must be a very hard language. Because most of the time, English men would rather not speak at all.'

'Sorry,' he muttered. 'Tough day.'

She sniffed.

'I'm in a rather difficult situation.'

'So am I,' she said pointedly. 'One minute you kiss me, the next minute you won't talk to me. It's really very confusing.'

He sighed. 'Sometimes my work . . . there are things I don't like.'

She put down the pigeon she was working on. 'So tell me about it.'

She listened without comment until he had finished. 'It's not the most recent vettings I'm worried about,' he explained. 'I've been letting those weddings go ahead. It's the earlier ones, the ones I did when I first came to Naples. Any one of those girls is at risk.'

'But it's obvious what you have to do.'

'Is it?'

'You have to make sure that none of those girls gets taken.'

'Livia, the round-ups will go ahead whether I'm involved or not.'

'But they will ask *you* whether the girls they have seized are really prostitutes. And then you must lie.'

'But in many cases, the files say that they are. *My* files, amongst others. I'm partly to blame for this mess.'

'Files can go missing.'

'They'll ask the girls how they support themselves. It isn't hard to work out the truth.'

'You must speak to Angelo,' she decided. 'He will know what to do.'

'Angelo?'

'The maître d' at Zi' Teresa's.'

'What's he got to do with it?'

'Jims,' she said, 'who do you think got me this job?'

'Me?'

'You *gave* me the job,' she corrected. 'Which is not the same thing at all. I'm not meant to tell you this, but it was Angelo who made sure there were no other applicants. Angelo who sees we always have enough to eat. Angelo who supplies everything I can't get at the market.'

'But why should Angelo care what I eat?'

'I think,' she said vaguely, 'he was just a bit concerned that when you first came to Naples you weren't eating properly. And it's well known that a man who isn't eating properly can't do his job properly either. *Panza cuntenti, cori clementi: panza dijuna, nenti priduna.* These days, apparently, you're much more – well, reasonable.'

'I see.'

'Although now you're angry.'

'No,' he said. And it was true, he wasn't. He was starting to see a possible way out of this mess, and Livia was right: Angelo might be just the person to help him do it. 'I'll go and talk to him,' he promised.

There was a ripple of vibration under their feet. The building shook itself with a rattle of doors and windows, the way it sometimes did when a heavy truck or a tank was passing. The throb rose to a crescendo, passed through them, and then was gone, a wave in search of a shore.

'Earthquake,' he said softly.

'It's the beginning of the summer,' she said. 'We get them when it's hot.'

'I wish I knew what to do.'

'Whatever you decide,' she said, 'it will be the right thing.'

He walked up the hill to the darkened restaurant. The notice announcing its closure was still displayed in the window, which in turn was draped in blackout blinds. He went around the back and knocked on the kitchen door.

Angelo opened it with a slight smile. 'Signore Gould.'

James had the feeling that he was expected. 'Captain Gould,' he corrected.

Angelo bowed. 'As you wish. Will you take a glass of wine with me?'

'I'd be delighted, Angelo.'

They sat either side of the empty bar, a bottle of Brunello between them. 'The last of my pre-war stock,' Angelo said as he filled their glasses. 'I've been saving it for a special occasion.'

'Is this a special occasion?'

'Oh, I think so.' Angelo held his glass up to the light. The wine was almost brown in colour, and when he swirled the liquid with a gentle tip of his hand, it clung to the sides of the glass. He put it to his nose and inhaled deeply. 'They call this vintage "the women's wine",' he said. 'When it was picked, in 1918, all the men had been killed in the Great War. So the women harvested the grapes themselves. The vines hadn't been irrigated, or pruned properly, or given any insecticides to help them grow. But sometimes a vine needs adversity to flourish. It was one of the best years Brunello ever had.' He touched the glass gently to James's. 'To peace.'

'To peace.' They drank.

'Now then. How can I help you?'

199

'I think I can persuade my superiors to reopen the restaurants.'

Angelo raised an eyebrow. 'That would be very welcome.'

'It shouldn't be too difficult. The food shortages aren't so bad now, and they'll believe me if I tell them that there's no longer a risk to public order or security.'

Angelo nodded. 'But of course you want something in return.'

'Two things, actually.'

'And they are?'

'First, I need you to spread the word that every restaurant has to employ at least one girl. Big places like this can employ half a dozen. They can work as waitresses, cooks, maître d's, whatever.'

Angelo considered this for a moment. 'It's an excellent idea,' he said. 'The girls will have jobs, so they'll be able to show that they have a source of income when the *rastrellamenti* start.' He caught James's look. 'News travels quickly in Naples,' he said apologetically. 'Does this mean that the girls who are engaged to soldiers will be able to marry?'

'I don't see why not. After all, a girl who works in Zi' Teresa's can hardly be said to be of bad character.'

'And the files? The reports that already name them as whores?'

'I think you'll find,' James said, 'that there was a German air raid a few weeks ago which caused extensive damage to my headquarters. Unfortunately, a large number of files appear to have been destroyed.'

'Ah,' Angelo said. He raised his glass to James. 'Now you are *furbo*, my friend,' he said admiringly. 'You have become a true Neapolitan.'

'Give priority to the girls who already have fiancés. There's a backlog of weddings we'll need to get through. But we'll have to be ruthless – once a girl is married, she has to give up her job and let another girl take her place. I'll employ Gina Tesalli, the one who's pregnant, myself. She can help Livia in the kitchen.'

At the mention of Livia's name Angelo smiled. 'So you'll be keeping your own arrangements as they are? I can always arrange for Malloni to come back if you'd prefer.'

'I don't prefer,' James said crisply. 'Mrs Pertini stays with me.'

Angelo inclined his head. 'And the second thing?'

'I want to know where Zagarella keeps his stolen penicillin.'

Angelo drew in his breath sharply. 'My friend, that is an altogether more dangerous undertaking. Why not leave him alone?'

'He screwed me over. Now it's my turn to screw him.'

Angelo shook his head. 'I'm not sure I can help you.'

'Of course you can. It isn't only Allied officers who eat in your restaurant, Angelo. The *camorristi* come here as well. And you hear things – you hear everything.'

'It is more difficult, and more complicated, than even you can imagine,' Angelo said.

'In what way?'

Even though they were alone, Angelo glanced around before replying. 'This trade in goods stolen from the Allies. Your predecessor, Jackson, thought that the Americans were simply too incompetent to stop it.' James nodded. 'Well, if I have learnt anything in the past year, it is that your American friends are many things, but they are rarely incompetent.'

'What are you getting at?'

'Suppose you were the Americans and you wanted the Mafia to do you a favour – a big favour, something political. How would you persuade them to help you?' Angelo closed his fingers and rotated his wrist, the old Neapolitan gesture for corruption. 'Perhaps you would throw open your stores and say, "Help yourselves."'

'But what could the Americans possibly want from the Mafia?'

'I don't know. All I know is, there is a plan.'

James thought back to the document he had found in the Americans' offices. That, too, had implied that there was some kind of plan. But what?

'As you say, it's probably political,' he decided. 'In which case, it needn't concern us now. And they won't break cover to save Zagarella, not if the evidence against him is strong enough.'

Angelo considered. 'It will take money. A great deal of money.'

'That can be arranged.'

'There will be no receipts,' Angelo warned him. 'The kind of people I will need to pay will not want any record of their involvement.'

'Very well. But I want Zagarella himself. Not some underling.'

'I understand. Let me see what I can do.'

The next day James had to interview some men accused of killing an ex-partisan in the hills above Caserta, a small town to the north of Naples.

He found the police station without difficulty, and the local marshal explained what had happened. The partisan had been little more than a bandit, happy to steal from the Germans just as he had previously stolen from the Italian government, and even happier when the Allies offered to drop arms and explosives to help. Although the bandit had been able to melt away into the hills after his attacks, the townspeople had not, and they became the focus of the Germans' increasingly punitive reprisals.

Eventually the Germans let it be known that for any one of their men killed in the raids, ten citizens would be shot. This had no effect on the bandit, despite personal appeals from the mayor and the priest. As he now possessed a large arsenal of weapons, and a large retinue of blood-thirsty companions as eager as him to use them, he was soon able to attack an entire German supply convoy, killing four Germans in the process. The Germans, true to their word, then rounded up forty civilians – men, women and children, but principally the latter, as most of the men had already been taken away to work in labour camps – lined them up against the wall of the church and shot them. At the funerals, the weeping mothers kissed and sucked the bloody wounds on their children's corpses, a sign to the community that they considered this a blood feud, one that every male member of their family was obliged to extract vengeance for, however many generations it might take.

It did not take long. The bandit got lazy, and eventually found his supply of arms curtailed by the Allied invasion. Meanwhile the brothers, uncles and fathers of the victims began drifting back from various prisoner-of-war camps in the north. These men, many of whom were sick of fighting, now found themselves given the responsibility of killing the bandit, which they duly did, and were duly arrested for.

James spoke to the men, who confirmed the marshal's account. They seemed resigned to their fate, which would undoubtedly be life imprisonment in the Poggio Reale, a place scarcely more pleasant than the prison camps they had recently left behind. He also talked to the priest, who showed James the wall honeycombed with bullet holes where the reprisal had taken place.

'Can I ask you, Father,' James said, 'what you would do if these men told you about their crime in the confessional?'

The priest considered. 'I would probably say that they had committed a terrible sin, but that if they were truly repentant, God would forgive them.'

'And what would their penance be?'

'I would tell them to help rebuild the houses and farms that have been destroyed by the war.'

It seemed to James that this was a far more useful punishment than any the courts would mete out. 'Would they do it?'

'Of course. Nobody here wants to be in a state of sin.'

James went back to the police station in a thoughtful mood.

'Well?' the marshal demanded. 'Do you want to take them now, or will you send a truck?'

'Neither,' James said. 'This is a waste of time. I'm going to go back to Naples and destroy the paperwork.'

The marshal looked astonished. 'Isn't that rather risky?'

'Perhaps, but by the time anyone untangles what's really happened here the war will be over and I shall be long gone.'

A crafty look had come into the marshal's eyes. 'I'm afraid, sir, we are a very poor town. We cannot afford to show our appreciation to the extent you are probably expecting.'

'I wasn't,' James began. He checked himself. 'How much could you afford?'

The marshal ummed and erred, his eyes never leaving James's face. 'Eight hundred lire,' he said at last.

'Very well.'

The marshal seemed even more surprised at this than at James's decision not to charge the men. 'Really? You'll accept eight hundred?'

'So long as you can get it for me straight away.'

'I'll ask the priest. He can take it out of the church funds.' The marshal had jumped to his feet and was almost falling over himself in his haste to finish the deal. He returned a little later with the priest, who handed over eight hundred lire without comment.

'It will go to a good cause,' James said, folding the money and putting it in his pocket.

'Of course, of course,' the marshal said, clearly not believing him.

But the priest nodded and said, 'I'm glad to hear it. And even if it doesn't, it has already done good work here in Caserta. Thank you.'

Back at headquarters, James rummaged in the cupboard until he found the old biscuit tin he had inherited from his predecessor. Carlo and Enrico looked on, perplexed. Tipping out the pencils, he put the eight hundred lire into the tin without comment, then carefully replaced it in the cupboard.

That evening, when he went back to check, he found that they were already up to nine hundred and fifty. Carlo and Enrico had got the message.

Although the damage from the air raid had been repaired now, somehow the courtyard had remained as the communal dining area. None of the Americans seemed keen to dispense with Livia's services, and James was beginning to realise the usefulness of a favour owed. It also meant he could eavesdrop on the Americans' conversations. Although he had heard no more about any dealings with the Mafia, he had picked up several useful items of gossip.

It worked two ways, however. That night, Eric came to sit next to him as he devoured a bowl of Livia's spaghetti.

'If I didn't know different, James, I'd say you've been avoiding me,' he said. 'How's tricks?'

James shrugged and waved a hand in the air. Conveniently, his mouth was full of spaghetti, and a shrug seemed to cover the situation better anyway.

'You know, you've started to use Italian gestures,' Eric said mildly. 'That shrug was not the shrug of an Englishman.'

James swallowed his mouthful. 'Eric, it was just a shrug.'

'If you say so. By the way, I hear you're going after Zagarella again.'

'Where did you hear that?'

'So it's true?'

'If your sources told you it is,' James said, spinning another ball of pasta expertly onto his fork, 'then presumably it must be.'

'Oh, James.' Eric regarded him with amused disappointment. 'Such vagueness. Are we going to arrest him again? Only it seems to me that this time, we're going to need some cast-iron evidence if we don't want to look like idiots.'

'As it happens,' James said casually, 'I was thinking I might take care of this one on my own. No need to tie up more manpower than we have to.'

'But last time,' Eric pointed out, 'we did it together, and we still didn't nail him.' A thought appeared to strike him. 'You're not suggesting that CIC had anything to do with him getting off?'

'I would never dream of suggesting any such thing.'

'But you're thinking it.'

James hesitated.

'If we weren't Allies, I'd take offence at that,' Eric said. 'I suppose you've heard this ridiculous theory that we're somehow in league with the Mafia.'

'I don't pay any attention to gossip.'

'James, we're intelligence officers. Gossip is our trade. But that one, I can assure you, has even less foundation than all the rest of the nonsense that gets talked around here.'

Livia was coming out with another bowl of pasta. Involuntarily, James watched her. Eric followed his gaze and said, 'Speaking of gossip, there's been a certain amount of talk about Mrs Pertini.'

'What sort of talk?'

'They say she's stepping out with you.' Eric laughed mirthlessly. 'I'll tell you, that one did come as a bit of a surprise to me. Since I assumed from what you'd told me you had a girl back home in England.'

James couldn't think of anything to say.

'Didn't believe it at first,' Eric continued. 'I don't like to listen to gossip either, but Livia confirmed it herself. So I reckoned you'd either been lying to her, or lying to me.'

'Sorry about that.'

'That was when I realised that, underneath all that British candour, you're a lot more devious than you make out. I think we might have underestimated you, James.'

'Who's "we"?'

'But you'll be pleased to know that mine is a lone voice,' Eric continued, ignoring the question. 'As far as most of CIC is concerned, you're still just the Brit who writes the wedding reports.'

'I'm glad to hear it. Since that is exactly who I am.'

'Anything you get, James,' Eric said softly, 'I strongly advise you to share it with your friends and allies.'

'You brute,' James snapped. A red mist descended, and he leapt to his feet, his fists clenched. 'Livia's no whore.'

Eric raised his own fists. 'I never said she was.'

'You were talking about sharing her—'

'I was talking about sharing intelligence, you stupid limey panty-waist.'

'Who are you calling a panty-waist?'

'Why?' Eric sneered. 'Are there any other panty-waists hereabouts?'

James had absolutely no idea what a panty-waist was, but that was beside the point. 'Take that back,' he spat.

The two of them circled each other furiously, their fists up. A few of the men around them hollered and whooped, sensing entertainment. James swung, and then Eric swung, and soon they were hammering blows at each other.

'Stop it,' Livia screamed, running out of the kitchen. 'Stop it, both of you. You're behaving like children.'

Shamefaced, they stopped. There was blood on both their faces, but it was hard to say which of them had come off worse.

'They say all's fair in love and war,' Eric said, dabbing at his lip. 'Which is another way of saying all's unfair. Bear it in mind, James.'

Thirty-two

Sometimes Livia found herself comparing James with Enzo, and it never failed to amaze her that one can love two people in two such different ways.

With Enzo, she had fallen in love *com' un chiodo fisso in testa*, like a nail in the head. Yet looking back, that had been a schoolgirl's love, a crush; and although she mourned her husband, she found that she was no longer heartbroken at his absence. Sometimes she wondered, a little guiltily, what her feelings for him would be now if the war had never happened, and they had spent all this time having babies and struggling to manage in his parents' apartment. Would she still love him the way she had on their wedding night, or would she be like so many of those other women, who sighed the little rhyme as they scrubbed at their endless laundry:

Tempo, marito e figli,
vengono come li pigli.

Husbands, sons and weather,
Must be endured whatever.

Her feelings for James were very different. For example, she liked the fact that he was kind, even though he could also be correct, even a little pompous. She took a quiet pleasure in driving him to the point of exasperation sometimes, since it was always amusing to see him go red in the face, and as for his ridiculous attachment to army rules and regulations, well, she had soon seen to it that none of those applied to her. Fairness, decency, kindness, compassion . . . These were not qualities she would

206

ever have thought would have attracted her to a man, but after four years of war, it struck her that they were actually rather rare.

There was another big difference between the way she felt about James and the way she had felt about Enzo. When she first met Enzo, she had been a girl, unaware of how pleasurable the physical expression of love could be. For four years she had put the memories of their love-making out of her mind. Now, her kisses with James were stirring up recollections and desires that she had long kept buried. Of course, a woman was not expected to admit to such feelings, nor could she expect to experience those pleasures again until she was engaged to be married. But war, Livia realised, was changing that, as it had changed so many other things. It was effectively up to Livia to decide how much of a relationship she was going to have with James. It was a choice that few women of her background had ever had before, and the enormity of her freedom almost took her breath away when she thought about it.

Nevertheless, it was not a decision she intended to make lightly. Apart from anything else, she had already grieved for the loss of one husband. If she allowed herself to become too attached to James, the choices they would have to make later would be all the more painful.

But, as she ruefully acknowledged to herself, sometimes it was not a question of what you allowed or did not allow yourself to feel. Sometimes the heart makes its own decisions, and all you can do is decide whether or not you are going to act on them.

In the market James found some strawberries, the first he had seen since the war began. Excited, he spent far too much money on them. Back at the Palazzo Satriano, Livia was appalled.

'The season hasn't started yet,' she scolded him. 'They won't be ripe.'

'They look fine to me.'

She tried one. 'Just as I thought,' she said dismissively. 'No flavour at all.'

'But how is one meant to know when the season has started?'

'One just does, that's all.' She saw his crestfallen expression. 'But we can have them with a little balsamic vinegar.'

'Strawberries with vinegar?' He made a face. 'It doesn't sound very enticing.'

'Trust me. They'll be sweeter that way.'

As she sliced the berries into a bowl she said thoughtfully, 'You're a typical man, James. You want everything to always be ripe, so you can have it straight away. But waiting until the right time is half of the pleasure.'

He looked at her sharply. Were they still talking about strawberries? But she was rummaging in a cupboard for the vinegar, a tiny bottle of ancient black stuff she had swapped for some rations, and he couldn't see her face.

As she unstoppered the bottle and drizzled a little of the thick liquid over the fruit she said quietly, 'Anyway, you won't have to wait much longer.'

'Nearly strawberry season?'

'Maybe.'

Certain things, he learnt, always go well together. Balsamic vinegar and citrus fruit was just one example. Parsley and onion was another, as was chicory and pork, or radicchio and pancetta. Seafood was a natural partner for courgettes, mozzarella went with lemon, and although tomatoes went with almost anything, they had a special affinity with anchovies, basil or oregano.

'So it's a question of opposites attracting?' he asked.

'Not exactly.' She struggled to explain. 'Anchovies and tomatoes aren't opposites, really, just complementary. One is sharp, one savoury; one is fresh, the other preserved; one lacks salt, while the other has salt in abundance . . . it's a question of making up for the other one's deficiencies, so that when you combine them you don't make a new taste, but bring out the natural flavours each already has.'

She glanced at him, and she knew that he was thinking the same thing she was thinking. The merest smile, a lift of an eyebrow . . . a quick kiss, in parting, planted on the back of her neck . . . her hand, trailing his as she let it go. Like parsley and onion.

'So what does tuna go with?'

She smiled. 'Many things. But particularly with lemon.'

'So if I'm tuna, you must be lemon.'

'Hmm.' She thought about it. 'I think I'd like to be a lemon. At least with a lemon, you know when it's there. And I'd rather be sharp than too sweet.'

It never ceased to surprise him how many of her dishes were cooked without meat. Her pasta sauces often consisted of just one or two ingredients, such as garlic and oil, or grated lemon and cream. Many more were based on a vegetable, with chilli, anchovy or cheese providing a subtle kick. Often it didn't occur to him that he hadn't eaten meat until after the meal was over. His very favourite dish was her *melanzane parmigiana*, but it was only as his palate became more trained that he realised this, too, contained nothing more substantial than dense chunks of aubergine. As for gravy, he had never missed it once.

He mentioned this to her, and she laughed. 'We've never had a lot of meat to spare in Campania. Even before the war, it was expensive. So we had to learn to use our ingenuity.'

The money in the tin mounted daily. Most was put there by Carlo and Enrico – James thought it best not to enquire too directly into its provenance. He assumed they were selling titbits of information, dispensing unofficial licenses for street vendors, helping to settle old scores between criminals, and generally supervising all the other little scams by which those in power make themselves useful to those they have power over.

Meanwhile, it seemed only appropriate that the filing cabinet, which had once held so many records of weddings refused, should in its new incarnation as an oven be responsible for their disappearance. James stuffed the bottom drawer full of papers, weighted them down with kindling, and set a match to them. For lunch that day he enjoyed a very good wood-roasted fish, served on a platter of salt and herbs.

The girls all had to be re-interviewed, and new reports written of a more positive nature. James was careful, however, not to go over the top. His approval was couched in the kind of subdued, dry officialese calculated not to arouse suspicion. No direct mention was made of Gina Tessali's pregnancy, other than an oblique reference to her 'evident enthusiasm to become a good wife and mother'. Violetta Cartenza would, he wrote, 'be a great asset to her husband's regiment, having made friends already with a large number of servicemen in Naples'. Rosetta Marli was 'according to many reports, unusually industrious and obliging at her work'. Even Algisa Fiore was 'sober and demure', a fact she demonstrated by pulling him to her bosom and covering him with kisses when he explained what he was up to.

He had decided against adding to his war chest by asking the girls for donations. Occasionally, however, they pressed on him an envelope stuffed with lire: these he took back to the Palazzo Satriano, where he added them to the tin.

One day Livia cooked him a new dish for breakfast, a kind of spring omelette, filled with fresh peas and mint. Then she announced that she would go to the market while he worked. For lunch that day they ate borlotti beans with pancetta, and a fish James could not identify but which Livia said was called *orata*, and highly sought after.

'My predecessor told me that seafood had an inconvenient effect on the libido,' James said thoughtfully as he wiped his plate with a piece of bread.

'That depends what you think is inconvenient,' Livia said enigmatically. 'There's a Neapolitan saying, too: fish for lunch, no sleep during siesta. But I think that's just because it's such a light meal.'

It was certainly true that after lunch he felt no need for a nap. But that may also have been because Livia hadn't served any wine. He hung around the kitchen, trying to engage her in conversation, but she seemed disinclined to talk to him. Eventually he gave up and went and lay down on his bed.

He couldn't get her out of his mind. Every time he closed his eyes he saw images of her, sliding into his brain: Livia laughing, Livia cooking, Livia's slim hands deftly cleaning a fish or scrubbing a potato; the flash of her eyes as she danced the tarantella. He groaned, and tried to think of something else, but it was no good. In his fantasies she was standing in front of him, unbuttoning the top of her dress . . .

A sudden sound at the door made him open his eyes. It was Livia, slipping into his room. A number of responses rushed through his mind, but he settled for, 'Oh, hello.'

She smiled. 'Hello.'

He felt stupid. An Italian would have greeted her with a stream of compliments and effusive protestations of love. But now his throat had gone dry. 'Livia . . .'

She was kicking off her shoes. Now she was climbing onto the bed. 'Such a huge bed,' she said, looking around. 'I've never slept in a bed like this before.' She glanced at him, to see that he had understood.

He reached for her. But for a moment, she held his hand in hers, making him wait.

'Now listen,' she said sternly, 'because this is something we need to be very clear about. In the village I come from, it is absolutely forbidden to make love until you are married. And this is a very good rule. Some things should be special.'

'Oh,' he said. Now he was confused. Had she not come here to sleep with him after all?

'So everyone is a virgin on their wedding day. But everyone is also very experienced at sex.'

He was getting more confused by the minute. 'I don't understand.'

Her smile broadened. 'Don't worry, you will soon. Just think of it as a meal without meat.' She slipped into his arms, wriggling against him, and her laugh – that delicious, throaty laugh, thick with promise – was suddenly very close to his ear.

Technically, he thought, I am still a virgin. Nothing has changed.

He lay on his back, with Livia snuggled against his side. Her sleeping breath tickled his armpit. When he looked down he could see one pink nipple, pressing against his ribs.

A virgin, but not a virgin. What a very Italian distinction. A rule that was not really a rule, but which turned out to have a very good purpose. Because he would, he knew, have been a fumbling idiot if he had tried to be a Casanova with her on his very first time. Instead, she had been able to show him what she liked, and show him what *he* liked, and he had all the time in the world to map that sleek beautiful body with his kisses, to caress her with his mouth and fingers, to hear the lovely gasps of pleasure whenever he did something she particularly liked.

He felt her stir. As she did so, the memory of everything they had done made him stir too, his cock thickening where it lay against his leg.

'Mmm,' she said, putting her hand on it. After a moment she began to stroke, brushing him gently with her slim fingers.

'I hope,' he said, 'that I can go on being a virgin for a very long time.'

'That can probably be arranged.' She increased the movement of her fingers slightly.

'Though if you're doing what I think you're doing,' he said after a moment, 'you might be a little premature.'

'*L'appetito viene mangiando*. Appetite comes with eating.'

After a little longer, he found that she was quite right.

As they started to explore each other's bodies again, the sound of jangling bells came through the window. Church bells, he thought, but not like the bells that rang every morning for Mass. They were ringing wildly, and he tensed, fearing some sort of alarm.

'It's all right,' she said, not stopping what she was doing. 'You know what that is, don't you?'

'I've really no idea,' he confessed.

She laughed. 'They're wedding bells. Someone's getting married.'

211

Thirty-three

He tried to work, but it was no use – his attention kept wandering as he experienced a series of delightful flashbacks to the afternoon's activities. Getting up from his desk, he went into the kitchen.

Livia was cooking. 'Hello,' he said, grinning at her. He felt ridiculously pleased with himself.

'Hello.'

'I'm finding it hard to work.'

'Me too.'

'And I'm ravenous, too. What's for supper?'

'Wait and see. But since you're here, would you come and stir this for me, please?'

He took the bowl of egg whites she handed him and gave it a stir. She watched, rather critically, he thought.

'Yes,' she said after a moment. 'I see what you're doing.'

'Is something wrong?'

'Too much force. And not enough wrist.' She put his hand on his and guided him. 'Like this. As if you're pushing it gently away from you, not bashing it. And move your hand around. It shouldn't always be in exactly the same place.'

'Does it really make that much difference?'

'Egg whites are funny things,' she said enigmatically. 'Sometimes they fold, and sometimes they don't. You're just a little – well, over-enthusiastic.'

'Oh,' he said. He had just realised that this conversation was not actually about egg whites at all. He slowed his movements, and tried to copy what she had just demonstrated. 'How's that?'

She watched him. 'Yes,' she nodded. 'That's really quite promising.'

*

The next morning she returned from the market with a large piece of beef.

'I'm wondering whether to grill it or stew it,' she announced. 'What do you think?'

He was flattered – she had never consulted him about a menu before. 'Well, a simple grilled steak is always nice,' he ventured.

'Yes,' she said thoughtfully. 'Yes, a lot of men think that. But it all depends how hot the stove is. If the stove is really, really high, you can just throw the meat on without thinking about it – it cooks quickly, without getting dry. But if the stove isn't quite so hot, you're better off going for a stew and simmering it slowly. Do you understand?'

He was becoming accustomed to this code by now. 'I think so, yes. So tell me, is the stove hot today?'

'Today, the stove is still fairly fierce,' she admitted. 'But that won't always be the case. We should practice making a stew, just in case.'

'It's a damn strange thing,' Major Heathcote said, 'but A-force seem to be having trouble finding any women of low repute for this disease-spreading scheme of theirs.'

'Really, sir?'

'Yes. Odd, when you consider we're putting over five hundred servicemen through the VD hospital every week. Makes you wonder who they're all sleeping with.'

'Yes, sir.'

'I hear A-Force have handed over responsibility for the rastrallymenties to the Italian police now. Though, frankly, I'd be surprised if that produces any better results. These Eyeties are as tricky as a brass sixpence.'

'Some do seem to be less than scrupulous, sir.'

'Hmm.' The major looked at him shrewdly. 'How about you, Gould?'

'Sir?'

'No problems I should know about?'

'Everything seems to be under control, sir.'

'Good.' Major Heathcote paused. 'Between you and me, I'm not too upset that disease thing didn't come to anything. I'm not saying you had anything to do with that, but . . . just watch your step. We don't want you going native.'

For lunch one day, Livia served the British officers a steaming dish of snails, which exuded a delicious aroma of garlic and tomato. James

213

looked around for a knife or fork, but Livia had not put any cutlery out.

'These are a real delicacy,' she said. 'We call them *maruzzelle*. They're harvested from plants that grow by the sea, which gives them a special salty flavour. Then we just cook them like this in their shells.'

Horris picked one up and looked at it doubtfully. 'In England we don't really eat snails. Or slugs, come to that.'

'There's a lot of things you don't do in England,' she said. 'Or so I gather.'

'What's that supposed to mean?' Horris asked suspiciously.

James had also picked up a shell, enticed by the rich, deep, earthy smell emanating from it. 'How do I eat this?'

'Just as it is.'

James put the mollusc to his lips and sucked. At first, nothing happened. 'You may have to loosen it,' Livia added.

He wriggled his tongue into the shell and sucked again. This time, the flesh moved a little. He wriggled harder, sucking at the same time, and felt a slither as the meat popped into his mouth, followed by the buttery juices. It was heavenly, and he gasped with pleasure.

One by one, with varying degrees of squeamishness and dexterity, the other officers followed James's example. Livia, however, seemed particularly interested in how James was doing. 'There are more juices in the shell,' she instructed, watching him. He pushed his tongue in again, working the tip around the shell's crevices until all the sauce was gone.

'That's fantastic,' he breathed as he put the empty shell down. 'Livia, you're a genius.'

'Good,' she said. She sounded pleased. 'Have another.'

When the snails were all gone she brought out a bowl of fresh peas, still in their pods. 'Now, the way to eat peas,' she explained, 'is quite like eating snails. You need to open the pod with your thumbs, like this.' She demonstrated. 'And then you need to put your tongue in and lick the peas up with it, like this.'

James tried to copy her, but all the peas rolled off onto the floor.

'It's a funny thing,' Jumbo said, 'but when I was in officer selection, they used to tell us that there was a proper way to eat peas too. But that was something to do with using a knife.'

James tried again. This time he managed to lick up all the peas except the very last one, the smallest one at the very tip of the pod. 'Can't quite get the last one,' he complained.

'It's the last one that's important,' she said. 'Trust me.'

Peas skittered over the table like tiny green marbles as the British officers tried to wrap their tongues around the elusive legumes. 'Actually, the knife was a lot easier,' Jumbo sighed.

'Don't worry; it comes with practice,' Livia said.

James waited until she was clearing the dishes, then followed her to the kitchen. 'Livia,' he said, putting down the empty dish he was carrying, 'what's all this about snails and peas?'

'Hmm,' she said. 'Well, they're both very interesting. Let me put it like this. Sometimes it's nice to have the peas first. Usually, though, you want to start with the snails, and then go onto a few peas, and then have a few snails again before you finish off the peas. But that's when you have to be sure to get the last one in the pod.'

'Well, that's as clear as mud.'

After lunch, though, when everything was quiet, she came to his room again, and suddenly it all did become clear. He realised then that the little cries of pleasure he had wrung from her previously were as nothing compared to the shuddering, gasping spasms he could elicit when he went from snails to peas, then back to snails, and finally worked his tongue under the very last pea in the pod.

It had never occurred to James that bed could be such a good place for talking. Sometimes in the long afternoon hours of the siesta it was hard to tell exactly where the talking ended and the love-making began, and those were the very nicest afternoons of all.

To begin with there were the secrets all lovers share: when did you first decide, and what does it feel like when . . . And then there were their upbringings, the comparisons between two countries that were completely different but also in strange ways similar. There were the friends they had each lost to the war, and the gossip about their new friends in Naples. Livia turned out to be a very good mimic – her take-off of Major Heathcote was quite brilliant, her only prop James's army hat as she strutted up and down stark naked, lambasting him – 'Captain Goo, you are a absaloo disgrease. Pull yoursel' two gather! You must be farm but fear wit dees Eyeties!' And then she would come back to bed, still laughing, and they would find other ways to continue the joke of his firmness with the Eyeties.

The body, he now understood, had its own language, somewhere between speech and silence. Sometimes it echoed the courtly, musical rhythms of Italian, at others the hard, urgent gutturals of Anglo-Saxon. And as with any language, one slowly became fluent, mastering the nuances, getting the accent right. There were so many unfamiliar intonations to practice: the gentle sibilance of a kiss, the delicate staccato of a tongue touching skin, the precise inflection of a gasp or moan – each one a complex burst of meanings, each one capable of being conjugated a dozen different ways.

In this language there were no phrase books and no dictionaries. You learnt to speak it by learning how to hear it, by trial and error, by saying back what had already been said to you. There was no one moment when you could say you'd finally got it, just a gradual realisation that no translation was needed any more – that what had been said was more important than how you'd said it, and that what you were doing together was not just sex, but the start of a long conversation.

Thirty-four

When the tin was full he took the money to Angelo. They had hit upon a simple way of transferring cash without arousing suspicion: James would eat a small meal, and Angelo would bring him an astronomical bill. James would then place a large pile of notes on the plate, thus reinforcing his own reputation as a fool who unnecessarily insisted on paying his own way.

Zi' Teresa's was fuller than ever these days. It might no longer be a place to secure a girl for your bed, but that was more than compensated for by the sheer beauty of the staff. From the sommelier to the cigarette seller, all were female and all were nice to look at, and if they also seemed to leave quite soon after they arrived, no one minded very much, since they were quickly replaced by others who were just as lovely.

One night, as James was leaving, Angelo murmured that he would like a quiet word around the back. James went to the kitchen door, where Angelo drew him to one side. 'A man will come and see you tomorrow,' he whispered. 'He has the information you require.'

The man who came next day was huge, a fat mountain of flesh who could barely fold himself into one of James's chairs. He did not introduce himself and he wasted no time on pleasantries.

'Zagarella has a mistress,' he said. 'She lives out at Supino, and that's where he keeps his stocks of penicillin. She has agreed to make sure he stays all night tonight, so you'll be able to arrest him in the morning.'

'Why is she doing this?'

The huge man shrugged. 'She has been shown a photograph of him with another woman. She is by nature very jealous.' He removed a piece

217

of paper from his pocket and held it out to James. 'The house is isolated. I have drawn you a map.'

Something about the man made James's skin crawl. The old adage about devils and long spoons came to mind. But it was too late for that now. He took the map and glanced at it. It seemed clear enough. 'Thank you.'

The man levered himself to his feet. 'Be very careful,' he said. 'Zagarella will certainly be armed.'

At that moment the door opened and Livia walked in. For a split second she and the fat man stared at each other. Then the fat man smiled.

'So this is where you have been hiding yourself, Livia,' he said.

'His name is Alberto,' she explained. 'He's been causing me trouble for years.'

'Well, he can't get at you here,' James said. 'You're under my protection now.'

'You don't understand,' Livia said flatly. 'To a man like that, information is power. And you've entrusted him with the most dangerous information of all – the information that you are breaking the law.'

'He's in this just as much as I am.'

'But you have more to lose.' She shook her head. 'Alberto's a pig, but he's a clever pig. You'll see, he'll find some way of twisting this to his own advantage.'

Seeing her looking so vulnerable stirred something deep in his heart. He took her in his arms. 'I swear you'll be safe,' he promised.

'Idiot!' she said, hitting him with her fist. 'It isn't me I'm worried about. It's you.'

He smiled at her. 'Then you really care about me?'

'*Porco dio!*' she fumed. 'Of course I do.'

'I wasn't sure.'

'Do you ever ask?'

'No,' he admitted.

'Well, now you know. So now you can promise me that you won't try to arrest this man Zagarella tomorrow.'

'Livia,' he said, 'I have to.'

'Rubbish.'

'It's my duty.'

'How can it be your duty?' she shouted. 'Your superiors would absolutely forbid it if they knew.'

'Don't you see – unless I do this, I'm just another corrupt intelligence officer.'

'So?'

'It's the opportunity I've been waiting for.'

'Oh?' she said. 'I thought *I* was the opportunity you were waiting for.'

'Of course you are. But I still have to do this.'

She threw up her hands. '*Tiene 'a capa sulo per spartere 'e rrecchie!** And I was stupid enough to think an Englishman might be different. Men are all the same, wherever they come from.'

'Livia—'

'Get out,' she cried. 'Go and get yourself killed. See what I care.'

They set off before dawn. The Italians had, as usual, dressed up for the raid in suits, spats and boaters, but something of James's mood must have communicated itself to them, and they were on less exuberant form than usual as the borrowed jeep rolled through the dark streets and onto the coast road heading north. The sun was rising by the time they found the place, a farmhouse just as remote as Alberto had promised. It was very still.

Too still, James thought. He didn't have much experience of farms, but surely they were never this quiet. Why were there no dogs barking? He motioned for Carlo and Enrico to draw their weapons.

He crept towards the front door. It was open. Stepping inside, he heard a sound – a baby, the muted half-cry of an infant that can't decide if it wants to sleep or to eat. He relaxed a little. At least there were people here, and alive. For a moment he had thought – but now he had to focus on the fact that a crying baby meant a waking mother. The element of surprise was vital. Pushing open the door where the noise had come from, he hurried through into a bedroom.

The man slumped against the wall was Zagarella, James was sure of that. He had been rising from the bed when someone had cut this red slice out of his windpipe, like a piece of watermelon. The woman in the bed had been stabbed as she slept: there was blood all over the mattress, a dark pool surrounding the body. And – horror of horrors – there was the baby, still attempting to suckle her lifeless breast. It lifted its head blindly as they entered, as if searching around for any mother who was not as cold as his was.

There was a movement beside him as Enrico crossed himself. James

* 'The only thing your head is good for is keeping your ears apart.'

heard the rumble of an approaching truck. Carlo went to the window.

'Men,' he said economically. 'Men with guns.'

'Soldiers?'

Carlo peered out. 'I can't be sure.'

'Come out with your hands up,' an American voice shouted.

'*Si*, soldiers,' Carlo said resignedly.

It was a disaster in every possible way. For a while he had wondered if Livia had sent the Americans after him, worried for his safety. But she swore she had not, and the Americans themselves said that they had simply received an anonymous tip-off. Even so, it required some fancy footwork to explain his own presence at the farmhouse in a way that satisfied his superiors' curiosity. A search of the farmhouse had not produced any clues. Nor had it turned up any penicillin, although there were signs that some crates had been hastily removed.

Jumbo's view was that James shouldn't worry. 'He's dead. You won.'

'But who killed him? And how did they know we were coming?'

'Probably a falling out between thieves. And as for the timing, that must be a coincidence. It couldn't have been the Americans, if you didn't tell them about the op in the first place.'

James knew he ought to feel triumphant. It was certainly a satisfaction to know that the pharmacist's boasts about the high-level protection he enjoyed had turned out to be hot air. But he could not help feeling uneasy. It was all too neat.

In an effort to find out more he took Dr Scottera for a drink at Zi' Teresa's. But the former fascist was not as hungry now as he had once been, and even the promise of egg-and-marsala failed to loosen his tongue.

'It's a mystery, Angelo,' James said gloomily when Dr Scottera had gone. 'Nobody knows anything.'

'You should ask yourself,' Angelo said thoughtfully, 'not "Who would want to kill him?" but "Who is better off because he is dead?"'

'Who?'

Angelo shrugged. 'Perhaps those who betrayed him were playing a double game. This way, they get rid of Zagarella, but they also get to keep his penicillin themselves.'

As the heat became fiercer, the atmosphere in Naples changed yet again. Arguments that in cooler weather would have led to florid exchanges of insults now ended quickly in stabbings. It was as if the citizens' passions were rising with the mercury, and it was all James could do to keep a lid on the waves of mass hysteria that quite suddenly gripped the city, like a panic, and then were gone again.

Rumours seemed to propagate like flies. A statue of Christ had climbed down from a crucifix in Pozzuoli and had led the congregation to the safety of the hills. The fascists were going to murder anyone who did not wear black shoes as a sign of their support. The king had demanded that all his loyal subjects wear their belts inside out. It was all nonsense, but even nonsense could be dangerous if it was allowed to get out of hand, and each wild allegation had to be investigated before it could be dismissed.

And yet James had to admit that it sometimes did feel as if something odd was happening. Take the case of the well at Cercola. He had a report from the British officer there that the water supply had been poisoned, and that the woman believed to be responsible had been arrested.

He drove out to investigate on the Matchless, grateful to exchange the stifling heat of the office for air moving on his face. It was certainly true that the water supply in Cercola had a fetid odour, like bad eggs. He tried a small mouthful, and immediately spat it out: it tasted vile.

'We thought at first someone had chucked a dead goat down the cistern,' the officer told him. 'But when we dragged it, there was nothing there. That's when we started to think it must be poisoned.'

James spoke to the woman who had been arrested, but it was clear that she had been fingered by the officer's informants only because they thought she was a *strega*, a witch, and any misfortune not explicable by other means should therefore be laid at her door. He had the woman released, and told the officer to ship in fresh water from the next village.

In the fields around Fico an entire flock of sheep was slaughtered, presumably by bandits. There was nothing very unusual about that, but according to the report of the local chief of police, the dead animals did not have so much as a scratch on them, nor had their killers taken any of the carcasses away. It was as if they had been killed by a fog.

In the Santa Lucia district of Naples the inhabitants were convinced that the Germans were setting off explosions in the catacombs. James had a priest admit him to the ancient tombs which stretched for miles under the city, and quickly came to the conclusion that there were no Germans down there – there was no light, no air, and anyone trying to hide in the pitch-black passages would quickly become lost. But he himself heard a distant booming sound under the ground, as if a cannon were being fired many miles away.

It seemed to him that these occurrences must be somehow linked to the earth tremors that now passed through Naples almost every day – more frequently, the older Neapolitans said, than at any time in living memory, a sure sign that the saints were displeased. He had long ago realised that the Neapolitans were essentially pagan in their religious observances, with saints fulfilling the roles of the lesser deities, but the fact that the Allies might be losing the support of the local population was a worry.

Yet he had Livia, and that was all that really mattered. After the lightest of lunches – *spiedini* perhaps, sticks of rosemary sharpened into skewers and passed through a few pieces of grilled octopus or fish; or a soup of fresh fava beans – they would retire to his room, where the feast that was on offer was infinitely more sumptuous. He came to know the different tastes of her body – the salty, delicate skin of her neck; the tips of her fingers, still bearing the flavours of her cooking; the sweet nectar of her mouth; the gentle perfume of her arms and thighs; her breasts, soft as fresh mozzarella. Even the taste of her sex was intoxicating, like the interior of some exotic fruit, bursting with sweet ripe juices.

He was sorry now he had fought with Eric. The truth was, they had simply had a hot-tempered falling out over a woman. Slowly, they started to become friends again, although there remained a slight awkwardness whenever the subject of Livia came up.

The first batch of fiancées was now all married, but a sizeable backlog had built up, and the bellringers of Naples were being kept busy. With the bars and restaurants open again, and few real restrictions on servicemen and Italians socialising together, there was also a steady trickle of new applicants wanting to see the wedding officer. James tried not to be a pushover, and if a girl was clearly unprepared for the life she would be leading after the war he would gently suggest that she came back to see him in a month or two, but in general he allowed love to take its natural course. How could he not, when he himself was so happy?

'James?'
'Mmm?'
'There's something I've been meaning to mention,' Livia said.
'Rightio.'
They were skinning tomatoes, and she paused to rinse some of the sticky skins off her fingers before she continued. 'Sometimes you're too polite.'

'Oh.' He thought about this. 'You see, one was rather brought up to *be* polite. Especially to the opposite sex and so on.'

'For example, while it's very nice,' she went on as if he hadn't spoken, 'that you always hold doors open for me . . .'

'Exactly. A case in point. A gentleman should always allow a lady to go first.'

'. . . there are certain *other* times,' she said significantly, 'when that doesn't apply.'

'It doesn't?'

'No.' She carried the pile of skinned tomatoes over to the sink. 'Well,' she admitted, 'sometimes it's nice that you make sure I . . . go first. But sometimes you shouldn't worry about it.'

'Ah.' He went and rinsed his own hands.

'When I cook a meal, I don't want everyone to sit there eating it with their elbows off the table, making polite small talk,' she explained. 'I want them to be greedy, and to stuff their faces, and to talk with their mouths full, and to reach across each other to try to steal the best bits off the plate, and maybe even make pigs of themselves a little bit. Because, you see, I have spent a long time preparing this meal, and half the pleasure of *that* is thinking about the pleasure other people will have when they eat it.'

'So you want me,' he said slowly, 'to make a pig of myself in bed?'

'Occasionally, yes.'

'No small talk?'

'No *polite* small talk. A compliment to the chef is always welcome.'

James is in bed with Livia, not lying down but sitting with their legs entwined, playing the game which, when James was a child, he always knew as 'slapsies', while Livia, it turns out, had known an identical game as '*schiaffini*', or 'little smacks'. The rules are simple. Each of them places their hands, palms together, in front of them, so that the ring fingers are just touching. Then they take it in turns to slap the back of the other person's hands. If the other person manages to avoid the blow, they get a turn instead. If they move before the slap has been initiated, or if the hitter lands a slap, the hitter gets another go.

And Livia, James is discovering, is quite extraordinarily good at slapsies. In fact, he only gets one to every dozen of hers, and even when he does manage to get a slap in, it's a light tap, sacrificing power for speed. Livia somehow manages to both land a blow before he can so much as twitch, and to make it such a resounding smack that the back of his hand now throbs as if it has been attacked by a dozen bees.

223

'Ow,' he says, as she slaps him again, and then a moment later, 'Ow –
Ow – Ow,' as she lands three more in quick succession. This time, he
thinks, he will be quicker to pull away.

'You moved,' Livia says, concentrating intently.

'No, I – ow.' While he was talking, she has taken the opportunity to
deliver a stinging crack with her left hand. 'Why are you so good at this?'
he sighs.

She slaps him again, with her right. 'Italian girls get a lot of practice at
slapping men. And I have very quick reactions.'

'Hah! My turn.' He hits her a hefty blow.

She protests, 'That's too hard.'

'But you hit me that hard.' This time he is a little gentler, and she
easily evades him, then slaps him back before he has even put his hands
together.

'Cheat – I wasn't ready.'

'So? I'm allowed to hit when I like.'

'Not in England, you wouldn't be.'

'Well, we're in Italy, so we're obviously playing Italian rules.' She slaps
him again, and he falls over backwards, pulling her with him. "Uh-uh,'
she protests. 'It's still my turn.'

'But I've stopped playing that game,' he explains, twisting her so that
she falls across his lap. 'And now I'm playing this one.' She arches her
back, and he smacks her experimentally across the buttocks, noting how
her eyes half-close with pleasure. So much of sex, he thinks, is actually
child's play. He remembers, though, not to be too polite, and this time he
ignores her yelps and protests until they turn into murmurs of satisfaction.

Afterwards he pulls on his shirt, and as he buttons it up she notices a
piece of paper in the breast pocket. 'What's this?' she asks, pulling it out.

'Oh.' He's embarrassed. 'It's a letter.'

'An important letter?' she asks, then answers her own question. 'Well,
of course it must be, if you keep it next to your heart.' She starts to
unfold it, then glances at him, suddenly serious. 'Is it from Jane?'

'Yes. She wrote that when she ditched me.'

'How long ago was that?'

'A long time. It was when I was in Africa.'

'But you pretended you had a girlfriend when you met me,' she
reminds him.

'Yes. That was stupid of me, wasn't it?'

'Very, because I knew you were lying, and that was what made me
think there must be another explanation. What was she like, anyway?'

He shrugs.

'Come on,' she protests. 'What was she like?'

'I don't really know,' he says slowly. And it's true: everything about Jane has vanished, like an English mist exposed to the fierce Italian sun of Livia's vitality. 'I think she was quite brave, though. Because it probably took quite a lot of guts to write that letter, and to decide that what we had wasn't good enough after all.'

'She was in love.'

'That always makes it easier,' he agrees. 'Anyway, tear it up.'

'I can't do that,' she protests.

'Then I will.' He takes the letter and rips it into a dozen pieces, tossing them into the air like confetti. It feels good. He is lying in bed with Livia, and nothing that happened in the past will ever matter again.

'One day you'll tear up my letters like that,' she says, suddenly sad.

'Never. Besides, we're never going to be apart, so you'll never need to write to me.'

One of his new wedding vettings was rather different from the rest. About a fortnight after the weddings started up again, Jumbo Jeffries stuck his head round the door. He was not looking quite so tired of late, something which he confided was partly due to a better diet, and partly because now that the war had moved on to a more aggressive phase he was obliged to spend more time away from Naples, blowing up bridges and slitting German throats. 'It's amazing what a few days' rest does for the constitution,' he explained. 'When I come back, it's as though I'm a new man.'

It turned out that Jeffries had come to see him about Elena. 'What with all these other girls getting married,' he said, stroking his moustache, 'it seems like a nice idea for us to tie the knot too. Actually, I was wondering if you'd like to be the best man.'

James assured him that he would be delighted, and said he would arrange for Elena to be vetted and receive the necessary papers forthwith – a mere formality, he promised his friend.

When the time for the interview came, however, Elena seemed a little preoccupied. Although her glass eye stared at James as unblinkingly as ever, her other gaze seemed to be fastened on the table.

'Is something wrong?' James asked gently.

Elena shrugged. Then after a moment she burst out, 'I don't want to marry him.'

'Ah.'

'I love Jumbo,' she said. 'I love him more than I've loved anyone. But I'm a whore, not a housewife. What will happen to me after the war is over? He'll want me to go back to England with him. It will be cold, and I've heard the food is disgusting. And we'll be poor as well. Jumbo's not clever like you: he's made for wars, not peace, and I don't think he'll ever be rich. I like my work here, and I like the freedom it gives me. Why should I have to give it up?'

It was a tricky problem. James asked her what she would do if a way could be found to avoid a marriage.

'I'd like to stay with Jumbo until the end of the war,' she said. 'After that, I should have another four or five years at the top, and with the money I save I'll open a whorehouse, the best whorehouse in Naples. Then,' she shrugged, 'my looks will be going, so perhaps I'll have to find someone to marry after all.'

'You could always tell Jumbo you don't accept his proposal.'

'But that will hurt his pride. He won't want to go on seeing me if I do that, and it seems a shame to end it sooner than we need to. Can't you help me somehow?'

It was hard to see how, but James promised to try to think of a solution.

After a few days he went back to see her. 'I've got it,' he said. 'We'll just have to pretend that you were married before, a long time ago, and you don't know what became of your original husband. Perhaps he ran away and abandoned you on your wedding night or something. Anyway, this being a Catholic country, getting a divorce will take a long time – perhaps you'll need a dispensation from the Vatican, and of course you can't get that while Rome's in German hands.'

'You're a genius,' she said delightedly. 'I'll tell Jumbo this evening. Now, how can I repay you?'

James assured her that he wanted no payment for making his friends happy.

'I know,' she said. 'But I want to do something for you. I suppose you don't want to sleep with me?'

James explained that, quite apart from any awkwardness it might cause with Jumbo, Livia would probably not be too keen on this idea.

'Then I shall repay you by talking to Livia,' she said mysteriously. He tried to find out what she meant, but she refused to be drawn any further.

The next day she and Livia closeted themselves in the kitchen, and cooked a slow *ragù* with the door firmly closed. From the shrieks of laughter coming from behind it, James gathered the conversation was going well, but when he asked Livia about it later she too became rather mysterious.

'We were just gossiping,' she said airily. 'Women's talk. You wouldn't be interested.'

The next time she came to his room, however, it turned out that she had acquired some rather intriguing new skills.

'I think I can guess who taught you *that*,' he said, after one particularly virtuoso episode. 'Though I can't quite imagine how.'

'She demonstrated on the courgettes,' she said. 'But it wasn't all one way. I showed her how to make my special *sugo*.'

'I suppose it's too much to hope that I still have any secrets left? Or does the whole of Naples know what we're up to?'

'Oh, Elena is very discreet, for a Neapolitan. She has to be, given her profession. Although I did find out why he's called Jumbo.'

'Ah.'

'Let's just say she picked a bigger courgette than I would have,' she teased. But he couldn't be offended, because it was soon time to start the virtuoso activities all over again.

He knew better now than to try to categorise what it was they did together, to file each afternoon's activities under one of Burton's myriad positions. When she climbed on top of him, gripping his hips with her fingers, and rubbed herself with a rocking motion back and forth along the length of his penis, or rolled him between her hands like dough, or knelt over him, as she did now, slipping him into her mouth, it was not as yet another item in a list, to be ticked off like a sightseer's experiences, or even a recipe that could be duplicated the next time it was made: it was simply *sfiziosa*, the whim of the moment; and like the moment, it was no sooner felt than it was gone again, never to be recaptured.

He was still, he supposed, technically a virgin, although the distinction had become so very technical that determining his exact status would have required a debate of almost theological complexity. There seemed to be an infinite number of graduations of sexual experience still left to work through, as many as there might be angels dancing on the head of a pin.

Sometimes, when their bodies were sated with love-making, they worked at Livia's English.

'I wud lick uh pant beater pliss.'

'A – pint – *of* – bitter.'

'Uh – pant – *urve* – beater. Pliss.'

'Certainly, Madam. I will pour your pint of bitter straight away.'

'Gems,' she said thoughtfully in Italian, 'will I like beer?'

He scratched his chin. 'Some girls do.'

'But why do they call it "bitter"? Bitter means sour, doesn't it?'

'Sort of.' He switched back to English. 'That will be sixpence, please.'

She sighed. 'Du u hev sharnge for m' tin-burb knot?'

'I have plenty of change for your ten-bob note.'

'This money is *pazzo*,' she complained. '"Bobs" and "tanners" and "haypenny bits". And what on earth is "half a crown"?'

'Two shillings and sixpence.'

'So a crown is—'

'Ah. There's no such thing,' he explained helpfully. 'Well, there is, but it sits on the King's head and is worth a fortune. Don't worry, you'll soon get the hang of it. You just need to remember to count in twelves, not tens.'

'Huh,' she said. She put her hand on his upper thigh. 'Enough English, for now.'

He ignored her. 'Tell me how you'd ask for a ration of margarine.'

'What's "margarine"?'

'It's – um – a little bit like lard. Or goose fat. You know, for cooking.'

'*Goose fat* is rationed? Why don't you just cook a goose and keep the fat?'

Perhaps English food was not the right subject to dwell on. He tried to think of something more appealing about his homeland. 'Shall I introduce you to the King?'

'If you like,' she said, stroking the sensitive dish of skin between his hip and his groin experimentally with her thumb.

'Good evening, your Majesty.'

'Gud ayvening, you matchstick.'

'May I have the honour of presenting my wife?'

'Ver' gled to meter you, your matchstick. And now I kiss you cock.' Livia giggled, and slid down the bed the better to fit her actions to her words.

James did not reply, partly because what Livia was doing was extremely pleasant, and partly because he had just called her his wife.

Of course, they both knew that there was only one reason why she was learning his language: because of the unspoken possibility that she would one day go to live in England with him, and order pints of beer in pubs. Yet it was still just that: an assumption, not yet discussed directly, and certainly not formally proposed.

Livia gave a little 'hah!' of satisfaction at what her kisses had achieved.

She ran her tongue all the way from the base to the very tip. Her eyes, mischievous and solemn at the same time, fixed on his as she kissed and nibbled and flicked and finally, with a sigh of contentment, took him all the way into her mouth.

At that moment he knew without a doubt that he wanted this to be his whole life. Her generosity, her passion, her sensuality – he loved her.

'Livia,' he began.

'Mmmm?'

He hesitated. Perhaps this was not, after all, the moment. A proposal made when your girl was giving you a perfect, languid blow job might be considered a slightly frivolous way of launching the serious undertaking of matrimony. There should be flowers, moonlight, candles – there should be a ring, for God's sake, and the suitor should have gone down on one knee, his boots and belt smartly polished, not be lying sprawled half-naked across a dilapidated four-poster, squirming with ecstasy as his lover went down on *him*.

He closed his eyes, his hips twitching involuntarily as she teased him with her teeth.

A proposal required planning and forethought. That was what he was good at, after all: he might as well get it absolutely right.

As he pulled her up and kissed her, unable to wait any longer, another thought slid unbidden into his mind. It would have to be a secret engagement. If the army forbade the wedding officer from marrying, they would hardly be happy if he got himself a fiancée.

Thirty-five

Despite the thick stone walls and the wooden shutters at the windows, the heat in the apartment was unbearable. James sat at his desk, trying to write a report. Every so often he stopped to wipe his face with a handkerchief. Even writing was difficult: the pen kept slipping from his grasp.

He heard a tiny sound and looked up. Livia was leaning against the open door, barefoot.

'Hello,' he said. 'How long have you been there?'

'Not long.'

'Did you want something?'

She pulled a face. 'It's hot.'

'Isn't it?' he agreed. He indicated the report. 'I've got to finish this, unfortunately.'

'You want me to go away?' She opened a button on her dress and began fanning her neck with her open hand.

'No, of course not, but – duty calls, unfortunately.'

'Yes, of course.'

He wrote another sentence, then looked up again. She was still there, and it seemed to him she had undone another button. 'I can't really work with you watching me,' he explained.

'Yes, I noticed.'

'And I really do need to finish this report.'

Five minutes later she was back. 'I brought you some cold lemon,' she said, putting the glass down in front of him.

'That's very kind.'

'It's too hot to work, isn't it?' she said, picking up one of his files and using it to fan herself with instead of her hand. A page flapped free and wafted to the floor.

'I can't do anything about the weather, unfortunately,' he said, picking up the stray page and taking the file back from her.

'And I've got nothing to do. The food is already in the oven.'

'Ah,' he said. He wrote a note describing the actions taken to suppress looting in the main art gallery, and turned his attention to the theft of an army film projector. 'Why don't you take a siesta?'

'That's a good idea,' she said, brightening. 'Will you take one?'

'I can't, unfortunately.' He scanned a note about a GI who had been charging wealthy Italians five-hundred lire not to have their cars requisitioned, and wrote 'Recommend arrest' at the bottom.

'Too busy fighting your war.'

'I suppose so.'

'What important military secrets you must be dealing with. Tell me, what is it today? Have you got a new invasion plan? Or is that one of Hitler's special communiqués you're reading?'

'It's not exciting,' he muttered. 'But it does have to be done.'

She watched him a little longer. 'Perhaps I'll take a bath.'

'That's a good idea.'

'Knock if you need to come in.' The bath was in the kitchen, so privacy was minimal.

'Don't worry. I expect this'll keep me occupied for a while yet.'

After a few moments he heard her padding to the door, followed by the sound of running water.

For five minutes there was peace, then he heard her singing in the bath. He did his best to ignore it, but it was impossible. With a sigh he got to his feet and went to investigate. The door to the kitchen had been left open. Livia was in the bath, almost submerged, only her breasts and knees breaking the surface, warbling. He watched her for a moment, closed the door, then went back to his office and closed that door too.

The next interval of quiet lasted almost ten minutes. Then, without warning, his door suddenly swung open. An arm came in. He just had time to identify it as Livia's, and to see that it was holding something small and round and red, before it hurled the red object at his desk. A very ripe tomato exploded on his open file.

'What the—' he began. A second arm hurled another tomato at his chest, where it scored a direct hit on his uniform.

231

'You bloody – *cow*,' he said, outraged.

There was a giggle from the other side of the door. 'You're the one who likes wars.' She ran off, and he heard the door to the kitchen bang shut.

He surveyed the mess with a sigh, and began to dab at the soiled papers with a handkerchief. Then his door opened again. He had just turned remonstrate when another tomato caught him full in the forehead.

'That's it,' he fumed, striding into the kitchen after her. She was using the bottom half of her dress as a receptacle into which she was loading half-a-dozen tomatoes. 'This is not acceptable,' he snapped. She threw a tomato, which he intercepted in mid-air before it hit him. She hurled another, and he caught that too. They were good catches, and he could see that she was rather surprised by them.

'I think you'll find,' he said tersely, 'that the skills of an Uppingham first eleven wicketkeeper are more than a match for your nonsense.'

'But both your hands are now full,' she pointed out, throwing another tomato. This one caught him on the chest.

He hurled the tomato in his right hand back at her. It exploded on her shoulder. 'Ow!' she yelled.

'Serves you right.' He threw the other one. It, too, was bang on target.

She retaliated with a bad lob that missed him and spattered harmlessly on the wall behind. With a cry of annoyance she ran at him and simply squashed all the fruits in her lap between the two of them, covering them both with a red mess. He grabbed her wrists, pulling her arms behind her back, and then she was kissing him, and the urgency of their fight became something else entirely. She was biting at his mouth with sharp little teeth, her hands were under his shirt, alternately scratching and stroking, and then his own hands were impatiently lifting off her dress. She pulled away from the kiss just long enough to say, 'Yes, James, now,' as the dress came over her head. She wasn't wearing anything underneath, and her skin was still damp from her bath. She reached for his trouser buttons. And then she was guiding him inside her – so warm, and so easy, like dipping your fingers into olive oil. He stopped, savouring the moment, and she smiled as she brought her arms up and slid them round his neck. Languidly, she lifted one leg and wrapped it round his buttocks, setting in train a whole new series of pleasurable sensations.

'So,' she murmured happily, tilting her head for another kiss.

From the other room an impatient voice called, 'Gould?'

'*Fuck!*' James said. 'It's the fucking CO.' He pulled out of her and grabbed his trousers. They were covered with tomato pulp. '*Fuck!*'

Livia giggled.

'It's hardly funny,' he hissed.

'Here, I'll scrape it off,' she offered. 'No, look – take a towel. He'll think you were having a bath.' She looked at the towel as he wrapped it round himself. 'Though you might want to hold it a bit more loosely at the front.'

Major Heathcote wanted to discuss an involved, and to James unimaginably tedious crisis involving accommodation for staff officers. James hurried him along as much as he could, trying all the time to conceal the squashed tomatoes on his desk, but by the time he went back to the kitchen people were gathering for dinner. Horris was telling an interminable story about a nine-year-old Italian boy who had been caught red-handed in possession of an entire lorry-load of cigarettes. Livia caught James's anguished glance and shrugged helplessly.

'Would you crush me some pepper, Captain Gould?'

He got the pestle and mortar out. Thumping the heavy stone pestle into the bowl, he felt a vicarious satisfaction as the peppercorns gave way beneath the force of his blows. Smash . . . Smash . . . Smash.

'Steady,' Livia murmured as she passed him on her way to the stove. 'You could hurt someone like that.'

He did not reply, but only banged the pestle even harder.

'Here,' she said, putting her hand on his and showing him. 'You're trying to crush them, not pulverise them. Like this. Slow and smooth.' She took her hand away and watched him for a moment. 'Yes, I think you've almost got it.' There was just a hint of wicked laughter in her eyes.

Only much later, as he ate dinner, did it occur to him that, technically, he probably wasn't a virgin any more. It didn't feel like much of a milestone.

Thirty-six

James was shaving when the seismologist came to see him. Or rather, he was trying to shave: the water supply, always spasmodic, appeared to have dried up again, and the trickle of rusty water that came from the tap was nowhere near sufficient for his needs. Irritably, he started to wipe the shaving soap off. There wasn't really enough stubble on his cheeks to justify a shave, anyway, something which still irked him – although it had been a revelation that Livia actually seemed to like his hairless face and torso, stroking his chest and back with exclamations of pleasure.

At the thought of Livia his irritation deepened. She'd gone back to her family for a few days, and although he would have liked nothing better than to go with her, conditions in Naples were too fraught for him to take leave just at present. At least she was safer where she was, away from the bombing. There had been a particularly unpleasant raid the previous night, and he was suffering from lack of sleep, to add to lack of Livia and lack of Livia's cooking.

There was a knock on the bathroom door, and Carlo put his head around it. 'There's a professor here to see you. A man by the name of Bomi. He knows all about earthquakes, apparently. Shall I send him away?'

'No, I'll see him,' James said, wiping his hands with a towel. 'Put him in the office, will you?' It might be useful to get an idea of when the earthquakes might stop. They didn't seem to worry the Neapolitans, but they certainly disturbed the servicemen, who were never sure if what they were experiencing was a tremor or the first salvo of a German raid.

Professor Bomi was a short, distinguished-looking man in a state of some agitation. He had initially tried to speak to the commander of the airstrip at Terzigno, he explained, and had been referred instead to the commander of the supply depot at Cercola, who had in turn referred him

234

to AMGOT, which had sent him around a dozen different departments, none of which had shown the slightest interest in what he was trying to tell them. And so, by an irresistible process of sifting, he had eventually ended up at the Palazzo Satriano. It had taken him three days to get this far, he said, and now he hoped James was going to do him the courtesy of actually listening to what he had to say.

With an inward sigh James settled himself in his chair and prompted, 'So this is about the earthquakes, I understand?'

Bomi shrugged. 'Possibly, yes. The earthquakes may be part of it, they may not. Pliny says that there were an unusual number before the eruption of 79.'

'I don't understand. What does Pliny have to do with it?'

'You have read my report, haven't you?'

James admitted that not only had he not read the professor's report, he had until that moment not been aware of its existence.

'But my report—' The professor checked himself. 'Never mind. I'm here now, and you're listening, that's the main thing. What my report says, essentially, is this: Vesuvius is becoming active.'

'Are you sure?' James glanced out of the window. The mountain looked much as it always had, although he noticed that the little wisp of smoke that usually hung over the summit was absent. 'It looks all right to me.'

Professor Bomi made an impatient gesture. 'That's because we're eight miles away, and you can't see that part of the cone wall has collapsed right into the crater. It's completely blocked. That's why there isn't any smoke.'

'Is it dangerous?'

'You have heard of Pompeii, presumably?' the professor demanded dramatically.

'Hang on a minute here.' James stared at him. 'Are you saying there's going to be another eruption like the one that destroyed Pompeii?'

The *professore* became markedly less agitated. 'Well, of course one can't say *that* for certain. The last time Vesuvius became active, in 1936, we simply saw some new lava flows – very fine lava flows, as it happens, although they didn't do much damage. But the time before that, in 1929, one flow reached almost to the sea and destroyed two towns. It's very unpredictable.'

'And what are you suggesting? Presumably your report makes some recommendations.'

The idea that anyone should actually act on his report appeared to take the professor by surprise. He shrugged. 'You must certainly evacuate everyone within twenty miles of the volcano.'

'But that would mean evacuating Naples. You're talking about dozens – possibly hundreds – of military installations. Tens of thousands of people. Where would they all go?'

'That's not my concern. I'm just telling you what might happen if they remain.'

'But what are the chances of this eruption you're talking about actually happening?'

The professor shrugged again. 'Who can say?'

James felt he wasn't really getting anywhere. 'Let me put this another way – what is it that makes you think that another Pompeii is more likely now than it was, say, six months ago?'

'Ah. A very good question.' The professor took off his glasses and polished them. 'Well, we've seen some very interesting portents recently. Not just the earthquakes. There have been some unusual sulphuric emissions. Wells have run dry, or been tainted. This may be a sign of tectonic movements.'

Sulphur. That explained the sour water James had smelt out at Cercola. A thought struck him. 'These emissions – could they kill sheep?'

'Possibly. Pliny describes a kind of poisonous miasma close to the ground. Grazing animals would be particularly at risk.'

So the sheep he had thought slaughtered by bandits might simply have been suffering from gas poisoning. 'This is Pliny the Younger we're talking about, presumably?'

'Exactly.' The professor beamed his approval at James's classical education. 'He witnessed the whole thing from his uncle's boat. Ever since, that pattern of activity – lava fountains, and a great plume of smoke that he described as being shaped like a pine tree – has been known as a Plinian eruption.'

'And if the volcano does erupt, which way will the lava flow?'

The professor threw up his hands. 'Who knows? It depends on the underground pressure, the way the land falls, even the winds. Do you have a map?'

James got a map of the area, and the professor showed him where previous lava flows had gone. 'San Sebastiano and Massa are the towns most frequently affected,' he explained. James remembered the frozen, black, glassy lava streams he had seen in San Sebastiano. 'Then Terzigno, Cercola, Ercolana and Trecase.'

There was an airfield at Terzigno, and Cercola was a military base. 'I'd

236

better warn them,' James decided. 'What about Fiscino? Is that in any danger?'

'Not especially, but who can say? The one predictable thing about a volcano is its unpredictability.'

For a scientist, James reflected, Professor Bomi seemed to take considerable satisfaction in his lack of knowledge. 'And when is the situation likely to resolve itself, one way or the other?'

'Who can—'

'Just give me your best guess,' James added quickly.

'There is some evidence that eruptions are most likely around the time of the full moon,' the professor said reluctantly. 'When the tidal pull is at its greatest. The best thing would be to keep the crater under close watch, but unfortunately my observatory has been taken over by the military.'

'Do you want me to see if I can get it back for you?'

The professor expressed such effusive gratitude that James began to suspect that a desire to observe any activity at close quarters, rather than the issuing of a warning, had been the main reason behind his visit. 'I'll see what I can do,' he said. 'But don't expect any miracles. There's a war on, and I doubt whether any amount of seismic activity is going to make people stop doing what needs to be done.'

When the professor had gone James went to the window. He had become so used to Vesuvius as simply a picturesque part of the view that it was a shock to remember that it was, in fact, a vast bomb – a bomb more powerful, and potentially more destructive, than any that man had ever devised. Now that he thought about it, there was a kind of brooding malevolence in the way the volcano squatted over the city, like some gargantuan looming stronghold, dominating the lives of every citizen. He felt a momentary twinge of fear for Livia. If it did erupt, what would happen to her? He wished there were some way of getting a message to her, but so far as he knew there were no telephones in her village.

He could, however, telephone the airfield at Terzigno. Eventually he got through to the American commanding officer, who informed him that an entire wing of B-25 bombers had recently arrived there – eighty-eight in all, the largest concentration of air power in the south. James asked if there was anywhere else they could be moved to, and explained about the professor's warning.

'You're not seriously saying we should change our dispositions just because some Italian's got the wind up?' the man asked incredulously.

James murmured that it might be as well to have some contingency plans, just in case.

'Only last week someone wanted us to evacuate because a statue in the local church had started crying,' the other man pointed out. 'These Italians are extraordinary. The German raids don't seem to faze them at all, but if they see two magpies in a row, or there's a ginger cat sitting on the steps of the church, they'll confidently predict that the end of the world has started.'

James had little more success with the troops stationed at the observatory, who informed him that the volcano was, if anything, less active now than it had been in the previous few months. 'Apart from a fairly unpleasant smell, all's quiet up here,' an officer told him. 'We don't even get these earthquakes they're reporting in Naples.'

'When you say a smell – is it sour, like something rotten?'

'That's right.' The officer seemed surprised. 'How did you know?'

'It's sulphur.' James managed to persuade the officer to let Professor Bomi have one room of the observatory back, but he felt increasingly uneasy about the situation.

He drafted a brief note which summarised the professor's predictions, together with a suggestion that contingency plans should be made for a limited evacuation of both the military and the civilian population, and submitted it to Major Heathcote. The major's response, not surprisingly, was an eruption on a scale which, had it been recorded by Pliny the Younger, might well have become known as Heathcotian, in which the words 'incompetent', 'foolhardy' and 'nothing better to do' featured several times. James was left in no doubt that the major did not consider the professor's observations to be a military priority.

To settle his mind, he spoke to Angelo, who smiled when he heard Bomi's name. 'Don't worry, my friend. That *professore* is always saying that a big disaster is overdue – he's been saying it for years, to my knowledge. But that's his job, isn't it? It's just like a priest saying that if you don't go to church the sky will fall in.'

'One day, statistically, he's going to turn out to be right,' James pointed out.

'Sure, but in the meantime he's worrying, so we don't have to.'

There was something wrong with the logic of this, but James had given up trying to fathom the fatalism of the Neapolitan mind.

As he sat alone in his room that night, he could not shake off the thought of Livia, perched up there on the mountain as if on the shoulder of a

238

sleeping giant. If it woke, what would become of her? What would become of all the Vesuviani? It was the most extraordinary folly that led them to repopulate the mountain after each eruption in any case. But that was Italians for you. They lived for today, cheerfully improvising a response to whatever calamities their lack of organisation or forethought had brought down on them.

But it wasn't his way. Abruptly, he pulled a notepad towards him. Bomi had said there would probably be two phases to the eruption, one in which the mountain spewed lava and ash, and another, potentially much more deadly, in which gases and smoke exploded into the air. That meant there would be a brief window of opportunity in which to deal with the situation. First there would have to be a reconnaissance to establish which towns and villages were directly threatened. Trucks would be needed to evacuate the population – no, not trucks, not immediately: the first thing would be fire engines, to deal with burning buildings. *Then* the trucks could come in – say a hundred of them. There would have to be military police to direct the traffic – perhaps even a temporary one-way system, one road taking trucks up the mountain, another bringing them back . . . He was making notes on his pad now, compiling a neat list of what would be needed. Temporary HQ . . . food distribution centres . . . fresh water . . . fodder for displaced animals . . . the list went on and on. People wouldn't want to abandon their possessions: the army would have to help them load up onto the trucks what they couldn't bear to leave. And then they must be prevented from going back too soon, by force if necessary. That meant army units, with weapons and ammunition in case there really was a panic. There would have to be temporary accommodation, perhaps in cinemas . . . He was planning a battle, he realised, a battle in which the enemy was a force of nature rather than a division of Germans, but the principles were the same. Establish objectives, work out a strategy, organise a chain of command. It was strangely exhilarating.

It was several hours before he was done. His plan was over twenty pages long, meticulously detailed. But it had been, he realised, a complete waste of time. He had become that most contemptible of creatures, a jobsworth; an armchair general, buried in his paperwork. The best that could be said of his plan was that it had filled the Livia-less hours between work and sleep.

He tossed the document onto the floor and put it from his mind.

If she was honest, Livia had to admit to herself that one reason she had gone back to Fiscino for a few days was because she needed to think about what was happening with James. What had started as an affair based on friendship and flirtation – and yes, since she was now being honest, an opportunity to fulfil a long-neglected physical need – was quickly becoming much, much more. It was not only because James was inexperienced that she had insisted on a courtship along traditional lines. She had imagined that by putting a limit on their physical intimacy, it would also put a limit on her emotions. But it hadn't worked out like that.

Sometimes her growing passion frightened her – not because she didn't want to fall more deeply in love with James, because that was exhilarating and wonderful, but because she could see more clearly than he could what the consequences might be. And soon, inevitably, she would have to make a decision. Would she be one of the thousands of Italian girls crowded onto the war bride ships, heading off for a new life in a cold, foggy country? Or would she be like Elena, whose self-sufficiency she admired, but who would be left all alone after the war? And what would it mean for her family if she did go back to England with James – for her father and Marisa, and the restaurant, which couldn't possibly survive without her?

She sat outside on the terrace and talked it over with Marisa, whose view was that she should make the most of it. 'You could always start another restaurant in England,' she suggested.

'I don't think I could,' Livia said. 'James says they've had rationing for so long, they don't remember what proper food is. They boil their vegetables for twenty minutes– can you imagine? – and they only eat tomatoes once or twice a year, always raw, in salads. How can one cook for people like that?'

'If you love him,' her sister declared, 'that's all that matters.'

Livia made a face. 'It's easy to see *you've* never been married.'

Marisa threw up her hands. 'And when did *you* become so practical?'

Livia was about to reply when her attention was distracted by a cloud of black, fluttering objects that poured out of the woods above the house. 'Bats,' she said, puzzled. 'Why are they coming out in the sunlight? And so many of them, too.'

Marisa followed her gaze. 'They've been doing that all week,' she said. 'At night we don't see them, but during the day they come out in swarms and fly over the trees. I've never seen anything like it.'

'Something must have disturbed the caves where they sleep. Perhaps it's the bombings.'

'Perhaps.' Marisa paused. 'Livia, I've been seeing things.'

'What sort of things?'

'Fires. Burning. People. I can't see the faces, but I know they're terrified.'

Livia caught her breath. 'Vesuvius?'

'I don't know. But have you noticed the summit isn't smoking? And then there's Priscilla's milk.'

'What's wrong with it?'

Marisa took her into the kitchen, where there was a bucket of water containing the previous day's *mozzarelle* and a pail full of the latest batch of milk. Livia tried the mozzarella first. It broke open in her hands as it should do – soft white chunks, as light as bread. But when she put some in her mouth it had a faintly sour taste.

'Sulphur,' she said at once. She tried the milk next. It had the same taint.

'This is last night's milk,' Marisa said. 'This morning, she wouldn't give any at all.'

'It must be coming up into the grass,' Livia said.

'What does it mean?'

'I don't know. Perhaps something is happening underground, something that has disturbed the bats' caves, and it's somehow making sulphur seep out of the ground as well. But I think we should tell someone.'

'Who?'

'I'll try to get a message to James. He'll know what to do. We could go up to the observatory – there's a radio there.'

They set off after lunch, keeping to the woods where it was shady. In addition to the strange behaviour of the bats, there were other unusual phenomena. A stream which brought spring meltwater down the side of the mountain had dried up. But further up the path, a meadow that was normally dry was now soggy and wet, steaming where the sun caught it. And the *upupa* birds, the hoopoes which normally filled the woods with their bubbling call, were strangely silent.

Emerging from the trees, they followed a goat track that spiralled around the south flank of the mountain towards the summit. Occasionally they crossed black, glittering lava flows from previous eruptions. Livia tried to imagine them as molten rivers of fire, burning everything in their path, but it was impossible. The mountain was simply too peaceful.

It was early evening by the time they finally reached the observatory.

It was a grander building than its name suggested, built in the ornate style in which the Bourbons designed all their public buildings, somewhat incongruous here on the summit of a mountain. Beneath them, the bay stretched out to the horizon, and Naples itself looked very small.

The observatory was full of the usual military clutter – radios, binoculars, camp beds, makeshift tables and chairs. As the two girls entered, a British officer got to his feet and doffed his cap politely.

Livia explained why they were there. He listened attentively, asking an occasional question.

'So to summarise,' he said when she had finished, 'you think that the behaviour of the animals may be linked to an increased possibility of eruption?'

'Exactly,' Livia said.

Emboldened by his interest, Marisa said, 'And I've been seeing things – premonitions.'

Livia had feared that the officer might be put off by Marisa's visions, but he only said, 'Really? Would you tell me about them?'

Marisa explained what she had glimpsed, and he nodded. 'I see. Well, what do you think we should do?'

Livia asked if he could get a message to James at FSS headquarters, and he said that he would include it in his evening report. 'In the meantime,' he added, 'would you stay and have a drink with me? There's a bottle of wine around somewhere, and the sunsets up here are spectacular.'

Livia explained that they needed to get back to Fiscino before dark. Thanking him profusely, they left.

When they had gone the officer picked up his binoculars and followed their progress down the track. What a shame, he thought wistfully. He had been sitting up here for tedious hour after tedious hour, scanning the horizon for German planes and warships, and the two beautiful Italian girls had been a welcome distraction. Now they had gone there was once again absolutely nothing to do. He had no intention of passing on their anxieties to HQ – he knew what the intelligence people would say if he started including that sort of nonsense in his report. There was an Italian professor due to come up here to take a look at the volcano sometime, once his papers had been processed. He'd tell him about the bats. It was just the sort of thing a professor would get excited about.

The girls were almost out of sight, walking in that lovely sensual way Italian girls had. Then they reached a bend in the track, and were gone. The officer sighed, and redirected his binoculars towards the empty sea.

It really was a most remarkable sunset. It would be a beautiful night, as well: they were due a full moon.

In Naples, people were more fearful than usual, but only because of the moon. These full moons were called 'bombers' moons', when cloudless days gave way to bright, silvery nights which needed no flares to illuminate the German aircrews' targets. Many citizens, fearing the worst, went to the air raid shelters to sleep.

In his bedroom, James stared out of the window at the silhouette of Vesuvius. He had heard nothing from Livia, and nothing from the professor, so perhaps he was worrying unnecessarily. But he could not shake off a sense of dread. Touching his breast pocket, he found the bone the priest had given him in the cathedral. He wished he had thought of giving it to Livia, then checked himself. You're becoming as superstitious as an Italian, he thought. He closed the shutters and climbed into bed.

He awoke just before dawn to the sound of bombs falling. No, not bombs, he thought: there were no air raid sirens. It must be a summer thunderstorm. A series of deep booming cracks were rolling across Naples, each one collecting its own echoes as it did so, so that after a little while they seemed to become one continuous rumble, punctuated by further booms. But it was a strange time of day for a storm. He went to the window and pulled back the shutters.

Yesterday, the top of Vesuvius had been round, like an egg in an eggcup. This morning the tip of the mountain had been sliced off, and a great bulbous cauliflower of ash-grey smoke sat on top of it, glistening in the first faint light of dawn. From here it appeared motionless, but the rolling waves of sound indicated the continuing force of the explosions within. Underneath the ash cloud, the top of the mountain was actually glowing red-hot, like a wick inside a candle. Two jagged, fiery trails spilled from the rim. James stared, mesmerised by the immensity of what he was witnessing.

The phone was ringing. He ran through to the office and snatched it up. A distant voice said, 'I wish to report some observations of unusual activity in the vicinity of Mount Vesuvius.'

'It's erupted, you idiot,' he shouted. 'Get off the line.' As he put it down it rang again.

'I don't suppose you did anything about those contingency plans?' Major Heathcote asked.

'As it happens, sir, I did.'

'Now might be a good time for me to take a look at them.'

James went and pulled on his clothes, his mind racing. Eric ran in and headed straight for the window. 'Holy smoke,' he said, awed. 'It's true.'

'The first thing is to get out there and find out which way the lava is heading. Then we'll need to evacuate the area. It's all in the plan.'

While James dug out his plan and organised a stenographer to make copies, Eric got on the telephone. 'They've got lava fountains in five different places,' he reported. 'Mainly around San Sebastiano and Massa.'

'Can we get trucks?'

'There are forty K60s at Cercola.'

'Let's get them moving towards San Sebastiano.'

'I'm onto it,' Eric said, dialling.

'And I'll go out there and see what's happening.'

'I'll come too. We'll take one of the jeeps.'

'A jeep will never get through the traffic,' James said. 'I'll take the Matchless – it's quicker.'

'I could get on the back.'

'It'll make it less manoeuvrable. And besides, if you come with me I won't have any room to bring Livia back.' He suddenly remembered. 'Oh Lord – there's a whole wing of B-25s at Terzigno.'

'Should we get them to take off?'

James shook his head. 'The eruption could last for days. We shouldn't move them unless we absolutely have to, or they might end up with nowhere to land. I'll take a look while I'm out there.'

He ran down the stairs and pulled the motorbike off its stand.

Thirty-seven

It was the most awesome thing he had ever seen. The sheer scale of it was breathtaking – nature's vast power effortlessly dwarfing the puny bombs and bullets of mankind's insignificant little conflict. He did not feel afraid. It was too mesmerising for that. Rather, there was a strange excitement at the prospect of plunging into the middle of it, of seeing what it was really like.

Beyond Torre Annunziata, at the foot of the mountain, he seemed to enter a dim fog, like an English winter's evening. For a moment he thought it was snowing; then he realised that the light grey flakes swirling all around him were not snow but ash. Already it was piling up on roofs, dusting the world with drifts of grey. He braked sharply to avoid a woman who was running across the road in her underwear to retrieve her ruined washing from a line. Instantly the Matchless skidded, sliding away from under him. He must be more careful, he thought, as he picked himself up and remounted: he hadn't realised the ash would be so slippery.

Refugees loomed out of the greyness, pushing their possessions in carts. Individual scenes stood out in the mayhem: a child stumbling along on crutches; a very old man being pushed along by his daughters in a wheelbarrow; a pig and a gramophone crammed together into an old pram. One family were trying to hitch a panicking donkey to a cart. As James passed it threw itself to the ground, toppling the cart and all its contents into the road. He swerved amongst pieces of broken china.

The nearer he got to the eruption, the more chaotic things became. The stream of refugees became a rout, fear visible in their faces as they tried to flee the roaring cloud of smoke and ash which now hung directly overhead, like a giant pulsing coral, its underneath turned pink by the glow from the crater. Below it, it was quite dark. The headlight of the

245

Matchless made little difference, clogged as it was with yet more grey ash.

At Ercolano he overtook a slow-moving procession of military trucks. They were the vehicles Eric had ordered from Cercola, hopelessly lost. He offered to guide them, and they followed him up the winding road.

He felt a light shower of sand. For a moment he thought it was being thrown up by the trucks. Then he realised that, in addition to the soft grey ash, tiny black fragments of grit were now falling from the sky – a light, insubstantial kind of stone, each piece no bigger than a match-head. Soon this hail of black grit was quite persistent. He felt it tapping against his uniform as he drove, working its way inside his collar and boots. Some of the bigger bits were hollow, like brandy snaps, and glowed red as they fell.

As he rounded a bend he caught his first proper sight of the lava. There were at least two separate streams – tendrils of glistening fire, pushing down to the north and west, their progress through the pine woods marked by trails of burning, smoking vegetation. He also became aware of a rumbling sensation. At first he assumed it was coming from his engine, then he realised that it was actually emanating from the mountain itself – like an unimaginably deep musical note, lower than the lowest organ pipe, so deep that you actually felt it in your stomach as a kind of pain.

On its way downhill one of the streams of lava had passed right over the road, completely blocking it. He pulled up about a hundred yards away. Even at this distance, the heat was immense. He had been expecting torrents of liquid rock, but this was more like a tumbling landslide of hot coals, nearly twenty feet high, juddering silently forwards, pushed down the slope by the pressure of yet more coals behind. The lava had a sort of crust on top of it, like the skin on a rice pudding. Presumably it was already cooling where it came into contact with the air. The skin wasn't static, though – as the lava oozed slowly down the hill, veins of red, and occasionally brighter fissures of brilliant gold, opened up momentarily, revealing the vast heat underneath.

He turned and indicated to the trucks behind that they would all have to use the other road. Anxiety about Livia gnawed at him constantly, but he tried to put her out of his mind. He would go to her as soon as he could, but first he had to make sure that the towns and military bases were being properly evacuated.

In San Sebastiano an extraordinary sight met his eyes. A twenty-foot-high wall of lava was pushing, very slowly, through the town, cutting a smoking swathe through the houses. Within the front edge of the lava James saw tumbled fragments – a tree trunk, glowing red like a lump of charcoal; a stone window frame, even what looked like the incinerated carcass of a cow. Further back, the dome of a church, somehow detached from the rest of its building, was being carried along by the lava like a saucepan lid on an overflowing river of porridge.

James watched as another house took the brunt of the lava's pressure. For a minute it seemed to resist: then, with an audible crack, the walls of the house eased away from each other and disintegrated, the stones added to the rest of the coals, the beams and timbers twisting as they burnt, like matchsticks.

The inhabitants of San Sebastiano were kneeling about fifty yards in front of the lava, clustered around a white-robed priest who was holding aloft the statue of Saint Sebastian from the church. The priest was chanting a prayer in Latin, his words almost drowned out by the crackle of flames and the din of the eruption. Many of the congregation had flowerpots or saucepans tied to their heads. James soon realised why: the hail of sand was falling less densely now, but the individual fragments were getting bigger. A stone the size of a fist smashed to the ground directly in front of him, where it lay smoking fiercely. If something like that hit a B-25 it would have much the same effect as a shell from an anti-aircraft gun. The airfield wouldn't have this rock-storm yet, he guessed: it would spread out gradually from the centre of the cloud, like rain in a storm. If he could get a message to them, they might still get the bombers to safety.

Behind him, the convoy of trucks pulled into the square. 'Evacuate everyone you can,' he called to the driver of the first one. 'Women and children first. I'm going on to the observatory.'

'Here, take this.' The man offered him a mess tin. James crammed it onto his head and stuck the handle down his collar to keep it in place. He waved his thanks and turned the bike round.

The stones were falling everywhere now. Several bounced off his makeshift helmet, and it was a relief when the observatory finally loomed out of the greyness. More stones clattered and bounced on its roof. Inside, a group of soldiers were crouching around a radio set. 'Thank God,' James gasped as he staggered through the door. They stared at him. He supposed he must look a bit of a mess by now, what with the tin clamped to his head. He glanced down at his uniform: it was completely covered in grey ash. 'I'm an officer,' he said. 'Captain Gould. I need to get a message to Terzigno airfield.'

'Radio's down,' one of the men said. 'There's been no reception since this thing started.'

'Damn.' There was nothing for it: he would have to go to the airfield himself. He turned to leave.

'Sir?' the soldier asked.

'Yes?'

The soldier spread his arms hopelessly. 'What shall we do?'

'Keep trying Terzigno. If you get through, tell them to get their planes into the air.'

He drove back through San Sebastiano, where the evacuation was proceeding in a reasonably orderly fashion. Somebody, somewhere, was evidently implementing the plan: there were fire engines fighting the worst of the fires, and military policemen directing the convoys of trucks, while human chains of soldiers rescued possessions from the houses in the lava's path. James kept going, taking the road that led around the mountain. The column of cloud was directly above him now, clearly visible through the falling ash. He remembered the seismologist saying that Pliny had thought it resembled a pine tree, but here, underneath it, it looked more like a vast Medusa's head floating in the sky, her face turned towards Naples.

In front of him, and a little higher than he was, another lava stream was oozing down the mountain. It seemed from this distance to be barely moving, yet it was soon clear that it was actually covering quite a lot of ground. He had the disadvantage of following a winding road, while the lava simply followed gravity and the contours of the landscape. When it came to a sudden drop the lava flowed sluggishly over it, like treacle dripping off a spoon, before resuming its downward path.

He lost sight of it momentarily as he rounded a corner. Another corner . . . He slammed on the brakes.

Just ten feet ahead, the road disappeared under a red river of smoke and fire. The Matchless skidded from under him. James rolled clear, the mess tin taking some of the force as his head banged the ground, but the momentum of the bike was still carrying it on its side towards the lava. He heard the tires burst as they came into contact with the hot coals. Flames licked at the frame. Desperately he crawled away from the heat. As he did so he heard the petrol tank going up with a soft 'crump' behind him.

Slowly he got to his feet. Well, at least he was alive. Apart from the clatter of tiny rocks as they fell to the ground, and that ever-present rumble, it was eerily still.

To get to Terzigno, he was going to have to outpace the lava on foot. He set off at a jog.

In Fiscino, the realisation that the volcano was erupting caused the same kind of mayhem as it had elsewhere. People rushed to and fro, frantically gathering together their possessions. As smoke and ash began to spew out of the mountain's summit, some chose to flee down the road to Boscotrecase. But most stayed, anxiously waiting to see what would happen.

In the darkness, the rim of the volcano could be seen above them, glowing white-hot from the heat inside it. Gradually, the glow swelled and spilled over the edge as the first streams of lava began pushing through the woods. One seemed to be heading in their direction, but it was hard to be sure. The villagers redoubled their prayers.

As the hours passed, the lava snaked from side to side during its slow descent, but every time it seemed to be heading away from Fiscino, it would eventually turn and tack back in that direction. Eighteen hours after the eruption started, the anxious villagers could see the lava only a quarter of a mile above them, like a fiery golden road winding up to the summit of the mountain. Now it was possible to say with certainty that it was heading directly for their village.

The sound of truck engines cut through the roar of the eruption. A line of Allied trucks was rumbling up the road from Boscotrecase, their blackout headlights almost invisible in the gloom. The front one stopped, its engine still running, and a soldier leaned out. 'We've come to evacuate you,' he yelled. 'Jump in, capeesh?' He gesticulated at the back of his lorry. '*Rapido, molto rapido.*'

A few of the villagers ran to the lorry, where willing hands hauled them up. 'Wait,' Livia cried. 'If we go now, the village will be destroyed.'

'There's nothing we can do,' Don Bernardo said gently. 'Except pray, and we can do that just as well from a place of safety.'

'We can dig a trench.' Livia looked around. 'A moat to channel the lava away. It's worth a try, isn't it? It's either that or let our homes burn.'

'Livia's right,' Nino said. 'We can dig.'

'What about praying?' someone wanted to know.

'We can dig and pray at the same time.'

'We can't hang around for you,' the truck driver warned. 'We have to get on to Cercola. If you want to be evacuated, it's now or never.'

'We'll take that risk,' Nino said. The truck driver didn't wait to be told twice.

The remaining villagers took their pickaxes and spades and climbed to the vineyards above the village. 'Here,' Livia said, pointing to a slight depression in the land. It followed the fall of the mountain, but at an oblique angle. 'If we can make that deep enough, and wide enough, it might just take the lava to one side of the houses.'

They used sticks to mark out a twenty-foot-wide ditch. 'So,' Nino said, spitting on his hands and hoisting his pick.

Livia swung her pickaxe over her head, punching a tiny bowlful of stony earth out of the ground. Could this ever work? She swung again, and again, her pickaxe flashing in the firelight; one of a dozen that rose and fell rhythmically as the people of Fiscino battled the mountain.

They all dug – men, women and children, although there were still precious few of the former. It was slow going. The ground was stony, and the work hard.

As they dug, the sky bombarded them with a hail of tiny stones. Livia looked up to wipe sweat from her eyes and realised with a shock that the lava was now only a few hundred yards away, close enough for her to smell the burning pine trees. 'The channel isn't deep enough,' she said helplessly.

'Get some mattresses. Anything to hold it back,' her father called. She ran to the shed and harnessed Priscilla to a cart, then piled it high with mattresses and furniture. Forcing the terrified animal to haul the load towards the lava was no easy matter, and it was several agonising minutes before she was able to dump her load against the sides of the ditch. The others were picking up boulders and branches, desperately trying to give the ditch a raised edge.

Above them, the lava reached the fields on the outskirts of Fiscino. It leant against a stone cowshed and crushed it like a box. Fruit trees yards ahead of it ignited spontaneously, the flames roaring through the branches and stripping them, leaving only the blackened trunks for the lava itself to devour. Livia could feel the heat scorching her face, and her throat was dry from the smoke. The heat went from uncomfortable to unbearable in a matter of minutes. One by one, as the wall of coal bulldozed everything in its path, the villagers were driven back from their places.

Sparks danced in the air, thousands of them, cascading onto the village like tiny burning arrows. The hay barn where she and Enzo had first rolled around together went up with a terrible crackling sound, the bright yellow of the burning hay a stark contrast to the deep red of the lava. More sparks poured from the burning roof, and on the ground, fires raced across the dry grass. The villagers tried to beat the ground fires out with spades, old sacks, even their clothes, but the flames were as nimble as cats, scurrying between their legs. They ran to the well with buckets, forming a human chain to douse the fires, but after a few moments there was a shout from someone who had allowed some water from his bucket to splash onto his skin. It was scalding hot. A few minutes later the well itself was dry, a great hissing coming from its depths as the mountain sucked the liquid into its core and breathed back only steam and smoke.

Now we are defenceless, Livia thought to herself.

Then the lava seemed to pick up speed. The wall of fire touched the ditch and paused, hanging there for a second, before spilling down into the narrow trench, filling it. A ragged, exhausted cheer went up from the villagers. Moments later, a red ooze of fire appeared at the trench's nearest edge and spilled over it. Most of the ditch wall was holding, but a tiny section no more than six feet across had collapsed and was acting like the spout of a saucepan, a rivulet of lava pouring from its rim towards them.

'The cart,' Nino shouted. 'Get the cart.'

Priscilla was still harnessed to the cart. Livia helped her father to get the harness off the panicking animal. They put their backs to the cart and tried to push it towards the gap in the ditch. Others joined them. The cart rolled into the ditch and caught fire. The villagers leapt back – all except Nino, who held on for just a moment longer than the others, steering the cart towards the gap.

Suddenly, as Livia watched, her father seemed to burst into light. Flames sprouted from his back like wings, and black smoke gathered around his head. Livia heard a terrible scream, and realised that it was coming from her own mouth. She ran, together with Marisa, to drag Nino clear, forcing herself into the scorching heat as if into a solid wall. They pressed themselves against him to extinguish the flames.

The cart burnt fiercely for a minute, and then that red bulge of fire was surging inexorably over it, gathering momentum as it headed straight for the centre of the village.

It was another hour before James reached the airfield at Terzigno, out of breath and exhausted. At first the guards assumed that he was a refugee, seeking medical treatment: it was only when he wiped some of the ash and mud from his uniform that he was able to make them understand that he was an officer, and that he needed to see the base commander on a matter of urgency.

By the time he was shown into the commanding officer's presence he was outwardly more composed, though his frustration was growing with each precious minute that passed. It was hard to make the man believe that an incipient fall of rocks from the sky was really going to put all his aircraft out of action, and when he had succeeded, harder still to organise eighty-eight aircrews for take-off, many of whom were not even on call. By the time the first bombers taxied down the runway the hail of light stones had started, pattering down onto the tin roofs of the temporary airfield buildings like a torrential storm and bouncing off the wings of the B-25s as they queued to take off.

'Doesn't seem so very terrible,' the CO commented, giving James a sideways glance. 'Still, better safe than sorry, I suppose.'

'This is just the beginning,' James said. 'In half an hour, those stones will be ten times their present size.'

'Well, that should give us—' the commander began. But his words were drowned out by a sudden cacophony as the patter of falling stones turned into a deluge. It felt, James thought, as if they were being buried alive – as though the Nissen hut they were standing in was a very small box in a very large hole, and some giant hand were shovelling huge quantities of gravel on top of them. Speech was almost impossible. Out on the airfield, one more plane managed to take off, its wings visibly shaking under an onslaught of rocks the size of walnuts. Initially the stones bounced on the runway: then the first layer settled and provided a thick, black carpet which absorbed those which came after, rapidly increasing in depth. The planes queuing for take-off ground to a halt, one skidding wildly as it fought for speed before pitching nose-forward.

The commander opened the door of the hut. Half a dozen stones immediately bounced inside. Quickly closing the door, he bent down and picked one up. 'Light as a ping-pong ball,' he yelled. Then he let it fall from his fingers. 'Blast! It's hot.' Across the airfield, the crews of the stranded B-25s were sprinting for the safety of the buildings, their arms raised over their heads against the pummelling rocks.

'Do you have a vehicle I can take?' James yelled. 'I need to get back up the mountain.'

The base commander looked at him as if he were mad. 'Why?' he shouted.

'There are some civilians I have to check on.'

The base commander waved his arm at the black deluge of clinkers. 'You must be joking. You won't get ten yards. Nothing could get through this lot.'

'I still need to try.'

The commander shook his head. 'You're not going anywhere until this is over. That's an order.'

There was little the villagers could do now except wait for the lava's approach. They made a stretcher to carry Nino, mercifully unconscious, to safety, where Marisa cleaned up the scorched, withered flesh as best she could. Even his breathing was painful, as though he had sucked the flames deep into his lungs. Then they organised a human chain to rescue the most precious possessions from the houses that were threatened. Livia saved from the *osteria* a couple of mattresses, clothes, some of Marisa's medicines, and the serving dish that had belonged to Agata's own mother, which she had always used to serve the Sunday *ragù*.

It took twenty minutes for the lava to travel the last two hundred yards. First the vines on the terrace caught fire, the leaves withering in the immense heat as if vaporised. Then the doors and window frames of their neighbour's house burst into flame. The lava nudged a corner of the *osteria*, and rolled up alongside it as if against a bank. For a moment it seemed as if the building might actually withstand the lava: then the juddering and jiggling of those hot coals, as big as boulders, seemed to pass into its fabric. It too juddered and shook; the roof splintered and capsized; the lava wrenched the kitchen wall from its foundation. It came cascading down in a tumble of stones and furniture, all of which fell into the blaze as the lava continued on its inexorable way downhill.

Minutes later the hail of light stones from the sky suddenly turned heavier, carpeting everything – the lava, the burning building, the woods, the watching villagers – with a thick layer of clinkers. The villagers were forced indoors, but there was one small mercy: like shovelling sand onto a fire, the flames of the burning buildings were instantly smothered by the all-enveloping grit.

Standing in the doorway of a neighbour's house, watching, Marisa put her arm around Livia. 'We did all we could,' she said gently. 'Now we need to look after our father.'

253

Thirty-eight

In fact, the eruption of Vesuvius in 1944 caused fewer casualties than anyone had a right to expect. The evacuation of over two thousand people from the area of Massa and San Sebastiano proceeded smoothly, thanks to the efficiency of the relief plans and the heroic efforts of hundreds of Allied volunteers who helped implement them. In San Sebastiano, which was almost completely destroyed, the lava eventually came to a halt only yards from the church, a clear sign – to the inhabitants at least – that the saint had once again intervened to protect his own. Many smaller villages and farms, however, were not so fortunate.

The fall of lapilli – the technical name for volcanic hail – continued off and on for eight days and nights, like some biblical plague, closing roads and making the whole area impassable. Then, with a final deafening roar, a great cloud of gas and ashes exploded thousands of feet into the air. Ten days after it had started the eruption was over, the vast ash cloud drifting slowly south-east as far as Albania, where it contributed to some of the most spectacular sunsets anyone could remember. The top of Vesuvius, which had been smoking gently for more than two centuries, was now completely still, its peak truncated by around sixty feet.

Livia and Marisa applied a poultice to Nino's shredded feet and hands, but although Marisa had braved the falling rocks to fetch a dozen bees to sting the skin around his wounds, he was beyond the reach of folk remedies. Soon he was in shock, running a temperature and thrashing around in sheets that were damp with his sweat. Livia sat up bathing him with salves, but there wasn't enough water to cleanse the wounds properly, and he became increasingly delirious as time went on.

'I don't know what else to do for him,' Marisa confessed as they watched him shiver. 'I think the wounds are becoming infected.'

'How bad is it?'

Marisa hesitated. 'It's possible he'll die.' Livia buried her face in her hands. 'Livia, he needs a proper doctor. Burns are difficult.'

There was no way of getting him to Naples during the eruption. Even if there had been, the journey would have killed him.

'The only thing that can help him now is penicillin,' Marisa said. 'But I don't know where we could get hold of any.'

Livia smoothed a damp cloth over Nino's shoulders. She knew someone who could supply her with penicillin, but it was too dreadful a prospect to contemplate.

All the next day, as her father's condition worsened, she sat up with him. Gradually she watched him weaken, his thrashing replaced by terrible juddering tremors. The charred skin on his legs was slowly turning white. His breathing was shallow and fast as he drifted in and out of consciousness.

They were still effectively cut off from the outside world, marooned on their volcano by the endless expanse of grey clinkers, as surely as if they were castaways marooned on an island by the sea.

'I think he's getting worse,' Marisa said. 'I'm sorry, Livia. All I can do now is make him more comfortable.'

Livia made a decision. She stood up. 'Wait here with him.'

'Where are you going?'

'To get him penicillin.'

The rocks had stopped falling, but grey ash and black volcanic grit covered everything – every plant and path, every tree, even filling the dried-up streams. It was like moving through a lunar landscape, utterly bereft of any features. Or perhaps, she thought, it was like a landscape from a dream, a world in which things that ought to be impossible suddenly take on their own inescapable logic.

I have no choice, she told herself as she trudged through the great grey drifts. I have no choice. For my father to live, this part of me has to die.

It was nearly a mile to the farmhouse where Alberto Spenza lived. It was an old place, very remote: a good place for the *camorra* to store contraband. She knew he would never have allowed himself to be evacuated, since it would have meant leaving all his black market spoils behind. Sure enough, she saw his Bugatti parked in a barn, although even there it had not escaped the eruption unscathed. Stones had broken through the roof and dented the paintwork, and the bonnet was covered in ash.

Alberto was cleaning his car with a cloth. When he saw her approaching he straightened up, though he said nothing.

She stopped in front of him. 'I need some penicillin. Urgently.'

'Why?'

'That's my business.'

'Then it's my business too. Since it's my penicillin.'

'I need it for my father.'

His fleshy lips made an 'o'. 'You know it's expensive?'

'Yes.'

'And you'll need enough for a couple of weeks, if he's very ill. How are you going to pay me?'

'We have some money saved up. You can have it.'

'Whatever you have saved, it won't be enough.' He was playing with her, drawing it out. 'But perhaps we could come to an arrangement.'

'What sort of arrangement?'

'That depends on how much you want the penicillin.'

'Alberto . . .' She hated to beg, but she had no choice. 'Just let me have it, and I'll pay you back somehow.'

'I don't want your money, Livia.'

'What, then?'

He simply looked at her and waited.

She had known all along what his price would be, and she had come knowing she had no choice but to pay it. 'All right,' she said. 'I'll do what you want.'

'Come inside.' He offered her his hand. After a moment's hesitation she accepted it, and they walked together into the house.

In the kitchen he led her to his larder and threw open the door. It was full of every kind of luxury imaginable: *foie gras*, lobster bisque, jars of *cassoulet* and bottles of Armagnac.

'One of the advantages of fighting a war alongside the French,' he commented. 'They still believe an officer should be fed in a way befitting his rank. And then, of course, there are the Russians.' He pointed to a small stack of tins. On the labels, under the strange backward-twisted script, was a picture of a fish. 'Caviar.'

'I don't know what to do with any of this,' Livia said helplessly. 'I've never cooked with these things before.' She felt a sense of panic as she thought of Nino, his temperature creeping ever upward. She just wanted to do what she had to and leave with the penicillin, but she knew that if she made her impatience obvious Alberto would spin it out even longer.

'Use the caviar as a sauce for *maccheroni*. And the *foie gras* can be seared, like a steak.'

She fetched a pan in which to boil water for the pasta, then opened the tins. The foie gras, when she tasted it, was so rich it almost made her gag, while the caviar was oily, sweet, and very salty. She added some butter and nutmeg, but otherwise she kept the accompaniments to a minimum.

All the time she cooked she was aware of Alberto watching her. Avoiding his gaze, she tried to lose herself in the familiar rituals of the kitchen: stirring, seasoning, heating. Anything was better than dwelling on what she was going to have to do.'

'It's ready,' she said at last.

'Lay two places. Today you're joining me.'

She set two places at the table. On his plate she placed a huge mountain of pasta, while on hers she put just a spoonful.

'Why so little?' he asked.

'I'm not hungry.'

'Perhaps one of the other courses will be more to your liking,' he leered.

He had opened a bottle of French wine, and now he poured two glasses and pushed one towards her. Then he tucked a napkin into his shirt and began forking the pasta into his mouth with exclamations of pleasure.

'To the cook,' he said, raising his glass. He drank without bothering to finish his mouthful of food first.

He continued to work his way through the huge pile of pasta, washing it all down with frequent refills of wine. 'The goose liver too,' he grunted. 'I'll have them both at once.'

She went and got the seared *foie gras* from the stove. Alberto took a forkful of meat, following it with another mouthful of pasta and a swig of wine. He rolled a mound of pasta onto his fork and pointed it at her. 'Now you.'

'Me? Now?'

'Why not? Today I'm going to have all three courses together.' He gestured at the table. 'I'm sure you know what to do.'

As if she were watching someone else, Livia saw herself get up from her chair and pull her dress over her head. When she was naked she climbed

257

onto the table. After that she forced herself not to think about anything at all.

When it was over she went to the sink and rinsed her mouth out with his fancy French wine.

Alberto got to his feet and went to the larder. He took out a small package, and tossed it to her. 'Your penicillin.'

She looked at it. 'But this is only one ampoule,' she objected. 'You said yourself, I need enough for at least two weeks.'

Deep in his eyes, she saw a glint of triumph – the triumph of a man who knows he has come off best from a deal. 'Then you'll just have to come back tomorrow.'

'And tomorrow you'll give me the rest?'

'No,' he said. 'Tomorrow I'll give you one more. And the day after that, another one.'

'You pig,' she said furiously.

He reached out and pushed his thick fingers through her hair. 'You should be flattered, Livia. You are the one dish a man can eat and eat, but never have enough of.'

She was almost home when she felt the waves of nausea overwhelm her. She bent double beside the path and vomited Alberto's rich food into the volcanic grit and ash.

Nino, in his delirium, felt the prick in his arm, and then Livia's soft hair brushing his cheek as she bent over him. 'Shh,' she said. 'It's only another bee sting. A bee sting. It'll make you better.'

The airfield was cut off from the outside world for the duration of the eruption, with even the radio producing nothing but howling static and garbled, hiss-swallowed voices. Then, as the lapilli storm eased, contact began to be re-established. Faint voices from Naples promised that bull-dozers had begun the job of clearing the roads, but the reports also made it clear that the job of getting back to normal was going to be a long one. An area of twenty square miles had been blanketed with clinkers. Roofs had collapsed under their weight. Vineyards had been flattened, crops destroyed, livestock wiped out. People spoke of seeing villages half submerged, their roofs poking out of the black stones as if they had sunk into the ground. And that was in addition to the damage done by the lava itself, which had melted the tracks of the funicular railway as well as burning the towns and villages in its path.

James found himself in the unaccustomed position of being considered something of a hero. Quite apart from the fact that he had been ready with an evacuation plan, the story of his epic journey from San Sebastiano to Terzigno was, apparently, becoming the stuff of local legend.

'You know what these Eyeties are like,' Major Heathcote explained by radio link. 'Superstition and miracles at every turn. Now they're saying that to get to Terzigno, you must have flown over the lava. The fact that it's quite impossible just makes it a better story as far as they're concerned. Anyway, although you and I both know that you were simply doing your job, the Germans are making a big deal out of the fact that our side had to bomb some monastery or other at Cassino, and it can only help our relations with the Italians to have saved so many civilians from Vesuvius. We're going to organise a little ceremony, with a news photographer there to picture the general shaking your hand. You might even get a ribbon.'

'Really sir, there's no need—'

'I know, Gould. Everyone hates a fuss, but the Bureau are insisting.'

It was gratifying, but the only thing he could think about was whether Livia was safe, and if so where she was. To begin with, he assumed that Fiscino must have been evacuated along with the other villages. Then he began to hear stories of one group of Vesuviani who had refused to leave.

Not knowing for sure whether she was among them was agony. His love for Livia up until then had been a thing of sunshine and optimism. Now the fear that she might be injured or even dead filled him for the first time with all love's terrors. He had been mad, he realised, to let her go from his side, even for a minute. But he was trapped both by the volcano and his orders. He waited impatiently for the roads to reopen so that he could go and check on her.

If she's all right, he promised himself, I will ask her to marry me. Even if we have to keep it a secret from the rest of the world, she needs to know how I feel.

Nino was no better, and no worse. Day by day, like two armies battling it out deep in his blood, the infection and the antibiotics struggled for supremacy. To begin with the contest was too close to call. But gradually, the fact that he was no longer deteriorating was in itself a sign that the infection was not following its usual course, and Marisa became more hopeful.

Every day that week, Livia went back to Alberto Spenza. Every day she kept her part of the bargain, and every day he handed her one more ampoule of penicillin.

259

By the fifth day, she no longer felt sick afterwards. It was simply what she did.

Back at Fiscino, she went to the room where Marisa was sitting by Nino's bedside.

'He's sleeping,' her sister whispered.

Carefully Livia prepared the precious syringe of penicillin, and slid the needle into her father's shoulder.

For the first time he opened eyes that were not vacant with fever, and saw Livia beside his bed. He smiled at her. 'Hello,' he murmured. 'What are you doing?' He twisted his head to look.

'Shh,' she said soothingly. 'It's only another bee sting.' When the syringe was empty she pulled it from his shoulder quickly, so that he wouldn't see what she was doing. Moments later he was asleep again.

'He looks well,' she said, softly, so as not to wake him.

'He's getting better,' Marisa agreed.

'Can we stop the penicillin now?'

Marisa shook her head. 'If the infection comes back because we've stopped too soon, it will kill him for sure.'

'How long?'

'It depends how strong he is. Another few days. A week, perhaps.' She shot her sister an anxious look. 'Perhaps it depends how strong *you* are.'

'I can do this,' Livia said angrily. 'I can do whatever I need to do to save him.'

'He wouldn't want you to blame yourself.'

'Maybe not. But the fact remains, it was my fault. It was me who wanted to stay and dig, instead of going with the soldiers.' She felt the tears spring to her eyes, and wondered that she had any left to cry. 'If it takes another week of penicillin to save him, then a week of penicillin is what he'll have.'

She could barely even begin to think about what would happen when he did get better, and what the consequences of her deal with Alberto would be. It was, she suspected, probably going to change everything. That was part of the price. All she knew was that it was all her fault. She had forfeited any right she might have ever had to be happy.

At last a bulldozer from Naples reached the airfield, opening up the road to Vesuvius. James immediately applied for leave. His request was granted, and he was even loaned a four-wheel drive jeep, courtesy of a grateful Fifth Army.

Most of the routes up the mountain were still blocked, and it was only when he gave a lift to some refugees returning to San Sebastiano, who showed him the hidden tracks that led through the woods, that James was able to get to Fiscino. As he neared the village he realised that one of the lava flows had come very close to it. Several of the houses had been damaged, and he felt a great pressure in his chest as he realised that one of them had been the *osteria*. But then he could see Livia, picking through the debris, and he was out of the jeep and running towards her, calling her name.

'So you see,' he explained, 'if it hadn't been for you, I would never have come up with the plan, and if it wasn't for the plan, hundreds – who knows, maybe thousands – of people would have been caught on the mountain.'

'Well done,' she said. 'You must be pleased.'

She seemed strangely subdued, even allowing for the fact that her home had been damaged. 'But you were really all right here?' he asked anxiously.

'As I told you, my father was the only one who was badly burnt. He had a fever, and for a while we thought we might lose him, but he's getting better now, thank God. Marisa's been looking after him.'

'You've all had a lucky escape.'

'Yes, I suppose we have.'

She was barely meeting his eye, and she hadn't even kissed him. He wondered if she was angry that he hadn't come to look for her. 'I tried to get here sooner,' he said. 'But then the rock-falls started, and no one could move.'

'We had them too.'

'But you were really all right?'

She shrugged. 'We coped.'

'Livia,' he said gently, 'aren't you even a little pleased to see me?'

'Of course,' she said. 'But now I have to prepare my father's lunch. He's staying at our neighbour's house, over there. '

As he walked across to the other house with her he said, 'I've got a few days' leave.'

'That's good.'

'I could stay here. If you'd like me to, that is. To help you clear up.'

'People would talk.'

'Does it really matter if they do?'

'Not to *you*, perhaps,' she snapped.

261

'You *are* cross with me. Livia, what's wrong?'

She shrugged miserably. 'You can stay if you like.'

'Really?' he said, confused. 'You do want me to?'

'I want you to.'

His heart lifted. She was just upset because of what had happened, not with him.

When she had given her father his lunch, James took her for a walk. As he put his arm around her he felt her flinch. Hopefully, he thought, what he was about to say would give her something to be happy about.

'You know,' he said, 'it's possible that all this may turn out to be a blessing in disguise.'

'Why?'

'I'm fairly sure there'll be compensation to rehouse your family some-where else, because of this.'

'What do you mean, somewhere else?' she said with sudden anger.

'Well, now that the *osteria* has been damaged, you can consider where the best place to situate yourself really is—'

'We're already situated here,' she snapped. '*This* is where we live.'

'But if you simply repair the damage *here*,' he explained patiently, 'sooner or later there'll be another eruption, and next time your family might not be so lucky.'

She gazed out over the pine woods towards the sea. 'Yes, we have been lucky,' she said quietly, 'but not because we were spared. We were lucky because we lived here in the first place.'

'I understand,' he said, not understanding, 'but now there's the future to consider. Staying here would hardly be a sensible—'

'Why would I want to be sensible?' she cried. 'I told you once, one life here is worth ten lived somewhere else. And if you don't see that, you're simply an idiot.'

He was flummoxed, and just a little angry, though he tried not to show it. To the rest of the world he might be a hero, but to Livia he seemed to have become the lowest of the low. 'Well, that's you Italians all over,' he said drily. 'Always choosing the grand gesture over common sense.' He searched for the most hurtful thing he could think of. 'Just bear in mind that next time, the Allies might not be around to clear up your mess.'

She laughed scornfully. 'We managed perfectly well before you came, thank you very much.'

They were rowing now, and he couldn't understand the cause. 'Livia,'

262

he said patiently, 'let's not quarrel. I'm desperately sorry about your father, and the damage to your restaurant, but you must surely see that it opens up choices you didn't have before—'

'You mean I could choose to come to England,' she snapped.

It was exactly what he meant, though he had been intending to work up to it gradually. 'So that's what this is about, is it?' he said stiffly. 'You were worried that I might use this eruption as an excuse to propose to you and drag you away from all this. Well, you needn't have any fears on that score.'

'Good. Because I can't think of anything worse.'

She had gone too far, and she knew it. But she was too miserable to tell him why she was so miserable, and she made no move to stop him as he strode angrily to the jeep, climbed into the driving seat, and set off down the mountain in a spray of volcanic stones.

She watched him go. A tear sprang to her eye and she blinked it angrily away. Then she got to her feet and began to walk down the grit-filled path that led through the woods.

She found Alberto sitting at his kitchen table, waiting for her. The aroma of fresh coffee filled the house, and a full *napoletana* sat on the table, along with a bottle of brandy, but Alberto was unshaven, as if he had been sitting there a long time.

She knew what was expected of her by now, and she went to the larder to see what he had chosen for her to cook. But he stopped her with an outstretched arm.

'I'm not hungry.'

She kicked off her shoes and began to undo the buttons of her dress.

'You can leave your dress on.'

She stopped, and lifted the dress up so that she could unfasten her drawers. 'That's not what I meant, either.' Abruptly he got up, went to the larder and handed her a fistful of penicillin ampoules. 'Here. Take them, if you want them so much.'

'All of them?'

'They're a gift.'

'Thank you.' She reached for her shoes, to put them on again. 'So I can go?'

'If you want to. All I ask . . . All I ask is that you come back sometime of your own free will.'

'Alberto,' she said, 'you know that's not going to happen.'

His eyes flashed. 'Then come back and pretend. Pretend that you're not simply here because you have to be.' He gestured at the ampoules in her hand. 'You can have all those, but just remember what I did for you.'

For a moment she hesitated. Then she leaned forward and kissed him on the cheek. 'Thank you,' she said.

By the time James reached the bottom of the mountain his anger had turned to misery. He had mishandled the situation completely. He had had no choice but to go to Terzigno on the day of the eruption, but he had failed to explain that properly to Livia. He would have done better to let her vent her feelings of anger at being abandoned, rather than retaliating as he had done. But he had been stung more deeply than he had let on by that sarcastic reference to taking her back to England.

He had known for a long time that what Livia and he had together was more than just a wartime love affair. Livia's English, it was true, was idiosyncratic, but he had vetted plenty of girls whose command of the language was much worse, and language, after all, could be learnt. It was also true that Livia would experience a culture shock in England. The England he knew, with its dried-egg rations, Woolton pies, National Dried Milk and margarine would never do for her. But after the war, things would surely start to change, and it was only reasonable to expect a wife to make certain sacrifices for the chance of a better life.

But Livia, it seemed, had not been thinking along the same lines at all. For a moment there was the awful suspicion that he was just a stopgap, that any Allied officer with a good job to offer and occupation money in his pocket might have been an equally acceptable cushion during these difficult years. He had thought she loved him – no, he *knew* she loved him. But the fact remained that in wartime Naples, with its atmosphere of fleeting intimacy and casual sex, love had come to them easily – much more easily than it would have done at home. Perhaps it had all been *too* easy. After the war, when a more conventional morality re-established itself, would they actually discover they had the basis for a life together? Or would a relationship that had so far been based almost entirely in the bedroom and the kitchen turn out to be inadequate for an English drawing room, and the whole grown-up, practical business of married life? Had she, in short, done him a favour by choking off the proposal he had been about to make?

Her reaction today had thrown him. Livia's volatility, which had always been part of the reason he loved her, suddenly seemed as alien and perplexing as the flavours of an Italian meal. He had vetted so many women as prospective war brides; yet when it came to making up his own mind, he was suddenly assailed by doubts.

Livia sat by a window, watching the sun set over the Bay of Naples and thinking. She had been sitting like this for over an hour.

Despite her misery, she had been telling the truth when she told James that she couldn't be a war bride. There was no way she could leave here now, when so much had to be done. She and James had, at best, until the end of the war together, and then he would go back to England without her. What would happen after that she didn't know, but it was clear to her that her first duty was somehow to help her father rebuild the farm and the restaurant, to provide for him in his old age.

But quite apart from that, it was not going to work with James. She saw that now. The locked box in her mind where she was shutting away her dealings with Alberto was already refusing to stay locked. What she had done would always be there, seeping its poison into their relationship. She either had to tell James everything, or accept that it was over.

But to tell him everything was simply another way of ending it. She thought back to Enzo, how he had hated it when another man so much as looked at her. James was outwardly less possessive, but he was still a man, and a man moreover with strong views on sexual conduct. However much he sympathised with the women he dealt with in Naples, the women who had prostituted themselves, she knew that he would never have allowed himself to fall in love with one of them.

No: it was going to end, and she would probably be lucky if she even ended up having someone like Alberto to fall back on.

The only choice she had now was of *how* it would end. Would she tell James about Alberto, and have it finish in anger and recrimination, or would she simply tell him it was over, and spare herself the added pain of a confession?

She watched the sun slipping under the sea, turning the sky to fire. Her eyes filled with tears, spilled, and filled again.

She made a sudden decision. Jumping to her feet, she went in search of paper and a pen.

Thirty-nine

Strictly speaking, the obligations of the Allied Military Government of Naples Province did not extend to acts of God, but four years of war had given the Allies an unshakeable belief in their ability to deal with any crisis. The Americans were still full of confidence and can-do optimism, while the British, perhaps, remembered their colonial past and the responsibilities it had once brought with it. Individual soldiers of all nations, from New Zealanders to Free French, suddenly recalled small acts of generosity by ordinary Italians in the theatre of war – a bottle of wine brought out by a housewife during a long, hot march towards Cassino, a smile or a wave from a pretty girl, a brief moment of conversation in which the war stopped and ordinary humanity reasserted itself for a few minutes – and now, almost without thinking about it, they decided to return the favour.

It began with the evacuation plan, but the evacuation was only the beginning. At Cercola a soup kitchen was set up by the Red Cross which dispensed food to over a thousand refugees. At Pollena-Trocchia a food distribution centre was established. Allied NAAFIs, cinemas and mess huts for miles around were turned into makeshift accommodation for the homeless. Every unit loaned what it could, from bulldozers to clear the roads, to trucks for transporting livestock. The Lancashire Fusiliers held a whip-round, and raised enough money to restore a whole village. Not to be outdone, the Royal Engineers simply loaded their vehicles with timber and hardware and one by one began rebuilding houses that had been damaged. Sappers enthusiastically dynamited buildings made unsafe by the earth tremors – so enthusiastically, it was said ruefully later, that they created more work for the engineers than was strictly necessary – and the RAF dropped food parcels. The RAVC, the veterinary corps, turned up with horses and mules, while Logistics donated a whole shipload of potatoes, originally transported from Canada as food for the troops but now a valuable seed crop.

Most extraordinary of all, however, was the reaction of the fighting units. Men who had spent months in the grimmest of conditions at the front volunteered to spend their precious leave helping to clear roads, rebuild houses, and shovel clinkers off the fields by hand. The enthusiasm with which they did so made it seem almost as if they actually preferred rebuilding to drinking and whoring, and more than one commanding officer was heard to observe that he wished a volcano would erupt more often, so beneficial was the effect on morale.

Back at the Palazzo Satriano, James found an air of purposeful activity. Two large flagpoles had been erected on the outside of the building, from which the Stars and Stripes and the Union Jack fluttered proudly side by side. In the entranceway, two military police stood on guard duty. An Italian man in overalls was busy painting over the racy frescoes with the contents of a large bucket of whitewash.

James spotted Horris. 'What's going on?' he asked.

'The general's visit. Thanks to you, the Film Unit are going to make a newsreel about it. Apparently we're now a wonderful example of Allied co-operation.'

As James passed Carlo and Enrico's office he glanced through the open door, and stopped dead. It had been quite transformed. Papers had been filed, the desks had been dusted, and both men were wearing the bow ties and spats they usually reserved for expeditions involving tommy guns. In addition, they were now both sporting small waxed moustaches, and their hair was brilliantined in the manner of some of the flashier American GIs.

'Hey, kid,' Carlo said in an American accent. 'How you doing?'

'Fine,' James said faintly.

Carlo snapped his fingers. 'Then I plant you now and dig you later, cat.'

Bemused, James continued to his own office. It was evidently being used as a receptacle for everyone else's junk. Boxes of papers were piled everywhere, and a huge chandelier had been dumped on the table. Its pieces had been decimated by German air raids and, like a tree in the autumn that had shed its leaves, it was now more iron than glass. He tried to heave it onto the floor, but it was surprisingly heavy.

Major Heathcote strode into the room. 'Better get this place cleared up, Gould.'

'Yes, sir.'

'The general will be with us Thursday, at noon.' The major eyed James's uniform, which had barely been standard issue before the eruption, and was in a considerably worse state now. 'Don't forget to draw a new uniform.'

'No, sir.'

The major hesitated. 'Incidentally, Gould, about this relief operation. It seems to have caught everyone's imagination – I suppose because it's the first positive news there's been for a while. Anyway, the Bureau thinks it best to emphasise that it was a team effort. So as far as the public are concerned, you and Vincenzo came up with the plan together. And I, as the officer in charge, had overall responsibility.'

James found he did not care in the least who took the credit for the relief operation. 'Really, sir, it's perfectly all right.'

'That's the spirit, Gould. Of course *we* know it was mostly your work, but it looks better for the people back home this way.'

After the major had gone James began to tidy up. There was a lot to be done, and it was a couple of hours before he had made much impression.

Suddenly he smelt something. A wonderful, rich aroma was wafting through the apartment. He would have recognised it anywhere – it was the smell of Livia's *fettuccine al limone*. With a burst of happiness he rushed through to the kitchen.

The girl who was cooking turned round with a polite smile. 'Oh,' he said, disappointed. 'I thought you were Livia.'

Horris was standing next to her, chopping a large pile of courgettes. 'I took the liberty of engaging Maria here on a temporary basis,' Horris explained. 'Just until Mrs Pertini comes back.'

'Yes, of course. Give me a shout when it's lunchtime, then.' Horris and Maria were looking at him clearly, waiting for him to go. 'You probably want to slice those at slightly more of an angle,' he said to Horris. As he closed the door he heard the two of them start to talk again in low voices. A little later, there was a muffled giggle.

The following day both the new flags had vanished from their flagpoles, and the traders on the Via Forcella were offering a new line in luxury striped underwear. After that, the poles were moved to the inside of the building, where two replacement flags hung, limply but safely, side by side in the windless courtyard.

The courtyard itself had been spruced almost beyond recognition. The

Americans' jeeps were cleaned, polished, and lined up as if in a car salesroom. Tables, hurricane lamps and other evidence of al fresco dining were carted away, and the chairs were rearranged on a podium for visiting Italian dignitaries to sit on. The Psychological Warfare Bureau was putting on a show, and everything had to be stage-managed to reinforce the impression of a grateful populace thanking their liberators.

For five days Nino slept, occasionally opening his eyes to see who was washing his wounds or changing his bandages. Sometimes it was Livia, but more often he found Marisa sitting by his bed.

'*Dov'è Livia?*' he murmured. 'Where's Livia?'

'She'll be back later. Now sleep.'

Each day, Livia used up another of the ampoules of penicillin Alberto had given her. Then, suddenly, Nino was well enough to sit up. His daughters brought him broth made with the last of the chickens, and milk still warm from Priscilla's teats. They pulped the last of the precious tomatoes to make a *passata*, halfway between a juice and a food, easily digestible and full of vitamins. He was weak, and Livia dared not stop his penicillin yet, but it looked as if he was going to be all right.

That afternoon, she went back to Alberto's for what she hoped would be the very last time.

The Bugatti was parked outside his farmhouse, its dents repaired and its bodywork gleaming.

She stepped inside his door. Alberto was waiting for her in the kitchen, but today he was wearing a dark suit. A dress hung from a hanger on the kitchen door.

'This is for you,' he said, taking it down and handing it to her. 'Put it on.'

'Don't you want me to cook?' On the table were ingredients for a meal – a live lobster in a saucepan, a bottle of wine, a pile of aubergines.

'Later.'

He watched without comment as she took off what she was wearing and pulled on the dress. It was a short dress, pencil-thin, made of silk covered in hundreds of tiny black glass beads.

'I need a mirror,' she said, looking around.

'I'll be your mirror.' He adjusted the neckline. 'There. You look perfect, Livia.' He held out his clenched fists. 'Choose one.'

She frowned. Was he going to hit her? She tapped his left fist, and he opened it to show her a silver necklace.

'Turn around.'

As he fastened it she felt his breath on her neck, deep and regular. Then he stepped back and handed her a bonnet.

'Now we're going for a drive.'

The road to Massa was still covered with clinkers which crunched under the car's wheels. Alberto drove slowly, careful not to damage the bodywork.

The town was deserted, many of its buildings destroyed. But in the main square they found a truck parked with its engine running. Two men were carrying goods out of the houses that remained – candlesticks, mirrors; anything of value – and throwing them into the back.

'Those people are looting,' Livia said, horrified.

'It certainly looks like it.' Alberto stopped the car. 'Guiseppe, Salvatore,' he called. 'How's it going?'

One of the men shrugged. 'There's not much here. These people were all poor.'

'Maybe you're not looking in the right places.' Alberto jerked his thumb at Livia. 'Look what *I* found.'

The men eyed Livia. With a laugh, Alberto put the car into gear and swept away from them.

Livia closed her eyes. For a moment she had thought that something truly awful had been going to happen. But that was the point, she realised. Alberto was making it clear that until he had handed over the penicillin, she was his, to dispose of as he wished.

'Where are we going now?' she asked.

'Into Naples.'

As Alberto drove through Naples, he seemed to be struggling with a decision of some kind. Once or twice he tried to engage Livia in conversation, but she ignored him and stared out of the window.

Eventually he drove into a quiet road at the back of the Questura and stopped the car. A *carabiniere* standing guard at the door nodded to him.

'A friend of yours?' Livia said at last.

'Yes. I do a lot of business with the people in this building.'

'And what's that got to do with me?'

'Today you're the business I'm here to do.'

She did not ask him to explain. Whatever he had in mind for her, it was bound to be unpleasant. She would simply shut it out of her mind until it was over.

'Livia,' he began, 'I want to ask you something.'

*

James sat at his desk, resplendent in a brand-new uniform. His boots were polished to a mirror finish, his brass belt-buckle shone, and his cap was hanging in readiness on the back of the door. He was pretending to work, but work was actually impossible, not least because of the constant interruptions from other members of the section who kept sticking their heads round the door to wish him good luck or to say 'well done'. In the next office, Carlo and Enrico had abandoned all pretence of employment, and were rearranging their straw boaters and bow ties, using the newly cleaned windows as mirrors. From somewhere Carlo had acquired some reflective Ray-Ban sunglasses, of the sort issued to American aviators, and he was admiring the way they hid his eyes.

A howl of microphone feedback came from the courtyard. 'Testing,' an amplified voice said hesitantly. James went and looked out of the window. Even now, in the last few minutes of preparations, more bunting was being hung above the microphone where the general would deliver his speech. A man from the Forces' radio station was wandering around with a tape recorder, and the cameraman from the Army Film Unit was trying different angles, ensuring that no bomb damage was visible through his viewfinder.

James picked up a letter from his in-tray and scanned it. It was headed 'Commune of Cercola'.'

> *Dear Sir,*
> *The administration of this commune, in expressing the gratitude and*
> *thanks of the citizens of Cercola for the work done for the public benefit*
> *during the recent eruption of Vesuvius, feels bound to mention in*
> *particular the prompt intervention of the Allied authorities for the safety*
> *of about 500 families, who were transported with their household goods in*
> *Allied vehicles, and the abundant distribution of rations . . .*

He added it to the pile of similar letters. The thanks were genuine, he had no doubt, but once those who had benefited from the Allies' help realised that they were being encouraged to make a song and dance about it for propaganda reasons, they had all tried to outdo each other in the effusiveness of their gratitude. Many of the letter writers were even now gathering on the raked seats downstairs, decked out in the extravagant plumed hats, robes and chains of office which denoted a minor Italian dignitary.

Eric put his head round the door. He, too, was wearing a new uniform in readiness for the general's visit, though he had at least had the decency to be embarrassed by the suggestion that the idea for the operation had been anything to do with him.

'See you downstairs, buddy,' Eric said. 'General's car's on its way.' James nodded. 'I'll be right down.' He opened another letter.

Dear Captain Gould,
I just wanted to let you know that Corporal Taylor and I have had our baby. He is a beautiful little boy, nine pounds, with blue eyes and dark colouring, very hungry. If you will let us, we would like to call him James, in recognition of all that you did for us.
  Regards,
  Gina Taylor (née Tesalli)

He smiled, and opened the next.

Dear James,
I am sorry that we parted on bad terms when you came to see me at Fiscino after the eruption. However, it doesn't matter now. What I am about to write has nothing whatsoever to do with our quarrel.
  I have decided that I am not going to return to Naples to resume my position as your cook. My life has taken a different course now, one which however much I regret I cannot undo. It is probably for the best, in any case. I enjoyed our time together, but I would never have been happy in England with you. In fact, I could never be anywhere but here, looking after my father, and I have decided that I shall do that for the rest of my life rather than marry again. My reasons for this are complicated, but there is no chance whatsoever of persuading me otherwise. You would do much better to forget all about me.
  This has been a painful letter to write, and I only ask one favour of you: that you do not make it any more painful for me by trying to change my mind.
  With best wishes for a happy life,
  Livia

He stared at the letter. It was not possible. He read it again, twice. His first reaction was that she did not mean it, that she was simply angry with him. But that last paragraph seemed to leave little room for apologies. And the tone – it seemed resigned, even wistful, rather than furious. He peered closer. Was that a tear stain, blurring her final salutation?

Then the awful reality of it hit him. She was ditching him. He would never kiss her again, never see that mischievous smile, or her eyes flashing with passion, never hear the words tripping out of her mouth as she talked nineteen to the dozen. He would never again taste her sweet flesh, never stand shoulder to shoulder with her, chopping courgettes. She wanted him out of her life.

This is all wrong, he thought desperately. This is all completely wrong.

Livia was aware of Alberto looking at her in a strange way, but she kept her gaze fixed on the bonnet of the Bugatti. She shrugged. 'If there's something you want to ask, then ask.'

'Will you marry me?'

Her head did swivel then. '*What?* After everything you've done? You're even crazier than I thought.'

'It got complicated. I was angry. You're so beautiful, Livia, but so damn superior. No, wait.' She was trying to protest. 'Sometimes I wanted to cut you down to size. But everything I did, I did because I love you.'

'That's ridiculous.'

'I love you. That's why I had to do anything, anything in my power, to have you.' He paused. 'Even if it meant hurting you. But I see now that it wasn't your body I had to have. Livia, you've seen how much respect I have around here. After the war I'll be a rich man. I need a woman by my side. I need *you*. I'll give you everything you want. And I promise that I will never, ever harm you again. I will treat you like the princess you are.'

'What about . . .' She swallowed. 'What about the restaurant?'

'Of course we must rebuild it. More than that – I'll put money into it, we can build it up into a proper business. With me behind it it'll become successful again, you'll see. We'll make money there. There'll be jobs, good jobs, for Marisa and your father, and if your father wants to retire there'll be plenty left over to make him comfortable.'

She stared out of the windscreen with unseeing eyes. What Alberto was offering was more than she would ever be offered by anyone else, she knew. Logically, there was no alternative.

'Gould.' It was Major Heathcote, standing at the door. 'For heaven's sake, man, get a move on.'

'Yes, sir.' Despite his shock at the letter, he automatically fell into step beside the major as the CO hurried downstairs to the courtyard. Some of the Italian dignitaries, seeing the two British officers striding out together, broke into a round of applause. There were even a few shouts of 'Bravo.'

'Not yet, not yet,' the major muttered, glaring at the clappers. 'Wait for the general.'

They halted, then stood easy. The Italians applauded again, more politely this time. 'It's not a bloody parade,' the major muttered disgustedly under his breath.

Outwardly James was impassive, but inwardly he was reeling. She had ditched him. Why? It made no sense. What could possibly have made her change her mind about him?

The general's armoured car swung in from the Riviera di Chiaia, and two smartly dressed military policemen presented arms on either side of the entrance. A moment later, all the Allied servicemen in the courtyard snapped to attention as one. The Italians, having clapped politely when they saw two men halting, went wild. There was a two-minute standing ovation, laced with many cries of '*Vivono gli Alleati.*'

The general's car was turned off and the great man got out. Major Heathcote stepped forward and saluted.

'At ease, guys,' the general said through the din of cheering Italians. 'Is that camera rolling?'

The Army Film Unit director said that it was.

'Great. These the guys?' The general came around so that he was standing between Eric and James. Flashbulbs went off. Then he raised his hand for silence. An expectant hush fell on the crowd.

'Alberto,' she said, 'I'm sorry. I just can't. It's a generous offer, but the answer's no.'

He sighed. 'I thought you might say that.'

'I just can't,' she repeated.

'Does this have anything to do with the Englishman?'

However afraid she was for herself, she was even more fearful for James, knowing that Alberto would have him killed without a moment's hesitation if he deemed it necessary. She shook her head. 'I'm not seeing him any more.'

She felt his eyes on her. After a moment he grunted and pointed towards the police station. 'In there,' he said, 'there are people who have been given the job of rounding up women with syphilis and sending them north, behind the German lines.'

She felt a cold spasm of fear closing around her stomach. 'What's that got to do with me?'

'I told them I've got a girl they can take.'

'But they'll find out—'

From an inside pocket he produced a piece of paper. As he unfolded it she saw that it was some sort of certificate. 'An Allied army doctor has examined Livia Pertini and found that she is carrying the infection. It's already signed. All I have to do is fill in the date.' He paused. 'Unless, of course . . .'

'So that's the choice you're offering me, is it?' she said. 'Marriage, or that?'

'I would rather you had agreed of your own free will. But everything I said still stands. Livia, I have to have you.'

'You certainly know how to make a romantic proposal, Alberto.'

'Which is it to be?' he said doggedly. 'You have to choose.'

'We came not to conquer this ancient country, but to free her,' the general said into the microphone, his voice rolling around the courtyard. 'And these fine officers at my side are a shining example of our respect for you. Through vigilance, enterprise and democratic endeavour, they have shown that we are ready to combat tyranny in all its forms.' He expanded on his theme. Soon James was almost convinced that the volcano had been, if not actually caused by Hitler, then part of an international conspiracy, which the general pledged himself to fight from whichever direction it appeared. 'The conflict against Hitler,' the general declared, 'is just the opening battle in the wider war on tyranny.' At one point, he hinted at 'dark forces' at work in the civilian population, 'ready to seize upon disaster to sow discord and undermine democracy.' He was talking about fascism, but his words, James realised, could equally be taken to refer to the communists.

'Finally,' the general said, 'to the tyrannists I say this: with men like these in our fine army, you cannot hope to undermine our ideals. And to these brave officers, I say: the free nations of the world salute you.' The audience, most of whom had not understood a word but who had realised from his tone that the end had been reached, burst into applause.

'What was it you guys did, exactly?' the general murmured as he pinned a ribbon to James's chest.

'Organised the civilian evacuation from Vesuvius, sir.'

'Oh, yes. Good work.' The general saluted them, and they saluted him back. 'Either of you speak Italian?'

'I do, sir,' James said miserably.

'Say a few words, would you?' He gestured at the crowd.

'Sir?'

'A few words of thanks. Though if you could mention the war on tyranny, that would be good.'

'Yes, sir.'

The general held up his hand for silence. Instantly, silence fell. James leaned towards the microphone. 'I just want to thank the general for his kind words. And to, er, reiterate that the war on tyranny is, er, very important to us.' The echo of his amplified voice interrupted him, putting him off his stride. He looked at all the expectant faces. Suddenly he knew that he could not go through with this nonsense any longer.

'Look,' he said, 'I'm not a hero. I'm not even a good soldier. The truth is I only came up with the evacuation plan because of a girl.'

The Italians gave a collective murmur of interest. Political speeches were all very well, but romance was much more fascinating.

'She lives on Vesuvius, you see. That was the point – I wanted her to be safe. But when it came to it, instead of seeing that she *was* safe, like a fool I went to Terzigno to make sure the aircraft were all right.'

As one man, his audience gasped with anguish at the thought of James's folly. Those in the back rows craned forward to get a better look.

'What's he saying?' the general said in Eric's ear.

'It's, uh, a little too fast for me to follow, sir.'

'I made the wrong decision,' James said slowly. 'I realise that now. Her house – her family's restaurant – was damaged. I still don't know exactly what happened during those ten days, or what she went through, but I know it was enough to somehow make her change her mind about me. And although I'm not going to take off this ribbon here and now, because the man standing beside me would have me shot, I would throw it in the sea tomorrow if I could only have her back.'

'This is fascinating, James,' Eric murmured out of the side of his mouth in Italian, 'But if were you, I'd start to wrap it up.'

James looked at the crowd of Italian faces gazing sympathetically back at him. The emotions he had for so long been choking off suddenly, inexorably, welled to the surface, and his eyes filled with tears. 'I love her,' he said simply. 'I love her more than anything. And now she's asked me to forget her. But that's the one thing I can never, ever do.'

The audience sighed. In the front row, a mayor wiped his eyes on a corner of his ceremonial robes.

'And now,' James said, 'if you'll excuse me, I'm going to go and get drunk.'

276

The Italians broke into applause. Many were openly weeping. One or two even got to their feet, running forward to hug James and press their tearful cheeks against his own.

'Extraordinary,' the general said, looking around him with an air of bemusement. 'Quite extraordinary.'

Zi' Teresa's was deserted apart from a barman polishing glasses. James went to the bar and ordered Scotch.

'We're not open,' the barman began. But Angelo, seeing who it was, came out from the back and motioned for the barman to leave them.

'Would you like some company, James?' he said as he placed the glass in front of him.

'Just the bottle.'

Angelo raised his eyebrows. James took Livia's letter out of his pocket and pushed it towards him. 'Here. You might as well read it.'

Angelo read the letter in silence. Then he reached under the counter for an unmarked bottle of pale brown liquid. 'Scotch is not what you need at a time like this. And in any case, that stuff you've been drinking never went anywhere near Scotland.' He threw the contents of James's glass in the sink, unstoppered the new bottle and poured two small balloon glasses of the pale liquid. James picked one up and sniffed it.

'What is it?'

'Grappa. Triple distilled, blended in the cask, and over a century old. If, God forbid, we were in France, it would be called cognac, and the Germans would have stolen every bottle I had.'

James shrugged and knocked it back in one gulp. Even in his present mood, however, he could not entirely ignore the unctuous, venerable fumes that caressed his sinuses and lingered as a soft, rich, smoky aftertaste on his palate – a taste redolent of cobwebbed warehouses, damp cellars, incense-filled churches and dusty wooden beams. Just for a moment, he seemed to see his problems as this ancient liquid would see them: tiny and insignificant and fleeting.

As if reading his mind, Angelo said, 'When this spirit was locked away into the first of its many oak barrels, Italy was not even a nation, and your Queen Victoria was still a child. Sometimes it helps to take a long view.' He poured James another shot and touched his own glass against it. 'To history.'

This time James drank a little more slowly.

'So,' Angelo said thoughtfully, 'Livia has decided she will not marry you. She has chosen duty over love.'

James pushed his glass towards the maître d' for a refill.

'It occurs to me that the two of you are probably more alike than I ever realised.' Angelo poured James's drink and picked up his own glass. 'And now, I should imagine, you are feeling rather bad.'

'I let her down,' James said. 'I wasn't there when she needed me.'

'I see.' They drank in silence for a moment. 'You are being too hard on yourself,' Angelo said thoughtfully. 'You were simply doing *your* duty. Livia, I think, will forgive you for that.'

'Forgive me? She never wants to see me again.' He buried his head in his arms and groaned. 'Angelo, I've been such a fool.'

'That's true,' Angelo agreed. 'However, it may not matter.'

'What do you mean?'

Angelo turned his glass a little, inspecting its depths. 'Sometimes, when you look into a grappa as old as this, you can almost fancy that you see the future.' He took a small sip, rolling it around his tongue for a moment. 'And when you drink it, you can almost believe that you can change what that future will be.'

'What are you getting at, Angelo?'

'Simply this. Have you ever actually told Livia that you love her? That you want to spend the rest of your life with her? That no obstacle, however insurmountable it seems, will ever be enough to keep you apart?'

James sighed. 'No,' he admitted. 'It was a difficult situation – you know that. As the wedding officer . . .'

'James, James. Remind me why Britain is in this war.'

James shrugged. 'We decided that certain things were worth fighting for, I suppose.'

'Such as?'

'Well – fair play. Sticking up for people who can't do it for themselves. Not letting ourselves be pushed around by some tinpot military dictatorship.'

'Yet when it comes to your own heart, you are prepared to let other people tell you what to do, to have your life dictated to by the military, even at the expense of kindness, of decency, of fair play – and yes, even of love.' Angelo nodded. 'You decided that our country was worth fighting for, and we're grateful. But what about our people? What about Livia? Isn't *she* worth fighting for?' He placed his finger on the letter, and pushed it back across the bar towards James. 'You can keep this letter next to your heart. You can carry it round with you until it's faded and torn and coming apart at the seams like a piece of old lace. Or you can say that a piece of paper is not a decision, that a love renounced in circumstances like these has not been renounced at all, only tested, that this parting will not be permanent until both of you accept that it is. In short, my friend, if you really think the cause worth fighting for, then you can choose to fight.'

'But she says not to try to change her mind.'

'She's a woman, James. If you do change her mind, she'll thank you for it. And if you don't,' he shrugged, 'it doesn't really make much difference, does it?'

'By God, Angelo,' James said, staring at him. 'You're absolutely right.'

Forty

He strode out of the restaurant and jumped into the jeep, disturbing the gang of *scugnizzi* who were in the process of carefully removing the headlamps. As he sped off, metalwork tinkled on the road.

The roads might be open, but the landscape was still eerily dead. Ash swirled around his wheels as he zigzagged up the mountain. Here and there great blackened swathes through the woods showed where the lava had done its worst.

When he got to Fiscino everything was very quiet. He pulled up outside the ruin of the *osteria* and turned the engine off. There seemed to be absolutely no one about.

'Hello?' he shouted. Then he saw a face he recognised at one of the neighbours' windows. 'Marisa,' he called. 'It's me, James.' She came to the door. 'Where's Livia?'

'She's not here.'

'So where is she?' She hesitated, and he said, 'I have to speak to her.'

'She went to Alberto Spenza's house.'

'The gangster? What's she doing with him?' She hesitated again, and he said impatiently, 'Never mind. How do I get there?'

After a moment she pointed to an opening in the woods. 'Take that path, and follow it for about a mile.' Then, in a rush, she said, 'She went there yesterday, and she hasn't come back. I'm worried about her. I've been seeing her – seeing her somewhere dark.'

'Don't worry, I'll find her,' he said, setting off at a run.

Behind him, Marisa nervously twisted her fingers, wondering whether she had done the right thing.

He jogged down the track until he came to a farmhouse. There was a gleaming red Bugatti parked in the barn, and the front door was open. 'Livia?' he called.

There was no reply, so he stepped inside. A smell of stale cooking wafted from the kitchen. On the table were the remains of a meal – and what a meal: the table was littered with the most astonishing luxuries. He saw a dismembered half-eaten lobster and what looked like open tins of caviar, carelessly scattered around. A bottle of Mouton Rothschild lay on its side, almost empty. Two half-full glasses stood by two empty plates.

'Livia?' he said again.

There were sounds coming from upstairs. A creaking bed. A woman's cry, either of pleasure or pain. He ran upstairs and kicked open doors.

There were two people in the bed, the fat man and a woman. He saw a mass of dark hair, a naked back, and a dress thrown over a chair, but the woman straddling Alberto Spenza was not Livia.

'Get up,' Alberto said to the woman. Obediently she moved to one side. He wrapped himself in a sheet and lumbered to his feet.

'Where's Livia?'

Alberto crossed to the window and glanced out. 'So you came alone,' he commented. 'That was rash.'

With a snarl James advanced on the Italian. 'Tell me where she is, you bastard, or I'll—'

'Or you'll what? I have the ear of influential people. What do you think, that one girl is more important to them than their war on tyranny?' He smiled mirthlessly. 'But if you have really lost something of value to you, you could always ask at the police station. Perhaps someone has handed it in.'

'What are you talking about?'

'She won't be coming back. But if you do ever find her, you might like to give her this.' He picked up the dress and threw it to James. He recognised it as Livia's.

'She was a good fuck,' Alberto said conversationally. 'I hope the Germans appreciate her. And you, my friend – I hope you enjoy having more horns than a dozen baskets of snails.'

With a curse James ran towards him, and found himself looking down the barrel of a pistol. For a long moment they stared at each other. Then, without another word, James turned and left.

The Italian called after him, 'Careful as you go through the front door. Those horns might hit the lintel.'

*

281

Seething and humiliated, he retraced his steps up the track to Fiscino. He could guess something of what Alberto had done now, although he still couldn't imagine how or why Livia had let herself get mixed up with him. And what had he meant about the Germans, and the basket of horns?

Marisa was waiting for him. 'Well?' she said anxiously. 'Was she there?'

'No,' he said curtly. He threw down the dress. 'Only this. Marisa, I think you'd better tell me everything.'

When she had finished he closed his eyes. 'Why didn't she tell me all this?'

'How would you have reacted if she had?'

It was a good question. Although he was moved by the enormity of the sacrifice Livia had made, another part of him was appalled that she had been able to do it at all.

'I suppose there's absolutely no doubt,' he said, 'that she slept with that brute?'

She hesitated. 'I could lie, and say that perhaps she didn't. But we'd both know it isn't true. She did what she had to do.'

He took a deep breath. At the thought of Alberto and Livia together – doing not just what James and Livia had done together, but all those things that they had not yet done – he felt sick. A basic, primal jealousy boiled in his veins.

'James,' Marisa said quietly, 'it's you she loves. Whatever she did, she never stopped loving you. You have to go on believing that.'

The sound of truck engines drifted up from the road. Three big army lorries were driving up the hill, very slowly, as if lost. When they got to the cluster of houses that was Fiscino, the first one turned round. But instead of going back down the hill again, as James had been expecting, it began to reverse towards the *osteria*.

James watched, puzzled. The truck stopped, and a soldier jumped down from the cab, but he was simply guiding the truck closer to the damaged building, shouting instructions to the driver.

'What are you doing?' James called.

'Hold on,' the soldier yelled, banging the side of the truck. He turned to James. 'Captain Gould?'

'That's right,' James said, mystified. 'What's going on?'

'We're in the right place, then.' The soldier saluted. 'Private Griffiths, Royal Engineers. I heard you on the radio, sir.'

'The radio?'

282

Griffiths nodded. 'That speech you made when the general came.'

'Oh – but that was in Italian—'

'That's right – I'm pretty fluent, now. I was listening with the wife, anyway, so she helped me out. You'll remember the wife, sir. Algisa Griffiths. Though her maiden name was Fiore.'

James stared at him. 'Private *Griffiths*. Of course – you once killed three Germans with your bare hands and a spoon.'

Griffiths looked a little embarrassed. 'Ah. That was a slight error of translation, actually. There was a spoon involved, but there was also a machine gun, only I didn't have the word for machine gun at the time.'

'But what on earth are you doing here? And who are all these other people?' More and more soldiers were jumping down from the trucks.

'Well, that's Corporal Taylor,' Griffiths said, as another man stepped forward to shake James's hand.

'Gina's not here, of course,' Taylor said. 'She's looking after little James, but she sends you her best. Very pleased to meet you at long last, sir.'

'That's Bert, Violetta's husband. And over there's Jim – he's brought Silvana with him . . . Magnus and Addolorata . . . Ted and Vittoria . . .'

'But what are you all doing here?'

'We heard you say that you and your girl had been having a spot of trouble. So we put the word out and – well, we thought we'd come and see if you needed a hand. Ah, there's the timber.' A second truck had backed up to the *osteria*, and men were sliding out lengths of wood. Private Griffiths surveyed the wreckage of the kitchen with a practised eye. 'Looks worse than it is. I used to be a builder, before I joined the Engineers.'

James sighed. 'You're very kind, but my girl isn't here.'

'Well, you'd better go and sort it out with her, hadn't you? You can leave this lot to us.'

James hesitated. 'Can I ask you a rather personal question? As a married man?'

'Of course.'

'I think you know that Algisa – well, before she met you, there were—' He stopped, unsure exactly how to put this.

Corporal Griffiths said calmly, 'She went with soldiers, sir, and that's the truth of it. And I'm very glad she did.'

'Glad? Why?'

'Because if she hadn't, she'd have starved,' he said simply. 'And then I'd never have met her.'

'Was it – difficult for you?'

'It was hell. But not half as difficult as living without her would be. At the end of the day, that's all that matters, isn't it? What we feel for each other.'

'Yes,' James said. 'Of course.' He put out his hand. 'Thank you, Corporal Griffiths. You've been a great help.'

He turned and hurried back to the jeep.

At the Questura, the main police station, he was shown into the presence of the chief of police. James explained why he was there. The man called for the relevant files and looked through them lugubriously. Eventually he turned a file round and pointed. 'It's written here,' he said. 'There seems to be no doubt. Livia Pertini. Arrested in the act of soliciting, and examined by a doctor the same afternoon. She was taken to the camp at Afragola to join the other girls.'

James's blood ran cold. 'So where is she now?'

The policeman glanced at his watch. 'I should imagine they will already have left by boat for the journey north.'

'We have to stop them. There's been a terrible mistake.'

The chief of police folded his hands over his stomach. 'Are you her boyfriend?'

'Yes, as it happens.'

'Ah.' The chief of police nodded thoughtfully. 'You were not aware that she was supporting herself in this way. This happens.'

'She is *not* a prostitute. Nor is there any question of her being diseased.'

'If you say so. But it's out of my hands now, it's a military matter.'

'There has been corruption. I demand a full investigation.'

The chief of police gave him a hard look. 'Be careful what you accuse us of,' he said mildly. 'Unless your proof is absolutely cast iron.' After a moment he nodded. 'I thought not.' He started gathering the papers together. The interview was clearly at an end. 'What will you do now?' he said conversationally.

'As matter of fact,' James said, 'I'm going to go and fetch her back.'

The chief of police smiled. 'I don't think you understand. She is being taken behind the German lines.'

'I understand perfectly.' James stood up. 'And however long it takes, I promise you I will find her.'

She had been taken to a cell, still shouting, and pushed inside. The door slammed shut. Livia had hammered on it, calling them dishonest sons-ofbitches and vermin, but her only answer was a laugh on the other side of the door and the sound of footsteps walking away. She yelled some more.

'There's no point,' a voice behind her said. She turned. Three young women were sitting on a bench under the cell's only window. They were all around her own age, dark haired and pretty. The one who had just spoken said, 'They won't come back. Renata tried to bribe them, and even that didn't work.'

The youngest of the three nodded and said, 'I told them they could have a free go, and I'd give them a thousand lire each as well. But they took the money anyway, and they were too scared to go with me because of the infection. Where did they arrest you?'

'Nowhere,' Livia said. 'I refused a *camorrista*'s offer of marriage, and he didn't like it. I need to talk to someone in authority and get myself examined by a doctor. They'll soon discover it's all a lie.'

'They won't let you see a doctor now,' the third girl said. Her voice was very quiet, as if she were terribly shy. 'They think we'll do or say anything to avoid being sent north. Once you've got the certificate to say you're infected, that's it as far as they're concerned.'

After a couple of hours the door opened and they were escorted onto a truck by a *carabiniere* who refused to answer any of their questions. Then they were driven out of Naples. Eventually the truck arrived at an army compound near the sea. Soldiers stared at the four women as they drove through the camp, but there was no humour or curiosity in their glances, only appraisal. Livia got the impression that they all knew why the women were there, and that they were not the first the men had seen passing this way.

Sure enough, they were taken to a makeshift prison block which already contained a dozen or so women in four separate cells. The four new arrivals were put in a cell, where a British officer visited them and calmly told them what they would have to do.

'Basically, when you get to Rome you'll be taken to the German military brothel, where you'll sleep with as many Germans as possible. You won't have a great deal of choice in the matter, because we're going to give you identity papers but no money. You'll have to earn what you need. But presumably you're used to that.'

'What will happen if the Germans realise we're infected?' one girl asked.

'You can assume they won't be too happy about it.'

'This is outrageous,' Livia protested. 'We're women, not weapons. You must at least give us access to medical treatment.'

'Actually, you're criminals,' the officer retorted. 'Prostitution being a civil and military offence.' He threw some bags onto the floor. 'We've taken the liberty of packing some things for you. Can't have you looking a mess when you get to the Eternal City, can we? We'll be leaving by boat in a few hours' time.'

'There's been a terrible mistake,' Livia said. 'I'm the friend of a British officer, James Gould. You must get a message to him.'

'Every girl in Naples is the friend of a British officer,' the man said. 'And if you think I've got nothing better to do than pass on messages, you're mistaken. Your officer friend will be much better off without you.' He turned and left the cell, locking the door behind him.

One of the girls opened the bags. They contained dresses, hats and shoes, but little else.

'This is ridiculous,' Livia fumed, kicking one of the bags.

'What did he mean, a German military brothel?' the girl with the very shy voice asked.

'The Germans do things differently from the Allies,' the girl called Renata said. 'You're not allowed to stop men on the street. You have to go to a place that's run by the army. There was one in Naples, when the Germans were here.'

For the first time Livia realised just how bad her predicament was. She was not only going to be taken behind the German lines, but she was also going to be taken to a brothel. What would happen if she refused to do what was expected of her? She said, 'Presumably we can tell the Germans we're sick. They won't want us in their brothel then.'

'No, but then they send you to a prison camp,' Renata said. 'They don't treat women with infections, only soldiers.'

As the night went on the girls told each other their stories. None of them had been prostitutes before the war. The girl with the shy voice, a nineteen-year-old called Abelina, had fallen in love with a German officer. 'No one told me I shouldn't,' she whispered softly. 'After all, we were on the same side then, and Jurgen had nothing to do with the SS or with Hitler. We would have been married by now if the Germans hadn't withdrawn. But after they left, everyone in the village said I was a slut for going with him. No one would give me food or work, so I had to earn money this way instead.'

Bianca had been raped by the Allied soldiers who liberated her village, a group of Moroccans from a Free French regiment. 'They did it to all the women,' she said. 'But I was the only one who was engaged. When my fiancé found out he said he'd have nothing to do with me.

No one else would help me after that, so what choice did I have?'

Renata was the youngest, but she was from the Neapolitan slums, and after the war started she had become a whore because there were no other jobs available. She had heard about the *rastrellamenti*, and knew that they could be avoided by getting a proper job, but she was the only breadwinner in her large family, and a waitress's wages weren't going to keep them all in food. When she'd been caught, she'd assumed she could bribe her way out of trouble – but by that time the *carabinieri* wanted to get the operation finished with.

Livia listened to them recounting their stories – so matter-of-factly, without self pity or false sentiment – and felt a strange kind of anger, different to any she had ever felt before. It was not like the explosive fury she had felt when Pupetta was killed, or the terrible hopelessness she had felt when her father lay dying. Instead, she felt a deep, passionate conviction that none of them should be there, any more than her; that this war – which, according to James and others, was a good war, a war that had to be fought – was nevertheless being fought in the wrong way, by generals so determined to win that they had forgotten how to be compassionate and fair. People were often good, and did good things, such as the things that had been done to help after Vesuvius erupted, but as soon as those same people were given any authority or power, they abused it, or ignored the human consequences of their actions. And the people who ended up suffering most were always the women, because they had no authority or power to start with.

The solution, of course, was for women to somehow achieve power for themselves. But she couldn't see how that would ever happen, not in Italy.

She saw now that this war, which she had thought was being fought between the forces of fascism and the forces of democracy, was actually about a whole series of different conflicts. There was the conflict between those who wanted women to stay at home, and those who thought that women should be able to work. There was the conflict between those who wanted young people to show more respect, and those who wanted old people to show more tolerance. There was the conflict between those who embraced the Americans, with their movies and their slang and their gangsters and their jive, and those who wanted Europe to be more European. There was the conflict between those who thought that ordinary people should know their place, and those who thought that ordinary people needed to be set free. There was the conflict between those who thought that government meant public service, and those who thought that government should have more power. But most of all there was the conflict between those who wanted everything to go back to the way it was before, and those who wanted everything to change, and in that conflict – a conflict whose battles were yet to be fought, and whose armies were still massing their troops – she knew which side she was going to be on.

PART FOUR

Forty-one

The boat left from the harbour at Gaeta, speeding without lights through the water. There were about a dozen women on board, escorted by two men from A-Force, one British and one Italian. From the way the two men spoke to each other Livia realised they had made this journey before. There was no shelter on board and the women, in their flimsy dresses, were soon drenched. Huddling together for warmth, they said little as the boat bounced and twisted over the waves.

Livia watched the outline of Vesuvius recede into the distance and wondered if she would ever see Naples again. There were no lights because of the blackout, but she could imagine all too easily the little cluster of houses at Fiscino, her father and her sister . . . And James. She wondered what he was doing now, and if he even knew that she was missing.

Suddenly there was a shriek. One of the girls – Bianca, the one who had been raped by Moroccan soldiers – had run to the edge of the boat and thrown herself overboard. The British officer swore and cut the engine, bringing the boat about. The other women crossed themselves, muttering prayers under their breath as the men searched the water. But without lights there was little chance of finding her. After a few minutes the officer gunned the engine again, and they left the area.

The other officer drew his pistol after that, and announced he would shoot anyone who tried to throw themselves out. It was, Livia thought, a ridiculous gesture – Bianca had meant to kill herself, not to escape, since they were miles from shore, and a bullet would hardly be a deterrent in such a case – but no one else tried to follow her example.

Livia had given up trying to make plans. Fear had dulled her mind to the point where she was incapable of thought. What lay ahead – the Germans, the inevitable eventual discovery, the recriminations that would surely follow – was too horrible to contemplate. Easier just to wait, to be told when to sleep, when to exercise, when to eat, when to move.

But a small voice in her brain reminded her that this torpor was only temporary, that sooner or later there would be chances for escape. When those chances came, she would take them.

The night was moonless, but the sea gave off a faint phosphorescent glow, and she could tell when they were nearing land again because the shoreline stood out black against the purple sky. The boat slowed to a walking pace, and the British officer went to the bow to peer into the water, looking for mines. For several minutes they proceeded like this, and then the officer was evidently satisfied, because he turned and raised his hand.

The boat accelerated: there was a 'chunk' sound as it hit something in the water, then a flash from under the boat – like underwater lightning, Livia thought: it flickered and was gone again. A great bulge of water seemed to rear out of the sea, barging the boat into the air. She heard screams, splintering wood, and only then, it seemed, the crack of an explosion. Cold water poured over her head and she was swimming – swimming, she suddenly realised, in the wrong direction: what she had thought in the darkness and confusion was up was actually down, and now her lungs were bursting. For ten agonising seconds she thought that she wasn't going to make it, that she was going to have to open her mouth and inhale nothing but salt water, but then, like a cork, she felt herself popping to the surface. Her head struck a splintered bit of wood, she felt oil from the engines coating her hair, but there was air, and her tortured lungs gratefully sucked it in.

Around her others were coming to the surface too, grabbing onto bits of wreckage. Livia looked around. The shore was less than a hundred yards away. Wearily she turned onto her back and began kicking in that direction.

Eight of them made it to the beach, including the officer who had been standing in the bow when the mine exploded. He was bleeding heavily from his chest: it was a wonder, Livia thought, that he had possessed the strength to swim at all.

They made him as comfortable as they could, taking off his wet clothes and making a shelter from branches. Only Renata, the Neapolitan girl from the slums, refused to help. 'He wanted to shoot us,' she said. 'As far as I'm concerned, he got what he deserved.'

'He was carrying out his orders,' Livia said. She fetched some more branches. It made no difference: the man died before daybreak. They had no spades to bury him, but they said a prayer together over his body.

'Now what?' It was Abelina who asked the question. 'Shall we find a German and give ourselves up?'

'And then what do you think will happen?' Renata said scornfully. 'As far as they're concerned, we're worse than spies – we're saboteurs. Being shot would be the best we could hope for.'

'But we didn't choose to come here.'

'Do you really think that will make any difference? Most of the Germans didn't choose to come here either. No, I know what I'm going to do.'

'What's that?'

'I'm going to find a town and try to earn some money. Where there are men, a woman doesn't have to starve.'

'What about you, Livia?' Abelina asked. 'What do you think we should do?'

Livia thought for a moment. 'In my village, there were men who had walked back from prisoner-of-war camps in the north. They slipped through the German lines without any trouble. If they can do it, so can we.'

'We don't even know where we are,' Renata objected.

'We know we have to go south. And we're women – at least no one will be trying to shoot us.'

'But look at the way we're dressed,' someone said. It was true: they were wearing the kinds of clothes their captors had thought appropriate for whoring, not walking.

'Well, I'm going to chance it,' Livia said. 'Anything's better than doing what those officers wanted us to do. Who's coming with me?'

'I will,' Abelina said.

To Livia's surprise, Renata too said, 'Oh, all right. I might as well give it a try. I can always stop somewhere on the way if I change my mind.'

Another girl whose name Livia did not know said, 'It's too far. I'm staying around here.'

The other three girls also decided that it was too far, and too dangerous, to try to get back to Naples, although they none of them seemed to have any clear plan of what they would do. It was as if they had been ordered around so much, and for so long, whether by the men they slept with, their pimps, or the A-force officers, that they had lost the power of independent action. Out of fear and inertia, Livia realised, they were probably going to end up doing just what the Allies had expected of them. Livia did her best to change their minds, but there was no point in trying to drag them off against their wills. The journey would be hard enough without that.

Livia, Abelina and Renata walked inland until they came to a village, where they asked directions. It turned out they were just west of Rome. Hearing this, Livia's spirits lifted a little. They were probably only seventy miles from the front line, and then it was another seventy miles after that to Naples.

It soon became clear, however, that there was a big difference between Renata and the girls from the country, Livia and Abelina. The former had never had to walk further than a mile or two in her life, and after half a day she was complaining of blisters and exhaustion.

Livia was exhausted too. 'We can rest,' she said, 'but we can't stop for long, or we'll never get back.' They sat down on the grass and took off their shoes.

Then they heard the sound of vehicles coming towards them. Livia would have hidden, but the trucks were on them before they could move – a convoy, each lorry filled with German soldiers. The men in the back of the trucks waved delightedly at the girls, the drivers tooted their horns, and Renata stuck out her thumb. The last truck slowed down and stopped.

'What do you think?' Abelina said anxiously. 'Is it safe?'

'Well, I'm going with them.' Renata ran towards the back truck. After a moment Livia and Abelina followed her.

The men at the back of the truck pulled them up, their faces cracking open into broad grins as they shouted things back and forth to each other in German. From the laughter, Livia guessed that the comments were lewd ones. And there was nowhere to sit – the soldiers were point-ing to their laps, and suggesting that the girls sit on those. Livia shook her head, only to go sprawling as the truck moved off.

She felt hands pulling her up, and a huge soldier gently but firmly pulled her onto his lap. Opposite her, Renata and Abelina were already seated on two other soldiers. The one she was sitting on smiled at her and said 'Ich Heinrich.' He pointed at Livia interrogatively.

'Livia,' she said nervously.

'*Bella* Livia.' It seemed to be the only word of Italian he knew. '*Bella*.' He bounced her on his knees as easily as if she had been a baby. When she gasped, he stopped, and looked apologetic.

They sat on the soldiers' laps for twenty miles, and in return had to endure little more than the occasional shy kiss, some out of tune singing, and much raucous laughter. When the trucks finally pulled over and set the girls down, all of them were sorry to see the Germans go.

There had been no food all day, and by the time they had walked another ten miles it was getting late. They had nothing to lose, so they stopped and knocked on doors in the next village. The people were poor, their crops devastated by the war, but despite the girls' appearance they gave them a little bread before showing them to a barn where they could spend the night. Near the barn there was an apricot tree. Livia filled her stomach, and went to sleep thinking about the apricots of Fiscino.

The next day they were on the road again soon after dawn. All day they walked. It was baking hot. There were no soldiers to give them a lift today, and apart from a dogfight between two aeroplanes at midday, no signs of the war. Only the absence of any animals in the pastures, and the fact that none of the vines had been tended, indicated that there was anything unusual about the peacefulness of the landscape. But it was noticeable that the villages they passed through were strangely silent. Often not even a dog barked.

Across the valley a pillar of smoke hung on the horizon. As they got nearer Livia began to wonder what had caused it. Something to do with the war, she wondered, such as burnt-out vehicles? There seemed to be no obvious dangers, so they kept on the way they were going.

It was only when they got much closer to the smoke that they found out what had caused it. It was coming from a village. There was no one about as they entered the outskirts, yet someone, Livia was sure, was cooking. She had not eaten for so long that her senses were finely attuned to the smell of food, and she could swear that the wind was bringing her a waft of roasting meat, like when a *bufala* was roasted on a spit. Her mouth watered. 'There's food,' she told the others. 'Let's see if we can beg some.'

They rounded a corner, and saw that the smoke was coming from the church, which was on fire. It was only then that Livia realised there was something wrong with the smell. It was like roasting meat, certainly, but there was something acrid behind it, something that caught at the back of the throat, and it was coming from the burning church.

'Oh, no,' she said, horrified, her hand at her mouth.

The door to the church had collapsed, blackened. Inside, the roof had burnt through, and the sunlight that streamed in made it easy to see what was there. Some of the twisted, blackened bodies had been incinerated, but others had only partially burnt. Some were clustered round the altar, which had itself been reduced to a charred stump by the fire. Others were lying by the door, as if they had been trying to escape. Most, Livia noticed, were women and children.

As she turned away Livia saw an old woman sitting in the road. She was rocking back and forth, as if she were cradling a baby, but there was no baby in her arms. Livia crossed to where she was, and sat down next to her. 'What happened here?' she asked gently.

'Partisans,' the old woman said numbly.

'Partisans did this?'

'No. It was the Germans. They said that we let the partisans take our food.' The woman struck her own head. 'What could we do? We asked the partisans to go away, but they kept coming back. So the Germans came and put everyone in the church. They threw grenades in. Then they set fire to the church.'

'How did you escape?'

'They left me here to tell the partisans what happened. I'm the only one they spared.' The old woman blinked. 'My family, my neighbours, my granddaughter – they're all dead. They even burnt the dogs.'

There was nothing they could do for her. They left the empty village and walked downhill in silence. On the horizon, on other hills around the valley, half a dozen more plumes of smoke curled into the air. When darkness fell, they huddled together under a tree, but none of them slept much that night.

The next morning they walked again. Livia no longer felt hungry. Every time she recalled that smell she felt ill. Occasionally they passed evidence of more military activity – a troop truck lying twisted by the road, a huge crater showing where it had been blown onto its side; a sudden scattering of machine-gun casings and empty ammunition boxes; a man tied to a tree, naked, his swollen body riddled with bullets and left to the birds and foxes. Only when Abelina began to faint from lack of food did they dare to knock on doors. Remarkably, they were given some – a woman took them into her kitchen and gave them a little boiled rice. Livia thanked her profusely: she could see that the woman would not be eating any better herself, and presumably even to offer food to strangers here was to risk German reprisals.

The woman waved away her thanks. 'I've got a son fighting in Russia,' she said. 'If I turned you away, perhaps he would get turned away. If I feed you, perhaps God will make sure that someone feeds him.'

That night, Livia sat and watched what she thought was a summer thunderstorm lighting up the horizon to the south. It was only when she noticed there was no pattern to the flashes that she realised she was looking at the two sides shelling each other on the front line.

The next day they saw a convoy of German armoured cars on the road ahead, and decided to make a detour rather than risk being seen. Getting hopelessly lost, they spent the whole day negotiating a steep ravine in order to get back to the path only metres from where they had started.

The way was all uphill now. Livia's muscles felt like lead, and her head felt thick and groggy. Looking at Abelina, she could see that she was in an even worse way. Her skin was shiny with sweat, her gait was unsteady and her eyes unfocused. Livia went to offer her an arm, but as she did so Abelina stumbled and fell. Livia felt her forehead: she was burning. She must be getting another bout of the infection. Renata came forward to take Abelina's other arm, but they made even slower progress as they half-carried her between them.

A man's voice said, 'Where are you going?'

Livia looked around. She could see no one, and for a moment she thought she must be hallucinating.

'If they are a trap,' a second male voice said, 'they are a very nice-looking one.'

Two men stepped out from the bushes. They were wearing a few scraps of faded uniform, but their feet were shod in the traditional sandals of mountain peasants, with straps that criss-crossed their calves, and at their throats were bright red neckerchiefs. Each had a rifle, and they were pointing them at the women. 'Where are you going?' one said.

Livia was too tired to be frightened. 'We're trying to get to Naples.'

The man considered this. 'Well, you can't go this way,' he said. 'You'll meet a *tedescho* observation post about two miles down the road.'

'Is there a way to get round them?'

'Only by going over the mountain.'

'We need somewhere to rest,' Livia said. 'This girl is ill, and the rest of us are exhausted. Is there somewhere we can stay the night?'

'What do you think?' the man asked his companion in a low voice.

The other man must have agreed, because the first one turned back to the women and said, 'You can come with us. But if I think you're signalling to anyone, you'll get a bullet in the back.'

He stepped forward into the road and gestured for them to follow him.

'Come on, ladies,' he said humorously. 'We've got a long climb ahead of us.'

They walked for another hour, taking it in turns to help Abelina. Eventually they reached a dense chestnut wood where their guide called a halt.

'Well, this is it,' he said, looking around him. 'Welcome to our *casa*.'

Livia didn't understand. Why were they stopping? Then, looking around her more carefully, she saw that there were a number of wigwam-like tents dotted among the trees, each one camouflaged with leaves and branches. People were emerging to look at the newcomers. Some were in uniform, some wore peasants' clothes, and some wore what looked like homemade sheepskin jackets. All of them wore the same red neckerchief as the man who was their guide.

A young man detached himself from one of the groups and walked towards them. 'Welcome, comrades,' he called. 'My name is Dino, and you are now under my command.'

Dino was young, about twenty-two, but he had the confidence and charisma of a natural leader. Initially he was suspicious of the three women's sudden appearance in his camp.

'If you're working for the fascists,' he said flatly, 'you'll be dead before dawn.'

Livia explained again that they were simply trying to get to Naples.

'Now is a bad time to try to cross the line,' Dino said. 'If the Germans don't get you, the Allied artillery will. You'd do better to wait a few weeks. Then the Germans will be forced to retreat past us.' He waved expansively towards the south. 'After that there'll be nothing between you and Naples.'

'Can we stay here while we're waiting?'

'We can't afford to keep visitors. If you eat, you work.'

'Of course.'

'What can you do? You look like whores, if you don't mind me saying.'

'Some of us are,' Livia admitted.

'Then you are the victims of capitalism and you will not be exploited here. Can you cook?'

'I can,' Livia said with a shudder, 'but at the moment I'd rather not.'

'Can you shoot?'

'Yes. I'm from the country – I've been shooting hares since I was a child.'

Dino unshouldered his rifle and handed it to her. 'Shoot that tree,' he said, pointing to a chestnut fifty yards away.

Livia's hand shook as she raised the gun to her shoulder. It was heavier than her father's, and she was weak from lack of food. But she planted her feet properly, as her father had taught her, and breathed lightly as she squeezed the trigger. The recoil thumped her shoulder, and a split second later she heard the crack as the bullet hit the trunk.

'Could you do that to a German?' Dino asked laconically.

She thought of the burnt, blackened bodies in the church. She could shoot the people who had done that. Then she thought of the innocent, shy soldiers who had given them a lift, and sung out of tune. Could she shoot *those* men? And what if they were one and the same people, the singers and the murderers?

'Yes,' she said, 'I could.'

Dino nodded. 'Good.'

He took her to a tent and showed her a heap of stinking clothes to look through. She chose what uniform she could find – a pair of khaki trousers and a rough serge shirt.

He handed her a red neckerchief. 'Whatever else you wear, always wear this. We are *Garibaldini*, and we wear the revolutionary flag. The *Bagdolini*, the monarchists, wear blue neckerchiefs. If you would rather be a blue, you don't have to stay here – we can send you to a different group.'

'So you're communists?'

'Yes. Do you know anything about communism?'

'Nothing at all,' Livia confessed.

'We'll teach you. If you want to stay with us, that is.'

'I'll stay,' Livia said.

The partisans had cooked a stew made from mule meat and chestnuts. Livia had thought she was starving, but when she was given a bowl of the stew, she found herself quite unable to eat it. It was not that it was badly made – considering how little they had to work with, the cooks had done a remarkable job, tenderising the mule meat with slow cooking and flavouring it with forest herbs and myrtle leaves, as well as chestnuts and a few mushrooms. But the smell of meat, once so delightful to her, made her gag. She picked out a piece of mushroom and a few chestnuts, then set the plate aside.

The men in the camp were of many nationalities. Some were local farm hands, forced to make a choice between joining the resistance or being taken by the Germans. Some were escaped prisoners of war, Russian, Polish and British, tired of walking south to rejoin the Allies. There were women, too, and these fell into two distinct groups. There were the hangers-on, the girlfriends and cooks, their long skirts grubby from the forest mud. Then there were a smaller number who were fighters. They wore the same clothes as the men and were treated by them as equals. Some of these women smoked pipes, which made their tiny tobacco allowance go further, and like the men they had elaborate *noms de guerre*, which were sewn into their red neckerchiefs. It was this group of women which Livia had joined.

The next day, she got her first taste of resistance fighting. The partisans went to a road the Germans were known to use and set up an ambush – a captured German landmine hidden in the dirt at the side of the road, which would be detonated by someone pulling a wire at the right moment. The other partisans, around forty of them, arranged themselves in ditches and behind trees, waiting. When the convoy of trucks approached, their headlights reduced to tiny blue slits to avoid drawing air attacks, Dino let half of it go through before giving the order. The explosion blew one of the trucks right off the road into a ditch. Immediately the partisans rose up out of the darkness, firing at the trucks that had been forced to stop, which themselves disgorged men with weapons who fired back.

Within moments, the air was a cat's cradle of bullets flying back and forth. Livia, crouched behind a tree with her own rifle, heard the thuds as German bullets smashed into the trunk. There were so many of the enemy, and they had the better weapons. Some of them were trying to set up a machine gun behind one of the trucks, but one of the partisans' few grenades took care of that. Then Dino gave the order to withdraw, and the partisans melted away into the woods. They had lost two men, but thought they had probably killed half a dozen. They would not know for sure until the Germans carried out their reprisals. Since the Germans always executed ten civilians for every soldier killed, knowing how many had been murdered in reprisal was an efficient way of keeping score.

Every afternoon, when the German patrols were at their most active, the partisans stayed in the camp and formed into small groups for seminars on communist theory. For Livia, it was a revelation. All her life, politics had been a subject for men, which women were kept well away from, and which seemed to consist in any case simply of moaning about the corruption of so-and-so and the impossibility of getting a fair deal in this world. Now, for the first time, someone actually sat down and explained the basic building blocks of society to her – the difference between the factory owner and the factory worker, and why the former was always trying to reduce the wages of the latter, but with the proviso that it was nothing to do with him if the factory worker ended up starving or out of work; and why women were treated like property, and why the many always ended up working for the few. With a suddenness that took even her by surprise, Livia became a convert. At last there was an alternative to the poverty and exploitation she had been surrounded by all her life. Italy was a country blessed with resources: all they had to do was distribute the wealth fairly, instead of allowing it to be siphoned off. If proof were needed that the communist system was an effective one, you had only to look at Russia. It was Russia whose armies had turned the tide of the war for the Allies, Dino pointed out, and that was because the Russian soldiers believed in the system they were fighting for. If the Italian communists could show that they were equally organised, they would inevitably form the first post-war government, and the country could begin to reorganise itself along more egalitarian lines.

What was more, the communists actively encouraged women to see themselves as men's equals. Just as no one should be allowed to own another man's labour through a contract of employment, so no one should be allowed to own a woman's body through a contract of marriage. Marriage and prostitution, Dino explained, were two sides of the same capitalist coin – if anything, prostitution was the less immoral, because a man who hired a woman gave her freedom back to her when the transaction was over, like a man employing a labourer by the hour, whereas marriage was slavery.

Livia did not totally agree with this – it seemed to her that there were some men who saw marriage as a partnership of equals, not as the acquisition of property, but she had to admit that such men were rare, and that the law and the church, whatever they might claim, were fundamentally united in treating a woman as her husband's chattel. The partisans were the first organisation she had ever come across that treated both sexes the same. 'The rifle does not care who fires it,' as Dino put it. 'And the German corpse does not care who shot him whether male or female.'

Looking back at the events of the past few years, it seemed to Livia that there was a simple inevitability about her new-found interest. It had been politics that had trapped Italy between the Allies and the Germans; politics which had taken her husband away from her, but also politics which had dictated that she marry so young in the first place. Politics had influenced the Allies' invasion of Italy; and it was the corruption of local politicians which had allowed people like Alberto to gain and wield power over her. Politics had ennabled the A-force officers to treat the women they rounded up as though they were of no more account than a box of ammunition, to be fired at the Germans. Now, as Dino said, the ending of the war, together with the death of Mussolini, would bring a political vacuum in which for the first time ordinary Italians had a chance to take on the big businessmen, the Mafia, the state and the church to create the kind of society for themselves that they wanted.

All her passion channelled into this new outlet, Livia drank in every word, and soon she began asking questions. Asking questions was always encouraged, because it was only through dialectic, or debate, that truth emerged, just as history was a process of revolutions and counter-revolution which gradually led to progress. Soon she was raising points that Dino couldn't answer, and she was having to work out the answers for herself. But that was all right, because communism provided you with a set of mental tools which helped you to answer most questions in the end.

One thing in particular continued to trouble her, though, and she took the opportunity to raise it with Dino privately.

'What about the reprisals?' she asked. 'On the way here, we saw some terrible things. The Germans are killing innocent people because of what you do.'

'Yes,' Dino said. 'They have committed many atrocities in this area.'

'Couldn't you . . .' Livia hesitated. She had no wish to be told to leave the only shelter she had, but she needed to ask. 'Couldn't you let the Allies do the fighting, and then there would be fewer reprisals against Italians?'

'And wait for the Americans do our dirty work?' Dino's face darkened. 'This matter has been considered at the very highest level, and by the Allied commanders. Our orders come from them, and they say they need us to continue. In any case, what's the alternative? Do we let ourselves be blackmailed by the Germans into doing nothing while other people fight over our country? Italy disgraced herself when we helped those fascists in the first place. Now we have to be the ones to get rid of them.'

Despite their political differences with the Allies, the partisans regarded themselves as part of the Allied forces, subject to the same discipline and orders as any other unit. Sometimes their orders came by code from London on the World Service. After the news, the announcer would read out a list of messages for 'our friends in foreign lands'. 'Mario, your brother's cow is unwell' meant attack a fuel depot. 'Your grandmother has influenza' was an order to do a traffic count. 'The sky is red' meant to increase activity.

There was one endless topic of conversation amongst them: when would the Fifth Army arrive? It was said that in Rome the graffiti artists were even making jokes on the walls: 'Americans, hold on! We're coming to liberate you soon.'

For their part, the Germans remained confident that resistance activities would never amount to much. Everybody knew what Major Dollman, one of their commanders, had quipped to his superiors: 'As far as the partisans go, we are quite safe. The Italians dislike rising, whether from their beds or against an enemy.'

It was hard to keep the lice out of her hair, so Livia had one of the other women cut it short. Most of the fighting women had already done the same. As the weeks passed, she began to look more and more like them.

As for James, she tried not to think about him any more. That part of her life was surely over. It had been a pleasant but brief interlude in a series of tragedies, and when she tried to remember the time they had spent together it seemed as unreal as a dream.

Forty-two

James huddled in a foxhole, his neck hunched against the shower of falling earth that trickled into his collar. The earth was falling because a shell had just exploded twenty yards from where he crouched. His ears were still ringing from the blast. Another shell hissed overhead. But that was all right, because it was one of the Allies'. Every night, like some crazy game of tennis played with high explosives, the two sides bombarded each other's positions like this, shell for shell. It was only in the last week that the Germans had started becoming more inventive, sending over butterfly bombs during the night, which wafted silently into your trench, or lobbing phosphorous rockets towards the harbour, far at the rear.

'Wish they'd shut up,' Roberts grumbled next to him. He was fiddling with a radio. 'It's almost time for Sally.'

'You shouldn't listen to that rubbish.'

'It's the only rubbish there is.' The radio whined as Roberts tuned it in. And then there she was, murmuring seductively through the static – the sweet voice of Axis Sally. 'Hi, boys,' she announced. 'How are we all tonight? Wasn't that rain a bummer? Me, of course, I'm nice and snug here in my little tent – it's you I'm feeling sorry for. There's going to be a thunderstorm later, I'm told. And there's fifty thousand of you out there now, with nowhere to keep yourself dry. Fifty thousand. Heavens, that makes Anzio beach the largest prisoner-of-war camp in the world – and you know what? It's entirely self-supporting.' She chuckled at her own joke, then her husky voice became lower and more sympathetic. 'Did you hear about poor GI Ableman? We picked him up in no-man's-land a few hours ago. Seems he'd stepped on a Schuh mine. Nasty things, Schuhs. Now his guts are all hanging out. The medics are doing what they can, of course, but they don't seem to think there's much hope for him. So here's a little song to cheer up his pals.' A foxtrot came on.

'What a bitch,' Roberts said with feeling.

'It's all written for her,' James said. 'The Germans have propaganda specialists, just like we do.'

'"The largest prisoner-of-war camp in the world." You've got to admit, she has got a point.'

James grunted. Of course she had a point. There was no two ways about it: Anzio was a hellhole. Of the fifty thousand men Axis Sally had referred to, thousands were already dead. When he volunteered for the front line he had imagined fighting his way towards Rome town by town to look for Livia. But in the three weeks he had been here, they had barely advanced three hundred yards before being forced to retreat again. In Naples it had become commonplace to talk about the war turning against the Nazis. Here on the ground, things looked very different.

The music finished, and the sweet tones of the Germans' propagandist came back on. 'Let's face it, boys,' she said. 'The only way you're not going to be cold and wet tonight is if one of our bullets gets you first. How's the trenchfoot, by the way?' Another song started.

'Bloody awful, since you ask,' Roberts said, trying to pull his feet out of the puddle at the bottom of the foxhole. With no way of keeping their boots dry, many of the men suffered from feet that were literally rotting away.

Just as Axis Sally had predicted, it started to rain again, a heavy summer storm that swept more mud and debris into the foxhole. The water smelled foul. The fetid water, in fact, was another reason for the trenchfoot. With little space to bury the dead, and no coffins, bodies were simply placed behind walls made of compo ration boxes, shored up with a little earth. Only the day before James had found his way along the trench blocked by a rotting arm sticking out of the mud wall, the hand clutching at air like a beggar's. He had lifted it at the elbow and passed on.

It was his turn to go forward to the observation point. He strapped on a reel pack, a contraption like a rucksack that would play a telephone wire out from a spool on his back as he wriggled forward. Gingerly he climbed up the firestep and slithered like a turtle over the edge of the trench into the mud.

It was generally agreed that it was best to crawl forward on your elbows, dragging your legs behind you: that way you kept closer to the

305

ground, and so were less likely to get your head blown off. He wriggled in the direction of the German lines for a hundred yards or so, pausing every now and then as a shellburst illuminated the night sky and made movement even more dangerous than usual. It occurred to him, as it often did in this situation, how remarkably beautiful the Italian sky was in wartime. Each type of explosive generated its own particular light. Tracer bullets flashed across the darkness, their coloured trails like brilliant stitching in a piece of canvas. Very lights fizzed and sparkled like red fireworks. Then there were the 'Screaming Meanies', the multiple-launch rockets the Germans favoured over mortars, streaking past in salvos of four or eight at a time, sparks dancing in their slipstream like embers from a bonfire. The 'Chandelier' was a flare that floated slowly to earth on a parachute, lighting the terrain for spotters, so bright and white it seemed to turn the landscape below into the negative of a photograph. 'Bouncing Betties' exploded above the ground in a puff of dense black cordite, scattering landmines. 'Anzio Annie' was a German gun so large, and fired from so far away, that you never heard the sound it made as it was fired, only a noise like a freight train as the shell passed overhead, followed by a vast flash like summer lightning as it pulverised the harbour, and finally, seconds later, the rolling thunder of its bang.

As James moved forward he could still hear Axis Sally, coming from the direction of his own trenches. 'Say, boys, do you ever wonder what your girl's up to right now? Most likely she's having fun with one of those draft dodgers I've been reading about. You don't blame her, do you boys? A girl's only human, and you can hardly expect her to sit at home and wait for you . . . Here's a song for every soldier whose sweetheart is finding solace with someone else.' James gritted his teeth and slithered on. It was true, he did think about what Livia might be doing, although in her case it was something much worse than fooling around with a draft dodger he was picturing. He tried to banish the thought from his mind. Right now, the only thing that mattered was getting back to his dugout in one piece.

To his left, there was a sound like the yapping of a little dog. Someone was firing a Schmeisser into the darkness. There was a faint cry, and the firing stopped.

He paused to check that his telephone wire wasn't snagging. He was so close to the German positions now that the enemy would be able to hear the faintest noise, even the tug of a telephone wire on a stone or a loose board. The Germans, of course, had their own spotters out in no-man's-land. It was not unknown for two men, one German and one

Allied, both slithering forward in complete silence, to bash their heads against each other as they collided. Then it was a case of hand-to-hand combat until one of them was dead.

James rolled over onto his side and, careful not to raise his head, brought his binoculars up to his eyes. Soon an explosion to his left illuminated not only the sky but also the German position. They were fortifying the area known as Dusseldorf Ditch, he noticed. And Munich Mound looked as if it had taken a direct hit.

To his right he heard whispering. A German patrol, he guessed, engaged on much the same mission as he was. He kept very still. That was the strange thing about these nights: everything was conducted in whispers and murmurs, so as not to draw enemy fire, but the fire when it came was often so deafening you felt your ears pop.

The whispers appeared to have passed by. He picked up the telephone handset and said very quietly, 'Twenty Jerries at Dusseldorf.'

A disembodied voice said, 'Roger that. Keep your head down.' A minute later, four mortar shells landed simultaneously on the ditch where James had noticed the refortification work.

He stayed where he was, phoning in every ten minutes with targets. A machine gun being set up at Cologne Cowshed – not a cowshed any longer, just a pulverised mound of stones – got pulverised some more after James had phoned in its position. A flack wagon at Berlin Bend beat a hasty retreat as British mortars zeroed in on it. He had just picked up the telephone to send in another target when he heard a voice at the other end saying, 'Time to come back, chum.'

'Already?'

'Change of plan. We're moving.' He could hear the suppressed excitement in the man's voice. Perhaps it was true what everyone was saying, that the big breakout was going to happen any day now. James turned over onto his back again, wriggled round until his head was facing back towards his own lines, and began the long squirm back through the mud to the relative safety of the Allied trenches and his dugout.

The dugout had been his home for the three weeks he had been here. Built by a previous division, it was about five-feet square and had a roof of railway sleepers heaped with sandbags. The sleepers had been papered with old editions of the Stars and Stripes newspaper, and a further layer of sandbags had been placed around the floor, where they acted as stepping stones during the frequent floods. A raised board on a pile of sandbags was the only bed. For the hours of daylight James shared this little space – and, indeed, the bed – with two other men, Roberts and Hervey. He knew almost nothing about them, but he also knew them better than anyone he had ever met. Hour after hour spent confined with them, under almost constant bombardment, had laid their personalities and characters as bare as if they had known each other all their lives. It was not a carefree life, but it was a surprisingly simple one. He owned nothing, cared nothing for money since there was nothing to spend it on, spoke to complete strangers as if they were his friends, and had not washed or changed his clothes since he had last been sent to the showers two weeks ago.

When James had first put in for a transfer to the front line, Major Heathcote's initial reaction had been disbelief. The Italian campaign was entering its bloodiest phase so far, and although news of them was never allowed to reach the newspapers, hundreds of Allied soldiers had deserted. Others had shot themselves in the foot or thigh rather than carry on fighting, and still more were suffering from psychiatric conditions such as shell shock and neurasthenia which had not been seen since the trench warfare of the Somme. For someone with a cushy job in Field Security to volunteer for precisely those conditions which were sending other men mad made no sense whatsoever.

Eventually James had realised that the simplest way to get what he wanted was simply to tell the major what his real reasons were for wanting to go north. Disbelief had quickly turned to shock. The news that the wedding officer, far from discouraging marriages to Italians, was actually searching for a particular Italian girl so that he could marry her himself was proof of what the major had long suspected – that James was possessed of an underlying streak of moral degeneracy, and that the sooner he was got rid of the better. James was given just a few hours to pack his things and clear his desk. There was no time to revisit Zi' Teresa's for a last grappa with Angelo; no time to send word to Fiscino, or to watch the sunset turning the Bay of Naples into a saucer of blood. There was no time for a glass of marsala-and-egg with Dr Scottera, no time to stroll one last time down the Via Forcella. He barely had time to scribble a note for Jumbo, in which he explained briefly what had happened and asked his friend to make enquiries amongst his A-force contacts about Livia's whereabouts.

As he made his way to the harbour, from where he was to leave for Anzio, a fragment of a sentimental ballad drifted through his head, one of the songs the sheet music sellers had sung in the municipal gardens beyond his window:

E tu dice: 'I' parto, addio!'
T'alluntane da stu core . . .
Da la terra da l'ammore . . .
*Tiene 'o core 'e nun turnà?**

Whatever happened – whether he managed to find her or not – he had the sense that something was over, that a part of his life was drawing to a close.

In the harbour he located the hospital ship which was to transport him to Anzio. It had been delayed by bad weather, and was only now disembarking – an endless line of stretchers being carried ashore by Italian porters, the men on them swathed in bandages. He glanced at some of them, shocked by the grime and filth in which they were still caked. They looked more like exhausted schoolboys being carried off a games pitch than soldiers: mud encrusted their limbs like plaster casts. Dirt caked their lips, their hair, even their mouths and eyes. Here and there a stretcher was stained bright red with blood where the auxiliaries had been unable to stem the bleeding from their patient's wounds. How was it, James wondered, that he had spent so long in Naples, yet never before seen one of these ships unloading its cargo of smashed-up humanity?

It was only an hour and a half up the coast to Anzio, yet it was like entering a different world. The ship lingered a few miles off the coast, waiting for darkness, and James was able to enjoy a sunset the equal of any he had seen in Naples. Then, with a low throb, the engines picked up pace and they eased towards a tiny gap in the distant shore, framed by boats of all sizes – destroyers, motor boats, even a couple of frigates, and the soft, bobbing barrage balloons that always made James think of flying elephants. He stood on deck and watched as the shore grew near. There were no lights anywhere, and it was very quiet. It seemed impossible that this was really a battlefield.

High over the beach, a lone Messerschmitt appeared, circling as idly as an insect. 'Better get inside,' a rating called. 'That's Bedcheck Charlie. He might take a pop at us, if he can't find anything better.'

James kept an eye on the plane. 'Why's he called that?'

'He's the first one out every evening. They use him as an alarm clock.'

Sure enough, the Messerschmitt turned and dived towards one of the

---

*'So you say, "Farewell, I'm leaving!"/Going far from what the heart clings to. . ./From the land where you found love . . ./But would you rather not come back?'

destroyers. James was too far away to see the cannon firing, but puffs of smoke showed where the anti-aircraft guns were firing back. After a moment the aircraft circled away, strafing the beach as it flew inland.

Suddenly a huge spume of water erupted from the sea a hundred yards away, followed by another, and another, like the blowing of some leviathan-sized whale.

'It's started,' the rating said. 'Always the same. That'll be a couple of 122s.'

As if in response to some invisible signal, the dusk became alive with lights – rockets streaking towards the beach from far inland, and sparks dancing like fireflies in the darkness, which James realised belatedly were the flashes of rifle fire.

'Skirmish,' the rating said. 'Welcome to Anzio.'

James went inside the bridge. Neither the captain nor the crew seemed particularly concerned by the shelling, although they steered a zigzagging course towards the harbour. James could see a long line of men waiting on the quayside to meet them, quite motionless despite the bombardment. Most were on stretchers. To his left, a motor boat suddenly took a direct hit, lighting up the sky and spreading burning oil across the sea. There seemed to be nowhere on the beachhead that was out of range of the Germans' guns. More shells whistled overhead, and the plumes of water as they hit the sea seemed to James like the stabbing of a giant with a needle, randomly hoping to skewer them.

'When we get to the shore,' the captain shouted over the din, 'don't wait. We'll want to get that lot loaded as quickly as possible.'

James nodded. As soon as the boat bumped the quayside he leapt for dry land. A roar like an approaching train heralded the approach of the biggest shell so far, followed by a vast geyser of seawater that, minutes after the bang, fell down on him from a great height as a shower of tiny drops. He shook himself off and looked around for someone to report to. A subaltern was standing by a stack of artillery shells. Incredibly, he was rolling a cigarette. James ran up to him, his shoulders hunched against falling shrapnel, and said, 'I've just arrived.'

The man gave him an amused glance. 'You don't say.' His face was black with cordite and dirt.

'Where do I go?'

The subaltern pointed with his cigarette towards a hole in the ground. 'Down there.'

James lowered himself into the hole and found that it led, via various stairs and ladders, to an underground room. Staff officers were shouting

310

down telephones, and a map table in the centre of the room was lit by a couple of hurricane lamps. As James watched, the ground above them shook, and a trickle of sooty earth poured from between the rafters onto the centre of the map.

Eventually he found someone who could tell him where to go, and he set off to find the unit of mortar men he had been assigned to. A muddy track led towards the front line. To add to his disorientation, a greasy, acrid smokescreen was belching from a dozen smoke generators down-wind, and it was an effort to follow the handwritten signs that loomed out of the darkness. Many of them seemed to refer to jokes of which he, as a newcomer, was ignorant. 'Beachhead Hotel – two hundred yards – special rates for new arrivals.' 'Waggoner's rest – no resting.' 'You are here – but not for long.' Gradually they became more sinister. 'Danger – shelling – make no dust,' and 'Absolutely NO daylight traffic beyond this point.' The shelling had temporarily paused, and the loudest sound he could hear was the singing of three or four nightingales.

Suddenly a Very light lit up the sky above him. A rattle of machine-gun fire, very close, made him start, and he ducked down automatically. He was only about a hundred yards from the front now, he calculated, easily close enough to take a stray bullet in the neck. And he still had absolutely no idea of where he was meant to be going. He had a vision of simply blundering out into no-man's-land by mistake, and being shot almost before he had arrived. Then he saw a ladder going down into a trench, and a handwritten sign saying 'London Underground this way'. It led fifteen feet down to a narrow network of trenches, crowded with hollow-eyed, grime-encrusted men, along which he was passed – like a latecomer at a theatre, disturbing the whole row – until he eventually found himself in a small dugout, lit by a smoky lamp made out of a cig-arette tin. A sergeant saluted him, and a captain held out his hand. Roberts and Hervey had been here four weeks, with one brief rest period in the pine woods down by the beach – still within range of the shells – and on one thing they were agreed: Anzio was the arsehole of the world.

'Good thing you had room for me in here,' James said as he stowed his kit in the driest corner he could find. Then he realised his mistake. 'That is – sorry. I wasn't thinking.' He was, of course, taking someone else's place.

Hervey nodded. 'Stevens,' he said quietly. 'Got hit by an anti-person-nel mine two nights ago. We buried him behind the stream.'

He took James back along the trench, pointing out the various posi-tions their company occupied. From somewhere in front of them came the sound of voices shouting in German. Hervey shouted, '*Ruhe da, wir koennen nicht schlafen.*'

'What did you say?' James asked.

'I told them to shut up and let us sleep,' Hervey said.

The life expectancy of artillery spotters, James gathered, was not high. Each night they took it in turns to go out into no-man's-land, crawling from observation point to observation point, checking on the men under their command and calling down mortar fire on any German activity. Their days were spent trying to sleep, catching crab lice – the record for the dugout was eighty-five in a day – writing letters, racing beetles, and waiting for nightfall, when their one meal of the day would arrive on the ammunition trucks.

On his second night, James was slithering into the mud of no-man's-land when he saw a German helmet moving cautiously across the skyline. A moment later, the head elevated itself a little. James drew his pistol and steadied his aim. The German's head was in his sights. All he had to do was pull the trigger. For a moment, he almost did pull it. But then he considered. His orders, at that precise moment, were not to kill but to observe. If he fired, he would be depriving some family of their son, perhaps some wife of her husband, and he could not say for sure that it would make one jot of difference to the war. In fact, it might simply give away his own position, and call down retaliation from the German mortars.

After a moment, he eased the safety catch back on, and slipped the pistol back into its holster. He would do his job, and if he needed to kill in order to do it then he would do so. But he was not going to murder indiscriminately.

As the weeks passed, and the promised advance kept being delayed, his world shrank until the dugout, and his little patch of battlefield, became all that he could think about. Dimly, in the back of his mind, he held to the notion that there was a reason to get beyond that ridge, that river, to strike beyond the beautiful white-and-blue hills which could be seen in the distance, blocking the way to Rome. His life with Livia was another life, and if he thought about her at all it was as a kind of mirage, a vague, desperate yearning for laughter and gentleness and the smell of steaming *fettuccine al limone* – for anything, in fact, that was not covered in mud, lice and blood.

James crawled on his elbows back to the dugout, there he found Roberts packing up their equipment.

'You heard? We're off,' Roberts said.

'Where to?'

'Cisterna, apparently.'

James's heart quickened. Cisterna was on the way to Rome. 'So this is the breakout?'

'Looks like it. 'Bout bloody time, eh?'

They joined the rest of their company and headed towards the assembly point. Moving back from the line like this was a strange experience. To begin with you walked in a crouch, just as you did in the trenches. Then, as you got further out of German sniper range, you walked a little taller and more upright, until by the time you reached the rear you were walking properly for the first time in weeks, a great elation sweeping over you as you realised that no one was actually, at that precise moment, trying to kill you.

At the rear a railhead had been set up, bringing ammunition up from the harbour. James whistled when he saw it. The last time he had been back here, the ammunition stack had been the size of a shed. Now it was as large as a church, and had clearly been even larger before the artillery-men had started taking what they wanted.

'It's the big one, all right,' Roberts muttered.

They were given food, then stood to and waited. It was the usual pre-attack chaos – you were either in the way, or in the wrong place, or wanted urgently somewhere else for something that turned out to be not terribly urgent after all. As they passed a supply truck Roberts nudged him. 'See that? Water canteens. We might borrow a couple of those. If there's one thing I've learnt about advances, it's that you get thirsty.' No one was looking. They each took an extra canteen, draping them on their backs along with all their other kit.

Hervey spent the time writing a letter to his girl. When it was done he passed it to James to read and initial. Every letter had to be censored, and if you wanted it sent quickly, you got it censored by the men you fought alongside. There was now little James did not know about Caroline, who worked in an office in Whitehall. He scanned the letter quickly. 'Dear Caz, By the time you get this you'll know there's been a big one. Everyone here's excited. I just hope I don't let the other fellows down. I'm so glad Gould and Roberts will be with me, you know how much I rely on them. Hope that thing with your boss got sorted out. I'll write as soon as I can but don't worry if it takes a while, I'm betting the postal service won't be up to much for a few days after this.' James initialled it and passed it back to Hervey. He didn't feel like writing. His parents were the only people he wrote to, and there was nothing he could say that would help them picture his life as it was now. He and Roberts spent their time blacking their faces with mud.

The attack must be getting closer: they had to make way for the First Armoured Division, moving slowly forward with the Special Forces. 'That means we'll wait for daylight,' Roberts said. James nodded: it was well known that the tanks would rather be able to see what was in front of them when they advanced, even if it meant losing some of the advantage of a surprise attack in the dark.

Eventually the order was given for their section to move forward. They stood two abreast in a crowded trench, waiting for something to happen. Behind James a soldier was insisting that the Italian women preferred it from behind, whereas English girls liked to do it standing up. The conversation went on and on interminably. Then, just before dawn, the barrage started and talk was impossible. For forty-five minutes every big gun in the beachhead pulverised the German positions.

Still they waited, shuffling forward now along the trench, their ears ringing. Ahead of them the fighting had already started, but the sheer pressure of numbers meant they couldn't all get into the battle at once. How very British, James thought: even when about to risk their lives, there was a queue. But this was less orderly than a queue for a bacon ration. All around him men were relieving themselves or even defecating as their nerves got the better of them. Meanwhile, the first wounded were already coming back along the line, looking dazed or relieved depending on the severity of their injuries.

'Doesn't look too bad,' Hervey muttered.

'Those are just the ones who can walk,' Roberts pointed out. 'The other poor bastards are still out there.'

Forty-three

Eventually they got to the front of the line, and then they were up out of the trench and advancing at a run. It felt odd to be standing upright out here, when for so long they had only crawled and slithered and wriggled through the mud. But all around there were thousands of others doing the same thing. Bodies lay on the ground – Allied bodies, both dead and wounded. There seemed not to be any stretcher bearers, or perhaps they had just been overwhelmed by the sheer number of casualties. James followed the man in front of him. When he stopped, James stopped: when he lay down, James lay down; when he advanced again, so did James. Ahead of them, fighter planes circled over what was presumably the thick of the fighting.

A terrified German soldier ran towards them, his arms in the air as he tried to surrender. Someone pointed to the lines behind them and told him to keep running. Then shells started dropping nearby – small German 88s. James flopped into a crater and waited along with a group of doughboys for someone with a mortar to catch up with them. Somehow he and Hervey had got separated from the rest of their section. Eventually a mortar team turned up. 'Position?' gasped the mortar man as he wrestled with his weapon. Hervey cautiously raised his head to look. As he did so, a shell took half his head away. He fell backwards without a sound, a look of wonder in his eyes. Blood pumped through his mouth. James tried to grab him but felt Hervey's head collapsing in his hands, like a broken egg. A burst yolk of blood slithered through his fingers. 'Quick,' he said to one of the doughboys. 'Give me your sulfa.' The GIs all had medical pouches on their belts, with bandages and tins of sulphanilamide powder. The doughboy shook his head. 'Ain't no point,' he said. 'That boy's a goner, and I might need it myself.'

315

'Give it to me.' Something in his voice made the other man shrug and hand over the tin. James sprinkled the powder over the wound, but the infantryman had been right, it was a waste of time. Hervey died even before James could get a bandage on him. He wiped the blood from his hands onto his trousers.

The mortar man got four mortars off and told them it was all he could do. Reluctantly James left Hervey's body and climbed back onto the battlefield. They crawled towards the German lines, several more of them taking direct hits, until a Spitfire overhead spotted their predicament and managed to get close enough to fire directly into the gun emplacement. Someone else shouted an order, and then they were up again and running. James almost fell into a trench, and realised it was a German one. He climbed out the other side and kept moving. Another trench. A German soldier, running in a crouch from left to right, turned and hurled something at James. It smashed him right on the chin. 'Christ,' James said, reeling back and feeling his face. The man had thrown a tin of rations at him. The tin rolled back into the German trench. James just had time to realise that it was not in fact a tin of rations but a grenade when it exploded, the blast knocking him backwards. He struggled to his feet, raised his rifle and shot the fleeing German in the back, but missed.

They were behind the German lines now. He passed a group of forty or fifty prisoners being guarded by a single GI. Then the inevitable counter-attack came – dozens of Tiger tanks cresting the brow of the hill and streaming down towards the advancing Allied infantry. The prisoners watched them with interest, like spectators at a sporting event. James retreated to the German trench and helped a mortar man knock out two of the Tigers. Then, as abruptly as they had arrived, the tanks were retreating again, their guns swivelling round to continue firing to the rear as they left the scene.

That was the pattern for the whole day – advancing in a large, chaotic group: taking casualties: dropping into a foxhole until sheer pressure of numbers forced the Germans back. Occasionally there would be holdups. Minefields, in particular, caused terrible casualties. They were dealt with by 'snakes', long tubes full of explosives which were pushed onto the minefield by a tank and shot at until the snake exploded, taking the mines with it. The path through the mines was then marked with white tape.

They had covered about five miles. James found himself moving forward unopposed with a group of about thirty others. Overhead, a Spitfire mistook them for Germans. It came around with its guns blazing, the lines of bullets walking up the road to meet them. They dived for the ditches on the sides of the road. When they got up, four men were dead. 'I'll shoot that stupid bastard if he comes around again,' a corporal was saying. But they had nothing to shoot a Spitfire with: they just had to pray he wouldn't come back.

A little later, James saw the men in front of him suddenly begin to shake their limbs and dance, waving their arms in the air like puppets and spinning their bodies around as if executing a jig. He had seen enough fighting to know what it meant: there was a Spandeau machine gun somewhere, the impact of the bullets tossing the soldiers around even as they died on their feet. The Spandeau ballet, they called it. Again he took cover in a ditch. He felt wetness on his thigh: a bullet had pierced the spare water canteen he had taken from the truck earlier. He held the canteen to his mouth and let the remaining liquid gush into his mouth.

'Come with me.' An officer was tapping him on the shoulder. James nodded to show that he had understood. The officer stood up and together they charged the machine gun position. The officer reached it first, took aim, and collapsed as a bullet took him in the chest. James, behind him, just had time to steady his rifle. He fired, and the German machine-gunner slumped forwards over his gun. The belt feeder put his arms up. '*Kamerad*,' he called. 'Surrender.' James motioned for him to leave the machine gun and walk forward. As he did so, someone James never saw shot him. James was no longer particularly upset by accidents like these, although each time they occurred he was reminded that sooner or later something equally unpredictable would almost certainly happen to him.

To his enormous pleasure he met up with Roberts, who although suffering from a shrapnel wound to the ear was still advancing. 'I'm not walking back through those bloody minefields,' he told James. 'I'm waiting until we take Cisterna and there's trucks to take me 'ome. Don't reckon it'll be long now.' He nodded to where the town could be seen ahead of them, in the bend of the hill.

By the time they got to Cisterna hundreds of Germans who had given up were being marched to the rear. Despite the sound of gunfire coming from the buildings, a route had already been marked into the town with white tapes, past a number of burnt-out tanks. A few women peered anxiously from doorways. Children waved shyly. A group of exhausted soldiers squatted by a radio. 'What kept you?' one of them said laconically.

As they entered the town they passed an officer listening to a small group of Italian women. The Italians were trying to explain something to him, pointing down the street and gesticulating. 'Any of you boys speak dago?' the officer called at James's group.

'I do.'

'Tell me what this lot are saying, would you?'

James turned to the women. '*Buona sera, signorine. Cosa c'è?*'

'We are trying to tell this soldier that there are fifteen Germans hiding in Cosima's cellar,' one of them said.

'Where is this cellar?'

The woman gave him directions, which he passed on to the officer. 'Do these Germans have guns?' the officer wanted to know. James translated, and the women nodded.

'*Sì*. Many guns.'

James nodded. 'Thank you, *signorine.*'

'Good job,' the officer said as the women departed. 'What's your name?'

'Gould.'

'Fancy a cushy posting, Gould? My lot are going to need a translator when we get to Rome.'

James shook his head. 'Sorry. Once I get to Rome I'll be busy.'

Three days later they were there. The forward units drove into the city expecting fierce resistance and were met instead by a relieved population throwing geranium flowers into their jeeps, pressing bottles of wine on them and giving them whatever gifts they could – which, in the case of the women, was often simply themselves. After a few days large signs appeared where once the Germans had posted their orders: 'Women of Rome, remember your honour.'

The speed of the advance had taken their own commanders by surprise, and for five delirious days the troops frolicked, swimming in the Tiber, taking full advantage of the Romans' hospitality, sightseeing, sending V-mails home, or simply catching up on their sleep in the sun.

James had no time for any of this. His first task was to discover the location of the German army brothel. It was not hard – the locals were only too happy to identify the place, at number 95 Via Nardones. It was a tall, stone building, presumably once a hotel. James ran up the steps and entered a large reception area. The desk was deserted, and the mess of papers scattered around suggested that the occupants had left in a hurry. His boot slipped on a sheaf of flimsy chits, and he bent to examine them. They were printed tickets, with spaces for the name and number of the soldier, the name of the nurse who had certified him free

318

from disease, and the name of the girl. A little further on he found one that had been filled in. The girl's name was Eva. Her price, it seemed, had been twelve lire.

'Hello?' he called up the stairs. He listened: it seemed to him that he could hear someone moving about.

He went up. There was a long corridor, the rooms all numbered. Notices printed in the elaborate gothic script favoured by the Germans hung on the walls.

James opened the first door. The room was empty, and looked as if it had already been ransacked by looters. A metal-framed bed had been turned over onto the floor and the mattress cut open. Horsehair spilled onto the threadbare carpet.

He caught a low murmur of voices. It was coming from one of the rooms on the opposite side of the corridor. He went across and checked them one by one. In the second, four girls were cowering on a bed. Their heads had been completely shaved, very badly – there were bloody scabs on their heads were the razors had nicked them. They looked up at him with fear in their eyes.

'It's all right,' he said in Italian. 'I'm just looking for someone.'

'The Germans have all gone,' one of the girls said in a lisping voice. 'They went on Monday.'

'Was there a girl called Livia here?' he said. The girl shook her head.

'Are you quite sure?'

'There's a register,' another girl said. 'In the office. You can check if you want.'

'I can't read German. I wouldn't know what I'm looking for.'

'I speak it, a little,' the girl said. She led him next door to where a large black filing cabinet had been tipped over onto its side. James managed to get it back the right way up. Inside, the files were still surprisingly ordered. And they were nothing if not comprehensive, he noted as he flicked through. Hundreds of girls had passed through the Wehrmachtsbordell on Via Nardones, and each one had been the subject of immaculate record-keeping. Every health check, every complaint, every day's illness had been written up and filed away.

'What does *damenbinden* mean?' he asked, seeing a word that recurred regularly.

'Pads for menstruation. They kept a diary of when our periods were due, so that we couldn't pretend to be sick.'

So many girls. 'What happened to the ones who left here? Where did they go?'

A shrug. 'The Germans took them away.'

There were no Livias and no Pertinis in the files. 'And you're sure that these are all the girls there were? There couldn't have been some they didn't keep files on?'

She shook her head. 'They kept a file on everyone.'

Sighing, he turned to go.

'Please . . .' the girl said.

'Yes?'

'We have no food. No money. If we go outside, the women spit at us. The men. . . the men are worse. Can you give us something?'

All he had on him was a few hundred lire in occupation money and a couple of packets of gum. He handed it all over.

'Are you looking for this Livia?' the girl asked as she unwrapped the gum. She put some in her mouth and chewed it vigorously, pausing every few seconds to swallow. She was, he realised, completely ravenous.

'Yes, I am.'

'She's lucky,' she said sadly.

'Only if I find her.'

He walked back along the Tiber, lost in thought. Everywhere he looked, the celebrations were continuing. A party of GIs were dancing with a group of Roman girls. In the Piazza Navona, the people were making a bonfire of German flags, documents, abandoned uniforms, even the beds the Germans had slept on. German proclamations were being ripped from the walls of buildings and added to the fire. A pretty girl ran up to James, kissed him on the cheek, and then ran away, laughing at her own daring.

It was a city in celebration, but he had not found her.

When he got back to the barracks where his unit was billeted Roberts told him someone had been looking for him. 'Big bloke. An officer. Said he was A-force.'

'Captain Jeffries?'

'I don't know, but he'd about a dozen Jerry watches down his left arm.'

'Yes, that'll be Jumbo,' James said fondly.

He found his way to the hotel in which A-force had set up a temporary headquarters. 'Ah, James, there you are,' Jumbo said, as if the breakout from Anzio had been little more than a hike. 'Say hello to my good pal Buster.'

Buster was another Jumbo, though with a broken nose. 'Buster's responsible for the partisans in sector four,' Jumbo explained. 'That's this bit.' He pointed at a map on the wall. 'Tell him what you heard, Buster.'

'I've been asking all the partisan commanders for an update on their strength,' Buster said. 'One of them sent a message to say his motley crew was gathering more recruits all the time. He made a light-hearted reference to the fact that they even had a group of Neapolitan prostitutes with them, waiting to cross the German line.'

'Could one of them be Livia?'

'Of course it's her,' Jumbo said confidently. 'How many other Neapolitan prostitutes can there be? Well, quite a few, I suppose,' he added, answering his own question. 'But not up here. Not trying to cross the lines.'

'If she *is* with Dino,' Buster said, 'she's done rather well. He's a good man.'

'Is there any way we can get her out of there?' James asked.

Buster shook his head. 'None whatsoever, I'm afraid. The whole sector's stiff with Jerries.'

'On the other hand,' Jumbo said cheerfully, 'we can probably get *you* in. Ever used a parachute?'

That night, the BBC's daily transmission of messages to the partisans contained some intriguing new material. Having told Mario his sister's cow needed milking and Piero that his wife thanked him for the hat, the clipped tones of the BBC presenter said, 'And finally a message for Livia, who is staying with Guiseppe. Please remain where you are. The tuna is on its way.'

High in the mountains, Dino's radio operator wrote down the message and frowned. It did not correspond to any code he had ever been given, but he would pass it on anyway. Perhaps it was something to do with the big guns they had been waiting for.

About fifteen miles from the forest where Dino and his partisans were hidden, the Germans were also listening to the BBC broadcast. They had cracked this code long ago, but 'tuna' was a new one on them. They, too, suspected it might be some fearsome new weapon about to be delivered to the partisans. The message was taken to the German commander, who ordered that patrols in the area should be stepped up immediately.

Forty-four

The fuselage of the B-17 was crammed and very noisy. It was crammed because of the huge piles of crates containing guns, ammunition and food strapped down in the bomb bay. There were no seats: James and Jumbo were wedged between a couple of crates, holding onto the webbing which lined the rear of the plane. James was clutching a knapsack and a small suitcase. One of the smaller bomb doors had been left open, and occasionally they could make out rivers and lakes as the Italian countryside passed underneath them, illuminated by a sliver of moon.

'We'll be going in at two angels,' Jumbo shouted over the din. 'It'll be fine.'

James nodded with what he hoped looked like confidence. He had never done a parachute drop before, and from what Jumbo had told him he gathered it was best done from as high as possible. Two angels – two thousand feet – was hardly time to open the main parachute, let alone sort out the reserve if something went wrong. But as the plane banked and turned north towards the mountains, he felt his heart racing with an excitement that was due to more than just nerves. He hoped desperately that Livia had got his message, and that she had not already moved on.

Officially Jumbo was the one being dropped to liaise with the partisans, and James was merely there to assist with the unloading. According to the report the pilot would file later, James would overbalance and fall out of the plane whilst pushing out a crate. It was, Jumbo assured him, a fairly standard way of moving people around without going to the bother of getting official permission.

After twenty minutes James felt the plane start to descend. Jumbo got to his feet. 'Time to get this lot unloaded,' he yelled.

They cut the webbing and pushed the crates towards the bomb doors. As they swung open, a small bonfire on the ground flickered into life, tiny as a firefly. 'There's the signal,' Jumbo shouted. 'Heave.' They pushed the first crate out. It wobbled in the slipstream, then sprouted a khaki-coloured jellyfish of silk, slowing its descent. James only hoped that his own jump would be as straightforward. But there was no time now to think about that. Together they pushed the boxes out one by one, until Jumbo gave the signal to stop. The plane banked, and came around again. 'Heave,' Jumbo yelled, and they resumed their work. Eventually the crates were all gone.

'How are you feeling?' Jumbo shouted.

'Fucking terrified,' James yelled back. Jumbo evidently thought he had said something quite different, because he gave him an encouraging nod and a thumbs up.

Clutching his suitcase to his chest, he stepped to the open door. Below him, the hillside seemed very distant. He was struck by how very wrong it was, hurling oneself into the sky like this. Then Jumbo gave him a firm shove, and he was tumbling head over heels through the void. There was a moment's panic, then he righted and felt the blissful tug as his parachute filled with air.

Below him, crates floated slowly through the sky. He looked up. Jumbo was twenty feet above him, to his right. Beneath him, he could see dark figures already carrying crates out of the drop zone. And then he saw a familiar skinny figure, running towards the place where he was going to land, and his heart soared way above the clouds. 'I love you,' he called down to her. 'I love you.' It sounded rather wonderful in Italian, so he shouted it again. 'Livia, I love you.'

Gently the ground came up to meet the two angels, one of whom was later heard by the partisans to be laughing even as he hit the ground and rolled. And then she was in his arms, the silk of the chute billowing around him as he held her, saying over and over, 'Livia, I'm so sorry. I'm so sorry. I let you go, but I'll never let you go again.'

They sat on a tree trunk, a little away from the camp. 'I brought you some things,' he said. He opened the suitcase. 'From the black market in Rome. Bread from a bakery on Piazza Trilussa. And – look.' Carefully he took out his prize. 'A whole mozzarella. It must have come into Rome from some farmer in the countryside. How extraordinary is that?'

'We need guns, not food,' she said sternly.

'From the look of you, you're in dire need of both.' She was even thinner than when he last saw her. He broke open the mozzarella and held some out. 'Try some.'

She ate a little. 'It's not very good,' she complained. But she ate some more. 'It's a bit stale,' she added. 'And not very well made. Thin and watery. Not like proper mozzarella from Campania.'

'It's the best I could find.'

'You shouldn't have wasted your money.' She ate a bit more. 'After the war, I'll need to find a replacement for Pupetta. It takes years to make a decent milker, you know. This cheese probably came from some decrepit old ox.'

There was only a very small bit left, so he broke it in two and tried some. Perhaps it wasn't as fresh and full of flavour as hers had been, but it still filled his mouth with the sweet, creamy tang of wet pastures, dense with lush grass and herbs.

'And it's small,' she added, finishing off the last bit. 'Trust a Roman to sell you an undersized mozzarella. I hope you didn't pay more than a few lire for it.'

James, who had paid all the contents of his wallet for the cheese, shook his head.

They sat together for a long time, his arm protectively around her shoulders.

'James,' she said with a sigh, 'there's something I need to tell you.'

'I know about Alberto. Marisa already explained.'

'But you still came?' she said, surprised. 'You'd be forgiven for wanting nothing more to do with me.'

'It isn't like that any more, though, is it? This war's made everything different. We're going to have rethink everything now – decide for ourselves what's right and what's wrong.'

She nodded. 'The people here say we have to rid ourselves of bourgeois hypocrisy.'

'Well,' he said thoughtfully, 'that's maybe taking it a bit far. You don't have to be bourgeois to be a hypocrite. And you don't have to get rid of one to get rid of the other.'

'Dear James,' she said. 'Always so rational.'

There was a long pause. He wondered what she was thinking. She said, 'There's something you need to understand, though. Things are different for me now. Coming here – fighting – seeing what's been happening – it's made me look at things in a different way. Here, I'm a communist first, and a soldier second, and a woman – well, probably not even third: being a woman comes way down the list.'

'But you won't always be a soldier.'

'I think perhaps I'll always be a communist now. And that means being a soldier, in a way. Who do you think is going to put it all back together, after the war is finally over and you people go back to where you came from? Someone's got to stop people like Alberto from doing what they like with this country. '

'Ah,' he said. 'Do I take it you still think England isn't the place for you?'

'I can't leave Italy. Not after this. Not after what the people here have been through. I'm sorry, James.'

'That's interesting,' he said. 'Because I won't be going back to England either. Or at least, not for any longer than it takes me to demob and get myself back over here.'

She looked at him, unsure that he really meant it.

'I want to stay in Italy,' he said gently. 'With you, if you'll have me. Without you, if you won't. A person can't choose where he's born. But he can choose where he spends his life, and I want to spend mine here.'

There was a problem with the supplies that Jumbo and James had brought. The crates contained rifles and pistols for small-scale actions, whereas what the partisans required if they were to take on the might of the retreating German army were Sten guns, grenades and semi-automatics.

'We've been asking for these weapons for months,' Dino explained, his face dark with anger. 'How can you have got it so wrong?'

'It's just an administrative cock-up,' Jumbo soothed him. 'Probably someone else somewhere is complaining about an unwanted delivery of Stens. I'll get onto HQ and order up what you need. In the meantime, there's plenty of planning to be getting on with.'

The leaders of the other partisan forces in the area were called to a meeting, at which Jumbo produced a map and, with James as translator, explained what each section was to do. There were questions, but no dissent. The partisans' military discipline was absolute. In addition, James saw, Jumbo was good at this. He had the ability to see the coming battle in physical terms, as a combination of weaponry and geography: moving *that* group towards *that* piece of high ground, which would provide cover for a different section taking *that* river . . .

The only muttering came from Dino, who pointed out again that the plans depended on his group of partisans having enough heavy guns to stop the Germans in their tracks.

'Exactly,' Jumbo said. 'And heavy guns we shall have. They'll be dropped by plane long before the Germans get here.'

The German retreat coincided with a heatwave. Even here in the hills the heat was oppressive, and many of the partisans went bare-chested apart from their red neckerchiefs. Some of the women partisans wore men's vests in lieu of shirts. James noted, though, that they never seemed to have any trouble with the men. They were all kept busy with preparations.

Fire trenches were dug, and here James was able to give advice based on his experiences at Anzio. A few of the men grumbled when he insisted that some of the trenches be dug ten feet deep, with tree trunks and sandbags for extra reinforcement in the roofs. They simply could not conceive of the explosive power of a German '88. Despite the grumbling, however, the digging always got done in the end. Dino made sure of that.

Dino himself, though, was still fretting about the delivery of the big guns. 'We can dig the emplacements,' he told Jumbo, 'but when will we get the weapons to put in them?'

'Soon,' Jumbo assured him. 'HQ will make sure that we have them in plenty of time.'

Privately, though, he was becoming rather anxious himself. 'I'm hearing some very odd stuff on the radio,' he confided to James. 'Apparently we've just withdrawn seven divisions from Italy to open up a new front in the Med.'

'But that makes no sense at all,' James said. 'Why let them outnumber us, just when they're almost finished?'

'It beats me too,' Jumbo admitted. 'I'm just hoping – well, that someone hasn't decided to make things more difficult for the Italians.'

'Why would anyone do that?' James asked. Then he was suddenly struck by a thought. 'Actually, I already know the answer to that.'

'What is it?'

'Jumbo, I think we need to get the commanders together. We need to tell them why those big guns they're waiting for might never arrive.'

'When I was in Naples,' James explained, 'I saw a document. A top-secret document. At the time I didn't understand why it was secret – it was just an assessment of what the political situation in Italy was likely to be after the war.'

He paused, gathering his thoughts. Dino, Jumbo and the partisan section leaders waited for him to continue.

'Basically, it said that amongst the Italians the most organised and disciplined political group are the partisans. The writer thought that after the war the King would abdicate, and the communists would take power. He wasn't very happy about this – he foresaw a communist super-state stretching from Moscow to Milan, as he put it.'

'So?' Dino asked. 'This is hardly a secret.'

'The report wasn't just an assessment,' James said. 'It was an action plan.'

There was a long silence while the partisans digested this. 'You're saying that we are being betrayed,' Dino said at last.

'I'm saying that it would suit some people if the *Garibaldini* have their numbers and strength reduced by the Germans. As far as they're concerned, the war in Italy has already served its purpose – it's tied up twenty-five German divisions that otherwise might have ended up in France. Now the war is almost won, they're pulling Allied divisions out of Italy, leaving the communists to take care of the Germans – and vice versa. It's what my CO used to call a two birds, one stone scenario.'

'Jumbo?' Dino said quietly. 'Can this be true?'

Jumbo nodded. 'It makes sense, I'm afraid. At the end of the day, the army commanders have to do what the politicians tell them.'

'You'd better call off your attack,' James said. 'Whatever supplies are dropped, I'll bet they won't include the big guns you need.'

'We can't call it off,' Dino said. 'Knowing that our deaths will serve some politician's purpose makes no difference. To our shame, we welcomed the fascists into this country. We can't simply sit back now and watch the German army go by without striking a blow against them.' He looked at the other commanders. 'Are we all agreed?'

One by one they nodded their heads.

James and Livia did their turn at patrols, just like everyone else. One night, there was a crackle of gunfire from the darkness ahead of them. Some partisans had run into the Germans. James and Livia dropped to the ground, lining up their guns to provide covering fire as the main body of the partisans retreated to a better defensive position. The fire fight was brief and intense.

'You fight well,' Livia said grudgingly as they got to their feet.

'So do you,' James said. 'Though somehow that doesn't surprise me.'

'I must say, these partisans are turning into quite a nice little operation,' Jumbo said proudly, coming back along the road to join them. 'When we started out here they couldn't even load a weapon on their own. Now they're quite capable of showing me a thing or two.'

The German traffic on the roads through the mountains was now mostly going north, away from the front. But these were supply lorries and logistics units. The partisans waited, biding their time for the fighting divisions to appear. There was a palpable air of tension in the camp, the familiar mixture of lethargy and terror that precedes any battle.

James took the opportunity to walk with Livia in the woods. It was the only way to get any privacy. They found a cherry tree, and gorged themselves on the firm, sweet fruit while they talked. Livia had still not responded to James's statement about wanting to come back to Italy after the war, and he had decided not to press her. Instead, they discussed her new-found political beliefs.

'First Italy must be free. Then her people must be free,' Livia explained. 'The factories and farms must be given to the proletariat, not the other way round.'

James ate another cherry. Livia's tendency to talk in slogans since she had joined the *Garibaldini* was rather trying, though understandable in the circumstances. 'What if the proletariat don't want them?' he objected. 'Or what if they take them and loot them?'

'The proletariat only steal because in an unjust system they have been given no choice,' she said sternly. Then she remembered how annoyed she was when people stole things from her. 'Of course, there will have to be leaders,' she conceded. 'The Party will need to provide direction to the people.'

'And will these Party leaders be elected?'

'Democracy has already been shown to be a flawed way of distributing power.'

'Yes, Hitler spotted that as well,' he murmured.

'Well, perhaps there will be elections then,' she said. 'The communists will win anyway, so it doesn't really matter.'

'But then you'd have democratic communism.'

'So? What's wrong with that?'

'It's just that I thought you communists didn't believe in all that.' He had to admit, though, democratic communism was a deliciously Italian idea, and in Italy it might just work. 'And what about religion? Presumably you'd close down all the churches, like Stalin did?'

'Of course not,' she said, shocked.

'So you'd have a sort of Catholic democratic communism?'

'Why not?'

'And what if the proletariat don't want their women to go on being emancipated?' he asked innocently. 'Presumably you'd go along with their wishes?'

'If the proletariat don't want that,' she said, 'they can go hang themselves.' Then she saw what he was doing. 'You're teasing me.'

'Of course not,' he said. 'I never rib Italian girls. They're much too serious.' She punched him on the arm. 'Ow.' She had, he noticed, rather a hard punch, her body wirier than he had known it previously. She punched him again. 'That hurts,' he protested.

'So what are you going to do about it?'

'I'll just have to punch you back,' he said, punching her lightly in the same place.

'That's not a punch,' she said. 'This is a punch.' She hit him in the other arm, even harder. This time, though, he grabbed her arm and tried to twist it behind her back, and then they were wrestling. Her laughing eyes were very close to his, and her laughing lips were close enough to be kissed. He slid his hands under her vest, and suddenly there were her breasts, brown from the sun, the nipples red as the inside of a fig, ready to be kissed and gently rolled between his teeth.

'Stop,' she said, pulling away a little, 'I want to talk about politics some more.'

'Oh,' he said, rearranging himself. 'Well, all right then.'

'James?'

'Yes?'

'I'm teasing you.' She came back to him, her shoulders arched to offer him her breasts again, and then her cool fingers were slipping inside his own trousers.

A little later, when they were both naked, and she was doing something rather nice that he remembered from their afternoons in Naples, it was he who stopped her. 'Actually, I had something else in mind,' he murmured.

She came up to kiss him again. 'Like what?'

He picked his shirt off the branch of the cherry tree where it had ended up and undid the breast pocket. 'It wasn't only cheese I brought with me from Rome,' he said. 'I brought some of these along as well.'

She looked at the packet of rubbers in his hand. An eyebrow shot upwards. 'Oh? So you simply assumed I'd sleep with you?'

'Not assumed. Hoped,' he said humbly. Then he saw her expression. 'You're teasing me again, aren't you?'

'Of course,' she said, taking the packet from him and tearing it open with her teeth. 'But I am genuinely cross with you as well.'

'Why's that?' He gasped as she took the condom and put it on him.

'Because if you'd told me about these when you first arrived,' she said, slipping one leg over his, 'we wouldn't have wasted so much time talking about communism.'

Afterwards they lay in each other's arms, letting the sweat dry from their bodies in the shade of the tree. There was red on Livia's stomach, but when James looked more closely he saw that it was only a smear of fallen fruit, crushed under her as they made love. He bent his head to lick it off, and felt Livia stir.

'What are you doing?' she asked.

'Nothing,' he said, and went on doing it.

'That doesn't feel like nothing.'

'What does it feel like?'

'It feels – quite nice.'

'Then I shall go on doing it.' He licked until all the fragments of crushed fruit were quite gone, then looked around. There were more cherries all around them, and he gathered two large handfuls. 'Now,' he said, 'I wonder what we can do with these?'

A lone German fighter plane circled overhead in the endless blue sky. James opened his eyes drowsily and looked at it. He wasn't concerned: they were too well hidden to be seen. After a few minutes the plane dipped its wing and drifted away.

In a day or two, he thought, we may both be dead.

He looked at Livia, nestled against his arm, one of her hands closed protectively around his balls. Her shoulder blades, sticking out from her spine, were as symmetrical as the wings of a butterfly. When this is over, he thought, she'll need feeding up. He smiled at the contradictory nature of his two thoughts. However much one expected to die, there was something in the mind that just refused to accept it as a certainty.

He remembered the person he had been when he first came to Naples, before he met her. What an unbearable prig he must have been, he thought ruefully.

'What are you thinking?' Livia asked sleepily.

'I was thinking about Naples. What are you thinking?'

She cupped his balls lightly. 'I was thinking that if it wasn't for testicles, there would be no war, but also no sex. I was just wondering if God made the right decision when he invented them. And I had decided that, on balance, he probably did.'

'Your thought was much more profound than my thought,' he said, impressed. He lay back. 'This is like living on Vesuvius, isn't it?'

'In what way?'

'Because we might get killed at any moment, and we don't know when.'

She rolled over, propped up on her elbows, so she could look into his eyes. 'Yes. So how are you finding it?'

'I think,' he said, 'that a life like this is worth ten lived any other way. So long as it goes on including you, of course.'

She was silent for a moment. 'James?'

'Yes?'

'After the war, if you ask me to marry you, I'll say yes.'

He thought for a moment. 'But that doesn't make sense,' he objected. 'Why not say yes now?'

'You haven't asked me, for one thing.'

'Livia Pertini, will you marry me?'

'No.'

'But you just said—'

'I said ask me after the war. It's bad luck to say yes now.'

'How can it be bad luck?'

'Well, for one thing I'd need a piece of iron in my pocket, because bad luck doesn't like iron. And we'd need to have our heads covered, so that the evil spirits can't see how happy we are. And you should never make any decisions about who you marry on a Tuesday.'

'You made that last one up.'

'No, I didn't.'

'But it doesn't make sense to say—'

'If you're going to marry me, James,' she said sleepily, 'you're going to have to get a lot less attached to sense. Anyway, getting engaged the day before a fight with the Germans would just be tempting fate.'

On their way back to camp they met Jumbo, who was busy cleaning the partisans' only machine gun. He gave James an interrogative look, and James gave him a thumbs up.

Later James went to give him a hand. 'So everything's all right with you and Livia?' Jumbo asked.

'Better than all right.' He couldn't help beaming. 'She wants to wait until after the war, but I think we're going to get married.'

331

'Congratulations, that's wonderful. I hope you'll be very happy.' Jumbo worked on his gun for a few minutes. 'You heard about Elena's little problem, I suppose. This long-lost husband of hers.'

'She did mention something along those lines,' James said awkwardly.

'Now Rome's free I suppose we'll be able to get it sorted out.'

'I suppose so. Though, er, it might take a while. Probably a bit of a backlog.'

'Thing is,' Jumbo said, 'she can't really go on being a whore if she marries me. It's not what people really look for in a tart, is it, the fact that they go home to a devoted husband every night and cook him his dinner.' He caught James's look. 'I always had a pretty good idea. It just seemed like one of those things it was better not to mention.'

'I'm sure you'll work something out.'

'I suppose so. Shame this bloody war can't last a bit longer,' Jumbo said wistfully. 'Well, not from your point of view, I suppose. But I've had the time of my life.' He regarded the machine gun, which was now reassembled. 'There, that should take care of a few Jerries.'

Gradually the trickle of German units north became a torrent. Travelling mostly by night – the Allied fighters were still harassing them by day – they swept through the mountains as if a dam had burst, the growl of truck engines and the stamp of marching feet echoing through the darkness.

'Not yet,' Dino said. 'Wait for the infantry.'

So the partisans, concealed, watched the endless procession of grey uniforms pass by, and waited.

Two days later their spotters reported that a column of troops had been seen moving up from the south.

The partisans waited until dusk. Then a growling sound, wafted on the still air, heralded the arrival of the convoy. A little later, the sound of singing could be heard.

'Troops,' Jumbo said. 'Troops and trucks. Quite a lot of them, from the sound of it.'

'Good luck everyone,' Dino said. 'Wait for my order.'

The sound of the Germans got louder as they advanced slowly up the valley. Then, dimly, they could be seen as well. In the pale light, it was like a river of grey lava flowing uphill towards where the partisans waited.

The first trucks were almost past the partisans' position when Dino said, 'Now.' Immediately, rifle fire spat from the concealed trenches. The Germans scattered and took refuge behind what shelter they could. Only then did the second group of partisans, concealed on the ridge behind them, open fire, forcing the Germans to move back. But this initial success was short-lived. An armoured car began returning fire, and the disciplined and experienced German soldiers began to form into small fighting units.

If the start of the battle had been messy and noisy, now it was chaos. Men were firing as they advanced until the barrels of their guns glowed like hot pokers. James looked anxiously for Livia, but couldn't see her. Then they were in amongst the German position, fighting hand to hand, and there was no time to think or look for anyone except the men on the left and right of you.

He heard a familiar chainsaw noise cutting through the din. It was a sound he had come to know and dread at Anzio – the sound of a Spandau heavy machine gun. The Germans had swung down the sides of an MG42 truck further down the column and were firing indiscriminately, mowing down their own men and the partisans alike in their desperation to regain the upper hand. James dived for a ditch, where he found himself alongside Jumbo.

'That Spandau's going to be a problem,' Jumbo said. 'Think I've got the answer here somewhere.' He produced a German mine from his pocket. 'Any minute now, they'll need to change the barrel.'

'I'll come with you,' James said. He started to feed another clip into his weapon in readiness.

'Don't do that,' Jumbo said. 'Might be a bit hairy. Besides, you've got Livia to look out for.'

'Don't be an ass. You'll need cover.'

'Give Elena my regards,' Jumbo said, heaving himself over the side of the ditch. James cursed, slammed the clip in and followed, crouching low and firing in short bursts left and right. There was a sudden sharp pain in his left shoulder, knocking him backwards. He was just in time to see Jumbo coming under fire as he hurled the mine at the machine gun. Then there was a flash, and the gun truck exploded, turning into a fireball that consumed yet more German soldiers.

Within ten minutes it was over, the remaining German trucks either dashing back to the safety of the valley or captured. But victory had come at a ridiculously high price. The partisans had lost over half their men.

James went to find Livia, running from body to body to see if she was among the wounded. Eventually he found her sitting on the mountainside next to Jumbo's corpse. He sat beside her, and for a while they said nothing. When at last she spoke, her voice cracked with exhaustion.

'I want to go home.'

The next day, as they were burying their dead, another column of men was seen moving up from the valley. But this time their uniforms were not grey but khaki, and Allied flags fluttered from the radio masts on their vehicles.

James went with Dino to act as interpreter, his arm in a sling where the bullet wound had been dressed. He explained what had happened, and the commanding officer thanked them.

'By the way,' he added to James, 'where did you learn your English? You speak it pretty well, for an Eyetie.'

James opened his mouth to explain, then for some reason he heard himself say, 'Well, I was born in England. But I grew up in Naples.'

'Thought so. Anyhow, we'd best be getting after the Jerries. Thanks for everything.'

As they walked back up the hill, with its lines of neat crosses, Dino said, 'You didn't tell him you were British.'

'No,' James said shortly.

Dino gave him a thoughtful look. Then he stopped by the line of graves. 'So many crosses. But you know, there's room for another one.'

'Where?' James asked, not understanding.

Dino pointed. 'There, on the end. A nice spot to be buried, don't you think?'

'It's very pleasant.'

'Perhaps you could be buried there yourself, next to your friend Jumbo. What do you think? "Here lies James Gould, an officer of the British Army, who gave his life in gallant action with the partisans, et cetera, et cetera."'

'Dino,' James said, 'Are you saying I should just – go missing?'

Dino took something out of his pocket. 'Look,' he said, unfolding it. It was a partisan's red neckerchief. Embroidered in the corner was the name 'Giacomo'. 'He was a good man,' he said quietly. 'One of many good men who died here. I don't think he would mind you having it. It's almost as good as a set of identity papers, don't you think? One of these, and a letter from me thanking you for your help, will open many doors in Italy after the war.' Dino pressed the red neckerchief into James's hand. 'Take her home, Giacomo. Take Livia back to Naples.'

Forty-five

It is seventy miles – seventy miles of fought-over terrain, already picked bare by two armies. There is no food, but as they walk they conjure it out of the air.

'What are you making me for dinner today, Gems?'

'Today –' he screws up his face in thought, for this is a serious matter – 'today I shall be making an antipasto of *noci in camicia*, walnuts in parmesan butter.'

'And are the walnuts from Sorrento?'

'Of course. Thin-shelled and absolutely fresh. None of this dried-walnut nonsense the British go in for.'

'And how are you making the butter?'

'In advance, clearly. *Well* in advance – probably a couple of hours before dinner, so that the flavours of the basil and the parmesan can mingle with the nuts.'

'Correct,' she says, 'but unfortunately I'm hungry right now. It's all this walking. Can't you make me a bowl of pasta? Something quick?'

'Of course. How about *fettuccine al limone*?'

'Perfect.'

'So I'm just going to boil some water and drop in the *fettuccine*—'

She interrupts. 'You mean you haven't made this pasta yourself?'

'Hmm. Well, perhaps I have. And I'm grating the zest of about a dozen lemons—'

'Tell me about the lemons.'

'The lemons are from Amalfi, of course, very big, and so pale they're almost white. And ugly. Ugly and thick-skinned, because the thicker the skin, the sweeter the juice.'

'Just so.'

'And now I'll just combine the lemon zest with the butter and the cream—'

'How much cream?' she says. 'How much butter?'

'*Quanto basta*. Just enough.'

She nods approvingly. 'Good. Gems, one day you may actually become quite a competent cook.'

'Thank you,' he says, ridiculously pleased by the compliment. 'And I'll serve it straightaway, just as it comes, or perhaps with a little pepper. How is it?'

'It's delicious,' she says. 'The best I ever had. Really, I don't know how I'll make room for the next course.'

'*L'appetito viene mangiando*. Appetite comes from eating.'

They have reached the top of a ridge, and they sit down for a moment. 'There are some woods down there,' she says, pointing. 'We should go that way. We may be able to find some mushrooms, or perhaps some fruit.'

'Yes,' he agrees. He does not say, because there is no need to, that the woods will have been scoured by many thousands of soldiers and other refugees before them. 'An apricot will be nice for dessert.'

'There are no nice apricots outside of Vesuvius.'

'I was forgetting. Let's pass on the apricots, then. Some peaches instead, and perhaps a jug of wine.'

They lie back, the sun warm on their skin. Livia takes off her shoes and rubs her sore heels. 'I bet the wedding officer is missing his motorbike.'

'I've no idea what the wedding officer misses.'

'What do you mean?'

'The wedding officer . . . that'll be some other poor chump by now. He's probably looking through my papers even as we speak, and thinking they're the most appalling mess. Ashes in the filing cabinet . . . a biscuit tin full of bribes . . . and God knows what he'll make of my reports, if he ever bothers to check up on them.'

There is silence for a while. Then she says carefully, 'But if you're not the wedding officer . . .'

'I can stay in the army, and still marry who I like. Yes, that had occurred to me, too. There's just one problem – I'll need my CO's permission. But I think I can take care of that.'

'Oh?'

'Eric won't be at all happy that we know what they're doing to the communists. I reckon if I threaten to kick up a stink, he'll make sure we get pretty much whatever we want. We might even be able to get your slippery *camorrista* friend put behind bars where he belongs.'

336

'What a devious mind you have, Gems.'

'I do, don't I?' he agrees. He lies back. 'But as Angelo says, a hungry stomach pardons no one. It's your turn to cook.'

'What about . . . let's see . . . Baked pancakes stuffed with mozzarella and green beans?'

'That sounds perfect.'

'Well, first we need some good mozzarella,' she says. She gets to her feet, and offers him a hand. 'Luckily I have some, from my own *bufala*, who is waiting for us just a little way ahead.' He gets up, and keeps hold of her hand as they begin to walk. 'And then you need good eggs for the pancake. But luckily we have an excellent chicken. And you will need milk, as well, again from the *bufala*, and then garlic to coat the beans in flavour . . .'

Epilogue

Time passes.

Time passes, and as the hot midday sun and cool mountain nights alternately bake and freeze the blackened landscape of Vesuvius, something remarkable happens.

Gradually, the streams of cold lava are colonised by a lichen, *stereo-caulon vesuvianum*. This lichen is so tiny that it is almost invisible to the naked eye, but as it grows, it turns the lava from black to silvery grey. Where the lichen has gone, other plants can follow – first mugwort, valerian, and Mediterranean scrub, but later ilex and birch trees, along with dozens of species of apricot.

Meanwhile, the clinkers and ash that covered the landscape like so much grubby grey snow are slowly, inexorably, working their way into the fields and the vineyards, crumbling as they do so, adding their richness to the thick black soil, and an incomparable flavour to tomatoes, courgettes, aubergines, fruit, and all the other produce which grows there.

Time passes.

Time passes, but people do not forget. Every year, on the anniversary of victory, they gather in the places that are special to them – an airfield, a war memorial, a café on a French bridge, a landing beach where they survived but others who were with them did not.

One of the places where they gather is a little *osteria* on the flanks of Mount Vesuvius, in a tiny village called Fiscino. This is a select gathering, and you are unlikely to see it mentioned in newspapers or on TV. But although it is select, it is not small. They come from all over Europe, and from the United States too – for those who live on the other side of the

Atlantic are glad of a chance to fly back occasionally and visit their families in Naples.

The men have names like Bert and Ted and Richard. The women . . . the women have names like Algisa, Violetta, Silvana and Gina. They are the war brides, the Italian girls who married Allied soldiers, thanks to a dispensation given with great reluctance by the men's commanding officers.

Others are here too, of course. There is Angelo, the former maître d' of Zi' Teresa's, long since retired, along with his wife and his sixteen grandchildren. There is Eric Vincenzo, who when asked what he is doing now is always somewhat evasive, but who is based in Langley, Virginia, the home of the CIA. And there is the elegant middle-aged lady who is always dressed, however unseasonably, in the finest furs. She is accompanied by her much younger husband, a millionaire industrialist, who addresses her with unfailing politeness as *carissima*. She only has one eye, the other being made of glass, and she answers to the name Elena.

Marisa is here, or *Dottore* Pertini, as we must now learn to call her. She has long had a thriving medical practice in Boscotrecase, where it is known that for certain ailments beyond the reach of conventional medicine, such as backache, arthritis or the infidelity of a spouse, she will be able to prepare you a compound not found in any pharmacy.

And her sister is here. She too is known as *Dottore* Pertini these days, though in her case it signifies that she has completed a university degree in political science. However, the fiery local councillor will always find time to cook, particularly when it is a meal such as this, a feast for family and friends.

And here is her husband, moving a little slowly as he works his way down the long trestle table that is set under the trees on the shady terrace, checking that everything is as it should be. His stiffness is the result of an old war injury, but it does not prevent him from making sure that the waiters are setting out the antipasto correctly – for it is he who took over the management of the restaurant and farm after Nino's death, and it is under his direction that it has become celebrated by all the food guides. It is said that he has been known to help out in the kitchen himself on occasion, and that his *fettuccine al limone* is even better than Livia's. The antipasto today will be *burrata*, creamy balls of mozzarella wrapped in asphodel leaves, made with milk from his own much treasured water buffalo, whose lowing floats occasionally across the fence from their tiny pasture next door.

But there is a ritual to this meal, as there has been every year since the war ended. As the guests bring their glasses of sparkling *prosecco* to the table, they are served first of all with bowls of a thin, insubstantial soup.

It is little more than pasta water, containing a few humble beans and flavoured with a little mutton fat, and it is, frankly, not very pleasant. The younger members of the group – those who are not old enough to remember the war themselves – make faces, and push it away after one or two mouthfuls. But the older ones eat it slowly and in silence, a faraway expression in their eyes as the taste transports them to another time, the memories crowding back to people the table with yet more visitors.

Then, when the soup is cleared, the mozzarella is consumed. Wine is poured; bread is broken. Conversations begin, turn into arguments, and eventually become conversations again. Civilisation resumes its normal course.

There are children here too – dozens of them, for in the period immediately after the war there was an explosion of procreation such as the world had never seen before. Some of them are a little shy, unaccustomed as they are to conversations carried out in more than one language. As the meal goes on, and on, and the adults still show no sign of wanting to do anything other than talk, these youngsters slip one by one from their chairs, gathering in small groups to play, or to look moody, or to flirt, depending on their age and sex.

Periodically they are called back to the meal, the centre of the gathering, to be argued with, or fed a titbit, or simply to join in one of the many toasts that are raised up and down the table, the young lifting their glasses in celebration of a victory about which they know nothing except what they have learnt in school and from their parents' stories.

And if they see Livia Pertini reach out a hand to touch her husband's arm as he passes, or see him bend his head for a fleeting kiss – habitually, almost unconsciously, breaking off his conversation to touch his lips to hers – they will, naturally, screw up their faces in mock-disgust, or pass some smart remark. For if they know little of war, they know even less of love. That is as it should be: each generation must be allowed to believe that it makes these discoveries for itself.

Besides, they have more important things to think about. Look, here comes another course, the long-awaited apricot *dolce*, carried to the table in triumph by the cooks.

www.theweddingofficer.com

Acknowledgements

Most of the events and incidents in this book actually took place and are taken from contemporary accounts, although I have aimed for authenticity rather than accuracy in my use of them. In particular, I have drawn on Norman Lewis's wonderful *Naples '44*, a journal of his time as an NCO in the Field Security Service. To take just the most significant example, his entry for 5 April reads: 'Twenty-eight investigations of prospective brides for Servicemen completed to date, of which twenty-two proved to be prostitutes ... One would like to be able to do something for these applicants to marry our soldiers. Of the twenty-two failed candidates most seemed kindly, cheerful, and hard-working at their household tasks, and their standards of good looks was very high.'

Amongst other things, Lewis witnessed the 1944 eruption of Vesuvius, which many observers believed would have been far more devastating had it not been for the relief operation carried out by American and British soldiers under the leadership of Lt. Col. James Kincaid. As it was, the eruption claimed most of the towns of San Sebastiano and Massa and destroyed almost an entire wing of B-25 bombers at the Terzigno airfield. Today, over a million people live on or around the volcano: seismologists say another eruption is probably overdue.

Lewis also describes 'a typically hare-brained A-force idea' to round up syphilitic prostitutes in Naples and send them to the relatively disease-free German territory in the north. This scheme, which had already been used with some success in France, was abandoned in Italy after a few attempts because of a lack of cooperation from the women involved.

Many thanks to the staff of the Imperial War Museum, London, who made it possible for me to study several unpublished accounts of life in occupied Naples, and who even provided me with a map, once issued to servicemen on leave, of the city as it stood after the bombing. Zi' Teresa's still exists, incidentally – I recently ate there a very good baby octopus simmered in squid ink and tomatoes.

The man who identified Beethoven as Belgian originally did so in the hearing of E. M. Forster, as recounted in his 1958 essay *A View without a Room*.

The quotations on pages 131–4 are from the twelfth edition of *Married Love* by Dr Marie Stopes. By 1940, it has been estimated, this guide to love-making had sold over a million copies.

I am also indebted to *Sophia Loren, In Her Own Words*, which describes a childhood in wartime Naples and Pozzuoli; *Dear Francesca* by Mary Contini, which contains many recipes and recollections of her grandparents' upbringing in Campania; and the wartime memoirs *The Gallery* by John Horne Burns, *From Cloak to Dagger* by Charles Macintosh and *Rome '44* by Raleigh Trevelyan. My sources about Neapolitan cooking include Sophia Loren's *Recipes and Memories*, and Antonio and Priscilla Carluccio's *Complete Italian Food*. A big thank you to Jamie for the tip about using a filing cabinet as an oven.

The suggestion that the CIC (later to become better known as the CIA) covertly tried to hinder the communist partisans has become known as the 'Operation Gladio' theory. I'm very grateful to Blaze Douglas for bringing it to my attention.

Several friends read the manuscript and made comments, including Bobby Sebire and Peter Begg. Particular thanks to Tim Riley for responding so unstintingly to my request for a really tough critique.

My agent, Caradoc King, encouraged me over a very good Italian lunch to start writing this story, and over another, eighteen months later, encouraged me to finish it. I doubt if either would have happened without his help. I also owe a huge debt to my publisher at Time Warner, Ursula Mackenzie, who told me to write whatever I wanted to, and my editor Jo Dickinson, who had to put up with the – sometimes unsteady – results as *The Wedding Officer* slowly took shape.

This book is dedicated to my father, one of that extraordinary generation of young men and women who decided in 1939 that democracy, decency and kindness were worth giving their lives for. For as long as mankind continues to tell stories, their story will be told and retold as an inspiration to us all.